D0596090

Up a Tree

A Novel and Shamanic Handbook

Jane Burns

Published in the United States by Out in the Barn Press, Southbury, CT

ISBN 978-0-9914179-0-2
eBook ISBN 978-0-9914179-1-9

Cover Art: Judith Bird (www.judithbirdart.com)
Cover Design: Deb Moran
Author's Photo: Joan Bennett

For my parents

Author's Note

Up a Tree is both a story about journeys and a guidebook for taking journeys of your own. When I first decided to write a book about shamanic practice, I was drawn to the idea of telling a story. Stories are a powerful way to inspire and uplift, and in many spiritual traditions, a great tool for healing and bringing people together. In this story, it is shamanism that is the hero, shamanism that saves the day and leads by example.

This book is aimed both at an audience of people who know and love the shamanic way of seeing and being, and an audience of readers who know nothing about the practice. At the time I wrote this book, I belonged to a writer's group, and the majority of our members had no knowledge or interest in the practice. I worried that these members would find the shamanic journeys, the interaction with talking animals and fantastical episodes experienced by the main character, Clare, to require too much suspension of their disbelief. These parts of the book, however, were resoundingly their favorite, and I realized once again that both story and shamanic experience are a universal language.

At the back of this book is a handbook, which contains twelve journeys and tips for honing your journeying skills, as well as rituals and creative exercises. These twelve sets of shamanic tools correspond directly to the twelve chapters of the novel. As a reader, you can decide if you want to read about Clare's experience chapter by chapter, and then try out each of her shamanic adventures for yourself. Or, you can read the novel in its entirety and then, undertake the handbook as a study guide or shamanic primer. Or, you can just enjoy the novel and leave the journeying to other folks.

When I wrote *Up a Tree,* I wanted to convey how the shamanic way of life is not an esoteric practice that lies peripheral to reality. It is a way for ordinary people to live their ordinary lives in an extraordinary way, a way of living more wholly and deeply, more peaceably and compassionately. A way of becoming the hero of your own story.

Deep Peace and Blessings!

Jane Burns
Southbury, CT
January, 2014

Prologue

Even then, in those first jarring moments, I had the feeling things were going to get a whole lot worse before they got better. Though I could not, for the life of me, imagine how.

"What time did you discover him?"

"Around six-fifteen."

One policeman leaned over Daniel's back, feeling both his neck and wrist for a pulse.

"Was he here all night?"

"He got up last night about midnight, said he couldn't sleep."

I thought briefly about the quiet of that moment, the simplicity of it, Daniel's body framed in the doorway, backlit by the lamp on the hall table. A nothing moment I would never have thought about again, being half-asleep and used to a husband with insomnia.

I compared the nothingness of that moment to the loud,

frantic, heart-stopping one it had become.

"I don't actually know whether he came back to bed at all, but he wasn't there when I woke up around six."

I was thirsty and nauseous and needed to sit down. I stepped away from the policemen as they began searching around the body, beneath the desk—looking for what, I wondered. I leaned against the fireplace in Daniel's study, as if there were a burning fire that could warm me. I was wearing two sweaters and a cashmere shawl, but I still felt cold. My eyes were tight and dry, and I couldn't stop blinking.

The nervous flutter of my eyelids made me dizzy. Everything was flashing by in a rapid series of stills. I couldn't keep the scene around me in focus: outside, there were the pulsing lights of the police cruiser, my two neighbors standing like sentinels watching from their snow-covered lawns. Inside, a policeman speaking on a cell phone in the hallway, the quiet briskness of the cops in their black nylon jackets, the swishing sounds of their jacket sleeves each time they moved their arms.

The absence of Daniel's heartbeat and the deafening pounding of my own.

I lifted my thumb and forefinger to my eyelids to hold them steady for a moment. "Had he been complaining about any symptoms?"

"A headache. Last evening, he said he was really tired, but then he couldn't sleep."

The policeman nodded. "The medical examiner is on his way. Have you contacted a funeral home?"

"I-I'll do that. I'm sorry," I said. "Would it be alright if I just checked on my children?"

The policeman nodded. "Sure," he said, resting his hand for a moment on my shoulder, a gesture of compassion that seemed routine and empty.

I smiled weakly and walked away, my arms crossed over my stomach.

"Is Daddy going to be alright?" asked Kenya, my

daughter, as I came into the kitchen.

I looked at my friend Rowena who had come to the house to sit with my children. We had already covered this ground with Kennie. Rowena made a face and shook her head as imperceptibly as possible.

I sat down at the table and held out my arms. Kenya came over and sank onto my lap. I held her head against my chin. "No, sweetie. Daddy's not going to be alright."

Panic rose in her voice and she sat up to look at me. Her eyes filled with tears. "Why? What happened?"

"We don't know yet," I said. "We'll find out soon. They'll tell us."

She shook her head. "No," she said.

She waited for my response. I closed my eyes and took a breath.

"Yes," I said.

She shook her head and looked away. "You're wrong," she said, both defiant and afraid. "Everybody's wrong."

"It *feels* wrong, sweetie," I said, "but it's true."

"No." Her face crumpled and she began to sob.

I sighed and pulled her against me again. I began to rock back and forth—instinct kicking in. I hadn't rocked my twelve-year-old daughter in many years, but it seemed like the only thing I could offer her.

I looked over at my son, Ethan, who was sitting directly across from me, his hands cupped around a mug of un-sipped tea. He looked up at me, as if waiting for what I would say next.

Ethan was the first child I awoke after finding my husband dead in his study. I stood in the doorway of his room, watching him sleep, unable to cross the floor and wake him.

He was at peace, still floating in a world where his dad lived and breathed. I was the one who would change that world forever.

I went to the bed and sat down. After a moment or two, my son opened one eye. "This better be good," he muttered.

I cleared my throat and tried to speak. Nothing came out.

Ethan rolled onto his back. He looked more closely at my face and then leaned up on one elbow. "What is it?" he said.

"Ethan, honey," I said, and then paused. "Ethan, sit up, okay, so I know you're awake."

"What? What's going on? What's the matter?"

"I'm sorry, honey. I'm so sorry to have to do this. But, I need to tell you something—about Daddy," I wiped tears from my cheeks. "Daddy—."

Oh, how do I do this? How do I say this?

"He's what? Mom, for Christ's sake!"

I reached out for Ethan's hands and took them in mine. The skin was rough and the knuckles chapped. I rubbed my thumbs over his knuckles and squeezed his hands hard and waited until I could steady my voice. "I found Daddy in his study this morning. Something happened to him during the night, sweetie. I don't know. I don't know what. But, he's—he's dead."

"Dead? What! Mom, are you sure?"

I nodded. "I called the police and they're on their way. I'm sure, Ethan. I'm sure."

"I want to see him," he said, pulling his hands away and jumping out of the bed.

"Oh, honey, I don't think that's such a good idea. You know, he wouldn't want you to see him like this."

But my son was already halfway down the stairs.

"Dad!" Ethan called, as he ran away from me. "Dad?"

I followed behind him, unable to catch up, my slipper coming loose on the stair. Then, Ethan was in the study, calling out. "Dad! Dad!" he was saying. I reached down to pick up my slipper, thinking my heart was going to land right beside it.

Now he was staring at me across the kitchen table. "She needs to see him," he said.

I shook my head.

"Mom!" Ethan said. "She needs to see him."

I looked at Rowena. She nodded.

I closed my eyes and put my cheek against my daughter's head. Here in this moment it was suddenly quiet again, like before. I could hide here. I could smell the coffee Rowena had made me; I could feel my daughter's hair against my chin. I wrapped my arms more tightly around Kenya and rocked, as much for her as for me. The sounds of the ongoing catastrophe that had burst upon our lives that morning were muffled behind the door—distant.

Sometime later, the medical examiner came and I walked down the hall to speak with him. He asked me some questions, like whether Daniel took any medication and said that he would order a post mortem to determine the cause of the death. He gave me some papers to sign. He said they were making preparations to remove Daniel's body. I retreated back to my hiding place in the kitchen, as if it were the only room in the house undamaged by the sudden blast of Daniel's death.

I sat down and Kenya climbed back into my lap. I closed my eyes and went back to rocking. Just rocking.

"Clare," said Rowena.

I looked up. The policeman was standing in the doorway. "They're ready to leave, Mrs. Blakeley," he said.

I stood up and took Kenya's hand. "My daughter needs to see her father first. We'd like a couple of minutes alone with him. Is that possible?"

"Of course," he said.

I turned back to the table. "Ethan," I said, beckoning. "Come on, honey. Come along." It seemed totally ordinary, not the least bit surreal. As if he were three years old instead of seventeen. As if we were getting in the car and going on a play date.

They left us alone in the study. Daniel's body was strapped to a gurney; there was a blue sheet folded neatly across this chest.

Kenya knelt down next to him and put her face close to Daniel's. "Daddy," she whispered. She reached one hand over to his face and touched his eyelids one at a time. It was the way she used to wake him when she was a toddler and sneaked into our room in the early morning.

Ethan flinched and reached out. Then, he seemed to catch himself and lowered his arm back to his side.

Kenya pressed Daniel's forehead with the flat of her hand. She paused, as if taking his temperature and looked up at me. "Where is he?" she asked.

"He's gone up to heaven," I said. "He's with his mom and dad. And all the angels."

Good lord, what was I talking about? Did I even believe what I was saying to her?

"And Raphael and Ariel," said Ethan, which gave me a start until I realized he was talking about the pet rabbit and duck we used to own.

"No, I mean *where*," said Kenya, "if his body's here."

"Well, when someone dies, they lift up out of their body," I said. "They go up and up until they stop at the place where the spirits live." I lifted my arm towards the ceiling. We all looked at my hand floating in mid-air.

"And then they can't see you anymore, can they?" she asked.

"No, Daddy will still be able to see you," I said.

"How do you know?"

My eyes filled with tears. "It's always that way," I said. I nodded and smiled, rubbing my hand on her back. "Just like my dad still sees me."

Kenya nodded. Her hand slipped away from Daniel's forehead. She bowed her head and pressed her hands together in prayer. I had never seen my daughter pray and wasn't sure she even knew how, or that she was actually praying now. We all waited solemnly until she finally stood up and looked at me.

"Alright," she said.

Chapter One
Birch: Growth

How alright could it be? Could a tree lose a major limb and ever be expected to regain its balance and symmetry? I wondered if that was how we appeared now to others, my children and me—a lopsided family with a pronounced skew. Did we even qualify to be a family—a real family?

Well, what did it matter? It only mattered how we felt inside, how well we managed to wrap ourselves around this tragedy and bring to it some kind of grace and meaning. In my imagination, I could *envision* how that might happen, but I couldn't feel it yet. Not even glimpse it. Right now, recovery did not feel possible.

All I *could* feel was that I needed to retrieve something that was lost, and that I had no means of ever finding it. I hadn't seen Daniel go. I had fallen asleep in one life and woken up in another. We hadn't said goodbye, my husband and I.

We hadn't said our peace. He had left with a kind of violent suddenness at an awkward time in our marriage, a period of estrangement that I kept expecting to resolve itself. But not this way.

We had drifted apart when I was sick. Two years before, for a number of months, I had a strange illness that was never diagnosed—an unspecified auto-immune disorder that was first thought to be toxic shock syndrome. Another doctor said Epstein Barre. Lymphoma was suggested at one point. Lyme's disease. Mono. Lupus. MS. The list went on. The tests and scans were inconclusive, the disease elusive. We waded through numerous examinations and bloodwork, and after a time Daniel began to stare suspiciously at me as if I were either holding out on him or making the whole thing up.

As the weeks went on and the tests proved nothing and I failed to get out of bed day after day, he became sullen and dejected, as if I had found a different, more interesting life apart from him and our children.

It seemed odd to me that he was now the dead one. As if he were kind of thumbing his nose at me and saying: "You want to see dying? I'll show you dying!"

I knew that sounded crazy but I couldn't help connecting the two events. As a couple, we had never recovered from my illness. I got better, while the marriage became diseased. As I became well, Daniel grew more suspicious, as if he could no longer take me at my word. As if I hadn't had the guts to go through with my plan to leave him. Like I had staged this big dramatic exit and then changed my mind.

All in all, I couldn't help feeling a little envious of those widows who felt nothing more than a plain and simple grief at the passing of their husbands. That seemed far easier to deal with than the swirl of ambivalence and betrayal that hung around me and the space that Daniel once occupied. Had I failed him as a wife? I kept thinking I had provoked him somehow and that his death was a retaliatory strike.

Maybe this was normal. Maybe other widows felt this

way—abandoned and stung. Maybe even to blame. But, if this were true, it didn't explain anything. It didn't explain what I should do next.

So I decided to put everything I had into just making sure my children were okay, that they could survive the loss. I would sort out my own feelings later.

"Did you make this?" Ethan asked, peering into the casserole dish on the kitchen counter.

"Mrs. Cleary made it," I said, reaching past him to preheat the oven.

"How long before we don't have to eat the neighbors' food anymore?" he asked.

"Ethan! That's a terrible thing to say. People have been so generous."

He looked at me. "Seriously, Mom, I can't eat anymore of this stuff. You never know what you're getting into."

"Oh Ethan, come on. It's just a casserole. How bad can it be?" I went to the cupboard to get out some plates.

"Bad," piped up Kenya, who was sitting at the kitchen table with her laptop. "Like that chicken you gave us last night with all those red things in it."

"Oh, I know," said Ethan. "So nasty. What *was* that?"

"Chicken and peppers," I said.

Kenya wrinkled her nose. "Why can't we just have eggs and pancakes for dinner?" she asked.

I sighed and smiled at them. It was our first night in the house alone since Daniel died. My mother had flown back to Ohio that morning. Both children had both been so unbelievably strong during the whole process. Everyone said so.

"You're right," I said. "Let's have breakfast for dinner." I slipped the casserole back into the still crowded refrigerator and dug out a carton of eggs, some butter, milk and a package of bacon.

A strange kind of peace came over me. I thought, you

know, this will be fine. My children will be fine and I will be
fine. It will be sad and it will be slow, but it's going to be okay
—just like everyone said it would be—and if it feels somewhat okay this soon on, why there's no telling how simple this
whole terrible process might be.

I felt such a wave of relief in my body that I almost
buckled at the knees. I was tired to the bone, and thought
maybe I would finally sleep that night.

I was at the stove cooking eggs and bacon. A platter
stacked with pancakes was keeping warm in the oven.

"Mom," called Ethan from the family room, "Kenya's
being an a-hole!"

I sighed and rolled my eyes thinking it was one of their
ordinary squabbles. But then Kenya let out a scream that made
me drop my spatula and run.

I found her standing on top of the coffee table, hands
clenched above her head. Something shiny dangled from her
hand as she danced about in a crazy, erratic way. She seemed
to be both crying and laughing at the same time. I became
alarmed just looking at her.

Ethan was trying to grab whatever she had in her hand
and Kenya was leaping from the table to the couch and back
again, screaming like a banshee.

"She's got Dad's keys and she won't give them to me,"
said Ethan.

"They're mine!" she cried, swirling her arms as she
jumped. "Mine-mine-mine! Mine-mine-mine!"

She was like a wild bird that had been grounded and
cornered, her voice screechy and broken.

"Ethan!" I said. "Back away! Leave her alone. You're
making it worse."

"She stole them out of my room," he said.

Kenya stuck out her tongue and taunted him as if she
had regressed to four years of age again. "Nyaa-nyaa."

"Kenya!" I said sharply. "Sit down and *shut up!*"

Kenya stopped as if she had been slapped. Then she crumpled into a corner of the couch and began to sob.

"She's a total brat," said Ethan.

"Well, what were *you* doing with Dad's keys in the first place?" I asked.

"Mo-om," he said. "Duh? Kenya doesn't drive? I do. Dad's car is mine now."

"Who said?" I asked. "That was never decided. Daddy's car is very expensive to maintain, Ethan. I was actually planning to trade it in for something more economical."

"What! You can't do that! You're changing everything! Dad would never want you to sell that car!" Ethan yelled.

"Well, he's not here to decide that, now is he?" I said.

Kenya let out a wail and started crying even louder.

"Kennie, for God's sake, I can't think straight with you howling like that! What is wrong with you?" I said, my voice cracking under the strain of shouting.

"What's wrong with *her*? What's wrong with *you*?" said Ethan. "Mom, listen to yourself!"

"I can't help it," said Kenya, her voice choked with tears. "I miss Daddy."

"You're acting like she isn't even *entitled* to be upset about Dad," said Ethan, the one who had initially caused this eruption.

"I'm not doing any such thing!" I said, holding out my hand. "Kenya, I will take the keys for now, and we will all discuss this calmly at another time."

"No," said Ethan, plunking himself down between his sister and me and folding his arms defiantly. Kenya was staring at him, still crying, but more softly now.

I narrowed my eyes at him. "Okay, what are you playing at, mister? You started this commotion and now you're, what? Switching sides? I see what you're doing—you know you can weasel those keys from her more easily than you can get them from me."

Ethan wiggled his hands in the air. "Ooooooh," he said. "Mom and her super psychic powers! Help! Help! I'm melting under the rays." He held up his arms in mock deflection. Kenya segued from sobbing into giggling, her blue eyes shiny with tears.

Then, the smoke alarm went off.

"Oh, shit!" I said and ran back to the kitchen. The bacon strips were charred and smoking, the eggs stuck like mortar to the bottom of the pan. I quickly slid the bacon away from the burner and covered the skillet with a lid.

Ethan and Kenya followed me to the kitchen. My son reached up and pulled the battery from the smoke alarm. Everything became very still, and I felt the tension of our family row dissipate, as if the alarm itself had been a player in the argument and trumped us all by being the loudest.

I stood at the sink watching the water as it flowed into the pan of eggs, creating a cloudy, lumpy mess. I wondered why I hadn't waited for them to cool first and then scraped them into the garbage. I wondered why the bacon hadn't caught fire, and what else we could have for dinner now. I wondered if we would ever, ever be right again. Then I started to cry.

Ethan retreated quietly and went upstairs to his room. Kenya came up alongside me and put her arms around my waist.

I'm sorry, Mommy," she said. Her face was wet against my arm.

"I know, sweetie," I said. "Me too." I wiped my face on my sleeve and put my arms around her.

"Here," she said, setting Daniel's keys down. They made a gentle clatter as they settled on the countertop. The keychain carried a medallion stamped with the words "Somewhere Over the Rainbow." It was Daniel's favorite song. He used to sing it to Kenya when she was little. I understood now why she wanted them. I picked up the keychain and slid off the key to Daniel's car. There were other keys on the ring, one to the house and another to the garage door. I didn't think the others were important. "Why don't you just keep that?" I said, holding it out to her on my finger.

"I just feel bad that I don't feel bad," I said to Rowena, poking at my salad with a fork. "I mean, I don't even miss him. Does that seem normal to you?"

Today was the first day my kids had returned to school. Rowena was treating me to lunch at *Davide's*, a restaurant we both liked.

"What's normal right now?" she said, tucking pieces of lettuce that had fallen from her sandwich back inside the bread. "Don't be so hard on yourself."

Though Rowena had been my best friend since grade school, I liked to believe she was still objective enough to let me know when I was being awful.

"So, you don't think I'm like, a cold, heartless bitch or something?"

"I think you're not giving yourself a chance to work through this process. You're just getting started, Clare. How do you know how this is going to unfold for you? Before it's over, you're going to feel a thousand different things." She shook her head at me. "Do you want some of this potato salad by the way? It's amazing."

"No, that's okay. Look, I don't think I'm going to start feeling bereft all of a sudden, I don't care how much time passes. There's a part of me that is so furious with him for just up and dying. I know it sounds ludicrous but it seems so typical of him to pull a stunt like this."

"I think once the anger passes, the tenderness will come back." Rowena reached over and put a dollop of her potato salad on top of my plate. "You'll like it,"" she said.

I took an obligatory bite. It was good, but I still wasn't interested in eating it. I set my fork down. "I was waiting for that to happen before he died."

"I know," said Rowena, chewing on a slice of pickle.

"Well, that can't happen now!"

"Why not? You're talking about a healing process, and you don't need Daniel around to do that."

We sat in silence for a while. I gazed around the restaurant and caught the eye of our waitress. She approached our table, a wraith-thin girl with translucent skin and a scrawny blond ponytail. She looked like someone who hadn't eaten in weeks. I thought perhaps they should have hired a sturdier, corn-fed kind of girl to serve their customers.

"Can I wrap that for you?" she asked, pointing to my half-eaten salad.

I sighed. "Sure, why not?"

"Are you interested in any dessert?" she asked.

"Oh, not for me," I said, putting my hand to my stomach. "I'm full."

"Oh, really?" said Rowena, raising her eyebrows.

She smiled up at the waitress. "We'll have the cobbler with ice cream and two forks."

The cobbler was one of the reasons we always came to this restaurant, and Rowena was just trying to keep things as routine as possible. She picked up a packet of sweetener and poured a pinch of it into her tea.

"How are the kids?"

I shook my head. "I don't know. Ethan seems alright, I guess. Kennie seems...unstable."

"How so?"

I shrugged. My eyes filled with tears. "This is why I'm so angry, Ro. These kids have been dealt such a blow."

Rowena stirred her tea and watched me. "What about getting some guidance on this?" she asked.

I frowned. "What do you mean? Like, *therapy*?" I said.

"No, not therapy. I was thinking you should probably contact that spirit guide of yours again."

"Sumeh? Oh good heavens, Ro, I'm not sure any of that was even real."

"You got better, didn't you? Clare, you were really sick, and you got completely better. How is that not real?"

"I was desperate, alright? I had way too much time on my hands. Who knows, I probably just made it all up." I started to laugh, but quickly noticed Rowena wasn't laughing with me.

"I watched you go through that," said Rowena. "I watched you transform in front of my eyes. It was like you came back from the dead, Clare. *That* isn't made up."

It was hard to look at her just then. "Alright," I said, lining my knife and spoon up so they were precisely even. "If I get desperate enough, I'll consider it."

Rowena returned with me to the house. It was time to go through all the banking statements and Daniel's employee benefits to see where things stood for us financially. This was a process I didn't want to face alone.

I sat down in one of the dining room chairs I had pulled into the study. The chair Daniel died in was rolled into a corner of the room until I decided what to do with it.

I pulled on the bottom drawer of the desk, where Daniel kept our files, but it didn't budge.

"Are you sure it isn't just jammed?" asked Rowena, bending down to look at it.

"I don't think so," I said, still jiggling the handle. "And I bet I know where the key is."

"Oh, on the key chain you gave Kenya," said Rowena, smiling.

I got up from the desk. "Let me see if I can find it in her room."

I hurried up the stairs, hoping I would find the keys easily and not have to wait for Kenya to return from school. I didn't usually go into my daughter's room. We had a strong difference of opinion on cleanliness, and I found, in the interest of domestic tranquility, it was best if I avoided going in there as much as possible.

The room was cold and had an unfamiliar smell. Kenya had clearly been burning something in here. I noticed that the center of the room was free of the clothing piles that covered the rug everywhere else. In the open space of the floor, my daughter had created, with sprinkled salt, a circle about three feet in diameter. Inside the circle were a number of candles of different colors, slips of burnt-edged paper with strange incantations written on them, a penknife, a lighter and a black magic marker. There was also a ceramic bowl from the china cabinet that seemed to be filled with a large mound of multi-colored wax, as if each candle had been dripped separately into the bowl.

Okay, I thought. This is just my wildly curious and imaginative daughter doing something wildly curious and imaginative. Right? I bent down and looked more closely at the papers and read what seemed to be a list of odd derivations of people's names—including **Clay-re-**ages and **Ee-**tano-poulos-**than**o. What, was she trying to put spells on us?

My insides went cold. It was then I noticed that Daniel's keys were inside the mound of hardened wax. I sighed.

Rowena found me in the kitchen pouring boiling water onto the wax that held Daniel's keys. She peered over my shoulder.

"What is that?" she asked.

"Don't ask," I said.

I could feel her staring into my face. "Okay," she said, knowing me well enough to recognize this was one of those moments when I needed space. She walked to the other side of the kitchen and turned the kettle on.

I pried the smallest key away from the set and took it back into the study. The file drawer opened easily, and I breathed a sigh of relief.

I thought I would just look through things quickly, have a cup of tea with Rowena, and then figure out what to do

about Kenya. But the things I found were a bit more complicated than I might have ever imagined.

The first thing I discovered after I opened the drawer
was that our investment portfolio, which at one time had been
around four hundred thousand dollars, now had a balance of
twenty-seven dollars and thirty-four cents.

The next thing I found was a packet of cards and love
letters to Daniel from someone name Cynthia.

The third thing I found was the deed to a house in
Arizona with Daniel and Cynthia's names on the property.

I could hear Rowena in the kitchen humming and
making tea. By the sounds of it, she was emptying the dishwasher and putting my dishes away.

"Ro," I called, "could you come in here?"

After Rowena and I went through everything, it
seemed pretty clear that Daniel was planning on leaving me,
but the logistics of his departure were vague. Was he going to
just pick up and move to Arizona, quit his job and start from
scratch, leave his children? I thought he had probably stashed
money away to finance a move like this, but it didn't really
sound like Daniel to desert his kids. He might have been
finished with me and fed up with our marriage, but he loved
his kids and I couldn't imagine him leaving them like that.

"Daniel was an idea man, remember?" said Rowena.
"He never concerned himself with the details."

"No, that was my job," I said. "I guess he was kind of
in a bind here. Couldn't really ask for my help with this one,
now could he?"

"What are you going to do, Clare?" said Rowena,
chewing on the inside of her bottom lip. I only ever saw her do
that when she was nervous.

"I don't know," I said. "There's life insurance coming.
That will hold us for a while, but in the long run, I won't be
able to stay here. And I don't know how I'll put the kids
through college."

"You need to call your lawyer."

"I need to lie down," I said.

I slumped back on the floor and stared up at the ceiling. My chest and stomach had a punched out feeling that made me want to lay my hand there. But laying my hand there didn't make it feel any better. Inside my head a voice kept saying: "Oh my God, oh my God, oh my God!"

"I think you're in shock, Clare," said Rowena. "I think —."

"What time is it?" I asked, sitting up from the floor.

"Two-thirty, why?"

"I have to clear some stuff out of Kenya's room before she gets home." I got up from the floor and headed towards the kitchen.

"You need help?" Rowena called after me.

"No, thanks," I said, as I tucked a portable vacuum cleaner under one arm and a garbage bag under the other. Once in Kenya's room, I threw away the candles and the papers, confiscated the lighter and penknife, swept up the ring of salt, and placed the key chain, devoid of keys, in the center of her cluttered desk. Then I closed her door and went downstairs.

I knew Kenya well enough to know she would say nothing about this to me for fear of punishment. And I would say nothing to her.

I could not control what I found in Daniel's study, I told myself, but I could control this. I could clean it all up, just like that, and make it go away so that I would never have to worry about it again.

In the kitchen, I cleaned out the ceramic bowl and put it back in the china closet. As I scooped up the garbage to walk it outside, Rowena, who had been sitting at the table observing me and still chewing on her lip, said: "You know, why don't I just stay and make you and the kids some dinner tonight. I'll call Harry and tell him to get something on his way home from the train. Would you like that?"

"I know what you're doing, Ro," I said.

"I know you know what I'm doing," she said, dialing her husband on her cell phone, "but I'm doing it anyway."

The children were at school. I had cleaned up the breakfast dishes and tossed in a load of laundry. I went to the bottom of the stairs, sighed, and trudged up to my study.

I told Rowena I would consider contacting my spirit guide, Sumeh, if I ever got desperate enough. Well, I was officially desperate.

I looked through the drawers of my night table for the shamanic drumming CD I had used two years before when I was sick. Listening to this CD put me into a mild trance. After a few minutes of listening, I would feel myself dropping down into the earth and there, I would find Sumeh waiting for me. Sumeh guided me through my illness and told me what I needed to do to get better. Sometimes he would take me to meet other spirits: an eagle, a bear, and an old man named Eamon. Sumeh told me Eamon was a healer and an ancestor of mine. He introduced the eagle and bear to me as power animals.

They call this process journeying, and where I went when I journeyed and met Sumeh is a place known as the Otherworld. I had learned how to journey from a book called *The Shamanic Handbook* that I had purchased, coincidentally, a few weeks before I first began to feel sick. Once I had become sufficiently fed up with my doctors and frightened enough by the persistence of my illness, I picked up this book and taught myself how to journey.

Sumeh appeared immediately as soon as I entered my first journey. He sat down across from me and we began talking. He told me that I was at a crisis point in my life and that I needed to make some decisions. Whatever I decided, he said, would be honored.

I said that I wanted to get better and I didn't want to die, and he said if that were so, I would need to begin to live differently. I asked what that meant, and he said that I would need to start living for joy, that the soul longed for expansion. He said joy was my birthright and that I should never have forsaken it for disappointment and grief.

What was I grieving, I asked. The life you thought you were going to have, he said. When he said that, I began to cry and as I cried, I felt the toxic grip on my body begin to loosen. It was true—my life had become so routine and ordinary, I no longer valued it.

I told him I had forgotten how to be joyful, that I could no longer locate any joy in my life. He said, jump then. Jump for joy.

That evening, I went online and ordered a rebounder, a small indoor trampoline that I kept in the center of my bedroom floor for the next year. Everyday, I got onto the rebounder and told myself I was jumping for joy. At first I could only manage one or two feeble jumps. I felt childish and pathetic, and sat down on the floor and cried. But I had a mission which Sumeh had given me, and so I went back to it the next day and the next, jumping because I had nothing left to lose, jumping because I was fighting for a new way of living. Especially at times when I felt in despair over my illness or my future, I got up out of bed and climbed onto the rebounder and jumped.

Daniel thought I had clearly lost my mind. I could tell by the way he walked gingerly around the rebounder whenever he went to his side of the bed at night, staring down at it as if it were a huge, gaping hole in the floor.

But the only thing I really lost in those months of jumping was the person I had been. After several months, I began to regain my strength, and the symptoms of my illness receded.

Whenever I became frustrated by my slowness to heal, whenever I felt depression begin to creep in again around the edges of my life, Sumeh would offer his steady, quiet wisdom: "Though your perceptions and memory may not be as sharp, you are as knowing as I am, dear one. Think of us as two brothers; you are the older and nearsighted one. You say to me, Brother, what is that mysterious dark spot by the edge of the lake? And I say, why, Brother that is only a deer drinking water. Or you say, what is the meaning of that ominous black cloud along the ridge? And I say, not a cloud, Brother, only the cypress trees blowing in the wind."

Now, a year later, I was headed back to the Otherworld again, feeling equally helpless and lost, ashamed that I had left Sumeh without contact or sufficient gratitude for having brought me back to health.

I lay on the floor of my bedroom and placed a bandana over my eyes. I pressed the button on the player and turned up the volume of the drum.

Sumeh's face was the first thing I saw when I entered the lower world. He was standing there, his hands folded in front of him, the picture of patience. He was waiting for me, the same as before, as if he had been standing there all along. He was tall and slim in his long, white tunic, his hair dark and straight, his broad smile shining forth. His face was—as before—the kindest face I had ever seen.

"Hello, Brother," he said.

I began to cry.

"Hello, Sumeh," I said. "I guess I need your help again."

"Yes, dear one, you certainly do."

"I'm sorry I haven't been here. I'm sorry I only seem to come to you when my life is falling apart."

"Now is the perfect time to visit," he said, graciously, sitting down on a large flat rock. He gestured for me to join him, and then raised his arm. I heard the cry of an eagle overhead and noticed a brown bear lumbering towards us from the left. From the hills behind Sumeh, came Eamon with his long staff.

I wept as I greeted them all, my dear friends from the

spirit realm, and they gathered around, as if anxious to hear my news.

"I don't know where to begin," I said. "I feel very frightened and uncertain about my future."

"The future is always uncertain, girl," said Eamon.

"Well, yes, that's true, but things have become really unsettled since Daniel's death. I feel as if his presence and support, his love and the security that provided me have all been stripped away. Like a slate has been erased."

"*Tabula rasa*," said Bear, nodding. Bear was erudite—for a bear.

"Anyway," I said, "on practically every level, emotionally, psychologically, financially, I'm pretty much up a tree here."

"Best place to be," said Eagle, puncturing the ground with his talons, as if he were trying to find something to hold onto.

"Let's go to the trees," said Eamon, slapping his hand against his knee as he stood up.

We began walking up a path that led into a stand of birch trees. The trees were humming in a way that made me feel giddy as I walked among them.

"Birches are all about rebirth," said Sumeh, "the purification process. Where one thing ends, something else is beginning. If you understand what is beginning, you will know what is being asked of you. If you know what is being asked of you, you will better accept what has ended."

"That sounds too simple," I said.

"Everything *is* simple," said Sumeh. "You make everything harder just by expecting it to be difficult."

Eamon rapped his staff on an enormous birch, which had been nearly split in two by lightning. "This is the one," he said, "Up you go."

I walked up to it and looked into the darkness of the scar. I felt like I was looking at myself, only this birch was managing her calamity with a good deal more dignity and grace. I climbed up the trunk, using the lip of the scar as a grip for my hands. Sumeh and the others stayed below and watched me. I settled on a branch high up and looked at the blue sky behind the white branches. A warm breeze crossed my face.

I couldn't see the scar from here. At this height the tree seemed strong and healthy, as if nothing had happened to it.

"You grow beyond it," said Birch, reading my thoughts. Her voice was gentle and grandmotherly. "Right now you're just feeling the sting of the initiation,"

"What initiation?" I asked.

"You're being required to become something different now," said Birch, "and it's frightening you."

"You're right," I said. "So, what do I do?"

"You do what I did—you grow from your center outward. You commit to your own growth. You reach higher in order to be stronger. You dig your roots further into the earth and you give thanks for every next breath."

I nodded. "But aren't you still scarred? Don't you still feel wounded?" I asked the birch.

She started laughing. "The lightning that struck me is part of my story, as is the rain that bathes me, the wind that ripples through me in summer and strips my leaves away in autumn, the sun that nourishes me, the boy who carves his name into me. All of this shapes me into who I am. The scar is what made your guide choose me, what drew you to me, what has made me a good teacher."

I tried to imagine feeling this way about everything that had happened with Daniel's passing, the possibility that it might well be something neutral and benign. I shook my head.

"I see how what you are saying is true for you, but I don't see how it is true for me in *my* situation."

"It's always true. What's true for one is true for all. It would help if you leaned into it a bit more instead of pulling away from it in fear. How will you know what this challenge asks of you if you keep trying to avoid it?"

I shrugged, feeling sullen again and trapped in the mess of my dilemma.

"Go to the scar in my trunk," she said, "the scar that nearly cleaved me in two, and look inside it."

I hung upside down until my face was against the darkness inside the scar. My likeness to the Hanged Man of the tarot deck was not lost on me. As I put my face to the blackness, I sensed a warm, smoky breeze. Inside, I could see a woman dancing before a fire. Her dancing seemed to feed the fire and make it burn brighter. When she stopped, the fire dimmed. As she turned away, the flame all but guttered out. She stood in the cold darkness, the picture of desolation. Then she returned to the place where the fire had been, and she began to dance again, wearily at first, as if she had no faith the fire would be restored, but then more steadily as the fire rekindled and caught. As I pulled away from the vision, she was dancing wildly, joyfully, and the fire was reaching skyward.

"Is that me?" I asked the birch.

"If you wish it to be. The fire within is the only thing in life you ever need to tend to. Not finances or betrayals, not losses or things that have fallen apart. Focus only on the fire within and everything else will take care of itself."

I put my arms around the tree and hugged her. "I will try and remember that," I said.

I climbed down and joined Sumeh and the others.

"I want to ask something," I said. "I want to ask about my marriage. What happened there?"

"Two vines intertwined on a stalk," said Eagle, "when the stalk ends, what happens to the vines?"

"They each look for something else to cling to," I said.

"What did you find to cling to?"

I thought about this. "I think I found myself, or some kind of inner strength. Another world opened up for me here."

"And what did Daniel find?"

"He found somebody else."

It seemed so peculiarly simple. I saw the vine that was me grow sideways and reach for a tree. I saw the vine that was Daniel grow the opposite way and grab onto a stone fence. We couldn't even see each other anymore.

"So," I said, pausing, not certain I even could agree with this. "We didn't do anything wrong? We just did what naturally came next, growing towards what we needed to?"

"You can tell the story of your marriage a hundred different ways. The story you tell is entirely your choice," said Sumeh.

"A story either empowers or disempowers," said Bear. "If you tell a story of betrayal, you must be willing to become a victim. You put yourself into a prison cell and make a dead man your jailer. Your choice."

"What was the last thing your husband said to you," asked Eamon. "Do you remember?"

I flashed back to the dark of my bedroom the night Daniel died.

"Clare," I heard him say.

I could see my husband in shadow standing in the doorway. He was framed in yellow light from the hallway.

"I'm going downstairs to do some work."

"Now? What time is it?"

"It's late. Don't worry. I have some things I need to take care of."

"What? Are you feeling alright?"

"Bit of a headache," he said. "I'll take something for it. Don't worry."

"Don't worry," I said, shaking my head. "A little ironic, isn't it?"

"Last words are very prophetic," said Eamon. "You should listen to him."

"Eamon, he was talking about his headache."

Eamon just laughed.

Suddenly, I heard a loud bang. I sat up and removed the earphones. I looked around, uncertain whether the noise was real or imagined. Then I saw him, a male cardinal that had flown into the sliding glass door and landed on the balcony outside my study.

I crawled quietly across the floor to him on my elbows and knees. He was staring down at the ground in front of him, his breathing quick and shallow.

I put my finger on the glass. "You okay, buddy?" I whispered.

The bird panted and stared. Panted and stared.

"It's okay," I said. "You just got a sore head. Pretty soon, you'll be like new."

He raised his eyes and looked at me. He blinked as if to bring my face into focus. It was like he had a message, that he couldn't tell me. A wave of something ran through me.

"What?" I asked. "What is it?"

He gave me a look that was so piercing. I waited. We stared at one another. I thought of Daniel. I held my breath. The bird opened his golden beak and paused and I swear if he had spoken to me in Daniel's voice right then, it would have seemed like the most normal thing in the world.

The cardinal let out a high trill and flew away.

I followed him until he disappeared from view.

"Okay, Eamon," I said, smiling. "Point taken."

I leaned my back against the wall and stared outside. I felt better. Nothing was different in my life—still the same mess—but I didn't feel the same hopelessness. I no longer felt sick with overwhelm.

This was the lifeline I was being thrown—my dear helping spirits. Would I have even gone there without Rowena's urging? I remembered reading in *The Shamanic Handbook* how shamans were often initiated, how they needed some near-death experience or trial by fire before they finally agreed to take up their path. I thought of the lightning strike in the trunk of the birch.

I had no illusions about becoming a shaman. I was an art teacher, and felt content in saying that was my path. But I was in one of those places where everything that once held and supported me suddenly ceased to exist, and like the vine Eagle spoke of, I was grasping for a new direction.

I got up and walked over to my bookcase. I searched through the stacks of paperbacks piled two deep on the wide oak shelves. Behind a batch of Daniel's science fiction novels, I found my copy of *The Shamanic Handbook*.

"Okay," I said aloud, and walked to the reading chair in the corner.

Chapter Two
Poplar: Endurance

Kenya was grumbling again about getting up for school. In the last two and a half months, I had been pretty lenient about allowing her to stay home. She complained of not being able to concentrate, of feeling weepy and lethargic. There had been a few emotional outbursts in class and calls from the nurse, suggesting I come and bring her home. The school had generally been very understanding, and I think we were all trying to strike a balance between easing her back into her life and giving her time to heal. But, we seemed to be going nowhere.

If anything, I was finding that as time went on, Kenya was asking to stay home more often. When the simple "I don't feel like going to school today" was no longer a sufficient excuse, as it had been in the weeks just following Daniel's death, she began to complain of headaches, stomach aches, or cramps.

"I think I'm getting a period, Mom," she would say, as she tucked her knees and arms against her stomach and rolled away from me in her bed.

Kenya was small for her age and less mature than her peers. She hadn't begun menstruating, as the other girls in her class had.

I had some notion that if recovering from her father's death meant repeating eighth grade, it would not be the end of the world for Kenya. Obviously her schoolwork and grades were suffering, and I'd noticed that she had broken away from many of the friends she'd had since elementary school. How could they understand the loss she had suffered? Anyway, that was the worst-case scenario I already knew we could live with, and so, when she acted all weepy and pulled the covers up around her neck, I sighed, closed the door behind me and went to into my study to call the school's attendance line.

After making the call, I hung up the phone and stared despondently at the floor. It was as if my daughter were encased in glass. I handled her with caution and care for fear the glass would break and cut her. But I couldn't touch her. She didn't seem to hear me, and whenever I tapped on the glass to get her attention, she became startled like a fish and darted away.

It was my children's grieving process for Daniel, not my own, that occupied me. Their struggle to bear the weight of their sadness pulled at my heart. Ethan became more focused and hardened. Kenya became more fragile and unglued. I could not help them with their own grief because I could not reconcile the seeming absence of my own. It made me feel guilty and ashamed to have no grief. I was apparently stuck somewhere in the horror and indignation I felt when I discovered Daniel's duplicity.

There were two Daniels—the one I knew as my children's father, the man I had married and lived with for eighteen years and the one whom I discovered was building a life with someone else. I looked at one and then the other, trying to figure out which was the real Daniel, but the fact that there were two of him more or less implied that neither was correct.

On the one hand, I felt called to help my children recover from the loss they had suffered and on the other hand, I felt compelled to do everything in my power to keep them hidden from the man I had discovered in the desk drawer.

No one but Rowena and my lawyer, Hal, knew about him, and hiding this secret Daniel required me to keep a tight lid on my anger and anxiety whenever I was around my children.

Though I wasn't just angry with Daniel. I felt foolish and disappointed in myself for having not taken a more direct role in our finances. Daniel was a businessman, a corporate lawyer. Finances were his world, and my decision to play no part in this aspect of our life together seemed like a perfectly reasonable choice. Until now.

I wandered downstairs to the kitchen. The high school day began earlier than the middle school day, so I found Ethan putting his sneakers on, preparing to leave.

"Mom," he said, "can you make me some tea to take to school?"

"Sure, sweetie, what kind?"

"I don't know. Something with a lot of caffeine in it. I've got two tests today."

"I'll make you black tea and leave the bag in, then. What tests do you have?"

"Calculus and Physics," he said as he packed his shoulder bag.

I could see the inside of his pack from where I stood. Pencils and calculator were tucked neatly into the inside pockets. His notebooks were lined up in the order he would need them. No loose, crumpled papers, no old lunch bags, soda cans and candy wrappers like one was accustomed to find in his sister's pack.

"Kenya staying home again?" Ethan asked.

"She is."

Ethan looked at me and shook his head. I shrugged. Neither of us knew what to say or do about Kenya.

"We should help her," Ethan said.

"How so?"

"I don't know, like send her to a shrink or something."

"Oh, I don't know. That might seem like a betrayal to her. It would be like me giving up on her and throwing her problems onto somebody else's shoulders."

Ethan frowned. "Well, *you're* not helping her."

I poured boiling water into Ethan's thermos, trying to not show how much his comment had stung me. "Ethan," I said wearily, "look, I know you probably feel like you need to assume more responsibility around here with Dad gone, but I really don't want you to do that. Kenya isn't your problem. I want you to just focus on school and college and your friends and all the things you would be concentrating on if this hadn't happened."

"But it did happen, Mom! Why do you keep acting like it didn't?"

"I'm not acting like that at all! Of course it *happened*! I just feel like...we should keep...doing what we're doing. That's all."

Even *I* thought that sounded completely lame.

"Ya! Great plan, Mom!" said Ethan, rolling his eyes. He picked up his bag and slung it over his shoulder, grabbed the thermos onto which I had barely finished securing the lid.

The basement door slammed in his disgust with me. I heard the garage door opening and Ethan's car starting up, the garage door closing and the car roaring out of the driveway.

Then the house got still. Very still. I was failing them. I needed to be the strong and capable one in the family, the parent who could be relied upon to pick up the slack and then some. I should have a plan. I should have clarity and direction. But I was hopelessly stuck and paralyzed by my ambivalence and my fear.

I needed to get out of the house for a while.

I went upstairs and found a rumpled pair of jeans and a long-sleeved jersey, some clean socks in the laundry basket by the door.

I padded back downstairs and poured some tea into a thermos. I extracted my walking boots from the tangle of shoes beside the kitchen door. I put them on and grabbed a hooded sweatshirt of Ethan's from the rack, over which I pulled on my winter jacket.

Outside, it was misty and still, with a deep chill in the air. I headed for the woods at the end of the road, longing to be swallowed up into the mist behind the trees.

Winter had finally ended. Daniel's death had made it seem even bleaker and longer. The snow and cold had only exacerbated my desire to huddle inside myself and pull the covers over my head. How could I blame Kenya for feeling the same? Or Ethan for being so angry with me? Truth be told, I wasn't anymore present than Daniel was. I had abandoned them by becoming so lost in my own self-pity.

The day of Daniel's death had been more than two months ago, but my self-absorption and disconnection from my kids felt older, reaching much further back to when, I wondered?

I looked back on the days before Daniel died. He had been on a trip to New Orleans that week. I now guessed he hadn't been alone, that Cynthia had probably been with him. I was at home, wasting my sabbatical from the college, procrastinating on some new art pieces that were to become part of a local exhibit set to open this coming fall. I hated starting any new project—afraid I would go off in the wrong direction—and I remember being obsessed and moody about it.

I was going through the motions with Daniel and the kids, locked away in my own head, feverishly making sketches of sculptures that never made it off the paper. Maybe that was why I couldn't rally now and come ashore—I'd been adrift from them for a long time.

The morning mist clung to the black bark of the trees. I walked within it and yet it always seemed just that far off, pulling away from me as I walked toward it. It felt like I was walking through the foggy muddle of my own head.

I read once that the Celts believed that mist was a portal to the spirit world, because of its ability to hide and disguise things, because of its being not quite water and not quite air, not quite here and not quite there.

My breath felt heavy in the thick cottony air. The sound of it rose loudly in my ears until that and the crunch of brush under my boots was all I could hear. I was tired and so weary of the constant dip and peak of the sea of emotion in my life. It seemed like it would never end. I let my eyes roll off focus and walked the walk of a somnambulist through the damp trees and the mist that was not here and not there.

How can I bring myself back to them, I thought, feeling like my beleaguered little family was coming apart at the seams. How do I provide a grounded and stable environment for them? I hoped for a sign from nature—some message that would carry an answer to my questions.

Overhead, there was a flutter and bustle in the trees. I stopped and looked up. I felt a little dizzy from the deep breathing and brisk walking and put my hand against the trunk to steady myself.

A murder of crows was camped out in the trees above and they started to send up a racket as soon as I stopped to look at them. It was if they were talking about me, gossiping and laughing at my misfortune, my stupidity as a wife, my ineptitude as a parent. Easy for you to say, I called to them. You try it out and see how well you do.

They squawked louder.

I walked on, looking down at the ground for a stone, a feather, or a bone. A sign. The trail forked and I stood for a moment deliberating—the left trail would take me down to the pond, the right path to a high hill with an overlook. There was one boulder at the overlook I liked to sit on and think. But today didn't seem to be a day for sitting and thinking, so I took the trail down to the marsh.

I always liked visiting the beaver dam there—a preposterous mountain of gnawed sticks clustered together at the center of the marsh. The poplar trees along the shore of the marsh had been well-harvested, some felled and partly pulverized into heaps of dust.

I walked over to them and sat down on one of the fallen trunks to drink my tea. This one was newly fallen. I looked around at the havoc and destruction left by the beavers —I felt like I was sitting in the middle of some kind of sacrifice.

Poplars were called "talking trees" by the ancients because of the way their leaves clapped together when the wind blew. They were said to whisper the secrets of endurance.

Sitting here in their shattered midst, I thought they must know a lot about that.

I set down my thermos and put my hands on the trunk. Was there any spirit left? Did hope continue on after the harsh realities of life set in?

"Life sometimes *is* harsh," said the poplar tree that stood behind me. I turned around and stared up at the magnificent, slender height of it. "And sometimes it is soft, like this morning."

I closed my eyes and listened. Even without her leaves, this poplar could speak just fine.

"My sister serves a different role now," she said.. "She is a home to the beetles and ants, she is a fertilizer that will enrich the earth and give life to new things. Every change in circumstance asks us to become something else—to serve in a different way."

I thought about that. How was I to serve differently now? I didn't feel like I had performed so greatly at the last job I was given.

I sighed, stood up and headed down to the marsh.

When I reached the shoreline, I could see circles of water rippling away from the water's edge. That usually meant the beaver was nearby, skimming just under the surface of the water. Sometimes she would poke her nose up out of the reeds and weeds and stare. I waited for her to show herself. The beaver didn't care much for spectators, though, and sometimes slapped her tail on the water in protest if someone got too curious.

The fog was particularly heavy over the water and the far shore of the marsh was nearly obscured. A lone swan glided through its silken curtain. She whooshed back and forth, back and forth, as if she were looking for something. She let out a kind of whoop that echoed across the water, and it startled me. I wondered to whom she was calling. They said swans mated for life. Maybe she had lost her mate like me.

Her cry sounded sad and forlorn. I felt like I understood that cry exactly. I felt like I carried that cry in the scooped out part of my chest, but couldn't give voice to it. It made me wince to hear it. It made my eyes water. I guess my challenge wasn't so much about holding it together as it was about letting go.

I watched her for a while, but she didn't look over at me and she didn't cry out anymore. She seemed resigned to her solitude now, skillfully floating on the cold glass of the water.

I breathed in the quiet and calmness that surrounded her, hoping it would linger inside me, too.

The water around the dam was without ripple, and I guessed that the beaver had skirted away. I looked at the dam and marveled at its intricacy, the patience and persistence contained in every stick. I walked closer and looked down into the water where I had last seen signs of the beaver hiding. There were some sticks nearby that she may have been intending to take to her dam.

"Is it alright if I take one of these sticks?" I asked. (It was always respectful to ask.)

She must have retreated to the depths of the marsh, but I sensed her there, observing me—me and my lameness, my complicated life and petty concerns. My endless human drivel. I felt her lying in the cool shroud of the water, her babies and her carefully constructed home nearby, and I ached for such simplicity, such safety and predictability.

"What makes you think my life is any safer than yours?" I heard her say. "And why desire predictability? 'Might as well be dead."

"I guess so," I said. "But it's just so hard sometimes."

"The harder it is, the richer it is. Your life is still blessed. Just live it and rebuild it—one stick at a time."

Her words struck me—what *good* did it do me to see my life as broken by Daniel's death, as any more difficult than it had been two months ago? Apparently, knowing what I now knew, my life wasn't really what I thought it was anyway. Daniel's secret life was a harsh reality, yes, but at least I wasn't living in the dark anymore. Maybe what happened wasn't so much a curse, as it was a rescue.

I bent down and plucked a stick from the ground, running my thumb along the tip and the grooves the beaver had gnawed there. I turned the stick over. The bottom was stained darker from the damp earth and bore the pattern of a circle with many lines radiating out from it, a sun that shone rays of hope and promise. I held it in my hands and smelled its sharp woodiness. "Thank you," I said. "I'll try to remember that."

When I came in the door to the house, I could hear the phone ringing and I rushed to answer it. The caller ID indicated it was my mother, and as I sighed and reluctantly pushed the TALK button, my daughter Kenya let out a wail behind me. I jumped and nearly dropped the phone.

She was standing in the hallway crying, her hair in a torrent around her head, her face reddened and streaked with tears.

"Kenya, what is the matter?"

"I didn't—know—where you—were! I got up—a-and
—you weren't—here!" Her sobs were clipping the words as
she spoke them.

"Okay, okay," I said, realizing my mother was hearing
all of this. I put the phone to my ear. "Can I call you back? I
need to take care of Kenny right now."

"Well, I should say so," my mother answered.

"I'll call you back," I said, clicking the phone off and
putting it down.

I went to Kenya who was standing in the hallway,
crying into her hands.

"Sweetheart, I was just out walking. That's all." I put
my arms around her and held her, and she sobbed into my
shoulder.

"I didn't know where you were. You left me all alone."

"Darling, you were asleep. I just took a little walk."

"I wasn't asleep! I've been sitting here worrying."

"Okay. Okay. I'm sorry." I tried to make my voice as
soothing as possible.

"You left me all alone!"

"Surely you knew I'd be right back, wherever I was."

"No," she said. "I was scared." She buried her head
deeper into my shoulder and sobbed.

I sighed and held her tighter. "Okay, well, I'll always,
always be back. You can count on that."

There was a long pregnant pause.

"Daddy's not coming back," she said, her words muffled in the folds of my sweatshirt.

I needed wisdom and calm detachment, clear measured
thinking, and I needed it right now. I breathed into Kenya's
chestnut hair and bundled the length of it up in one of my
hands, twirling it slowly in the air and letting it fall down her
back.

"No, sweetie, you're right, he's not."

"Did he mean to leave us?" she looked up and stared deeply into my face.

"Of course not. That just happened."

"Why?"

"Well, that's a big question, Kennie. When somebody we love dies, we're left with a lot of big questions like that."

"Then, what's the answer?"

"I don't know. It might take us some time to get those answers. So we have to be willing to keep listening. What do you think Daddy would say if you asked him why he left?"

"I don't know."

"Well, think about it."

"He'd say he just had to, that's all. Like when he used to go on trips and I'd ask him that. He'd say he had to work."

My mind drifted to the New Orleans trip, the week before he died, the trip I now believed—along with other trips —had been taken with the woman he was planning to leave us for. I cleared my throat.

My mind started to wander and I should learn never to open my mouth when my mind does that.

"You make a good point, Kennie. They say when people die, there's a kind of work they do in the afterlife. What they work on is the life they just left. They make up for things they did wrong. They try and repair things and help the ones they left behind to understand how much they were loved. So, for now we could say that Daddy left because he had some work to do."

Kenya picked her head up and looked at me.

"What did Daddy do wrong?"

"Nothing, honey. That's not what I meant."

"You said that. You said people who die work on what they did wrong."

"Oh, yes. Well, I meant that in general. We're all human, you know, sweetie. Even though we might have the best of intentions, we all make mistakes."

"So, did Daddy?"

"I suppose so, but that's not important, is it?"

"Sure, it's important. I mean, if he did something bad, I would want to know about it."

I closed my eyes. I had just done a face plant on the elephant in the room. Time to change the subject.

"Hey, missy, look at those bare feet on a cold morning like this!" I said. "Let's get you some socks and a nice warm breakfast. How about some Cream of Wheat?"

"Rice Krispies."

"Alright, let's see if we have some."

I got out a bowl and spilled in some cereal and milk. Kenya crawled into the breakfast nook.

I put her cereal down in front of her and went to the laundry area in the mudroom. There were some clean pairs of socks on top of the dryer. I unrolled one pair and handed them to her. She was shoveling Krispies into her mouth.

"Mom," she said. She was staring up at the ceiling in a thoughtful way.

"What?"

"Do you wish sometimes things could be like they were before?"

"Yes, sweetie, I do."

"You do?"

"Of course I do. Why, doesn't it seem that way?"

"No. You just act mad is all. It's like you blame Daddy for something. Is it because you know something he did wrong and you won't tell me?"

"Kenya, honestly, you have such an imagination."

"You shouldn't be mad."

"I'm not!"

Not knowing what more to say to her, I stood up and went back into the mudroom where she couldn't see me anymore. I started refolding clothes in the basket and humming. Kenya was like a psychic sponge. She knew something was in the air, and I was doing my best to hold her at bay by jamming the signals.

Even as a toddler, Kenya's startling insight into things would scare the hell out of me. It never seemed like she really knew the weight or importance of what she was saying. Things would simply roll out of her mouth in three or five-year-old language, observations as incisive as the edge of a razor. I was half afraid that one day the sharpness of those words might cut someone—most likely me.

Whenever she overheard Daniel and me bickering, Kenya always took Daniel's side. Once I was complaining about how overly sensitive Daniel was being, protesting that I was entitled to my opinions of him whether they were flattering or not. From the backseat of the car came Kenya's croaky three-year-old voice:

"He wouldn't get so mad if you didn't act like such a man-man," she said.

It's not what you say, she was telling me, it's how you say it. You're being bossy and aggressive, and it's not necessary.

I remember at the time Daniel and I looked at one another and burst out laughing. It broke the vexed state we were in and brought us back to a lighter mood. That was Kenya's magic. Something that came, I suppose, from the mysterious land where she was conceived thirteen years ago while Daniel and I were on safari.

Now, here I was hiding from that magic, hoping it didn't find me, lying about what I knew, carrying secrets I never wanted to hold, folding clothes that didn't need to be folded and humming away—"What a Wonderful World", no less—which was way more lighthearted and optimistic than I ever might possibly feel again.

Once Kenya got engrossed in watching a movie in the family room, I slipped upstairs to my study, locked the door and debated about calling my mother back.

I didn't want to call her back, and didn't feel up to

dealing with her scrutiny.

We had a history, my mother and I. I had proved to be a willful and headstrong child, and this always seemed to overwhelm and terrify her. She had made it clear many times throughout my life that I was not a person who could be trusted to make a reliable decision or handle a challenging situation. I was Calamity Jane to my mother, not Grace under fire.

To my way of thinking, if she had simply left me alone to grow up and express myself naturally, I wouldn't have become so rebellious and stubborn in the first place. I always felt my strong, independent streak was in direct response to her critical and controlling style of parenting.

It was this loggerhead dynamic that I had replicated perfectly in my marriage to Daniel. I was not allowed to handle things like our finances, and my opinion about them was not valued or heard. If I became too animated at a gathering, too exuberant about my work, too silly and childlike with the kids, I would catch him staring at me as if there were something dangerous and inappropriate about my behavior.

"Children should be seen and not heard," my mother always said. She had wanted a quiet and well-mannered child, a neatly-dressed doll she could put up on a shelf for safe-keeping. Daniel had wanted a wife with no blemishes or edges. For both my husband and my mother, I needed to be carefully kept, like the toys in the famous Margery Williams' tale that would never become as real as the *Velveteen Rabbit*.

I groaned, sat down on the floor and dialed her number.

"Is everything alright there?" she asked.

"Yeah, yeah, fine." I forced a lighthearted laugh like Kenya's meltdown was all too silly to even spend time on.

"Well, it certainly didn't *sound* fine," said my mother.

"No, it is," I said as evenly as possible.

"Really," she said.

"So, what's up?" I asked, changing the subject.

"Well," she said, pausing for dramatic impact, "it seems your son, Ethan, has called me."

My mind drifted to an image of myself confiscating Ethan's cell phone and pulverizing it with my foot.

"Has he?"

"Yes, and he's upset, Clare. Very upset."

Oh, that my first-born would give my mother this much ammunition against me.

"Of course he's upset," I said. "His father just died. Actually I'm glad he called you. He needs someone to talk to. I'm just too close to the situation."

I breathed, hoping I had somehow managed to steal her thunder.

My mother was silent.

"Well," she said. "I don't think it's quite that simple, Clare."

"Oh, do you *think*? I kind of thought this little matter of my husband up and *dying* was going to be a piece of cake."

Another silence.

"Clare, I don't understand why you're getting so angry with me when all I'm trying to do is help you and the kids. That's the only reason I called. Not to tell you how to live your life, just to offer my help. I never said I had all the answers, but I think I can shed some light here."

"Really?"

"Yes," she said, "didn't I lose my husband unexpected-ly?"

"It's not the same thing, Mom. Daddy was retired. Dean and I were grown and gone."

"How is it not the same?" asked my mother.

"It's *not*, that's all, and if I needed your help I would call you up and ask for it."

"No, Clare, you would never do that. You always think you know all the answers, and it really isn't your best quality, sweetheart. You're as pig-headed as your father was."

"I'll take that as a compliment."

My mother sighed.

We hung on the phone in silence, both of us stewing in our own juices.

"So what's Ethan got on his mind?"

"He's worried about Kenya. He says she's not doing well at all, and that you're doing nothing about it."

"I'm doing *nothing* about it? And you believe that?"

"Ethan says you're drinking."

"That's a cheap shot."

"So you *are* drinking then?"

"I have a glass or two of wine with dinner. It relaxes me. My days are very stressful, Mother. I don't see what's wrong with that."

Of course, I knew it was usually more than a couple of glasses. I had pretty much decimated Daniel's carefully constructed wine cellar over the last two months. But I told myself this was a temporary indulgence—just to get me over the worst of it. Just to get me over the hump.

"So you're drowning your sorrows," said my mother.

"Oh my God! I am not drowning my sorrows, okay?"

"And Ethan also tells me you're not eating. I'm concerned you're not taking care of yourself. I don't want you getting sick again."

I rolled my eyes. "I'm not getting sick! I'm eating, okay? I'm fine. Kenya's fine. We're all fine."

"Have you taken her to see anyone?"

"She doesn't want to see anyone. She cries whenever I suggest it. Look, I've thought about this, okay? I want to give her some time. I don't want her to think there's something wrong with her."

"There *is* something wrong with her. And you aren't handling it properly."

"Now how do *you* know? You're not even here. She's just grieving and she's doing it a way that is very much Kenya. She's working through it a little bit at a time."

"How can it hurt, Clare, to have her speak with someone?"

"She'll feel like I'm abandoning her, and that is the worst thing to do to a child who has just lost her father."

My mother didn't respond for a moment. I could hear her breathing quietly, mulling over what I had said. I was not going to relent, and I felt she would probably concede in some typically condescending way, and then that would be the end of it for a while.

"I think maybe I should come for a visit," she said. "Just for a little while. I need to satisfy myself that everything is alright there."

My heart started to pound. I couldn't control myself.

"What do you mean satisfy yourself? *Satisfy* yourself? Since when did my life become your jurisdiction? Frankly, I don't give a shit *what* you think about how I'm handling things! You have nothing to lend to this situation but more grief and aggravation, and let me just be really clear, you are NOT coming here!"

I shut the phone off and smacked it so hard against the desk, the battery shot out of its backside, skittered across the floor and became buried in a stack of papers.

Then, I got down on the floor and hammered my fists onto the rug like a five-year-old, curled up in a fetal ball and started to sob.

After a while, the sobbing passed and I rolled onto my back. My tantrum had not been dignified perhaps, but it didn't feel unwarranted, and it had relieved a lot of pent up anger and grief. A wave of exhaustion came over me and I felt a thick blanket of sleep catch me in the crook of its arm and slowly pull me away.

I found myself in a room with a fireplace and mantle. Over the mantle hung a wide mirror.

"A mantle should have a picture, " I said, "not a mirror."

"Look into the mirror," said a voice, "and *then* it will be a picture."

I laughed and approached the glass. My reflection surprised me. In the mirror stood a tall, willowy being. She was made of fiery, white light. Silver and gold sparks sizzled in the air around her.

I put my fingers to the glass. "Is this really me?" I asked.

"Yes," said the voice, "this is who you are."

"But, I don't feel this way. I don't know this me."

"You will," said the voice.

"But how? When?"

I kept turning my head this way and that, marveling at what I saw.

I reached out my hand, thinking the mirror was a portal, but found I couldn't penetrate the glass. I wanted to get into that world of the mirror. I began to look for tools, thinking I could break in around the frame.

But the room I was standing in was completely empty. The house seemed to be vacant, and I had the sense I had just moved there from another state. I began to pry at the frame with my fingers and was pleased to find it came apart easily. Whole sections of it crumbled off into my hand.

The glass lifted up just a bit and I was able to reach my hand into a cool and clouded world. The silvery-gold woman smiled. I pushed my whole arm in and wiggled my fingers, just grazing her shining garment with my fingertips.

I was beginning to wonder how my head was going to fit through, and then, suddenly, there was a loud bang on the ceiling above me. Then, another bang and another, as if stones were falling from the sky onto the roof.

I opened my eyes and sighed. It was Kenya, kicking the door.

"Mom!" she shouted. "Why is your door locked? Mom! Let me in! Why is your door locked?"

"Kennie, for the love of God," I said, getting up from the floor, "I was sleeping, alright?"

My daughter kicked the door again.

"Stop kicking the door!" I said, opening it wide.

My daughter looked at me and frowned. She gazed past me into the room, as if to determine what I was up to. Then she stared into my face.

"You look like hell, Mom, " she said.

"No kidding," I said. "Imagine that."

Chapter Three
Blackthorn: Trouble

Since last fall, I had been on sabbatical from the college where I taught art. I was taking the time off in order to produce an exhibit of sculptures called "Shifting Realities." I had just started one piece—the bust of a half eagle, half man-- when Daniel died. Now, here it was April already, and I was returning to teaching in less than six months with not much to show for my hard-earned year off.

I drove through the cold rain down the narrow streets of Hilltown, turning onto the River Road, our main drag. The river burbled over rocks to my right, the hills that gave their name to this town rose on either side of me. I wound my way into town, where I stopped at the coffee shop for a large green tea.

We had a small town center that most folks found charmingly New England in appearance. We used to be a factory town—clocks and fine furnishings—with a glass works down the road still in operation. The remaining buildings had been converted into antique shops, cafes, a drug store and post office, the newsstand and variety store, and The Old Mill Inn, which drew traffic from out of town due to its Zagat four-star rating.

Now Hilltown was pretty much a bedroom community for Hartford and Springfield. Though some found it a bit secluded, I loved its rustic character and small town appeal.

My studio was located in what had once been the home of an optical company. I rented the side where the lab used to be. It had a high, suspended ceiling and windows that let in plenty of light but gave no view. The walls badly needed painting and the floor was covered with stained and peeling linoleum. I took the space "as is", and the landlord, Ed, gratefully reduced my monthly rent by fifty dollars.

There was a door that separated the space I rented from what had once been the optician's shop. The shop had been empty for years, but when I arrived at my studio for the first time in three months, I saw that there were lights on behind the display windows and a sign over the door that said FRAGMENTS OF THE IMAGINATION.

I parked my Volvo wagon in the gravel lot behind the building and walked around to the front, picking up trash as I went. I emptied my hands into the dumpster by the road and wiped them on my jeans, while walking to the new shop to have a closer look.

As I approached the windows, my mouth gaped open with wonder. The window cases were filled with objects made of stones, glass and metal pieces, jumbled together with a mixture of copper wiring, epoxy and putty. They were complicated, disturbing and appealing all at the same time. And they were good—really good.

Some were hanging; others were mounted on black wooden pedestals. Each had a sturdy but ravaged look, their forms only partially composed: a woman's shoulder, neck and arm wired together and encrusted in chips of porcelain, half of a dog, made with bent and rusty nails, a chunk of a horse's face, constructed of broken beer bottles, that showed one eye, one cheek and a half of the nose. They were beautiful and full of passion and pain, and I couldn't stop staring at them. They reminded me of oysters, bumpy and deformed on the surface, but succulent and potent within.

I looked up and noticed a man standing at the back of the display, staring out at me. His brows were pinched together as if he were trying to figure out what I was doing there. In his hand, he held a twisted clump of copper wiring that looked like a bouquet of headless flowers. The artist, I thought.

I beamed back at him like he was an old friend and started to wave exuberantly, first pointing at the objects and then putting my hand flat to my heart, grinning broadly and nodding my approval.

He pinched his brows a little tighter, his baffled expression unbroken.

I reached for the door so I could speak to him, but it was locked. Duh! Clare. It's 7:30 in the morning! My hand came back from the knob as if I had been burnt. I clasped my hands together, trying not to look as stupid as I felt.

He opened the door to the shop slowly and stood back.

"Oh!" I said, bursting in the door. "Your stuff is UN-believable!" I walked past him to a display table in the center of the shop. I scanned the shelves and the pieces that hung on the wall and down from the ceiling.

"Oh, my God! Sooo powerful! A-MAZ-ing !" I shook my head in disbelief at him and then realized he still had not spoken. Here I was, babbling on in my high-toned, exclamatory way, doing the "mom talking about art" routine my children both loathed. They would be cringing with embarrassment if they were with me right now. Correction, they would have fled to the car by now.

"Sorry," I said sheepishly. "I get a little...." I rolled my hand around on my wrist as if this explained something.

"No, it's fine," he said. "I'm grateful for the compliments."

He seemed a little shy and looked down at his shoes as he spoke. The behavior was inconsistent with the aura he had, one that seemed tough and seasoned, even powerful. He was probably fifteen or twenty years older than me, tall and broad-shouldered with scooped-back gray hair that ran in a long thin ponytail down his back. He had on worn, plaster-coated jeans and a faded black T-shirt. The face was still handsome, despite a flattened nose that was probably broken during a misspent youth and skin that was deeply lined and leathery from too much sun exposure. I thought of Jack Palance. He had those same snappy blue eyes that almost hurt to look at, and a voice that was husky from years of cigarettes.

"I'm your neighbor, " I said, pointing to the back wall of his shop.

"My—?"

"Your neighbor. I have the studio in the back."

"Oh," he said. "I thought you were dead."

"What?"

He blushed and looked so intently at his shoes, I thought he was reading lines from them.

"I mean, I asked Ed why no one was ever over there and he said there was a death."

"Me? Oh God, no, I'm not dead," I said, pointing to myself. I barked out a snort of laughter as I heard myself say it.

"No, it was my husband that—um—died—actually." I tried to compose my face so that it matched the solemnity of this revelation.

"Oh, that's too bad. Sorry."

"I'm Clare."

"No, I can imagine. That's rough."

"No, Clare. It's my name."

"Oh right, right, right," he said. He ran the "rights" all together like they made one three syllable word. "I'm Dill."

"Dill?"

"Yeah, like the weed." He said weed the way guys who were veteran potheads said it.

"Ah!" I stared at him. "Interesting name."

He nodded.

"Well, I love your artwork," I said. "It's very visceral."

He squinted at me. "I don't know what that means."

"Visceral? Oh, well, visceral means like something that has a deep, raw, emotional, twisting kind of feeling." I was pushing my fist into my stomach as I spoke. He stared at my hand like I was a going to bring forth a skein of intestine.

"I know what visceral means. I just don't understand why you say that about my work."

"Oh, well, because, when I look at these pieces..." I gazed around the shop, and went over to a nearby pedestal that held what looked like an old woman bent over in grief. Her head was a howling knob of glass and the copper wiring that ran down her spine was frazzled and reaching. Her legs stopped at the knees; wires sizzled from her outstretched hands. It made me shake to look at her. I felt like I *was* her. "Man," I said, "this one just knocks the wind out of me."

Dill shrugged but seemed pleased by my reaction. He fingered the wires in his bouquet and twisted their ends.

"I don't always know what I'm doing when I make them," he said in a confessional tone. "Sometimes they start out as one thing and then I realize they're something else."

"It's good not to know," I said, touching him on the arm, as if I were consoling him. "It's good to keep the wonder in it. Then there's something there for everyone who sees it. Do you know what I mean?"

He nodded and then shrugged again, still twirling the copper threads in his fingers.

"It's a great concept though, the whole fragmented thing. How did you come up with it?"

He looked puzzled for a moment. "I didn't. That's just the way it happened. I have these things in my head—memories and things—but they're all in pieces. You know?" He pointed to his head. "My mind is all in pieces."

Something in the way he spoke about himself made my heart ache.

"Oh," I said. "Did something happen to you?"

Dill looked at me for a while as if deciding whether he wanted to reveal himself anymore than he had. Then he turned to adjust one of the displays. "Just regular shit," he said.

"Yeah, well, shit happens, as they say. That's for sure." I was sounding so awkward, trying to cover the embarrassment I seemed to cause him. "I wasn't meaning to pry—it's just that your work is so powerful. My work—I don't know—I wish it had this kind of punch to it."

"What kind of things do you do?"

"I do sculpture mostly. I'm trying to complete a series of figures that are part human and part nature, part real and part spirit—kind of a study in shapeshifting."

"Sounds cool."

"I don't know. Sometimes I think my work is too distant, too obscure. Yours comes right up and grabs people by the collar. Have you done any shows?"

"Nah, I don't go in for that sort of thing. To me, this is a craft—a craft and a kind of therapy. Keeps me out of trouble."

He did look like he'd seen a lot of that.

"Well, it's brilliant," I said. "You've inspired me to jump back into my own work. I've been dreading coming down here, really dreading it. I feel so disconnected from the project I started last year—I'm not even sure it makes much sense anymore."

He shook his head. "You can't plan it. You have to do what wants to come out."

I rolled my eyes. "Oh, dear. Not sure I want to even see that!"

Dill let out a thick, wheezy belly-laugh, which took me by surprise. He was so controlled and careful, it was as if he himself were coiled up in some of that copper wiring.

"It can be scary," he said. "It can be scary as hell sometimes."

I smiled. "It's nice to have a neighbor," I said, holding
out my hand to shake his. "Art can be a lonely business."

My own studio was cold and dark and fusty by comparison. Moments before in Dill's shop, a warm throaty saxo-
phone and the tang of brewed coffee had wafted up from the
back counter and filled the room. The sparkle of glass and
metal had danced from every surface. But here, it was gray
and vacant and still. Deserted.

I tugged at the sheet I had placed over my sculpture the
last time I was here. It had the oddly foreign feel of a work
you created but haven't seen in a while.

"Hmmm," I said, not liking it. My brain started drawing comparison's to Dill's work. "Don't even go there," I
mumbled.

I sat down on the floor and leaned my back against the
wall. The piece didn't grow any more appealing with the five
feet of distance I put between it and me.

I had intended it to be majestic, wise and fierce. But,
this piece had none of those qualities. The facial expression
was strangely lifeless, and the shoulders, which I had wanted
to look part human and part birdlike, were lopsided—giving it
a slight hunchbacked affect. The wing was oddly angled and a
little too scrawny. But the expression of the half-human, half-
eagle face was the worst part—the pushed in cheeks and open
mouth making it look more ghoulish than fierce.

I crossed my arms over my knees and sighed heavily. I
didn't know what I was doing, but I was pretty certain at this
point that I had to start over, not just with this piece, but
maybe with this whole idea. Like Dill said, I couldn't plan it. I
needed to do what wanted to come out.

What wanted to come out was this boatload of anger

I'd been sitting on for almost three months. No, make that, years. In truth, I'd been mad about Daniel and the failure of our marriage for about as long as I could remember.

I tried to think what would be the artistic end-result of me letting all that out of my head. I got a cartoon image of my studio reduced to rubble, a burned out, smoking cavern in the ground. I shook my head and laughed.

"Oh, Daniel," I said, "you *re-e-ally* did it this time."

Perhaps Daniel had only defaulted into this wild curve ball of an untimely death because he'd painted himself into a corner with Cynthia. No easier out than a disappearing act, is there?

"Here, Clare. See what you can do with this one," Daniel seemed to say, as he lobbed it over the plate.

Daniel's death was like the *coup de grace* of our historically co-dependent relationship, where he took on way more than he could handle and I cleaned up the ensuing mess. My husband was a man of great vision who had no follow-through. Oddly, it was the characteristic that had first attracted me to him—Daniel, the dreamer. In the beginning, I had been only too happy to be the helpmate and enabler of those big-sky dreams.

But what I became instead was the dependable accomplice, the one who asked no questions and swept up the broken glass or wiped up the blood and the muddy footprints, the one who released the hand brake and watched all Daniel's blunders and mistakes disappear into the center of the lake.

Death is never as tough for the one who dies, as it is for the one left behind. I remember Daniel saying that to me when I had been sick, and ironically, he was right. The doctors, noting my steady decline and failure to respond to any of the treatments they were giving me, suggested somberly one day that if they couldn't "turn this thing around," it might well be fatal.

Daniel was not so much shocked or saddened by this prognosis, as he was, how can I say this, *offended* by it. "What am I supposed to do?" he asked me. "I mean, the kids will be sad for a while, sure, but they're young; they'll get over it. They have their whole lives ahead of them. But what about me? What do *I* do, Clare?"

I remember lying there, unable to look at him. He'd brought this question into me along with the supper tray. I stared at the white bowl on the tray, knowing without even looking, that it contained Campbell's chicken noodle soup, one of the three things I was able to tolerate during this latent phase of my weird and mysterious illness.

I wasn't sure what upset me more: the predicted swiftness, with which my own children would forget about me, or the implication that Daniel's own impending distress would somehow trump my own.

In the end, I didn't die. In the end, I had what they termed a miraculous recovery. But, apparently, it was my threatened exodus that broke Daniel's trust in me. As I had become a flight risk, he needed to hedge his bets.

And because I had never answered Daniel as to what he *was* supposed to do if I kicked the bucket, Daniel answered it for himself—you find yourself a replacement. *Toute suite.*

As I sat there staring at my failed attempt at man meets eagle, I had a flash of longing not for my illness, but for those days when I had been forced to check out and take to my bed. I remembered full well how bored and frightened and depressed I had become during those months, how much I had wanted to just climb out of my body and take off for parts unknown. But, those days looked oddly appealing right now.

I shook my head and picked up my keys and handbag. I had to get out of here. I was starting to think very morbid and self-pitying thoughts. I grabbed my sketchbook, hoping it would eventually help to snag some passing spark of inspiration that would fuel a new and more promising sculpture. The ghoulish and hunchbacked eagle-man was headed for the dustbin.

That evening after dinner, Kenya and Ethan went to their rooms to study. I cleaned up the dishes and folded a load of clothes that were languishing in the dryer. Then I watered the plants, took out the garbage, and swept the porch steps. I was trying to work off the edginess I was feeling since I'd decided to cut back on my daily indulgence of wine, the wine I had relied upon to calm me down each evening.

When I'd plunked a glass of water down in front of my placemat at dinner, Ethan had stared at it and then looked up at me.

"I decided to have water with dinner," I said loudly.

Kenya looked up from her plate. "So?"

"Nothing," I said. "I'm just saying, for those of us who are keeping track."

"Mom," said Kenya, shaking her head, "you're so random sometimes."

Later, while Ethan stood at the sink rinsing his plate, I sidled up to him and said: "You know, the code around here is kind of like 'what happens in Vegas stays in Vegas'."

He gave me this deadpan look. "You're comparing our house to Vegas?"

"You know what I mean, Ethan. You can't be going and telling Grandma things about us. You need to keep things private within the family."

"Grandma *is* family," he said, sliding in the rack of the dishwasher and closing the door.

How odd was it that my son looked at my mother as family and I didn't?

"Nuclear family," I said.

"Nuc-u-lar?" Ethan asked, breaking into a grin.

"Nuclear! I didn't say nucular."

"Yes, you did, Mom. I heard you."

"I didn't, and don't change the subject."

"Whatever," he said strolling out of the kitchen.

Now, I stood in the middle of the kitchen floor, tapping my foot and chewing on the inside of my lip. I debated about whether to run the vacuum cleaner, watch a DVD or check out what was on television. Baseball season had started a few days ago and I thought about tuning into the game with Cleveland —my old hometown.

But I still felt unresolved about the argument I'd had with my mother the week before and Ethan's growing lack of trust in me. Not to mention the troubling, albeit fleeting, thought I'd had that afternoon about how nice it would be to simply take to my bed, close my eyes, and head for the exit sign.

I decided the most prudent thing to do would be to journey. And, after all, I was trying to be on my best behavior today.

I poured myself another glass of water and went up to my study. I lay down on the floor, put a blanket over me, and laid a scarf across my eyes. I turned on my drumming tape.

I went to the lower world and instead of Sumeh, found my ancestral guide, Eamon, waiting for me. Truthfully, I was a bit afraid of Eamon. He had a fierce, craggy face and sharp, glass-blue eyes. He said very little, but kind of snapped at me whenever he did speak, and he usually called me *girl*. He always carried this walking stick with him, and as if Eamon wasn't fearsome enough, today I noticed that the staff had long black thorns sticking out of its gnarled head.

I asked him why he was there instead of Sumeh.

"You wanted to work on the difficulties with your mother, did you not?" he asked.

"Well, yes," I said.

He turned and walked away from me, so I followed behind, awaiting further clarity. Across a wide field, I could see a lone, dark tree. It was bent at the middle and grew out sideways as if to ensnare approaching travelers. Then, I spotted all the thorns jutting out from its branches.

"Blackthorn," said Eamon. "Makes a good hedge for the sheep.

We stood underneath it and looked up. He stretched his staff up into the snarl overhead and pointed to a long, solitary thorn at the end of one branch. "Go up and get me that one there, girl," he said.

I stared at him.

"Go on now. Don't be wasting my time."

I sighed and began to climb carefully. This was a very tricky tree to navigate. I decided it might help to open up a conversation with it.

"Won't you show me the best way to climb a blackthorn?" I asked sweetly.

"You have to be a lot wiser than the blackthorn," said the tree, "in order to climb one."

"Ah," I said, thinking I might be on to something.

"And no one is wiser than the blackthorn," said the tree, who had a voice like the wicked witch of the West.

"What's taking you?" said Eamon.

"Look, it's a little tough to get along up here—it's very prickly."

"Is it now?" said Eamon, laughing to himself.

I was losing patience, but I was determined to get him the dang thorn he wanted. I could see it piercing the air at the end of the branch I was teetering on.

"And grace," said the blackthorn in its raspy voice. "You need a good deal of grace."

"Okay," I thought, stretching out my arms like a tightrope walker.

"But you don't have much grace," noted the blackthorn, which made me slip and tear a long slice in my leg.

"Tricky business, isn't it?" asked Eamon.

"Look, is there a point to all this?" I asked.

"You're getting it," said the old man, sitting down on a nearby rock to wait.

I reached out my arm and grabbed the requested thorn in one fist. It snapped away from the branch. Then I made my way back down, jabbing myself again and again with almost every move.

I walked over to Eamon and handed him his thorn.

He examined it and then took out a thin black cord from his pocket. He looped the cord around the thorn, and tied the cord around my neck.

"What's this for?" I asked.

"To remind you," said Eamon.

"Of what?"

"Your ability to wound."

"I don't want it," I said, reaching to remove it.

Eamon stared hard at me. My hand dropped to my side.

"There are things in life that need to be obeyed, girl. There are things that need to be attended. Sometimes, it's the voice of fate that calls to us, and sometimes it's the voice of our elders. It might be unpleasant to hear what they have to say, but that's the way of it. Your mother gave you your life, and she deserves to be honored. When you are willing to trade your pride for kindness and gratitude, the thorn will fade away from lack of use. Now, do you see how hard it can be for a person to navigate a prickly personality, who thinks she knows it all?"

I nodded. There were tears running from the corners of my eyes, across my temples and into my ears.

"Good. Now go up and visit with your father."

"My father?" I asked, but Eagle had already arrived. Picking me up by one arm, he dragged me up into the sky like a rag doll.

We landed in the upper world at a stone gate. Behind the gate stood a large brown house with a broad, square face, a wide front porch and steps. I walked up to the door and entered a great breezy hall with thick pillars along each side. As I walked further into the room, my father stepped out from behind one of the pillars.

His hair was snow white and he was wearing a dark blue robe and sandals.

"What are you doing here?" I said, having not seen him in awhile. Though dead for twenty years, my father was a frequent destination in the journeys I took during my illness. Sumeh used to bring me to see him, but I hadn't ever encountered him in this place before.

"I live here."

"Here?" I asked. "In this huge place?"

"Sure, what's wrong with that?"

"It's a little over the top, don't you think?"

He laughed. "I like it."

"Hmmph," I said. "What's that you're wearing?"

"It's comfortable," he said, sounding a little like a housewife in a muumuu and flip-flops. "Are you upset with me?"

"Maybe. You seem—I don't know, different."

"I'm trying out some new things."

"Geez, that doesn't sound like you. You were always so set in your ways," I said.

"Exactly," my father replied. "But, there comes a time to embrace change—develop new strengths."

"I can relate," I said.

My father smiled tenderly at me. "You have faced difficult things before—you can do it again."

I thought about the snarly road ahead, and it didn't look much different to me than that blackthorn tree Eamon had made me climb. I sighed.

"Resistance is futile," my father joked, and we both laughed, remembering the days when we watched Star Trek together.

"Your mistake is that you expect too much of everyone —Daniel, your mother, your children, yourself. People do the best they can, Clare. They really do, and they shouldn't be held accountable for simply being who they are. It's all they know.

You need to respect that."

"I don't think Mom is respecting who *I* need to be."

"You must try and see past what she is saying. Your mother loves you deeply. Just because you don't see it, doesn't mean it isn't so."

"You're right. I don't see it," I said.

My father smiled at me. "You don't see a lot of things, Clare."

"Yeah, I'm feeling that pretty strongly right now."

"You don't see your own strength. You need to think carefully about the ways you choose to use your power," my father said. "To harm or to love—to hurt or to heal. It's a choice, sweetie."

I hung my head and looked at the thorn still dangling around my neck. It felt like a scarlet letter. I reached over and put my arms around my father's neck. He kissed me on the head.

Later on, after the kids had gone to bed, I went out into the hallway and pulled down the stairs to the attic. I climbed up into the unfinished space above and located my rebounder, which was wrapped in plastic and leaning against some boxes of old toys. I pulled it out of its plastic cover and dragged it down the steps as quietly as possible. Then I set it up in the center of my study, climbed on and began to jump.

Tomorrow I would relent. Tomorrow I would call my mother and invite her to come and visit. And when she arrived and made me so crazy I wanted to spit nails—or thorns—I would bite my tongue and listen. I would try and see past my mother's words to the intention that was behind them. Then, I would escape into my room, get on my rebounder, and jump until the insanity passed.

It worked once—it could work again.

Chapter Four
Fir: Constancy

I was lying on the foldout couch in my study, staring at the clock again. Sometimes I did this because I hoped it might bore me into falling back to sleep. I would lie on my side and watch the digital numbers change from seven to eight, nine to zero. The arrival of a new hour—when three numbers flipped over at once—was a moment I looked forward to with strange anticipation.

In the middle of the night, when life felt so supremely screwed up, those numbers clipping by so steadily in their crisp red coats seemed like a small miracle to me. There were nights when the inner workings of my alarm clock achieved a grace I found enviable. How does it do that, I would ask myself, realizing with mild concern that I was sounding not unlike Homer Simpson.

My mother was visiting—just visiting. It seemed like I

had to say that four or five times a day now. Everyone—neighbors, friends, folks at the local restaurants and shops—kept assuming she was staying for some reason: oh, are you relocating? Are you thinking of moving here?

She's *just visiting*, I would fire back, the heat of my words coming just shy of singe-ing off their eyebrows.

What were they thinking? Couldn't they see the desperate look in my eyes? Didn't they notice the level of stress, which had left a telltale high-water mark around my forehead? How I longed for the day I could release her to those fine people in airport security. Anyway, we were down to 9 days, 6 hours and 35 minutes until departure time, but who was counting?

I tried many times to remember the stern words of Eamon and the somewhat kinder advice of my father in regards to this challenging area of my life. More than once, I felt that hideous black thorn swinging like a noose around my neck. But, somehow my mother always proved more formidable than the strength of my resolve. If she couldn't get a rise out of me by pushing one button, she always found another one to press.

Tomorrow, no, make that today, we were going to one of those huge outlet complexes over the border in Massachusetts. My mother loved a bargain. She never bought anything if it wasn't on sale. She remembered the original and purchase prices of everything she owned, the number of times it had been marked down, and what additional discounts had been applied. My mother trotted out her shopping stats like some baseball fans rattled off the home run records and batting averages of their favorite players.

"Nineteen ninety-five," she would say, as she came into the kitchen modeling a new blouse. "Donna Karan. You don't believe me? Look at the label. 100% silk, and they retail at ninety dollars. I could have gotten four of them for less than what some poor soul paid for one!"

My mother and her tales of conquest on the retail battleground could melt the legs off a metal chair.

"I love your sweater," the perky checkout girl at Stop and Shop would say as she ran our food items under the scanner.

"Oh, God," I would mutter under my breath, "please don't get her started."

So, tomorrow I was taking her to the Lenox Village Outlets as a welcome distraction for both of us. We would agree on a meeting time and split up as soon as we entered the gates. Though my mother was always eager to school me in the ways of sniffing out a good bargain, I would insist on this separate arrangement. She would head off in one direction and I in the other, and when I was sure she was clean out of sight, I would buy myself a large cup of coffee, return to my car and read for two hours.

Or sleep, as the case may be.

So far, the visit had not gone well. Not that this surprised me—my mother and I had never exactly been chums. Growing up, I'd had no sisters with whom to commiserate, no one to join in my virulent dislike of her, who would cozily create with me in the wee hours of the morning inventive ways to eliminate her. My one brother, Dean, never got the whole mother-daughter dynamic and thought my mother was the easiest person in the world to get along with.

"What's your problem?" he'd say, "Honestly, it seems like she bends over backwards for you."

She bends over backwards for me? Where was he getting this stuff? Oh right—from *her*! The world according to my mother, and my brother ate up every crunchy tantalizing bit of it, like it was popcorn shrimp.

The other day, while we were folding laundry, she started chuckling to herself.

"Do you remember how I laid out five new dresses for you on your bed the day you started first grade and you refused to wear any of them? They were all Polly Flinders, one more gorgeous than the next, and you didn't like one of them.

Not one!"

"Okay for the eight hundredth time—I didn't want to wear *any* dress. I wanted to wear my pedal pushers, and you wouldn't let me! How is this relevant—I was five for God's sake."

Those pedal pushers were my lucky pants. I loved them. They were navy blue with white polka dots and I wore them with my red boat-necked jersey that had three-quarter-length sleeves and a little navy anchor embroidered on the front. I mean, it's not like I had no sense of fashion!

"We couldn't afford Polly Flinders, mind you. Not on your father's salary. I bought those dresses on close-out sales and put them aside for you, and you never even appreciated it."

"God, enough. It was forty years ago. Can you forget it?"

"You were difficult even as a baby—very difficult. I mean, you couldn't help it—you were born that way."

"That makes me feel much better."

"*Mary, Mary, quite contrary. How does your garden grow?*" My mother sang out, laughing as if she were harkening back to a warm family moment. "That's what I always said about you."

"No, really? This is the first time *ever* that I'm hearing that."

"I just never understood why you had to be so difficult, that's all. Doesn't all that New Age stuff you love so much teach you how to—what's that expression?—go with the flow?"

"Mother, I wasn't being difficult. I was being myself. I'm not a difficult person—I'm just different from you. Okay? I'm just trying to speak my own truth."

"Speak your own truth? Well, it's not like you need any lessons there. You certainly never minced any words with me, I can tell you that."

"Oh, for the love of God. Look, I get that I was a challenge for you, Mom. Can we just drop it now?"

"Challenge? Honey, you were impossible! What child turns her nose up at five Polly Flinders dresses? Five?"

"Me!" I say, slapping my hand on my chest. "Me, I did that! If you want to know the truth, I hated those fucking dresses! All five of them! There—are you satisfied now?"

And so it goes.

9 days, 4 hours and 53 minutes remaining. And if the springs in my rebounder hold out, we might just make it.

I fumbled through the morning and managed to get the kids off to school. Then I went back to bed. One of the few nice things about my mother was that she really enjoyed her sleep and wouldn't usually surface until 11:00 a.m. Before long, I fell into a deep sleep.

When the telephone rang at 9:30, I was trapped in some convoluted dream about a train station in Paris. I was banging on the door of the train, which would not open, but kept ringing and ringing.

I opened my eyes and reached for the receiver. It was Hal, my lawyer.

"Clare," he said, "did I wake you?"

"Maybe."

"Do you want me to call you back, then?"

"No, no, I'm good."

"Well, I'd like you to be awake for this conversation."

My heart flopped over in my chest and I sat up in the bed. "Why," I said, "what's wrong?"

"Cynthia's moved into the house."

"Moved there?"

"Yes. It strengthens her claim on it a bit more."

"But I thought she lived in Hartford."

"Well, she's relocated. Got herself a job out there in Arizona."

"Fuck," I said.

"We still have a case; you needn't get discouraged. I was just hoping she would go away quietly, but it's really not looking that way now."

"Jesus," I said, 'how did you find this out?"

"Her lawyer."

"She's got a lawyer?"

"Well, she needs a lawyer, Clare. I wasn't expecting her to go away *that* quietly."

"Fuck. I can't believe he's put me in this position. I just can't believe this."

"I know," Hal said, 'it's taking you a while to get used to that."

Hal waited for this information to sink in a bit, and then he said: "There's more."

"There's *more*?"

"Well, yes. The reason why her lawyer called me was to inform us that he'd filed a declaratory judgment on Cynthia's behalf in the state of Arizona that would clear Daniel's name from the title and give her sole possession of the house."

"She can do that?"

"She can file a claim, yes."

"Well, what can we do?"

"We can have a motion to dismiss filed in Arizona, basically stating Cynthia has no claim to the title, since the money used to purchase the house was Daniel's."

"The money used to purchase that house was also mine," I said.

"Yes, Clare, I know, that's the foundation of our case, but I don't think you're understanding what this claim means."

"What?"

"It means the case will be heard in two states now. In addition to that, Arizona is a community property state, while Connecticut is a common law state, so I have to figure out what *that* means for us...."

He paused and I could hear him tapping his pencil on

his desk. "You don't happen to know anyone who practices law in Arizona, do you?"

"Of course not!"

"Well, we have to find somebody. There's a guy I knew back in law school. I heard he'd moved out that way—maybe I can track him down."

"Hal, this doesn't sound good," I said. "This sounds very, very bad to me."

"Look, Clare, I told you from the beginning it was unlikely we would get all of Daniel's money back, but we'll probably get some of it back. We still have our claim on the money that went into purchasing the house and it's a good one. The settlement has just gotten more complicated, that's all. I wouldn't worry too much about it."

"Okay," I said, feeling like my lungs had just been trussed in piano wire.

"I'll get back to you when I know something more, alright?" said Hal, signing off.

I put down the phone and stared up at the ceiling. My eyes filled with tears. How the hell did I end up here, I wondered wearily, with this stupid, big-ass house in Arizona plunked down on my head from out of the sky? Yet, somehow there I was, sandwiched under bricks and mortar, my two scrawny wicked witch legs now shriveling and shrinking as they disappeared into the foundation. It was bringing a whole new meaning to the term "fixed asset".

I dragged some air into my lungs, which were feeling newly compressed under all those belongings Cynthia had moved in over the threshold. I imagined her padding around expansive white-tiled floors with muted desert vistas behind each plate glass window. I saw her unpacking an espresso machine and Bose sound system. I watched her delicately fingering a framed photograph and wondered for the first time ever if she missed Daniel. Maybe she was crushed by his death; maybe she was heartbroken.

I thought about how much easier it would have been

for both of us if Daniel had never begun this relationship with her. Here's where I spent time exploring the various implications of if-Daniel-had-never-met-Cynthia. For one thing, I'd have about four hundred thousand dollars more in my bank account. I wouldn't be concerned about how I was going to keep this house or send my kids to college. I wouldn't have lawyer bills and sleepless nights and painful memories. I wouldn't feel like someone had put his foot through my chest or that every muscle in my back had been shortened by two inches. I wouldn't have my mother visiting, because I'd be handling everything way better than I was. My son wouldn't think I was the worst mother on the planet and my daughter would have someone a lot stronger and saner to lean on.

I paused in my reverie. "Yeah, that just about covers it," I said aloud. "And now back to our regularly scheduled program."

Two days later, I sneaked away to my studio while my mother took the kids to a movie. I decided to start over with my work project and was busy shaping about twenty-five pounds of clay on a new stand. My revised sketch was that of a man with birdlike features and a winged back. His skull was to be feathered, his neck arched down. I had rolled out a slab of clay for the wings and was just beginning to cut out the shape. I sighed and rubbed the back of my hand across my forehead. I really disliked this part of the sculpting process— the clumpy mass on the board looked exactly like what was inside my head.

Joni Mitchell's *Hejira* was on the stereo and I sang along to "Amelia" as I sunk my fingers into the clay. It made me think of Daniel, that song, the Daniel who was like Icarus. It made me think of the crashing end we had come to.

I walked over to the stereo, hit repeat, and turned up the volume. Then, as I sang along to the music, wiping tears away with my sleeve, I suddenly realized something I hadn't understood before. Something about Daniel was trying to come through the half eagle-half man I had thrown out. That was why I couldn't get it right.

Then, an idea came to me. If poetry could do this, capture and evoke such intense emotion and bring such clarity, imagine if I could apply it to the sculpture itself, so that the sculpture would serve as both the metaphor and the canvas.

I sat down on the floor and thought about this and wiped my nose with my sleeve while the music blared and the lyrics saturated me. I hadn't written any poetry since college, but I thought it might well break the spell I was under. I felt so disconnected from my art, so creatively blocked by Daniel's death. Writing verse might actually be the bridge I needed—it might end the stalemate. In my mind, I could see a man running, arms stretched back, his tied-on wings unevenly tilted. Verses of poetry ran down the ribs of the wings and around his legs. Would I paint the words on or apply a pastiche?

There was rapping on the door that separated my space from Dill's shop. I realized I'd been hearing it for a while now, but I was so caught up in the images in my head, I hadn't moved to answer it.

I jumped up, snapped off the stereo, and ran over to the door to open it.

Dill was standing there, a quizzical look on his face, one hand on his hip, the other leaning against the doorjamb.

"You know," he said, "I like Joni same as the next guy, but I—."

"Oh my God, Dill!" I said, grabbing his arm and dragging him into my studio, "tell me if you think this makes any sense at all. I'm here listening to "Amelia," right? And I get this idea...."

Dill started to smile. I explained my idea to him, complete with all the gory details about Daniel and Cynthia and the house in Arizona, my failed marriage, my illness, my daughter's grief—even my mother's visit. And as I talked, his smile grew bigger and bigger and bigger.

"Well, there it is," he said, "there's all the stuff that needed to come out. You can always rely on art to tell the story. You have to trust it. It's your job to get out of the way and let all that you've seen and experienced just pour out."

"I know," I said. "I know. You're right!"

"Artists tell the stories no one else can, the stories everybody needs to hear. But it's hard to give birth to it, that's for sure. It's hard to give it a life of its own."

I smiled and folded my arms. "So, what's your story then? What is it that finds its way into all those amazing pieces in there?" I pointed through the doorway to his shop.

Dill blushed and looked at the floor. "No, no," he said, shaking his head, "that's a really long, sordid mess of a story. That shit would take hours to explain."

"Oh, I'm in no rush," I said, sitting down on the floor and pouring myself a cup of tea from my thermos. "Come on, Dill," I said, "let's swap war stories. I've got *all* afternoon." I grinned up at him.

Dill stared hard at me for what seemed like an entire minute. His face looked even more lined and serious than before. At one point, I almost started to apologize for putting him on the spot, and when he turned around finally and walked back into his shop, I didn't really expect him to return.

But he did, a cup of coffee in his hand. He sat down on the floor facing me and after a few more moments of jiggling his foot and staring into the floor, he began his tale.

"Forty-two years ago, I was a cocky, smart-ass kid who got kicked out of college for vandalizing a statue of the school's founder. Three months later, I got drafted into the service. And no surprise, I ended up in Nam.

He took a sip of his coffee and looked out the window at the cars passing by our building.

"Nam was like driving off a cliff. The car is going like a thousand miles an hour; you're in free fall. You don't know if you're going to end up dead or maimed or with any of your wits intact once you hit the bottom. Everything is going so fast, you can't think or breathe. All this craziness just flying at you all the fucking time.

"They tell you going in you're doing something good; you're helping people—saving people. I actually remember one CO saying that to us. But you're there for like five minutes and you know that's all shit. What's going on isn't helping anybody. What's going on is just full-out decimation on such a massive scale you can't even take it in. It's like it's bigger and faster and more unimaginable than your brain can absorb."

Dill touched the top of his head with his hand and held it for a while as if to hold something in that might be otherwise lost.

"But, lo and behold, I got out in one piece. Or so I thought. I came back home and I went about my business and I never talked about anything that happened over there—that was the code—you kept your mouth shut and your emotions in check. Right? But the thing was I *couldn't* keep my emotions in check. I was all over the place—like a walking time bomb. Everybody was afraid of me. *I* was afraid of me. The only way for me to deal with it was to become a drunk and a pothead. And the only thing good about *that* was it probably kept me from blowing my fool head off. Or somebody else's.

"Anyway, years passed, and I still don't even know how I lived through them, when I met this girl named Jen. She was probably too young for me, looking back on it, but she was pretty cool and she was smart as hell. She was an artist, made art glass right down the street here at the glass works. She saw what was going on with me, and she said, Dill, I think you need to work with glass." He paused and smiled at the memory. "So, she shows me how to blow glass, right? And, I don't know, I started to feel like the only time I could really be myself was when I was working in her studio. It was like this safe place where everything that needed to come out *could* come out. I felt free to capture whatever was going on in my head and put it into some kind of form for people to see. It became my new language."

He looked back over his shoulder and motioned with his hand at all the gorgeous, broken things he'd created. "This is who I am," he said. "This is the record of my life here. It doesn't matter what people think about it. It only matters that I keep doing it."

"Dill," I said, "I'm so sorry. I didn't mean when I said we would swap war stories that my stupid suburban housewife experience is even in the same league—."

"They are in the same league, Clare," said Dill. "Just different wars. Different battlefields. Same ravage, same wounds. It's the stuff of life and death, and you have to take in all its raw ugliness and spin it into something golden. Something fragile and beautiful. That's it. There's nothing else to do."

My mother was putting dinner on the table when I got home—salmon cakes, macaroni and cheese and stewed tomatoes. I felt like I was in high school again, coming in the door and smelling that smell. I smiled at her.

"Thanks, Mom," I said, removing my jacket. "Smells great!"

"Well," she said, "I'm not sure what it will taste like. But it was all I could find. The kids were hungry and they didn't know where you were."

"What do you mean, they didn't know where I was—I was at the studio."

"We all figured you'd be home hours ago."

I looked at the clock on the stove. "It's six o'clock."

My mother shrugged and I looked over at Ethan as he slid into his seat at the table. "Grandma was worried," he said.

"And did you tell her that I often stay this late at the studio?"

"You haven't been going to your studio," he said.

"Well, I have, actually. I was there a couple of weeks ago."

"First I'm hearing about it."

I looked at Kenya. She was sucking on a strand of her hair and staring at me.

"Kenya, please don't do that, sweetie. Look, will everyone just lighten up? I told you I was going to the studio. If you were worried, you should have called me on the cell."

"We did," said Kenya, still chewing on her hair.

"Kenya," I said, pointing to my own mouth. "You did? Well, I didn't hear it ring."

Kenya lifted her head back and spat the strand of hair out of her mouth.

"God," said Ethan, "you're such a freak."

"Kenya, please apologize. That was really—inappropriate." I looked at Ethan. "And you can apologize to your sister."

"Oh, can I? Thanks!"

"Ethan," I said, glaring at him.

"What?" he said, his mouth full of salmon, "I said thank you."

Kenya bent her face close to her plate and pierced exactly one piece of macaroni with her fork. "Asshole," she said under her breath, as the food met her lips.

"Kenya!"

She looked at me, her face dripping with holy innocence. "What?"

I let out an exasperated sigh. I couldn't even look at my mother. I poked at the food on my plate, which had smelled so appetizing only two minutes before. Then I took another deep breath and collected my wits.

"So," I said, "how was the movie?" They had gone to see a movie called *Tell Me No Secrets* about a pair of amateur sleuths.

"It was good," said Ethan. "Really funny."

"Yeah? What about you, Ken—did you like it?"

Kenya nodded. She was swinging her foot back and forth and hitting the metal support of the table—clink, clink!

I reached under the table and silenced her foot with my hand.

"Did *you* like it, Mom?" I asked my mother.

"It was alright. Pretty silly mostly, but the kids liked it. Kenya saw some of her friends there."

"You did?" I asked.

Kenya rolled her eyes. "Sarah Drucker." She stuck out her tongue and pulled on an imaginary noose around her neck. "Sarah Drucker is yucker."

"I know a better word that rhymes with Drucker," said Ethan. Kenya burst out laughing.

I gave him my most emphatic "stick a sock in your pie hole" face and turned again to my mother. "Sarah was in Girl Scouts with Kenny, and now they're in student government together," I explained.

"She is?" said my mother. "Why did she say she hardly recognized you?"

"Because she's a dork-face," Kenny said, sinking closer to her plate.

"Sarah's the leader of this pack of girls who all dress and talk alike," I said to my mother. "They're honestly pretty catty. I assume she was there with her entourage?"

Kenya pushed her hair back with both hands and plunked her elbows down on the table. "God, Mom, the only reason she even came up and talked to me was because I was with Ethan, and she goes, oh, is that your brother, how old is he, is he dating anybody? And I'm like totally trying not to throw up and I go, he's practically in college, you moron, you think he's going to go out with an eighth-grader? And she goes, oh, well for your information, the guy I'm dating now is seventeen and he drives a sports car and plays football for Boswell. And I go, yeah, he must have had his head planted in the ground a few too many times if he's going out with you! What a bitch."

I felt my mother wince.

"Ken," I said, frowning.

"Well, she is! You said so yourself."

"Sweetie, I never said that. Now eat your meal, okay? This is one of Grandma's specialties." I looked over at my mother. "You always made this meal on Friday nights."

"Daddy always liked it," she said, her eyes still on Kenya.

"My daddy liked hot dogs and beans," said Kenya.

"Yeah," said Ethan, "remember that? That was good!"

I groaned. "Daniel used to make this concoction," I said to my mother, "with canned baked beans, sauerkraut, some ketchup and cut-up wieners with refrigerated rolls all over the top. Then he baked it in the oven. It was something his mother made for him when he was little. He and the kids loved it!"

"You should make that again," said Ethan. "We could have it for dad."

I smiled at Ethan. "That's a great idea, honey. We can do that tomorrow."

"Maybe once a week we could have a meal that Daddy really liked and we could, like, set a place for him at the table," said Kenya.

"I like that idea, too," I said, smiling at her.

I thought for a moment that hearing this conversation would make my mother realize things were just fine here with my children and me in the wake of Daniel's death.

I looked over at her and found her staring awkwardly at the floor, pursing her lips as if to say: I am sitting at a table with a bunch of head cases, and I will just need to make the best of it.

My mother and I were holed up in the family room after dinner, and I was trying desperately to find something on television that would help pass the time. The children were upstairs in their rooms intravenously attached to their respective computers.

"So did the kids behave themselves for you?" I asked, flicking on the remote.

"Well, they behave themselves for *me*, yes," my mother said.

I looked over at her and then thought to myself, no, I'm not taking that bait. I kept surfing the channels.

"Do you like to watch the cooking channel?" I asked and then frowned as I saw what was on. "Oh, God. Not *Kitchen Samurai*. You know, when John Belushi did this routine on *Saturday Night Live*, it was considered comedy. I don't know what they're thinking."

"Just pick something, Clare. You're making me dizzy with all that flicking."

"Sorry." I settled on the rerun of a popular family sitcom and set down the remote. I picked up my tea and cradled it in my hands. "Wonder when the weather's going to warm up, huh? It was so cold last night. Were you warm enough? I meant to tell you there's an extra blanket on the top shelf of the closet."

"I was alright," my mother said. "Surely you can't be comfortable sleeping in that study of yours."

"Oh, I'd rather you take my room while you're here. The bed is better for your back."

"The kids told me you don't sleep in your bedroom at all anymore."

My kids were so discreet.

"Well, no, I don't."

"What's that about?"

"I just don't want to sleep in there right now."

"All his clothes are still hanging in the closet! I was absolutely horrified when I saw that."

What she didn't know was that I hadn't cleared the closet because I was afraid of what I might find there. The desk in the study had been a regular booby trap. I just wasn't up to dealing with the closet quite yet.

"I'll get around to it, okay?"

"How do you expect these children of yours to heal and move on if you can't? You're the one who has to show them how."

"I hear you. I'll clear out Daniel's closet next week."

"I'm just saying you have a tendency to dwell on things. And I know the toll it took on Daniel."

I started to take a sip of my tea, and then paused. "Wait, what?"

My mother shrugged and looked away. "I'm just saying," she said.

"Yes, but I don't understand what you're saying."

"Well, you didn't make things easy for him, let's just say that!"

Now, here was a piece of bait that reeled me in, hook, line, sinker, and my mother's right arm. I simply could not help myself.

"Are you somehow suggesting I sent my husband to an early grave?"

"Oh, Clare! For heaven's sake, don't be so dramatic! What a crazy thing to say. I'm just telling you what *I* know about Daniel—*from* Daniel."

"I'm not following you."

My mother smiled—an expression she herself would have described as the cat that ate the cream. "Well, Daniel used to call me from time to time over the years, you know, whenever things got rough between the two of you. And we would talk, no big deal. I think he just really needed someone to understand his point of view...."

She went on talking, explaining her no-big-deal relationship with my now dead husband, and I just couldn't take it in. I felt like another secret drawer in Daniel's desk had just popped open.

Daniel and my mother. Now, why had I never suspected these two and their cozy heart-to-hearts? On the one hand, there was Daniel, always defending my mother whenever I criticized her. On the other hand, there was my mother with her unusual insight into my husband and the motives behind his confounding behavior. Still, it never clicked.

Perhaps this liaison didn't occur to me because I simply could not imagine someone intentionally seeking out a relationship with my mother. But then, men always liked my mother. They found her charming for some reason.

And yet—and I have to say I loved the irony of this— as much as Daniel had deceived me, he had no doubt deceived his old pal, Lois.

"So when was the last time you heard from Daniel?" I asked.

"What? Oh, I don't know, a couple of months before he died, I guess."

"So he didn't mention his plans for the future?"

"What plans?"

"Oh, well, I'm surprised he never mentioned any of this to you, since you two were so tight and all, but yeah, it seems there was this woman named Cynthia, whom he fell in love with a couple of years ago, and they made some getaway plans, even bought a house together in Arizona. They had it all worked out. I'm not sure why he was even wasting your time discussing how rough it was here with me since he had no intention of even sticking around."

My mother sat quietly, looking at the floor in front of her. She was clearly stunned. I knew that expression—she was taking conversations she'd had with Daniel out of one reality and pasting them into this new one. The changes in meaning were apparently quite startling to her.

"He must have been very mixed-up," she said, shaking her head. "Very confused."

That my mother's sympathies remained unshaken infuriated me even more.

"Well, it should comfort you to know that you must have been helping him to decide," I said coldly.

"I don't understand how he could do that," my mother said.

"What? Lie to you? He was apparently quite good at it. Who knew, right?"

"Are you sure about all this?"

"Very."

My mother shook her head. "It's so hard to believe," she said.

"Yeah, I know, Mom, but I wouldn't dwell on it if I were you. I hear that can put a real strain on others."

"Clare," my mother said, shaking her head, "you shouldn't be angry with *me*. You never told me about this! I had no idea."

"No, Mom, you should have told me! You should have told me that my husband was calling you and talking to you about things of a completely private nature. Instead of joining in and talking about me behind my back—for years!"

"I was only trying to help, Clare."

"Don't give me that! You weren't trying to help. You were trying to be important! You were trying to have a say in something that was none of your goddamn business!"

"What are you screaming about?" asked Ethan, who, suddenly, was standing in the doorway, blinking at the brightness of the overhead lights.

"Nothing," I said. "It doesn't concern you."

"Then don't be so loud about it!"

He walked away. I could hear him in the kitchen getting something out of the refrigerator. He slammed the door shut, and then clomped back up the stairs to his room.

In a mild wave of panic, I wondered how much he'd actually heard of our conversation.

"Clare, you need to talk to someone about Daniel."

"I am," I said, "I'm just not talking to you about it."

I got up and took my teacup to the kitchen sink. I rinsed it and put it into the dishwasher.

My mother came up behind me. She was pulling her shawl up around her shoulders.

"I'm very sorry about this, honey," she said. "I'm even

more worried about you than I was before."

"Imagine that. Yeah, I'm worried about me, too. I'm worried about my kids and how I'm going to send them to college and support this family and pay off Daniel's credit card bills and somehow recoup the money that he sunk into a future with somebody else. To put it bluntly, there are only so many things I can handle on a given day, and you're not one of them."

I closed the door of the dishwasher and stood up. "You're not helping me. You're making everything harder. I want you to go back home, Mom. I'll drive you to the airport tomorrow."

It was Eagle who was waiting for me the next time I journeyed.

"Well," he said, "you got what you wanted."

"Look, I know I was wrong to send her away. I just needed to insulate myself from her constant stream of criticism."

"Was your action driven by protection, then, or revenge?"

As much as I liked to think the motive for sending my mother back home was self-preservation, Eagle and I both knew I was pretty wedded to the idea of getting even.

I had lain awake all that last night of her visit, feeding my indignation until it was about the size of Alaska. The following morning, I had barely spoken to her as I bustled her off to the airport, scooping her luggage off the kitchen floor and marching out the door, shoulders back, head held high. I tossed her bag into the trunk of the Volvo and slammed the lid.

"Ready?" I asked, my voice oozing with false gaiety.

We didn't speak until we were almost at the airport exit.

"What time is my flight?" my mother asked.

I looked at the clock on the dashboard. "Let's see," I

said, "6 days, 2 hours and 33 minutes from now."

"You didn't check on whether or not I could change my flight?"

"No, I did not."

"Well, what am I supposed to do now?"

"I'm sure you can figure it out."

"What if they don't have any seats available?"

"I don't know. You're pretty good at handling impossible situations. Look at the great job you did with me."

"Clare," said my mother, glaring so hotly at me I felt my right cheek beginning to melt, "you're being very heartless and unreasonable!"

In the end, I relented, parked the car and ushered her inside, where we found her a seat on a flight that was leaving in two hours. I walked her to a coffee shop and got her situated with a nice cup of tea, a muffin, and the morning paper. And by the time I left, her indignation over my shabby treatment of her was only about the size of Asia Minor.

"You make things more difficult than they are," Eagle observed.

"You're sounding just like my mother."

"Your mother is a wise woman. You just can't hear what she has to say."

"Maybe I don't *want* to hear what she has to say."

"Exactly," said Eagle, "but that doesn't mean there's nothing of value in her words."

"Well, Daniel certainly thought so, didn't he?"

"Why does that disturb you, that your husband sought out your mother's advice?"

"It feels like a complete betrayal. He took our problems outside the marriage and to her of all people!"

"Did you never speak of your marriage to others?"

"Okay, fine, I did. But this is different. He knew how I felt about my mother."

"Is it possible Daniel went to your mother simply because he thought she might have good insight into you, and that he never meant to offend you at all?"

I sighed. "Yes, I suppose."

"Then what is so wrong about that? Did you take the time to make sure your choice of confidantes met with his approval?"

Rowena, of course, came to mind here, Rowena, whom Daniel considered to be "insufferable." I sighed again. "No."

I rolled onto my side and listened to the drumming CD as it hammered into my head. The journey faded slightly as I gave way to the mounting despair I was feeling. The fabric of my life was all in pieces. I kept trying to patch it back together, but it was so worn and frayed, whenever I mended it one place, it tore somewhere else.

I really tried to make the visit with my mother work out. I did. I thought I could handle it, but I was not strong enough. I actually thought I'd made progress lately, let go of some of my anger even. Where did I get such an idea?

I reviewed the sad state of my life. Kenya and Ethan were confused and upset that my mother had left so abruptly, and were barely speaking to me. The suit against Cynthia had developed into some dark and terrifying labyrinth I'd probably never find my way out of. My work, after six months of sabbatical, amounted to no more than a nebulous, crazy idea I didn't even think I could execute. I was still sleeping in my study and my husband's clothes still hung in the closet like he owned the place.

Practically perfect. And, here I was lying on the floor, like a felled tree.

"There is no shame in falling," said Eagle. "You can gain a whole new perspective from down there."

I managed a smile, remembering now how Eagle first came to me.

Eagle was a gift from my spirit guide, Sumeh. During the months I was sick, Sumeh showed up each day as I journeyed. We would speak about whatever was going on with me at the time, my fears, concerns, and grief. These talks held me together at a time when I felt I had nothing else to hold onto.

Then, one day Sumeh said, "I'll be leaving you now in the care of the Eagle."

I knew from the book I was reading that Eagle was my power animal, but I didn't see the need to communicate with him. Everything was working pretty smoothly with Sumeh. Why upset the balance?

"It will be good for you to establish a bond here," said Sumeh, as he disappeared from view.

I waited for him to return, but Sumeh was faithful to his word. Each day in my journeys, Eagle would meet me instead of my trusted guide, and I would reluctantly ask him my questions. He would answer capably—and clearly, I might add—but I remained stubbornly aloof.

Then, came the bird of prey show. I had taken my kids to a fair in a nearby town. I was still feeling pretty weak. My limbs were still tingly and numb, my lungs strangely weighted as if I were breathing under water. It was an effort to move through the heat and the crowd.

We stopped at the bird show, so I could sit down for a while in one of the chairs by the stage. The bird handlers had brought with them several owls and a turkey vulture, a red-tailed hawk and a bald eagle with one eye.

The eagle's name was Captain. He had been shot out of the sky by a hunter and then found at the edge of a lake by a family out on a hike. The bullet had taken his left eye, part of his head, and a certain degree of his coordination, including his ability to fly. Though permanently grounded, he had been lovingly rehabilitated by his handlers and now traveled around as the star of the bird show.

Captain and I studied each other for a long time. When I listened to his story, my heart fell apart. As I absorbed the details of how he'd been plucked from the sky and observed how gracefully he had risen above his plight, tears ran down my face. Captain just cocked his head and stared harder at me.

I know what it's like to have your wings clipped, I said

to him.

I know what it's like to lose your joy, he said back.

I know what it feels like to just fall and fall and fall, I told him.

I know how hard it is to get up again.

After that day, Eagle and I got along just fine. On some level, we were the same, he and I. That's what I found in my journeying anyway—a union, a level where there was no longer any distinction between human and human, human and animal, human and tree or sky or stone or water. In my journeys I found the point where normal limitation didn't exist. Where everything was one.

I rolled onto my back again and blotted my eyes with my bandana.

"I just don't believe I will ever get free of this mess I'm in," I said.

"It's not holding onto you, dear one. You're holding onto it."

"Jeez, don't tell me that!"

"It's the truth, dear one."

"Okay, fine, how do I let go of it then?"

"You only need to decide that you want to. Choose something else instead.

"Like what, forgiveness?" I asked.

"Well, you might find that easier to live with."

"You're asking me to forgive something that is unforgivable to me. I wouldn't have done this to him. I would *never* have put him in this position. Never."

"I am not asking you to do anything. It was you who asked me. And don't say never. You are looking at one fragment of a long history that goes well beyond this lifetime. How can you be so certain you have never been deceptive? Perhaps, once upon a time it was your mistake to make. Perhaps, it was Daniel's soul that once felt the sting of betrayal. It is not an easy thing to live with from either side, is it?"

"So, this is all like some kind of karmic retaliation?"

"Retaliation desires perpetuation. Karma desires resolution—bringing things into balance so they *don't* perpetuate. Karma asks to be dissolved—by grace."

I sighed. "Alright," I said.

Eagle said, "Come with me."

I climbed onto his back and we flew for a while over a ridge of mountains. Then the landscape opened up and we landed in the center of a burnished plain with a 360-degree horizon. Two tall fir trees stood at the center.

A lone figure appeared in the distance, a man on a horse. It was Daniel, and as he approached, something awoke and rolled over inside of me—a grief that suddenly found its breath. It felt as if the part of me that was holding the full weight of the loss stepped out of hiding and opened its mouth.

I hadn't anticipated the force of the reunion. Daniel's face shimmered behind a blur of tears. He was gone, but somehow worse for me was the notion that I had lost him long before he died, and yet, somehow continued through our life together numb and unaware. How did I do that?

I called up the memory not of who we were in the last years, but of who we were at the beginning, when we looked at one another with such love and promise. Where did *that* go?

I felt, more than anything, that I wanted the return of our mutual respect and understanding—a return to the time when we were both on the same side. I wanted accord.

I wiped my face and sunk back into the journey.

Daniel dismounted and then he and the horse, Eagle and I all stood together in a loosely gathered circle under the fir trees. Eagle took command of the proceedings and explained that we had assembled in order to put an end to the discord between Daniel and me. He said that the power we had taken from one another during our life together would be returned and restored to us. There were ways in which Daniel and I had not allowed each other to be who we were, ways in which we had stood in the way of one another's growth, claiming control we were not entitled to.

I looked at Daniel. For once it felt like things were in balance, that he and I were on an equal footing.

He put out his arms. They were filled with ribbons of color that he placed on Eagle's wings. When Eagle brought them to me, they looked like pieces of the aurora borealis, and when they touched me, they turned into a cape of pale rainbow colors.

I extended my own arms and found them filled with a wreath of orchids that I placed around the horse's neck. The horse placed his muzzle on Daniel's head and the wreath shook down his neck onto Daniel's shoulders, where it came to rest as a cloak of purple velvet.

It was so peaceful in this space; I wanted to just remain here. My chest felt light and healed—the heartache was silent. Then Eagle asked if there was anything we wished to say.

Daniel said: "I am grateful for everything you ever gave me. Our life together was not easy and perhaps did not end well, but it meant everything to me."

I nodded, because I knew what he meant. Daniel and I were not some ill-conceived coupling. We actually belonged together. We had a life and children—maybe many lives and children—and that meant something, no matter how imperfect it was.

I thought when the moment came, I would have lots to say to him, but none of the things that had burned to be said seemed to matter now.

"I hope you're okay there," I said.

"I'm good. I was caught for a long time, but I'm free now."

My eyes welled up. I had never thought of Daniel as caught, but it seemed a good word for him.

"I hope you'll still help me take care of Ethan and Kenny," I said to him.

He nodded his assent, a flickering form in purple. I tried to hold him steady.

I thought about how much he was missing by not being

with them. "I'm sorry you can't be with them to watch them grow up."

Daniel smiled. "I'm with them all the time. I'm with them now more than I was before."

"Clare," he said, "I'm sorry about us."

Tears ran from the corners of my eyes and drifted into my ears. "I'm sorry too, Daniel."

Eagle said we should give one another a gift of good will. A clarinet came to my mind for Daniel. He had played one as a boy and always regretted leaving it behind. The one I presented him with was gold and shiny.

Daniel handed me a chunk of black, tarry substance. When it touched my hand, a diamond of brilliant clarity burst out from the center. It was my forgiveness of him, released at last.

We said our goodbyes and Eagle took me back to our meeting place.

"What now?" I asked.

"Make a bundle," he said. "Find things that represent the history of your relationship. Burn these things; then fill a cloth with the ashes and bind it. In the full moon, bury the bundle in a still body of water that will hold and transmute it —pick one with a muddy bottom."

That night while the kids were asleep, I pried open boxes of pictures, files and keepsakes. It seemed to me that much of Daniel's and my history could be traced through a trail of paper: from the letters he wrote to me in college, to gift cards and old valentines, birthday greetings and silly notes, through pictures of our holidays together and copies of our wedding invitation. We were the sum and total of everything from our banking statements and joint IRS returns to the photo of the couple holding hands at the Grand Canyon and the leftover engraved Christmas cards that were sent out to friends and family every year. I held and read and paged through all of it.

I made a pile—a very, very large pile and gathered it up into a brown grocery bag, which I pushed back against the wall of my closet. Over the next two days, while I waited for the arrival of the full moon, I dug through drawers and boxes and added things I felt helped tell the story of Daniel and me. If there was anything I needed to keep for the kids, or for financial or legal purposes, I made a copy first and threw that into the bag. I wanted a complete record.

On the day of the full moon, after Ethan and Kenya had gone to school, I swept out the fireplace and vacuumed it. Then I built a pyre of the papers, cards and photographs I had gathered. I lit the fire and burned the whole lot until it was reduced to a high feathery mound of speckled ash. Then I took a large square of cloth from a flannel shirt of Daniel's and filled it with the ash. I sprinkled the ashes with some crumbled dried roses and baby's breath I had found in the keepsake box, and topped the bundle with sweet grass, lavender and tobacco. Then I pushed my wedding ring down into the center and bound the bundle up with a string.

I felt that if I were ever to rebound from Daniel's death, I would need to mend the discord between us. I would need to let go of all the bickering and habits we had gotten lost in over the years. I would need to let go of the disappointment and guilt over how we had not attended to or accepted one another.

With bundle in hand, I went to the woods to find a place that would accept my offering.

It was a sparkling day. New spring leaves were slick and dripping with rain from the morning's shower. The sun caught hold of each drop and held it in glistening suspense before it fell from its own weight. When the breeze shot through the sopping trees, drops of water landed on my head and shoulders in quick dowses. It felt like a baptism.

I went to the beaver marsh and walked the perimeter as far as I could, singing softly to myself. Along the way I noticed two big fir trees growing not far from the water's edge. They reminded me of the ones I had seen in my journey with Daniel. I stood for a moment between them and put one hand on each trunk.

Gazing upward into their tall swaying peaks made me dizzy. I asked what should my intention be in releasing the bundle I had made. What should I create going forward? Clear view, said one. Constancy, said the other.

I felt that these trees marked the spot where the bundle of ashes should be given to the water. I walked to the water's edge, bent down and dropped it in, pushing it under with a stick. It sunk into the mud and roots and water with a satisfying burble and slurp, as if it had been swallowed by something primeval.

I left some corn and tobacco at the base of the trees and thanked them, and then sprinkled the rest of my offerings over the surface of the water. The war between Daniel and me was over now.

"It is done," I said, turning towards home, "and so may it be."

Chapter Five
Holly: **Battle**

It was one of those mornings. To begin with, Kenya was having a meltdown because her favorite tee shirt—a clingy little number with a hot pink skull and crossbones emblazoned on the front—wasn't clean. She stood in the hallway, arms folded, insisting she would not be able to go to school because there was nothing for her to wear.

She was dressing all in black these days, a trend I had mistakenly assumed was in mourning for her father's death. Ethan thought this was hilarious.

"Mom, you're so clueless," he said. "She's gone totally Goth. Don't you know anything?"

In a moment of desperation, I finally located a small black jersey of my own that Kenya—also out of desperation—grabbed from my hand and took to her room, slamming the door so hard, the hinges rang.

She caught the school bus at the very last possible second. Red lights flashed as she inched her way up the lawn, the driver of the bus and those in several waiting cars gaping at her nonchalance in disbelief. I closed the door and flopped my back against it with a huge sigh of relief, the way characters in TV sitcoms do when they manage, in the nick of time, to purge themselves of some annoying neighbor or in-law.

It was about 10:30 and I was just set to leave for the studio when the phone rang. It was Kenya's school.

"Mrs. Blakely?"

"Yes, this is she."

"Mrs. Blakely, this is Grover Potts, the principal here at Hilltown Middle School."

"Ye-es?"

"I have Kenya here in the office with me. Kenya was in a fight this morning with another student, and we're going to have to suspend her for the next couple of days. Can you come and pick her up?"

"Suspend her? But, is she alright? Is she hurt?"

"No, she's not hurt."

"Well, what happened? Who was she fighting with?"

"It would be better if you came here, if you could, and we could speak about it in the office. Are you able to do that?"

"Are you saying my daughter harmed this other student?"

"Mrs. Blakely," he said tiredly. "Can you just come to the school?"

"I'll be right there."

Well, now she had done it, I thought. Kenya and her temper tantrums—she had gone off on someone apparently—that was it, I was sure. She had always been a child to take out her emotional frustrations on a physical level. The numerous divots in her walls and furniture, the scuff marks along the bottom of her door, the starred windowpane that had met with a flying shoe one morning—all these were a testimony to her rages.

I hopped into the car and raced through the winding local streets to the school, feeling like I was hitting most of the curves on two wheels. I was talking to Eagle in my head and trying to get a read on the situation at school. But I was too keyed up to concentrate. When I got to the parking lot, I spun into the nearest space and leapt out of the car.

The hallway of the school was stuffy, the thick air holding captive the odor of various lunchtime meals—something that smelled like a cross between canned spaghetti, cooking oil and cake mix. Children's voices echoed off the tiled walls in an exuberant cacophony.

The office by comparison was carpeted, quiet and cool. It was clear that in order to do what they were hired to do, the administration needed to firmly detach from the pubescent energy that roiled outside its doors.

I approached the main desk, where a neatly coiffed, middle-aged blonde sat at a computer typing. She looked up at me and removed her headset.

"I'm here for Kenya Blakely," I said.

She gave me a short stare, then swiveled in her seat and stood up. I wasn't sure, but I thought I saw her roll her eyes as she turned away. She walked over to an office with a partially open door.

"The mother is here," she said.

I could hear the creak of a desk chair as the principal stood up and came to the door.

"Thank you for coming," he said stepping out into the reception area. We shook hands. He held out his arm. "Right in here," he said, with just the right measure of courtesy and solemnity.

His demeanor made me think of the mortician at Daniel's funeral and the doctors I visited when I was sick, a manner which seemed to say: "I am here to support you in these troubled times."

Kenya was slumped in a chair by the window. The first thing I thought when I saw her was that they had somehow called the wrong mother. Over the black jersey I'd given her that morning, she was wearing a silver fishnet tank top I'd never seen before. Over her jeans she wore a short black leather skirt and high boots. Were these *her* clothes or had she borrowed them from someone?

Tracks of mascara ran down her face, made all the more Pagliacci by the stark pale make-up and dark bow of lipstick she must have applied that morning in the girls' washroom. She had also teased, sprayed and pinned her long thick hair into a fountain effect that fanned out stiffly from her scalp. This was the hairdo of women who were suspected of putting their fingers into light sockets. A row of silver clip-on rings ran along half of her bottom lip and around one nostril. When did she find the time to do all this?

I stared down at her, unable to move, and Kenya blinked back at me—Kenya behind the face of a girl who looked like Edward Scissorhands.

"Have a seat, Mrs. Blakely," said Mr. Potts.

"I—okay," I said, groping for a nearby chair.

"Kenya," said the principal, "perhaps you'd like to tell your mother what happened here this morning."

Kenya Scissorhands began to speak and I tried to listen, having still not closed my jaw or located my little girl behind the wild hair and macabre face.

"Sarah Drucker called me Emo, so I hit her."

"Who's Emo?" I asked, thinking it might be the new Goth character on *Sesame Street*.

Kenya rolled her eyes and slumped further down in her chair. "Not *who*, Mom, *what*."

I looked over at Mr. Potts.

"Emo is apparently what they call children who dress like your daughter."

I looked back at Kenya. "So, if that's how you dress, then...."

"I'm not some Emo, okay? I'm wiccan. I'm a pagan."

"You're a pagan?"

Kenya rolled her eyes. "Ye-ah. I've been a pagan since like forever."

"No, you haven't. What are you saying?"

"Look," said Kenya, "she was making fun of me, so I grabbed her by the hair and wailed on her."

"You punched her?"

"Mom, she like totally deserved it!"

"Kenya, no one deserves to be punched! You just walk away from her if she bothers you. Don't try to convince me of the correctness of something you know isn't right."

I looked at the principal. "Is Sarah alright?"

"The incident took place in the hallway," he said, not answering my question. "Two of the teachers escorted the girls here. The Druckers have since come and taken their daughter home. They were quite shaken, as you can imagine, but if you wanted to know more, you could speak with them directly."

"I see," I said, not relishing the phone call I would need to make when I got home.

"As you yourself said, Mrs. Blakely, Kenya knows her behavior towards Sarah was wrong and behavior like this cannot be tolerated if we are going to provide a safe and conducive learning environment for the students at Hilltown. As I discussed with you on the phone, I think it would be best if you were to take Kenya home and keep her there for the remainder of the week—that's three days suspension. I think for her own safety as well as for Sarah's, everyone needs a little break from one another. Do you generally speak with Sarah online, Kenya, or get together outside of school?"

"I'm not exactly part of her posse."

"Well, it's our suggestion that the girls be isolated from one another for awhile until things can cool down. Mr. Gore has arranged separate projects for them on student government. Fair enough?"

"How is this going to affect Kenya academically?" I

asked.

"Kenya is not a student we are used to having here in the office. But we will be watching her, to make certain she doesn't develop...further disciplinary problems. At this point, though, nothing will be going onto her permanent record. She will be given extra time to make up any missed work. We just really want to diffuse the situation."

"Speaking of watching her, are you aware of the fact that Kenya only dresses like this *here*?"

"At the school?"

"At the school, yes. She didn't look like this when I put her on the bus this morning. If the way she dresses seems to be provoking problems for her, maybe the school could ensure she doesn't get the opportunity during the day to dress this way?" I twirled my finger in Kenya's direction.

"If the way a student dresses doesn't violate the school dress code, we really can't do anything."

"Well, how about if it violates her parental dress code?"

"I don't know how we can enforce that, Mrs. Blakely. That would be up to you. The thing is, we believe there is a deeper issue at play here. It would seem to me that your daughter's desire to dress as she does is arising out of some personal issues, not the school environment. I'd like to suggest that you speak with Dr. Woods about Kenya's behavior. Dr. Woods is our school counselor, and he's already spoken with Kenya this morning."

I looked at Kenya to get some sense of what was about to transpire but she was busy playing with her licorice-colored press-on nails.

"Fine," I said, sighing.

Mr. Potts got up from his desk and went out into the reception area. "Ask Jack Woods to come down, please, Heather." I heard him say.

We sat alone for a few moments while Mr. Potts engaged in a conversation just outside the door—something about adjusting lunch schedules so that the science fair could be set up in the cafeteria.

I couldn't stop staring at Kenya. My heart broke at how strange she looked. I'd been so preoccupied with my own anger and grief over Daniel I hadn't been able to take in the depth of my daughter's own distress. I realized we had both been hiding our true identities from one another: she, the closet pagan and I, the betrayed and forgotten wife. Maybe Kenya was just trying to show the outside world how dark and isolated life had become for her on the inside.

My daughter looked up at me and in spite of my heartache and fear, I smiled at her. She dropped her gaze and her small shoulders sank with relief. A trace of a smile flickered at the corners of her dark mouth.

"Mrs. Blakely?"

I turned to find a tall, athletic-looking man in a plaid shirt bending over my chair with his hand extended towards me. "I'm Jack Woods," he said.

He looked like he could be the model for Brawny paper towels. He had a thick crop of dark brown hair that stuck out from the crown of his head like a thatched roof, and brown eyes that sparkled like coke over ice. Okay, I thought, this wasn't going to be half the nightmare I assumed it would be.

"Clare Blakely," I said, taking his hand. My face felt flush.

"Mr. Potts had to step out to a short meeting so we're going to just talk among ourselves for awhile." He folded his long, muscular frame into the chair beside me.

"Kenya," he said, beckoning with his hand as if inviting her to play a game of Uno, "bring your chair in closer."

Kenya stood up and amiably dragged her chair into a circle with Mr. Woods and me. I could tell she liked him. As she moved closer, I got a better look at the outfit and streaked make-up, and gamely resisted the desire to reach into my purse for a wet wipe.

"So," he said, "I understand a lot has been happening for your family since the beginning of the school year. Kenya tells me her father passed away soon after the holidays, and I was real, real sorry to hear about that." He nodded at Kenya and then looked over at me. "I want to offer my condolences."

"Thank you," I said.

"I was telling Kenya that I lost my dad when I was just fifteen. So I think I can understand *some* of the things she's been feeling, but what I was explaining to her this morning is that while there are some parts of Kenya's grief that are just like what other people feel when someone close to them dies, there are other parts—the deepest parts—that are special and unique and known only to her. And those aren't so easy to put into words. Right, Kenya?"

My daughter nodded, but didn't lift her head. I knew she was trying not to cry.

"I like to use this analogy with the kids in explaining how emotions work sometimes. They all know what it's like to be in a classroom where somebody is acting out and trying to get the teacher's attention. And what happens when the teacher keeps ignoring that child?" He smiled at Kenya.

"He just gets louder," she said quietly.

"That's right! He just makes *more* noise and gets into *more* trouble. Emotions are like that, too. Some emotions are big and bossy and angry and scared and they need to be heard. They need our attention, and when we don't give them that attention, everything gets kind of chaotic. All of our other emotions feel the impact, just like all those other kids in the classroom who can't get their work done, or hear what the teacher is saying. Sound about right, Kenya?"

Kenya shrugged. "I guess," she said.

"I know Kenya has been resistant to the idea of therapy," Mr. Woods went on, looking directly at me, "but we've talked about it, and I think we've agreed she should give that a try. Of course, she knows she can come and talk to me anytime there's something going on at the school that's getting her down, but I can recommend some good therapists for her to see. Folks I have a lot of faith in."

"And you can't do that yourself? I mean, she seems so comfortable with you."

"Well, I can help some, but my responsibility to Kenya is really with respect to her school experience only, and this is something that goes beyond that. Wouldn't you agree?"

"Oh yes, I do." I said, rolling my eyes.

Jack Woods examined my face for a moment. Then he crossed his legs and sat back in his chair. "Kenya has chosen an avenue of self-expression that is very common for this age group. The social structure among teens is very well defined. I find that students align themselves with whatever group they feel reflects best who they are. It's an identity thing—it's her way of signifying how she sees herself in comparison to the rest of the group. We all do this, if you stop and think about it."

He crossed his hands in a kind of Zenlike pose in his lap. I made note of the fact there was no ring. It was hard to imagine this guy ever got ruffled about anything. But then again, this wasn't his daughter sitting across from us—it was mine.

"I suppose so," I said. "If you could give me some names...."

"Certainly," he said, grabbing his pen. "Why don't you give me your email and I'll send you some recommendations. And then if you let me know when you make the appointment, I'd be happy to call and speak to them in advance."

"That would be great," I said. I handed him a faculty business card from my purse.

He looked at it. "Oh, so you teach over at Middleton State? I've been doing some post graduate work there."

"Wow, no kidding," I said. A scene of Jack Woods and me having coffee at the university Starbucks flashed through my mind. I cleared my throat.

"Okay," he said, standing up and shaking my hand

again. "You'll hear from me by tomorrow." He looked down at Kenya. "Hey, you get some rest there, kiddo," he said, patting her on the shoulder. "Come and see me next week, okay?"

Kenya nodded.

"Thank you," I said, smiling up at him. "Thanks a lot."

He held out his broad hand in a flat wave and grinned at us before disappearing behind the door.

I sighed.

A second or two later, the blonde receptionist tapped on the door and opened it. "Mr. Potts is going to be tied up for a while. Did you want to just get Kenya's things and go on home?"

"Sure," I said.

I walked behind Kenya down the empty halls. Children and teacher voices wafted out from behind the door of each classroom we passed. Every class seemed animated and engaged. Lively discussion and even laughter ensued in most. I scanned the students in each room, hoping to find some evidence of the group to which my daughter had supposedly aligned herself, but no one else looked like her. No other grimly outlined face met my gaze, warning me to steer clear and mind my own business. No other child looked like she was on her way to a casting call for the next Tim Burton production.

We got to her locker and Kenya ran the combination, her black-lacquered fingernails beetling around the dial. She opened the door about six inches and stuck her hand inside, rummaging around for her backpack and jacket. It was clear she didn't want me to see what was inside.

I grabbed hold of the door and opened it all the way. A can of Aqua Net hairspray rolled out onto the floor. Inside there was a jumbled mass of clothes and shoes, books and papers, make-up, hair products and strange metal-studded accessories. It looked liked the innards of a trash compacter.

I sighed. "I think we need to sort through all this, Kenny," I said.

"Why?"

"Why? Because, first of all, most of this stuff shouldn't even *be* in your locker, and secondly, how can you function like this? How do you find anything?"

"Mom, it's fine, okay? I need all this stuff," she said, trying to tug the door free of my grasp.

I glanced around the hallway to see if anyone was watching us. I lowered my voice and kept a firm hand on the locker door.

"You *need* all this stuff? No, Kenya, you do not need all this stuff, and furthermore, I don't want you to even *have* this stuff. Where did you get the money to buy all this anyway?"

"I had it."

"No, you didn't," I said.

"Grandma gave me some when she was here. She told me I could buy whatever I wanted with it." She was digging her boot into the floor and looking around as if she were totally bored by our conversation.

"You're lying, Kenya, and I really don't appreciate it. Now help me clean this locker out right now. We're taking most of this home with us."

"No!" she barked. "It's mine and you can't take it!"

She pulled on the door to loosen it from my hand. It twanged as she lost her grip and stumbled backwards. She recovered her balance and grabbed onto the door again.

It seemed like the costume she wore gave her a level of boldness and recklessness that was new to me. I looked up and down the hallway again, waiting for some nosey parker teacher to stick her head out of her classroom to see what was going on. I leaned in and answered her through my teeth.

"I'm not *taking* it. We're just clearing it out of here. In the future, we will need to come to some agreement on what you will wear to school each day, and that's going to be decided at home, not in the girl's bathroom. Clear?"

"I hate you!" she said, narrowing her eyes and pushing

her chin up towards me. "I wish *you* were the one who died, not Daddy!" She turned and stalked off down the hall, wobbling on the heels of her boots.

I probably would have felt pretty sorry for myself just then if my self-pity hadn't been keenly trumped by my sadness for Kenya.

A door opened between us and a slender man wearing chemistry lab goggles and a quizzical expression poked his head out and watched Kenya go by. He looked at me. "Need any help?"

"No," I lied. "Everything's...fine." I nodded and forced a smile.

"Okay," he said, pulling his head back into his classroom, the quizzical expression unchanged.

"Crap," I said to myself.

I stared down the hallway at Kenya's dark retreating form. I closed my eyes and exhaled, calling up the mantra Sumeh had taught to me during my illness. *This is where I am now*, I said to myself, resting my forehead on the hand that still gripped the locker door. *This is my life*, I said, as I peered into the tangled, snaky hell of my daughter's locker, *and it is blessed. I am safe. My child is safe...*a black, plastic skull dropped out of the locker and rolled towards my foot...*and all is well.*

"Arg," said Rowena, as she listened to my tale the following morning. "What's been going on since you got her home?"

"She's been sleeping mostly. I managed to get some dinner into her last night."

"Did you call the other girl's parents?"

"Yes," I said wearily.

"How'd that go?"

"Which part?"

"There are *parts*?"

"Well, talking to Sarah's mother, Judith, was fine—I know her from Girl Scouts. We were having this conversation, and Judith was very sympathetic—she knows Kenny and she really gets it. She said she's seen the changes in her since Daniel died and understands what I'm grappling with. And then, the dad grabs the phone once he realizes it's me and he starts screaming about how either I need to do something about Kenya or *he's* going to do something about her, and I'm like, what? And he starts going into this whole thing about how he should press charges and send Kenya to juvenile hall and that will totally straighten her out, and then Judith starts trying to grab the phone away from him, and there's this like —scuffle—and then the phone goes dead!"

Rowena burst out laughing. "God, it's like that scene from *It's a Wonderful Life,* you know, when George Bailey grabs the phone from Mary and screams at Zuzu's teacher?"

"Rowena, my life isn't a movie, okay? And it isn't the least bit wonderful right now; it's a big load of crap, and I don't know what I'm doing anymore." I sighed. "Anyway, Judith called me this morning and apologized. She said not to worry about Larry—he's very *protective*."

"S-o-o, have you spoken with Brawny?"

"Who, the counselor at the school?"

Rowena winked. "Yeah, Woodsy."

"Ro, come on, this is serious. " I said.

"You come on! You like him, Clare. I can tell."

"Look, I was in a state of shock, okay? For heaven's sake, I would have felt the same way about anyone who came along at that moment and made some sense out of things. I just felt rescued, that's all—a woman can lose her head over that kind of thing."

"Really."

"Okay, fine! I thought he was very sweet and kind and yes, totally, *totally* cute, and I probably wouldn't mind curling up in his lap and taking a nap there for the next month or so, but that's just me longing for escape. Pay no attention to that."

Rowena smiled. "Uh-huh. Well, what's next, then? Have you made an appointment for Kenya at the therapist?"

"Not yet. I have to do that today. You know, in my heart, I'm really only concerned about her grief over Daniel. I don't care so much about the way she dresses or how unpopular she is. Kenya can survive the rigors of non-conformity—it's who she is. I think the wicca thing is just her way of saying: don't expect me to be like everybody else."

"It's hard to tell what Kenya's saying. I think maybe we need to let this situation evolve a bit."

"*De*volve is more like it. I have this sense there's another shoe about to drop."

"I hear Dr. Martens are all the rage with that set."

That afternoon, the mail dropped the other shoe when I opened a credit card bill of Daniel's that I was still in the process of paying off. When I saw the $639 charge to a store called BawdyWare, I initially concluded that Cynthia must have used Daniel's credit card number to buy herself a carload of spicy lingerie.

I ran to my computer, hands shaking, and did a search for the store on the internet—it was located in a nearby town—but when I navigated to the website, I realized right away that the type of things they sold were not likely to be Cynthia's taste. What I found instead was the answer to the question how was Kenya financing her Goth wardrobe?

I knocked on Kenya's door.

"Kenny?"

I heard the shuffling of things being put away in a drawer and then she came to the door. Her hair was teased up and banded in an array of rooster tails. The thick smears of dark eyeliner and black lipstick made the ice blue of her eyes otherworldly. My daughter, the teenage vampire, I thought.

"What do you want?" she asked.

"What do I *want*? How about if we start out by you

giving me Daddy's credit card."

"What credit card?"

"Kenya, don't be tiresome. The one you stole, the one connected to this billing statement." I waved the bill in my hand.

She stood there, thinking about it. "I didn't steal it! Daddy wouldn't care if I bought some things I wanted. Daddy always bought me whatever I asked for."

"Really? So should I have him wire me the funds from heaven, or what did you have in mind?"

"You're mean!" she said, starting to cry.

"How is that mean? What did you think was going to happen when you went on this little shopping spree? Did you really think Daddy was going to pay for it?"

She looked down and nodded. The rooster tails flapped back and forth.

I sighed, remembering how young she was.

"Okay, here's how this is going to go. You give me back Daddy's card and all the stuff you bought with it gets returned to the store."

"What? Why?" She was sobbing now.

"Because we can't afford it, that's why. Because it wasn't your money to spend in the first place."

"But it's my *stuff*!"

"Kenya," I said. "Enough of this. Give me the credit card."

She went to her desk and ripped open the top drawer. She rummaged wildly around in the tangled entrails of necklaces, hair bands and headphones, miraculously extracted the credit card, and slapped it into my hand. Then she darted around the room, digging into her closet and dresser, gathering up pieces of clothing and accessories. She threw these past me out into the hallway in such a fury they seemed to sizzle upon hitting the floor.

Finally, she picked up the desk chair, which had rolled to the center of the room, and heaved it into her open closet.

Boxes of papers, stacks of CD's and magazines rained down from the overhead shelf.

"Kenya," I said tiredly.

She turned around and glared at me. Tracks of mascara marked her cheeks and her fiery blue eyes flashed. "You think you know everything about me, but you don't know anything," she said, feigning triumph. "I'll show *you*, you just wait. I'll show you something you'll never forget!"

Then she slammed the door in my face and locked it. There was more thumping and bumping and a long wail that ended in sobs.

"Good God in heaven," I said, wiping my forehead with the back of my shaking hand.

The next week, I was in the studio applying a pastiche of poetry to the sculpture I had made of Daniel, Daniel as Icarus, running with wings aloft. Poetry lined the ribs of each fated wing.

I had inked the poetry onto pieces of thin muslin and the verse that now unfurled beneath my gluey fingers read:

> *He was a man ill at ease*
> *on the earth, a man*
> *given to ceaseless wondering,*
> *invention and the like. One eye*
> *watched while the other wandered.*

Just then my cell phone rang.

"Fuck!" I said.

I reached behind me for a damp rag and grabbed the phone from the pocket of my smock.

It was Hal calling with dismal news. The court date for the motion Cynthia's lawyer filed in Arizona was July 23rd. The date for *our* hearing was August 9th.

"The good news," said Hal, "is that I located my old

friend from law school. He lives in Tucson and he said he'd handle the case for us. Isn't that lucky?"

"Hal, how is that lucky? I don't want to battle this thing out in a courtroom halfway across the country with a lawyer I don't know."

"This guy is super sharp. We couldn't have found a better litigator."

"I appreciate that. I really do, but Arizona, Hal? I don't want to go to fricking Arizona to settle this case!"

"Clare, that's only if we can't move the date, alright? I know a couple of clerks. I can call in a favor, maybe and get our hearing moved up. Let me work on it, and I'll call you back. In the meantime, better book yourself a flight to Tucson just in case, okay?"

I clicked off the phone and dropped it into my pocket. I pinched the bridge of my nose with my still sticky fingers and shook my head. Then I stared hard at the sculpture in front of me.

"I hope you can appreciate all the shit you've gotten me into here," I said.

A good night's rest was hard to come by. Usually I went to sleep easily enough, but I never stayed there for long. At some point in the young hours of the morning, my eyes would snap open and my mind would begin grinding away like a great, glittery wheel of fortune, tick, tick ticking around the dial past my legal battles with Cynthia, my daughter's emotional fragility, my son's failure to get into the college of his choice, the lack of progress on my sculptures, my inability to move Daniel's stuff out of the house, the growing water stain in the corner of Ethan's room which had begun to raise blisters in the paint, and the unresolved feud I had going with my mother. On and on. Where it stopped, nobody knew.

Tonight, the crisis du jour was my house, which all started when I woke in the middle of a disturbing dream.

In the dream, Daniel had moved into the basement without my awareness and begun a massive remodeling project. I went downstairs and discovered to my dismay that one wall of the foundation had been removed. A severed pipe was spewing water onto the floor. I waded through piles of his belongings to a long barricade of boxes. He was apparently living behind it, in a small alcove near his workbench, and I found him there, leaning over a set of blueprints.

"Daniel," I said, "you don't belong here anymore."

"Don't worry," he whispered, "I'm making it so you won't even know I'm around. I'm building a secret compartment." He pasted a blueprint up on the wall and pointed things out to me. A simple rerouting of the heating ducts and plumbing would be required. A series of partitions invisible to the naked eye would be constructed behind the furnace.

When I moved closer, I could see that what he was showing me was not a blueprint at all but a large yellowed scroll on which an ornate family tree was displayed.

"These will have to change," he said, indicating some names near the top of the tree. He took an exact-o knife and began slicing them out. As he removed them, the other names on the tree fluttered and reshuffled themselves like cards in a computer solitaire game.

I turned to find a group of strangers dressed in ancient clothing nosing around the space left open by the missing wall.

"You have to close off this hole, Daniel."

"Yeah, well, not enough material for that," he called back over his shoulder.

"But what about all this water?" I asked, becoming more frustrated and alarmed.

He turned and grinned at me. I had never seen him so happy.

"That's for the moat I'm building," he said.

Now I lay on my side, replaying the dream, the feelings of alarm and unease still crouching in my stomach. No wonder I had such dreams. I lived everyday with those same apprehensions and fears of exposure and isolation, the same run amuck clutter and confusion, the same now-you-see-him, now-you-don't Daniel in my life.

My anger towards him had subsided since my work with Eagle, but still there was this lingering sense of incompleteness. Something that felt stuck and immoveable.

Maybe I should just start—throw open the closet doors and begin bagging stuff up. Pick out a few paint chips and refinish the bedroom. Buy some new prints for the walls, some new shades for the windows, fresh linens for the bed. Something bright and sassy, something that said, here I go, turning over a new leaf!

I sighed. No, the pretense of cheeriness was altogether more depressing than the idea of leaving things as they were. If I was going to proceed, I needed to pick a tone that was somber yet sophisticated—quiet but self-assured. Ochre, perhaps, or a sage green. A geometric design, not flowers. Definitely not flowers.

I realized I would need courage. Courage and a good swift kick in the pants. The best place to go for such gifts was Eagle.

I remembered a trick he had shown me once for resolving a troublesome dream—to enter it as if it were a journey.

I reentered my dream with Daniel. I saw myself standing once again in the basement. I could feel Daniel moving behind the barricade; I could hear the scritch-scritch of his pen on the blueprints. I could hear the blade of his knife cutting the paper. I felt like he was rewriting history back there. I peered over the top of the boxes.

Daniel was gone, but a scattering of names lay on the floor. I pushed the boxes aside and picked them up in my hands. I tried to read them but the ink had been blurred by the water. When I held them, my hands got hot, and soon I realized that that there were traces of blood on them. The slips of paper felt like pieces of skin, and when I tried to shake them off, they stuck to my hands.

I was feeling queasy, but instead of resisting the feeling, I walked more deeply into the journey. I had to find Daniel—where had he gone?

I wandered a bit more around the basement and then trudged back upstairs. The rooms were all empty and the door to the deck was open wide. Daniel seemed to have vanished. I went outside on the deck and asked for Eagle to help me. I wanted him to walk through the house with me and help me figure out what to do.

I saw him circling the woods behind the house. He landed; I could feel the pressure of his feet on my left shoulder. The queasiness in my stomach eased, and I felt myself breathing more quietly. I sunk deeper into my trance.

"I'm stuck," I said. "I don't like the way my house feels, but I don't know how to change it."

"Well," he said, "what it is you want to create?"

"I want a home that's peaceful. I want a place I can feel safe and clear in. Right now, the energy feels all jangled. It makes me uneasy."

Suddenly we were standing in Daniel's study. Daniel was slumped over in his chair, dead, the way I had found him that morning in January. The air in the study was so thick it felt like I was breathing in cotton. In a second it was all so obvious to me—it wasn't just Daniel's clothes that needed to be removed. His energy was still present here.

"The house needs to be cleared," said Eagle. "You can't build something new and vital on something that is still in ruins."

First, he said, we would call in a protectorate for the house, a power animal to help clear the space of any energy that didn't belong. We returned to the basement, where I found a beaver hard at work on sealing the broken pipe and rebuilding the foundation.

"There is a path of water that leads to this front wall," said Eagle. "It comes down from the hill across the street. The strength of the house keeps getting washed away."

It was true that years before the basement had leaked after every storm. Daniel had had a drainage system put in.

"But we cured all the leaks years ago," I said.

He looked at me and frowned. "You did not stop the flow of the water from swarming the foundation."

The beaver looked up from her work. I sensed it was the one I had met two months before at the marsh. I was touched by her willingness to help.

I could see a thatchwork of thorny leaves and berries forming and spreading across the walls, like a climbing rose bush.

"Plant holly along this side. It will cleanse the energy moving toward the house, bring in new light and protect the foundation.

I nodded.

When she was finished with the walls, she nosed around on the basement floor, sucking up all the water. Then she blew it out of her mouth like a fire hose. A force of water and wind took every bit of debris from the basement floor and sent it hurtling into space, where it burst apart like fireworks in the sky. The basement glistened and shimmered like a Mr. Clean commercial.

We went upstairs and walked from room to room. I was given very specific instructions about where to burn candles, where to smudge, where to place bowls of lavender and open containers of salt water. In Ethan's room, Beaver shook her head when she saw the wet corner and the bulging paint.

"Clean your gutters," she said.

When we at last reached Daniel's study, there was a small band of people standing behind his desk chair. One of them was Daniel's father. Another was his grandmother and an aunt who had passed away several years before him.

The air was still dense here and the thickness seemed to hang in gray, wispy clouds around Daniel's body.

"Your husband was suffering here before he died," observed Beaver. "He felt he had nowhere to go."

I thought about the dilemma he had created for himself with Cynthia on one side and me and the children on the other. I thought of a trapped fly, buzzing between a closed window and a screen. I remembered Daniel saying that when I met him on my journey: I was caught, he said.

Eagle began to clear the room. With his great wings he began to fan the gray patches until they formed a single clump. He took the clump in his beak and flew out the open door to the woods behind the house, disappearing into the sky until I lost sight of him.

Soon he reappeared, a gold speck falling from the sun. When he streamed in through the door, a great gold beam of light came in with him, a light that fanned out into the room, scouring and burning any dark traces of Daniel's energy that had been left behind.

Then the beam rolled itself up into a globe of gold that landed in the arms of Daniel's father. I looked at the chair and saw that Daniel's form had faded away. Daniel's father smiled at me and then led the others out of the room through a staircase in the ceiling. The portal in the ceiling closed.

"This room," said Eagle, "is the heart of your house. It connects to everything else. These doors," he said, pointing around the room, "are tributaries. This is a vital area and should be kept sacred. You cannot close it off; there should be life here, activity. Build an altar here." He pointed to the north corner. "Put family artifacts on it, precious things. And don't forget to honor your protectorate."

I felt satisfied. I thanked Beaver and Eagle for their work and came back to the presence of my room. I opened my eyes and looked over at the clock: 2:22.

The message in the dream seemed clear. I felt much better about moving Daniel's things out—something about them seemed loosened, dislodged. I was turning paint colors over in my mind and planning a trip to the nursery in order to purchase a holly tree. Then, I remembered one thing that still seemed unsettling about the dream.

What was the meaning of those names Daniel was cutting from the family tree and why had they stuck to my hands like flesh and blood?

Chapter Six
Apple: Beauty

I decided on a green that was the color of golden delicious apples. In the afternoon sun, the walls looked split pea-gold, and at night under lamplight, they turned key lime. I paired the green with accents of dark pinky red and couldn't believe how much I liked it. The room, which had been navy and taupe, took on a whole new look.

Rowena gave me the name of a home for veterans, and they came out one morning with a truck. I donated to them all the furniture and books from Daniel's office, our bed, two chests of drawers, and most of Daniel's clothing. (I had set aside some nice sport coats and ties for Ethan and some tee shirts for Kenya as keepsakes.) I put all of Daniel's jewelry in a baggie and took it to the safe deposit box. Everything else went to the dump.

I made the three trips there alone and each time I returned with an empty car, I felt physically lighter than before. I repeatedly asked myself why I hadn't done this long ago, but then, I knew why.

I spent time scrubbing the walls of Daniel's office with orange water. I did all the smudging I'd been instructed to do. I decided to paint the adobe colored walls of Daniel's office sky blue to honor the work Eagle and Beaver had done there. I thought about making the room into a hangout for the family, but Eagle said no, this was intended to be the space for my new office. I decided my existing study could now become a full time guest room.

All the change and bustle of new things in the house made me feel energized and happy. Ethan and Kenya observed the changes I was making and for a time, said nothing.

"When are you painting *my* room?" Kenya asked one day from the doorway after she stood there for some time watching me paint.

I was crouched on my knees and elbows slathering the baseboard in a creamy white coat. "What's wrong with your room?"

"Ah, hello, it's pink?"

"What's wrong with pink?"

"Pink is retarded. I want it black."

"No, no, honey, that's too dark."

"How about if I splatter Day-Glo orange on top of the black?"

"Kenya, be serious."

"I am serious. I'll paint it myself then. I don't need you."

I sighed and sat back on my heels. "Sweetie, we can paint your room if you want, but there have to be parameters. It has to be something *I* can live with."

"You're such a control freak, Mom. You never even go into my room. What do you care?"

"If we can agree on a color, you can paint your room. That's the deal."

"I could never agree to some stupid color you like. You'd just make it something nasty like this." She waved her hand around the room. "Jeez, if I had to sleep in here, I'd want to puke my guts out all the time."

"Kenya, why should you have a say in what color I paint my room? I like this color."

"Exactly, Mom."

I shook my head and bent down to continue painting. Maybe I was being unreasonable. I recalled a time two years before when I had battled with her over getting her ears pierced.

"You know," I remembered Eagle saying at the time, "what she's asking is really just a small thing."

I sighed. "You're right, Kenya. Why don't we go pick out some paint chips this weekend? You want to do that?"

Silence.

"Kenya?"

When I looked up, she was gone.

About an hour later, Ethan stopped by for a peek.

"What do you think?" I asked.

"Wow, snot green," he said. "I'm totally loving it."

"Don't be a smart ass."

"You asked, Mom."

"So, what have you been up to, Ethan? Have you spoken anymore with Mrs. Madison about your alternatives?"

Ethan's applications had been turned down at the three schools he had selected. The only schools that had accepted him were the "safety" schools suggested by his high school advisor. Now he felt completely uninspired about going away to college in the fall. I had encouraged him to speak with his advisor about finding some independent studies to do or ways in which to make the safety schools more appealing—even if just for the short term until he could reapply.

"Yeah, she suggested I go down and talk to an army recruiter," he said.

"WHAT!?" I jumped up so fast I lost my balance and

ended up planting my foot right in the middle of the paint tray. "You're not serious?"

Ethan started laughing. "Oh my God, Mom, you should see yourself! Oh, man, that's classic!" He held his stomach and leaned his elbow against the doorjamb to keep from collapsing.

"Ethan! Surely, you aren't considering that!" My heart was thrumming so hard in my chest I could barely catch my breath.

"Of course not," he said. "Sheesh! I was just joking around."

"That really isn't funny, Ethan," I said, bending down to wipe the paint off my foot. "You scared the crap out of me."

"Well, gee, Mom, why would you even *think* I was being serious? Don't you know me any better than that?"

I frowned. "I don't know anymore, Ethan. Seems like I've been getting a lot of surprises lately."

"No shit, Mom. You need to pay more attention around here." He jerked his head in the direction of Kenya's room and then slumped away from the doorway.

I looked down and realized I had spilled great globs of what now looked like snot-green puke all over my carpet.

The next morning I waded into Kenya's room to get a better idea what the impact of black walls might be in there. I thought maybe I could get her to agree on papering one of the walls in a black and white print or choosing another color, like eggplant or charcoal instead—anything to mollify the stark effect of total black.

I trudged through the piles of clothes, DVD's, books and papers strewn across her floor and tried to envision how I could coexist peaceably with a Goth décor. My foot crunched on a tin of adhesive bandages, and when I bent down to pick them up I noticed a box of rolled gauze that had been removed from the First Aid kit I kept under the bathroom sink. Blisters,

I bet, from those hideous boots she always wore.

Then I noticed the brown stains of blood on both sleeves of her pajama top. My heart started to beat very fast in my chest. I rummaged around the room in order to locate every jersey I could find. Of course, they were all black but when I touched the cloth or held them up to the light, I could see traces of dark stains on all of them, stains I had never even noticed when I did the laundry.

There had to be a better explanation than what I was already thinking. I looked around the room and thought back to the drawers I had heard her slam shut the day I confronted her about the credit card bill. I began by opening the bottom drawers of her dresser. In the second drawer, stuffed inside the pocket of a pair of jeans, I found three razor blades wrapped in a crumpled tissue. They were the kind of blades you bought in a hardware store that came wrapped with little sleeves of cardboard. She had probably found them on Daniel's workbench.

Daniel's workbench. The dream image of Daniel slicing names from his family tree spilled through my brain. I felt myself break into a cold sweat.

I had heard of children cutting themselves. I'd read articles on this stuff. Some psychologists linked the behavior to an ancient tribal practice, an initiation rite aimed at teaching and testing pain endurance. Kids often did it not so much to end their lives, but in an effort to substitute one pain for another—the one who administers the pain presumably controls it.

Was my daughter cutting herself?

I forced myself to search further through the rest of the drawers. Another pants pocket produced a bloody handkerchief that bore Daniel's initials and his father's old penknife. She had taken these from Daniel's dresser.

I sat down on the floor and started to cry. My stomach was sick with alarm and I could hear the drumming of my own heartbeat in my ears.

I don't know how long I sat there. I thought about

Ethan and his warnings about my failure to pay attention and Kenya and her threat that she would show me something I would never forget. I needed to talk to someone about this, someone who knew something.

I found my way to the phone and shakily called the school's number. I asked for Jack Woods in as even a voice as I could muster.

"Jack Woods speaking," he said, after a few clicks of the line.

"It's Clare Blakely."

"Mrs. Blakely, how can I help you?" he said cheerily.

"Remember your analogy about the disruptive kid in the classroom who's always trying to get the teacher's attention?"

"Ah, yeah?"

"Well, what do you do when that kid has a knife?"

There was a slight pause as I felt his mood get very serious.

"What's happening?" he asked.

"I found razor blades, bandages, and a penknife in Kenya's room. The sleeves of her jerseys are all stained with blood. I think she's cutting."

"Have you confronted her about this?"

"She's at school," I said. "I just found this out. My head is reeling. I don't know what to do."

"Kenya's been seeing Gina Scacchi for counseling, hasn't she?"

"She has, and she seems to like Gina, but I personally don't find the woman very helpful."

"You need to contact her about this."

"I know, I will, but every time I talk to Gina, she keeps reminding me that she's Kenya's therapist, not mine, like I somehow don't know that. I think it's her way of saying she has to maintain some boundaries of confidentiality, but I find it so irritating. Dealing with her this past month has just made me feel more out to sea."

"I'm sorry about that," he said.

"No, it's okay. I was just remembering how helpful you were that day Kenya was suspended for hitting Sarah Drucker, and I called hoping you could shed some light on this for me. I was hoping you could suggest how I might approach Kenya when she comes home. This is such a fragile situation. I don't want to make things worse."

"No, of course not," he said. "I actually did some work around this issue recently."

"With another student at the school?" I asked.

"No. I work at a clinic as part of my post-graduate work, and I was studying some cases there."

"Then you must have some insight for me."

I was glad I had thought to call him.

"Well, I think the most important thing to remember is to put your own fears aside for the moment and approach her from a place of strength and compassion. I know that's a challenge here, but if you confront her with feelings of horror or rage or even aggravation, if you make it about you, it will only make matters worse. Parents typically panic and want to control the situation immediately. But this is a case where the child herself has to learn to control the behavior in her own time—and it will require your patience and support. There's a new book out on this that's been getting rave reviews by the folks in the field. It's by this child psychology team, Newsome and Finster—you can probably find it online."

I scribbled the names down on a sheet of paper.

"She needs to be evaluated for the risk of suicide. You know that, don't you?"

"Yes, I'll take her to see Gina right away."

"You may want to take her to your pediatrician as well. Sometimes these things can be exacerbated by hormonal and chemical imbalances. And you want to make certain there's no blood poisoning or anemia."

"I'll do that."

"I'm so sorry, Mrs. Blakely. Kenya is such a bright and

wonderful girl."

"I know that," I said, my eyes welling with tears. "I don't think I gave her enough support after my husband died—I was so caught up in my own problems."

"I can see why you'd feel that way, but I always think it's better to just take things as they are and worry less about who's to blame."

"I guess."

"And you know you can contact me if you have questions or concerns, right?"

"I do. Thanks."

I hung up and pondered whom to call next. Rowena was away at a human resources conference, and I really didn't want to bother her with my problems right now. The company she worked for was in the midst of tightening its belt and Rowena was apparently learning how to deal with the effects of layoffs and dismissals on employees. I knew she had been stressed out enough by the turn her work was taking lately, and I didn't want to lay this in her lap.

The person I actually wanted to talk to most right now was Daniel. Daniel and I knew Kenya in a way others would never know her. That was the level of insight I felt I needed right now.

Had Daniel been trying to warn me, I wondered? I thought back to the dream and what he might have been asking. Was he saying he would be there, behind the scenes, planning, helping, protecting? I remembered he had been so joyful. Was he trying to tell me not to worry, that everything would come out fine?

At the time, I had felt impatient; I didn't want to listen to him. I was even resentful of his intrusion. Now I wished that I had been kinder.

I put in a call to Kenya's therapist, Gina. I left a message on her voicemail, asking her to call me. Then I called the pediatrician and made an appointment for a check-up—I didn't say why.

I picked up the piece of paper I used to take notes during my conversation with Jack Woods. I went to the computer and ordered the book he recommended plus two others. Then I did a search on "cutting" and began to read.

The words of other parents who had found themselves in my situation began to blare at me from the computer. Things that hadn't even occurred to me began to sink in and rattle me even more than I already was. I would not be able to keep Kenya safe; I could not watch over her every minute. If things got worse, I might even have to put her into a psychiatric ward just to keep her alive. I would not be able to control the duration or severity of this experience—that was up to Kenya. I would not be able to stop her.

I would not be able to stop her.

I shut off the computer. I needed to take a look at what choices I did have.

I could delay sending her to high school in the fall and let her adjust to things for a year. In the meantime, I could find courses and activities that would give her a better avenue of self-expression and take her away from the social pressures of school. I could find her the best therapist around, one who had experience and more importantly, success, with kids who cut themselves. I could get guidance and help through journeying. I could choose most of all to be a calming, steadying and reliable support for Kenya—that was the toughest one—and I needed to start doing that right now.

Kenya didn't get off the bus that afternoon when it stopped in front of the house. I called her cell phone and heard it ringing from behind her bedroom door. Great!

I decided perhaps my call to the counselor had prompted them to pull her from class or something. I called the school in a panic and asked for Jack Woods, who—I was told

—was not in the office I explained to the woman on the other end of the phone that my daughter was missing.

"It's a nice day," she said, "maybe she decided to walk."

"She lives seven miles from the school."

"Oh. Have you tried her cell phone?"

"She doesn't have it with her."

"Well, you really should try to make certain she carries it for situations like this."

"Yeah, well that doesn't exactly help me right now, does it? Listen, I need you to help me find her."

"One minute, please."

One minute? I thought. What does that mean? Is she looking for Kenya? Taking another call? Letting me just cool my heels here? God, I wanted to pound this woman.

I paced back and forth in the kitchen, imagining the worst. Kenya going off to the woods behind the school, pulling a blade from her pocket and applying it to the cuts that were already open on her skin. The image terrified me and I couldn't get it out of my head. I started to shake and cry.

Okay, I thought, if this woman didn't get back on the phone in one minute, I was going to get in the car and drive there myself.

"Mrs. Blakely? Kenya's here. She's making posters for the Pancake Breakfast. She said she told you about it."

A small light went on in the dim recesses of my tortured brain. Ah, yes, so she had.

"You're right," I said, feeling a rush of relief that nearly brought me to me knees. "I-I totally forgot. I'm *so* sorry to trouble you. God, thank you for finding her! R-really. Thanks so, so much."

I was sure the woman could tell I was crying. Loon, she was thinking to herself, complete loon.

I hung up the phone and wiped my face. Could I be *any* lamer? I was definitely capturing that calming, steadying and reliable part. Yep, that part I had down cold.

I waited in a small queue of cars outside the school. I stared at the mothers in the cars in front of me and behind me. I envied them for their lives, their normal, balanced, beautiful and perfect children. I wished wholeheartedly that I could have been any one of them, to sit as they did now, waiting for their fresh-faced, enthusiastic and promising teenager to emerge like a finely honed widget from the revolving door of the school.

Okay, so my child was a rebel, an individual in the purest sense of the word. No mold was going to fit snugly around this girl, no-sir-ee. This was a child who was unique in every way, and wasn't that a good thing? Wasn't that a breath of fresh air in this wasteland of mediocrity?

I looked again at the row of waiting moms and sighed heavily. Lord, give me a widget any day, I thought.

Kenya appeared, a stark black and white cutout amidst a sea of sparkly animated girls in colorful tops and pants. It reminded me of those tests they give to children: find the one that doesn't belong in each group.

She stood staring at the car for a few moments and then slunk towards it. She opened the car door and plopped into the passenger seat.

"Everyone in this school is so retarded," she said.

"How so?"

"Trust me, they are."

I pulled away from the curb and eased into the traffic leading out of the school.

"How are the posters coming?" I asked.

"I practically had to do them all myself. Tara and Jessica were supposed to be helping, but they both sat down and painted their fingernails instead, and then they're like, oh, we can't do posters *now*, our nails are wet, tee hee. God, they're so stupid; the only reason they even come to the meetings is so they can flirt with Dylan and Matt."

"Are you working on posters again tomorrow?"

"No way! I did my eight hours of volunteering. That's the *last* they'll ever see of *me*."

The phrase made me shudder, and I remembered why I was stalling.

"Kenya," I said. Then I stopped and pulled the car over to the side of the road.

"What?" she said looking over at me.

"I found some things today—things that are used by kids who cut themselves. I found them in your room along with some bloodstained clothes. I want to see your arms."

Kenya folded her arms tightly across her chest.

"I cut myself shaving," she said.

"You don't shave."

"I shave my *under*arms."

"Well, shaving your underarms would not explain the things I found. Let me just see your arms. If your arms are clear, then we can forget about it and go home, okay?" I held out my hands so I could take hold of her wrists.

She wrapped her arms more tightly against her chest.

"I want to go home," she said. "I have to pee really bad."

"Show me your arms first and then I'll drive you home."

"Drive me home or I'll pee on your car seat."

Kenya was a complete germ-a-phobe—there was no way she was going to wet herself intentionally. I decided to call her bluff and stay put.

Maybe a minute passed—a long silent minute.

She glared at me. "Fine! Then I'll walk."

I locked the doors and held my finger down on the button.

"Are you cutting yourself, Kenya?" I asked.

"Take me home or I swear I will start screaming at the top of my lungs right now."

"That's okay. When the police come and ask what's

going on, I'll tell them what I found today in your room and they will make you show *them* your arms. It's a criminal offense, you know—to cut yourself."

"You're lying," she said.

"Want to try it out and see if I am?"

"Here!" she said, pulling up her sleeves and flashing her arms at me. "There! You happy now?"

I caught a glimpse of several rows of inch-long cuts on the inside of her arms. It reminded me of the tick marks prisoners etched into their cell walls in order to keep track of their sentences. The skin from wrist to elbow was tender-red and raw-looking.

"Oh, Kenya," I said, reaching out to take hold of her arms.

"You said if I showed you, you'd take me home," she said, starting to sob. "I have to pee really, really bad!" Her voice escalated suddenly to a high screaming pitch. "We have to go now! Don't you understand?" She folded her arms against her stomach, bent over at the waist and rocked back and forth, crying.

I felt cruel. I felt like a monster. Here I was, trying to be sensitive and calm, trying to do the right thing. And I had only made the situation worse. I had betrayed her in some way —I didn't realize it, but I had. I was trying to protect her, but I'd sold her out for this one moment of control, these few small seconds of triumph.

She was the most precious thing in the world to me and instead of telling her that, I had effectively pressed my boot heel against her jugular until she was trapped, until she was forced to give up the only control she had.

I drove home stunned and silent, unable to console her or myself and when I pulled into the garage and unlocked the doors, she grabbed her backpack and burst out of the car.

"I hate you, you ugly stupid cow," she said, slamming the car door shut. "Fuck you!"

I went upstairs to Ethan's room and asked him to remove the locks on both Kenya's bedroom door and the door of
the bathroom she used.

He looked at me.

"I don't know how to do that," he said.

I handed him a Phillips head screwdriver. "Then you'll
need to figure it out," I said.

"What are you talking about?"

"Your sister is cutting herself and until we get a grip on
the situation, I don't want her behind a locked door."

His face went white. "She's cutting herself? Are you
sure?"

I nodded grimly.

"Jesus, Mom, how could you let this happen to her?"

I almost said: "I didn't." But then I felt he was right on
a number of levels, asking me that question. I even felt I owed
him a good answer. I just didn't have one.

"I don't know," I said. I laid the screwdriver down on
his desk and left the room.

I went downstairs and made a plate of sandwiches,
some ham and cheese with mustard, the kind Ethan liked,
some chicken and lettuce with mayonnaise, the kind Kenya
liked. I put the plate into the refrigerator and went upstairs to
my study.

I closed the door and lay down on the foldout couch. I
gazed out of the window and stared up into the arms of the
apple tree that grew in our front yard. The branches were lush
with blossoms at this time of year, petal pink and downy soft
—almost too beautiful to absorb. I felt like I could look at that
tree for a long, long time before I would ever be able to absorb
its beauty.

It was much the same way with Kenya's cutting. It
would take a long time to absorb that as well. I would need to
be hyper-vigilant again, the way I had been when she was a
baby, never letting her out of my sight, checking on her

throughout the night to make sure she was still breathing.

Right now, though, I just needed to lie here and catch my breath, inhale deeply and slowly, over and over and over again, until the knotted fist of my chest opened and relaxed. I needed to look up into those pink-white blossoms until my eyes ached more from their beauty than from the memory of my daughter's ravaged arms.

I lay there, warm tears coating my face, beckoning the apple's soothing beauty until it seemed that it was only the dripping pink of it that rained on me and rolled down my neck.

It was dark when I woke up. I could hear Ethan in the room next door, talking. Kenya's room. I sat up and blinked. The clock read 8:47.

I opened the door quietly and peeked out. Kenya's door was closed and I could hear her talking now as well. I tiptoed down the hallway and leaned gently against the door.

"She doesn't mean it that way," Ethan was saying. "You're just scaring her—that's all. You're scaring me too, Ken. You gotta stop doing that. Promise me you'll stop it. Will you?"

Silence.

"Listen," Ethan went on, "come and just talk to me if you feel like you gotta get stuff out of your system. I'll listen to whatever you have to say."

"You'll just make fun of me," said Kenya. Her voice sounded muffled as if she were leaning her face into her pillow.

"I won't," said Ethan, "I promise. Look, I'll promise to listen and help and you promise to stop cutting yourself. I promise on Dad's grave." His voice cracked. "Okay, Kenny? Deal?"

My heart and eyes felt so full. I put my hand up to my mouth to hold it all in.

More silence.

"Kenny," he said, so sweetly I couldn't stand it. I thought of those blossoms again—too much to take in. "C'mon now."

"Okay," she said. "But everything I tell you is just between you and me. You can't tell Mom. You can't tell anybody."

"Deal," said Ethan.

I backed away from the door and returned to the study, closing the door soundlessly behind me. I bent my knees to the floor and folded in half, pressing my forehead into the carpet. I let out a deep sigh of relief and wept with gratitude.

Kenya idolized her brother. She wouldn't have made that deal with me, but she had made it with him, and knowing Kenya, as long as Ethan kept his half of the bargain, she would keep hers.

Eamon was waiting for me when I entered the lower world the next morning. He was standing on the path, arms folded and hands buried into the open ends of his wide sleeves.

"You look monkish," I said.

"We have to hurry," he said, walking briskly away from me.

As usual I had to run to keep up with him.

"Your daughter is playing out a pattern of behavior that runs through your family—an inability to survive the death of a loved one and the desire to follow in his footsteps to the other world."

"What does that mean?"

"Being a survivor," he said. "What do you *think* the term means? A death is either survived, or it isn't."

"I never really thought about it."

"Well, think about it then," he said, striding up the mountain ahead of me.

It seemed like we walked for a long time, up, up, up. I couldn't get more clarity on Kenya; I felt too rattled by what Eamon had said. All I could do was wait until we reached our destination, wherever that was.

A cloud cover descended and we walked more. The ground underneath got craggier. Then the clouds parted and I saw a cabin ahead of us. There was smoke billowing from the chimney. The smell of peat pricked my nostrils.

Eamon opened the door and went inside, beckoning me to follow. Inside the cabin, an old woman, a man and a young girl warmed themselves by the fire. The man wore a kilt and the girl a tartan shawl.

The woman began to speak. "It began with the clan wars," she said. "We lost everything we had ever known—our homes, our land. Everything our ancestors had built up and claimed as their own rightful place on this earth. All gone. First, we turned on one another, clan against clan; then the invaders came and cleared out the rest. Life was not worth living."

The man leaned over and continued the tale: "It began as a protest among the young people. Those who were being cleared out began to kill themselves outright, saying it was nobler to follow the dead into the underworld than to stay in a world where we had no place to stand."

Then the girl spoke up: "There were ceremonies in the hills. We would meet under cover of night and take our own lives, slit our own throats. It was seen as the only courageous thing to do in the face of our destruction. We called it spilling."

Eamon turned to me: "The ritual has an enduring energy," he said. "Now do you see what's happening?"

It took a while to absorb what they were saying. I looked into their grave, hollow faces and saw something there that made me shudder. It was a look I had seen cross Kenya's face a couple of times, a kind of knowing that was almost too dangerous to share.

"What can we do?" I asked.

"The energy can't be destroyed," said Eamon, "but it can be changed."

"Okay," I said, "how do we do that?"

Almost as soon as I spoke, we landed in another place. We were outside on a broad, flat summit surrounded by mountains. A large circle of people stood around a blazing fire. The crowd parted and it became clear that I was supposed to step into the fire in the center. Everyone was looking at me with such trust.

When I looked down at my body, I could see it had been wrapped in layers and layers of linen, as if I were already dead and had been prepared for burial. Then the fire was all around me, and the faces of the crowd disappeared behind the wall of flame. I felt no heat, only a wild kind of buzzing inside and around my body.

Soon, my body was shooting up out of the fire and I could see all the people on the ground below me, looking up. It seemed like the experience was theirs and mine at the same time.

I looked down at my clothes, which were white and glowing; my hands and arms were luminescent. I landed softly on the ground and Eamon put his hand on my head in some kind of blessing.

Then the old woman from the cabin came forward. "I wanted to leave them courage, so our children would find strength in the living of life and whatever it brought."

The man who had been with her—her son it seemed— then spoke. "I wanted to leave behind an honorable path for them to follow," he said.

The girl now stepped out of the ring of people. "I wanted to leave joy, not a black river of grief."

"Build a shrine to the memory of these people," Eamon said, "and the lineage that connects your daughter to them. Honor their deaths, and bring through the legacies they wished to leave behind them—joy, honor, courage—the ideals our people have aspired to since the beginning of time. Take your daughter with you when you build it."

I had questions about how and where I was to build such a thing, but I felt myself slipping back to the beginning of the path on which I had first met up with Eamon. The drumbeat had shifted to callback and I was spiraling up towards the room. I opened my eyes and stared at the ceiling. I blinked and then blinked again.

"Good lord," I said.

Chapter Seven
Beech: Guidance

Kenya was better. Things around the house--and inside my own head—were much calmer and saner. Over the weeks that followed my discovery that she was cutting herself and the agreement I overheard her make with her brother, I instituted a number of changes into Kenya's life. But I also made certain—taking the advice of the book I had bought on cutting—that she was included in all the decision-making so she would feel she still had control.

I took her out of school at the end of May. Her poor grades, numerous sick days, and incomplete schoolwork did not qualify her for graduation anyway, and I didn't want her to feel embarrassed or saddened by the flurry of preparations and graduation rehearsals going on around her, or the excitement over the end-of-the-year picnic and the after-graduation dance she would not be eligible to attend.

We met with the eighth-grade teaching team, and mapped out exactly what Kenya would need to finish in order to meet the requirements for entry into high school. She had a year to complete the work and I was given the names of local tutors we could use to navigate her through it.

In the meantime, I signed her up for some art classes and some music lessons.

Kenya said she wanted to focus more on the guitar playing that had been largely abandoned since Daniel's death. The art classes were just studio drawing and beginners' painting, and when we went to buy all her art supplies, she seemed genuinely excited.

Because she was doing so well emotionally, I declined the anti-depressants offered by Kenya's psychiatrist. I thought we would stick with Gina for the time being, but if the cutting started again, I would look for someone new.

Almost everyday, I checked Kenya for marks. She let me check her without protest, even joked about it sometimes, hamming up the whole process by striking dramatic poses with her arms and legs, while I peeled back her clothes to look at her skin. Her arms had healed nicely, and all in all I felt we were back on track.

But when I woke her up on the Saturday of her first art lesson, she rolled over and complained of a stomachache. She seemed glum and listless and when I asked to see her arms, she sat up in bed and screamed at me.

"I'm not some kind of psycho, okay? You're the psycho! Do you know how ridiculous you look, pawing all over me everyday? You're like obsessed or something. It's sick!"

"Kenya, what's happening with you? I thought you were looking forward to your art classes."

"I don't want to go to some stupid art class! Just leave me the fuck alone, will you?"

She pulled the covers over her head and curled up underneath in a fetal ball.

I sighed. I couldn't believe this was happening. It was as if we had gone back to square one.

I left her room and closed the door behind me. I stood in the hallway thinking.

Ethan had been very busy lately. His high school graduation was approaching.

There were daily rehearsals and weekend parties, his usual track meets and practices, not to mention the close of the school year and his preparation for final exams. He hadn't been available to talk to Kenya, to listen to her, as he'd promised. I was certain that was what it was.

I went to Ethan's door and rapped softly.

Silence.

"Ethan?" I said, tapping. "Ethan?"

"God! What? I'm sleeping!"

I opened the door and went in.

"I need to talk to you," I said, leaning over the bed. "Kenya's acting weird all of a sudden."

He lifted his head and looked at me.

"All of a *sudden*? You're kidding, right?"

He slumped back onto his pillow.

"Do we have to do this right now?" he asked.

"Yes," I said. "What has she been telling you?"

"Mom, she hasn't been telling me anything. She doesn't talk to me."

"Ethan, I know you're not supposed to talk to me about it, but I heard the two of you make a deal together. She promised you she would stop cutting if you would listen to her problems."

"No, she didn't."

"Yes, she did. I heard her."

"No, Mom." Ethan rubbed his head and sat up in bed. "I tried to get her to talk to me. And at first she said, okay, but then she changed her mind. I thought it was because she didn't trust me to keep quiet, but she said no, that wasn't it. She didn't want to tell me because she said if she did, I would want to do it, too. I don't exactly get what she was saying, but I think she thought if she talked to me about how it made her feel, *I* would start cutting."

"What do you mean?" I asked. My heart was racing wildly in my chest.

"I can't explain it," he said, shaking his head. "She acted like it was contagious or something, or that it was some kind of a *cult*."

The face of the girl from my journey came back to me. "There were ceremonies in the hills," she said. "We called it spilling."

A chill went up my spine. I figured I'd better get to work on that shrine.

Kenya and I went to my studio later that same morning. Her mood had been more stable since she had come down to breakfast, and when I insisted she come with me, she didn't protest.

I brought Kenya's art supplies along. She sat across the room from me putting aimless strokes of color onto a pad that was propped against her knees. An open box of pastels was beside her. She wiggled her fingers—now muddy brown with many layers of color—over the box and pulled out a stick of lapis lazuli blue.

I decided I would undertake a sculpture devoted to the girl in my journey—the one who had taken her own life. I hadn't yet figured out how Kenya was to be involved in the process but I was told to bring her with me, so I did.

I sat on the floor, doodling and drawing without much success. I just couldn't seem to get to the core of it.

Suddenly, there was a hard rap on the inside door. Then the door popped open and Dill walked in. I was always a bit startled by that road-worn face of his and the studs of sea-glass blue eyes peering out at the world.

"Hey, Dill!" I said, laughing.

"Came to borrow a cup of sugar," he said, grinning broadly.

Then he stopped short as he spotted Kenya. "Oh, sorry," he said.

"Don't be sorry. This is my daughter, Kenya. Kenya, this is the guy who does all those amazing things in the window out front. This is Dill."

He looked embarrassed and held up two fingers. "Peace," he said.

Kenya's spine straightened up a full three inches. "Hey," she said.

Dill knew all about Kenya's story. I had poured my heart out to him one day when I was at the studio and felt too distracted to work. Dill listened intently to the whole saga, a child's grief that had spiraled into cutting, and then he riffled through some cards in a jar on his worktable.

He handed me one. It had a graphic of a blue butterfly on it. Lila Love Sky, Shamanic Practitioner, it read, followed by a phone number.

"Lila Love Sky?" I said. "Her name sounds like a bad sentence."

Dill smirked and rolled his eyes. "Okay, I guarantee you," he said, "you take your daughter to see Lila and you won't care if her name is Lila Stewed Cabbage."

I started to laugh. "Well, at least Lila Stewed Cabbage makes a grammatical sentence," I said.

"Seriously, when I first went to see this woman, I was like Humpty Dumpty. Somehow she managed to put all the pieces back together again." He held out his arms and spun around, grinning wide. "See? Good as new."

I smiled. "I'll think about it," I said, tucking the card in my pocket.

Now, here he was, giving me the same silly grin.

"You want some coffee?" he asked. "I just made some. And you," he said, looking over at Kenya, "I got a can of Witch's Brew with your name on it."

Kenya looked at him and blinked. Witch's Brew was a tea-flavored soda that kids her age loved.

"Sure," she said.

Dill turned and went back into his shop and Kenya scrambled to her feet and followed him. I watched them with curiosity through the doorway of the studio.

"What grade are you in?" asked Dill, reaching down into the tiny refrigerator beneath his counter.

"I'm not really in any grade right now," Kenya said, shrugging. "I-I kind of left school."

She dug at the floor with the toe of her shoe, that thing she always did when she was uncomfortable.

"Cool," said Dill, handing Kenya her soda. "That's awesome."

"Y-you really think so?"

I watched the sole of her shoe go flat onto the floor.

"Sure. Absolutely. You're taking a time-out, right?"

"I'm finishing eighth grade at home this year, and I'm taking art and guitar lessons."

Dill put two mugs onto the counter and poured coffee into them.

"How long have you been playing guitar?"

"Since I was eight. Then I kind of—um, stopped."

"I play guitar, too," he said. "I suck at it, mind you, and it's torture to hear myself play, but if I leave it for a while, I really miss it. You know what I mean?"

Kenya nodded, though I wondered if she did know what he meant.

"Tell you what, you bring your guitar with you next time you come down to the studio with your mom and we'll do some jamming together."

Kenya looked mildly stunned. "Seriously?" she said.

Dill patted her on the shoulder. "Seriously. You have to promise not to make fun of me, though. C'mon, let's take your mom her coffee," he said.

He picked up both cups and came striding towards me,

arms lifted away from his chest, a wisp of his long stringy hair floating out behind his head.

Kenya walked behind Dill, staring up at him with wonder, as if she had just met Jesus.

Later on, Dill went back to his shop and I picked up my sketches again. I was staring into all the many faces I had made of that girl, but none of them was quite right. I flipped through the pages and sighed. Kenya sat cross-legged on the floor, cradling her drawing pad in her lap.

"Why does he look like that?" she asked after a few minutes.

"Who, Dill? I don't know; he's had kind of a rough life."

"Not *Dill*. Daddy."

I looked up and found her staring up at the sculpture of Icarus, which was nearly completed and positioned on a pedestal between us.

I was surprised by her question. Yes, the sculpture was intended to be of Daniel, but the likeness wasn't strong and I couldn't figure out how she knew it was her father. She hadn't gotten close enough to read the poetry or to guess at the subject of the sculpture, but the image of this winged man running after something he would never catch still struck her as being Daniel.

"What makes you think it's Daddy?"

She rolled her eyes. "Duh. Because it is. He was always like that."

"Like what?" I asked.

"I don't know. Never satisfied with anything. He was, like, a dreamer. He had big dreams."

It amazed me that my daughter saw her father this way. I guess there was a time when I saw those things in him too. Maybe it was what I first loved about him, until the failure of those dreams and visions became a source of disillusionment and constant grumbling. But they were both part of the same Daniel, weren't they?

"You're right," I said. "It is Daddy."

"So you put those wings on him because he's an angel now?"

"Ah, ye-es," I lied. No, it was not why I had put the wings on him. Icarus was a man with dreams so grand they proved fatal. To me, those wings were a symbol of Daniel's foolishness, but art was a canvas broad enough to incorporate everybody's vision. So why couldn't they be angel's wings?

I looked down at my sketches and then back up at my daughter.

"Kenya," I said, before I could stop myself, "how would you like to work on a sculpture with me?"

She continued staring up at the sculpture of Daniel and just when I thought she was totally ignoring me, she shrugged her shoulders and looked back at her box of pastels. "I guess," she said.

"I feel like I need some help figuring out my subject."

She picked up a stick of marigold colored pastel, gripped it in her fingers, and began scraping it hard, back and forth over her pad.

"You mean that girl you keep drawing?" she asked.

I smiled. "Maybe."

After some more strokes of pastel, she looked up and held out her golden fingers. "Give me one of your pencils," she said.

I shot one across the floor to her.

She flipped the page back on her pad and began drawing. She sketched for about ten minutes, turning both her head and the pad this way and that, biting her top lip as she drew. Then she came over and sat down next to me.

I took the pad in my hands and held it up to the light. It was a sketch of a girl carved into the trunk of a tree. The face of the girl was watery, floating away in the ripples of bark. Beside her, as if it had escaped from her body, was a heart, lurching out from the surface of the trunk like an embedded stone.

"Oh, Kenya. Honey, this is so beautiful," I said. There were tears standing in my eyes.

Kenya nodded. "She can't get out of there," she said, her finger coming to rest on the face of the girl. Her finger left a smudge of gold on the girl's brow.

"I know, sweetie. But we'll get her out." I pulled her close and kissed the top of her head. "Don't worry, we'll get her out."

The following Monday, I rummaged through my desk until I found the business card Dill had given me. *Lila Love Sky*. I sighed and turned it over and over in my hand, trying to get a sense of whether this was the right path for Kenya. Of course, I acknowledged the success of shamanic techniques in my own life, but part of me still wanted to believe it was some sort of trick I played on myself, a harmless and quirky exercise—Clare just being Clare.

When I stuck with things and worked them through piece by piece in my journeys, yes, they did seem to unravel and magically resolve themselves, but wasn't this a more serious thing with Kenya? Wasn't there a whole lot more riding on this?

I reached into my desk drawer again and withdrew a scrap of paper. On it, I had written the names and contact information of two therapists in the Hartford area, both of whom had been heartily endorsed by Jack Woods. I had found their names on the internet when I was searching one day for therapists who had experience with teens who cut themselves.

I put Lila's card and the scrap of paper side by side on the top of the desk and stared at them. Then I picked them up and carried them into Kenya's room.

She was lying on her stomach on the floor, drawing. I looked at the sketch she was working on—the head of a deer, its antlers leafy like tree branches.

"That's nice, Kenny," I said, peeping over her shoulder.

She put her hand over the sketch. "I'm just doodling," she said.

"Oh, well, it looks pretty good."

"Whatever." She rolled onto her hip and looked up at me. "What do you want?"

I sat on the floor beside her and put the card and the scrap of paper down on the pad beside her hand.

"Let's say, if you could talk to someone other than Gina, I mean, someone new, would it be a therapist like these two people or someone like this." I pointed at the business card.

Kenya picked it up. She touched the blue butterfly with her thumb and stared at it. "Where did you get this?"

"Actually, I got it from Dill," I said. "He says she helped him get over something pretty major. He said she put him back together again."

"Really?"

"Yeah, really."

Kenya handed me the card. "I would go and see her," she said.

"Are you sure? I mean, she doesn't work like a therapist, you know. You wouldn't just sit there and talk. She would work on you energetically, so to speak, and it might be kind of different from—."

"Mom!" said Kenya. "I know what shamans do. Okay? I'm not an idiot."

I couldn't help smiling. "Okay, good. I'll call her."

I got up to leave.

"Hey, Mom?"

"Yeah?"

"When you're done with that card, I'd like to have it back."

"Uh, sure. I guess you could have it."

Kenya rolled her eyes at my puzzled expression. "It's

no big deal. I just like it, that's all."

I left a voicemail with Lila Love Sky, asking her for an appointment. I ended the call and exhaled deeply. Suddenly, I felt so much better.

As I was about to set the phone down, I noticed the message light was blinking red. I dialed my voicemail. The message was from Hal.

"So," he said. "Good news. You can cancel that flight to Arizona."

(Actually I hadn't made any arrangements for Arizona because Eagle told me I wouldn't need them.)

"I called in a favor," Hal's voice continued, "and we have a hearing scheduled for July 14th. Make an appointment with Julie for like a week or so before that date, so we can have you come into the office and go over things."

I clicked off the phone and set it down on the desk. I closed my eyes and breathed another sigh of relief. That was two whole sighs of relief in under a minute.

I smiled and whispered a thank you to anyone who was listening—God, my helping spirits, the angels, Providence, maybe even Lady Luck.

"Thank you, members of the academy," I said out loud.

No, I wasn't out of the woods with Cynthia yet, by any means, but the news still felt like a triumph.

Lila Love Sky lived a bit off the beaten track. We followed the river for several miles and then crossed an old stone bridge that had once been part of the mill. I had passed by this bridge many times but had never crossed over it before.

The road got pretty steep on the other side and darkened in the shadows of the overhead trees. Kenya and I looked at one another. I wiggled my eyebrows up and down and she laughed.

Up ahead, a sky blue mailbox signaled our destination. We turned and made our way slowly up the drive. Two stately columns of beeches lined either side, their coppery heads shimmering in the breeze. The cedar shake house was small and compact, and looked like it had been plunked down in Wizard of Oz fashion into a riotous sea of flowering plants. Wind chimes clanged from the perky red porch eaves. Luminous glass gazing balls peeped above the irises and azaleas, the bleeding hearts and roses. Wrens and robins flitted and squawked wildly as we walked up the flagstone steps, no doubt protesting our intrusion into their nesting territories, and as we approached the door—also painted sky blue—a sleeping marmalade cat sprung from its perch on the porch railing and bolted into the rhododendron.

"Wow," said Kenya, "it's like, I don't know, *enchanted* or something."

Well, I thought enchanted might be stretching it, but there *was* really nice energy around this place, I had to give her that.

I knocked on the door and as I waited, something in the nearby woods caught my attention. I turned to meet the eyes of an enormous stag standing in the trees, the tips of its antlers obscured by the surrounding leaf cover.

"Kenya," I said, pointing, "look, it's just like—."

"Hello!" said Lila, opening her blue door with a flourish. "Come in. Come in."

Lila Love Sky was a sight to behold: a mane of white hair that fell to her elbows, aquamarine eyes that flashed when the light caught them and skin so milky white you had to resist reaching over to touch it. Her eyebrows were thick and dark and the tip of her long pointy nose a bit lopsided, as if she spent nights sleeping face down in her pillow.

"Have any trouble finding me?"

"No, no," I said. "Gosh, it's so lovely up here. I've

never been up this far—you almost wouldn't know it was here."

"I try to keep it that way," she said, laughing.

"And you're Kenya," she said, turning to my daughter.

"Yes," said Kenya.

"I like your hair," said Lila. "Believe it or not mine used to be this dark. How do you get it to stay up that way?" She reached over and took one fanned out chunk in her hand.

"Lots of spray," said Kenya.

"And teasing, right? I used to tease mine, too! Way up like this." She held her arms over her head like a ballerina and laughed again. "Boy, those were the days, huh?" she said, winking at me. "I loved wearing my hair like that!"

She turned suddenly and walked away from us, her long red skirt flouncing as she moved. "We're in here," she said.

We followed her down a narrow hallway to a room with a wood stove, a large circular rug and a wall of windows. Clusters of brightly colored pillows dotted the floor. A native print cloth was positioned in the center of the rug. It was covered with stones, shells and crystals, candles, bones, and a variety of small animal figures.

"I put the stove on, because it was so chilly in here this morning. If you want tea, it's made. The bathroom is just there."

"I'm fine," said Kenya.

"Sit, sit," she said and plunked herself down on a pale blue cushion in front of the windows.

"Now, Kenya, my preference is to have your mom in here with us to help support the work, but you tell me what you're comfortable with."

"That's okay," said my daughter.

"Great! Now let's hear about what's been happening, what brings you here?"

"I don't know. I guess my mom thinks I should talk to somebody because of how I've been acting lately."

"Oh? How've you been acting?"

Kenya shrugged and looked at her hands. "Just messing up," she said.

"Kenya," I said, "I don't think you've been messing up. I think you're in trouble and I'm looking for a way to help you out of it."

Lila looked at me while I spoke and then back at Kenya. "Do you think you're in trouble, Kenya?"

Kenya shrugged again and looked out the window.

Lila watched her for a moment. "Okay," she said, "Tell you what. I have some helping spirits I usually talk to about these things. Would you mind if I had a chat with them about you—see what *they* think?"

"What kind of spirits?" Kenya asked. "You mean like dead people?"

Lila smiled. "Well, I don't usually think of them that way, but now that you mention it, a couple of them actually are dead people—long dead, though, like a few centuries or so. And some of them are animal spirits. Do you like animals?"

Kenya shrugged. "Some, I guess."

"Good, then. Before you leave here today, we'll get you a power animal of your own. Would you like that?"

Kenya looked up. "What kind of power animal?"

"Well, we'll have to wait and see who comes forward now, won't we?" She laughed a mysterious little laugh and winked at Kenya.

Lila stood, shook out two blankets, and laid them down side by side on the floor. Then, she crowned each with a pillow. "Slumber party!" she chuckled. "Kenya, I'm going to ask you to lie here between your mom and me, alright?"

She looked at me. "You said on the phone that you journey?"

"I do," I said.

"Okay, then you lie on this side of your daughter and I'll be sitting here on the other. Kenya, I want you just to close your eyes and think about how you've been feeling lately. And, Clare, I want you to journey and find out how you can support your daughter."

I lay down on the floor and closed my eyes. I could hear the hiss of the wood stove, the coo of a mourning dove, and then Lila picked up her drum and its penetrating beat filled the room. I took myself to my favorite tree, circled around it a few times and then sunk through the ground at the base. I could feel myself falling like water down a long hole, until I splashed onto the bottom and stood up.

Eagle was summoning me from a nearby tree limb. I climbed onto his back and we flew up high until the earth below was just a patchwork of green. I could see the foothills where Eamon had his cabin, the waterfall that cascaded beside Bear's cave. We flew for some time and then landed softly on a rock ledge, which seemed to be part of a floating canyon. As I looked to the other side, some clouds parted and Daniel stepped into view.

I raised my hand and waved. He waved back, leaned over and looked down into the chasm. For a moment I thought he might jump.

"What are you doing?" I asked.

"I have something for Kenya, but I can't give it to you."

"Throw it," I said.

"Can't."

"Then Eagle will come and get it."

Daniel shook his head.

I turned to Eagle to ask for help, but Daniel ascended from the ledge and disappeared into the clouds.

"You can't follow him," said Eagle, reading my thoughts. "Don't worry; he's figuring it out."

"But I'm supposed to be helping Kenya."

"Not here," he said and we flew back out over the cloud-filled canyon. Soon the air below us cleared and we landed on a smooth pale plateau that looked like the head of a drum. Kenya was dancing around in the middle of it. I stood on the rim watching her. Every so often, she would suddenly lose her balance and topple over. She would sit for a moment and then get on her feet again and dance some more.

"Why does she keep falling like that?" I asked.

"Because there's too much weighing her down," said Eagle.

"What can I do?"

"Take back the piece of soul you gave her."

"What? When?"

A picture floated up in my head. I saw myself lying in bed, during the time when I was still sick. I was worrying about Kenny and what would happen to her if I died. She was not a resilient child, and I did not believe she would thrive without me. I am her source of strength, I thought. She's only ten years old, and I am betraying her by leaving too soon.

I remember thinking I needed to leave her the fierceness of my love. I would give her that, and she would have it to draw on when she no longer had me.

"She never got the chance to prove her own strength," Eagle said.

When I looked back at Kenya, I could see there was something wrapped tightly around each of her legs that she kept trying to pry off. I went to where she was sitting, and knelt beside her. I reached down and removed two heavy braces, one from each leg.

She got up and started dancing again, around and around the plateau, her hair flying out behind her like a dark wave.

I gave the braces to Eagle, and he took them to a fire pit nearby, holding them there in his beak until they melted into a long molten ribbon of silver, which he then brought to me and wound around my heart. I felt its warmth ripple through me.

"The best way for you to support your daughter," said Eagle, "is to believe in her. To see the best in her, no matter what she is saying or doing."

I thought about all that had been happening lately with Kenya, the anger, the withdrawal, the failure in school, the cutting, all the hurtful things she had said to me. My heart and throat ached with it all. "I'm not sure I can do that," I said.

Eagle stared hard at me. "If you weren't able to do it," he said, "I wouldn't have suggested it."

He flew up and perched on a nearby tree. I felt like the subject had been closed as far as he was concerned. I sighed and thought about seeing the best in Kenya. It really felt too far for me to stretch. She seemed so weak to me.

In the distance, I saw Bear lumbering towards me. He took my hand and walked with me until we came to a stand of copper beeches.

"This is what you need to become," he said. "It will help you to see something different."

I approached one of the beeches and gazed into its branches. I opened my arms to it and felt suddenly lifted up through my trunk until my head seemed to bump against a ceiling of sky, and my feet poked deep in pockets of the earth.

I felt wonderfully majestic, gracious and beneficent. My leaves began to clamor. Each one had a story to share. Each one wished to be heard. I looked down at one leaf and nodded. It immediately began to tell the story of a child who spouted words of deep wisdom before she was three years old. Another told the story of a child who loved to dance and spun ribbons of gold with her feet as she twirled. A third leaf began to flap loudly in the breeze. It told of a girl who wore a storm cloud for a hat. And then another leaf spoke of a girl who shared her heart openly with the world by wearing it on her sleeve. It got bruised more often that way, but it grew strong in the open air. Finally, one small leaf shared a story about a girl who was lost in the forest and how the trees helped her to find her way out.

I listened intently, knowing these stories were all about Kenya. They were stories about what made her remarkable. I had lost a sense of what a splendid child my daughter was. Of what a special gift her life itself was. I wasn't seeing into the depth of her character, because I was so stuck on the bristly surface of her.

I looked down at Bear and smiled.

"What did you learn?" he asked.

"Every life is many stories. Each story has importance. It's wonderful to belong to those stories, to be a witness and a keeper of those stories. I'm *fortunate* to be part of Kenya's life, no matter what it looks like, so lucky. I mean, if nothing else, let the part I play in her story be life-affirming."

Bear smiled and beckoned me out. I shook myself free of the beech, though I felt reluctant to leave its generosity and strength.

"There's no "me" in beech," I said to Bear, "only "be.""

Bear laughed and nodded.

I heard Eagle calling me from above and as I looked up, the callback from Lila's drum began to beckon me back to the room. I waved goodbye and made my way up the tunnel. I heard the hiss of the stove and felt the wood smoke sting my nose. I blinked a few times and sat up.

Lila was jotting some notes down on a pad of paper. Kenya was just opening her eyes. I looked down and smiled at her.

"Take your time getting up, Kenya," Lila said to her.

"Are you alright, sweetie?" I asked.

"Yes," said Kenya, sitting up. "I had a funny dream, though."

"You did?" Lila asked.

"Yeah, it was cool. I was in this really beautiful place with lots of hills and trees and streams. First, I was just dancing and dancing and dancing around on this platform—kind of like a skating rink—and I felt so light, like I was made of air or something. Then, I looked up and I could see my dad smiling down on me."

Her eyes filled with tears. She wiped the back of her

hand across her face. Lila handed her a tissue.

Kenya dabbed her eyes, rolled and unrolled the tissue in her hand. "He said he was taking care of me. He said I was never, ever out of his sight. He said he loved me and I was still his little girl."

"Wow," said Lila, "that's a powerful message."

Kenya smiled weakly.

"I actually saw your dad in my journey, too. Would you like to hear about that?"

Two tears spilled down Kenya's face. She nodded.

"The first thing I did was consult with my power animals. They told me that when your dad died, you were so sad about his leaving, that you sent a piece of your soul to him, just so you could still be together. Do you know what I mean by that?"

To my surprise, Kenya nodded. She wiped her nose with the tissue.

"It was a very loving thing to do, Kenya, but it doesn't help your dad and it doesn't help you either. We need to bring that soul part back to you. Your dad has given it to a power animal of yours and right now it's in his custody. But if you agree to take this soul part back again, I'll go in and retrieve it for you. What do you think?"

Kenya looked up. "A power animal of mine?"

"Yes, a power animal I located for you with the help of my guides. Would you like to know what it is?"

My daughter nodded.

"It's a tall and very powerful deer, a buck with antlers out like this." Lila held her arms above her head.

Kenya nodded. "I know him," she said.

"You do?"

"Yes, he's been in my dreams a couple of times. He watches me, but then when I try and reach him, he turns and runs away."

"Well, he won't be running away anymore," she laughed. "I'm bringing him to you along with your soul part.

Are you ready for that?"

"D-does it mean my dad won't be watching out for me anymore?"

"No, it doesn't mean that. Your dad and you have a strong and deep bond that nothing can change. But it does mean that your dad will rest easier now and you will feel better. What do you think?"

"Okay," said Kenya.

"Good. Mom's going to drum for me."

Lila pointed to a drum resting against the wall. "Do you mind, Clare?"

"Not at all," I said. I reached for the drum, retrieved the beater from the webbing on the back and rested the frame against my knee.

"Now, Kenya, what I'm bringing back to you is really just missing energy—think of it as like air almost. I'm going to return that to you by blowing it here into your heart and here into the crown of your head. Would that be alright?"

Kenya looked over at me and I nodded. She turned back to Lila. "Okay," she said.

Lila lay down beside my daughter and I began to drum. I realized I loved the feel of the drum in my hand and wondered why I'd never purchased one. I made a mental note to buy one for myself.

As I drummed, I watched my daughter and Lila lying side by side on the floor. Part of me was saying, this is crazy, right? But down deep I knew something truly wonderful was happening here. That Daniel had come forward—we had all seen him—seemed magical to me. I could almost sense how much better off he was now. The work Lila was doing was helping him as well—just as she had said it would.

Minutes passed and then Lila rose, one hand cupped against her heart. She leaned down and placed her hand on Kenya's heart, put her mouth to her hand and blew hard. Then she lifted Kenya into a sitting position and blew again into the top of my daughter's head. She lowered her back down and rattled for a while over Kenya's body. Then she looked at me and nodded. I drummed out the callback and rested the drum on the floor beside me.

"So, Kenya," said Lila, "have you ever done any wood carving?"

Kenya sat up and wrinkled her forehead. She shook her head.

"Well, I saw you making these carved objects," said Lila, "some small things, some not."

"My mom makes sculptures," she said.

Lila looked at me. "You do? Maybe you can help her with this then."

She looked at Kenya. "Your power animal tells me you that when you feel sad or troubled, you should carve those feelings into wood in order to bring them out. The trees said that *they* will take the cutting for you. Do you know what they mean?"

Kenya's jaw opened in amazement, and then she nodded.

"There is something, too, in the significance of what type of wood you use. Different trees have different healing properties, different powers—you can probably find a book on that and study up on it. Your power animal said to remember that there is something of beauty in even the deepest, darkest emotion and he wants you to bring that beauty forward through the carving. That seems like a tall order for a girl your age, but he kept insisting you were up to it."

Kenya nodded. "No, I get it," she said.

Lila and I exchanged glances. We both smiled and raised our eyebrows in surprise at one another.

"How are you feeling, Kenny?" I asked.

My daughter looked up at me and it was as if someone had turned a light on behind her eyes.

"I feel pretty good, actually," she said.

Chapter Eight
Ash: Balance

"And she's better now?" asked Rowena.

We were sitting in our favorite coffee shop talking about Kenya's visit to Lila. We liked this coffee shop for its deep purple couches, its shabby-chic decor, its buttery, fruit-laden scones, and the fact that no one ever bothered us, no matter how long we stayed or how loudly we laughed.

"Yes. Much better. I mean, she's still Kenya, and that's enough to deal with right there, but she's more solid than I've seen her in a while, and a bit less edgy. She smiles more, talks more. Actually, she said she wanted to go back again, and I think that's probably a good idea. In the meantime, I made an appointment for myself. I've been feeling a little wobbly about this court case with Cynthia, and I can't seem to get any clarity in my own journeys."

Rowena had removed the lid from her coffee cup to get

at the rest of her cappuccino. She looked up.

"Eek, when's that ratcheting up?" she asked.

I sighed.

"There's a hearing Monday to determine the jurisdiction of the case."

"God, do you have to take the stand or anything?"

A guy at the nearby table turned and began to take more than a casual interest in our conversation, so I leaned in toward Rowena and lowered my voice.

"No, not yet. This is just a preliminary hearing. Opposing arguments are made before a judge and then the judge takes it under advisement and decides where the case should be heard—here or Arizona."

Rowena scraped a plastic spoon around the inside of her cup, withdrew a wisp of foamed milk, and put it into her mouth.

"And Cynthia's going to be there?"

"Apparently, yes."

She wrinkled her nose. "Aargh."

"Yeah."

"You up for that?"

I shrugged. "Ready as I'll ever be. More worried about the outcome than anything."

Rowena rested her hand on my sleeve. "Want me to go with you?"

"No, I'm good. I might take a rain check though for the actual hearing."

"What does Hal say about all this?"

"Well, he says it's a little tricky, because the legal points on each side are actually pretty well-balanced, so we need to rely on the strength of any emotional arguments we can make—the loss of college funds for the kids, the damage to my financial stability, the shock and depth of the deceit. All that poor grieving widow stuff."

"He's suggesting you take the kids with you?"

"No. He knows that's off limits. The kids don't know,

and if I can help it, they'll never find out. I mean, I just got Kenya somewhat stabilized. Imagine if they found out about Daniel's plans to jump ship. Wouldn't that add a delightful twist to their grief process?"

"It certainly added one to yours," said Rowena.

The squirty *pshhht-quaaw*! of the cappuccino machine blasted across the coffee shop. Two teenaged girls giggled conspiratorially together as they linked arms and ran past us to the ladies room.

"You might say that. But I'm a lot better now. All is forgiven." I angelically raised my eyes skyward and crossed my hands over my heart.

"Yeah, you look just like the Blessed Mother right there—I can hardly tell the two of you apart. Speaking of mothers, what's been happening with yours lately? Are you speaking yet?"

I curled my legs under me and slumped deeper into the sumptuous purple sofa. "Oh yeah," I said, "we're speaking—I call and she spends the entire time complaining about everything she can think of—her neighbor's dog, the women on the garden committee, the financial strain she's under, how she can't sleep at night. She's really laying it on thick."

"She feels guilty."

I burst out laughing. "My mother? No, I don't think so. She's too busy drowning in self-pity."

"I don't know, I think people who play victim all the time probably *do* feel guilty. Otherwise, why would they spend so much time exonerating themselves? It's like, 'thou dost protest too much' or something."

I shrugged. "Maybe. I never thought about it that way."

Rowena pulled her cell phone out of her handbag and squinted at the screen.

"How hard would it be to just let her off the hook?" she said, pushing a few buttons on her phone.

"What do you mean? I *have* let her off the hook."

"No, you haven't."

"I have."

"Clare," said Rowena.

Rowena and I had known each other practically all of our lives. Our mothers had gone to school together—my mother still called Rowena's mother by her maiden name, Gibbons. So, when Ro and I ended up in the same first grade class, our mothers carefully steered us toward one another and we never strayed.

Following high school, we both went northeast to college, she to Smith and I to Amherst, and afterwards, we both settled in New England. Currently we lived within fifty miles of one another.

Rowena adored my mother, as much as I did hers, which caused us more than once to wonder if we had been switched at birth.

"What," I said, "I actually applaud her efforts at keeping my marriage stable. She's loyal, my mother—to a fault."

"Uh-huh," said Rowena, tossing her phone into her handbag, "I hope you learn to be more convincing than that whenever you do take the witness stand."

I laughed. "Look, I get it. She is who she is. If I didn't know better—."

"Hello!"

I looked up and then up some more at the tall man who had materialized beside me. When I saw who it was, I practically swallowed my tongue. "Oh-h," I stuttered, "there you are!" I felt my face getting hot and dared not look at Rowena.

Jack Woods shifted his weight from one foot to the other and turned his coffee cup around in his hand. "Here I am," he said, laughing, "I'm just on my way to the school. I coach tennis there in the summer."

"Oh, right." I looked nervously at Rowena. "This-this is Kenny's guidance counselor from school," I said, realizing I was talking rather loudly, "Jack Woods. And this is my friend, Rowena Lawton."

Rowena's eyes popped open wide as she held out her

hand. I could see her giving him the once over as they shook hands. "Enjoying your summer?" she asked.

He smiled. "It's hard to cram everything in that you promise yourself all school year long you're going to do once summer arrives, but yes, it's been a great break so far." He looked back at me.

"How's Kenya doing?" he asked.

"Kenya's much better," I said. "I think we can probably put that chapter behind us."

"Wow! That's excellent. The therapy worked then?" He got down on his haunches so we could be at same eye level. He rested one tanned arm on the sofa beside me. I looked down at the hairs that sprang from his golden skin like a field of summer grass. I blushed and cleared my throat.

"Well, not exactly. I, uh, sought some—alternatives."

His face lit up. "I'm delighted to hear that. We so desperately need alternatives to talk therapy. What did you try, if you don't mind my asking?"

I glanced over at Rowena, who was grinning like an idiot.

"Well, we tried some shamanic healing for her and it worked beautifully."

"I've read about that! I bought this book about innovative and actually very ancient methods of curing disorders like PTSD, addiction, and depression. They talked about shamanic healing rather extensively. It's fascinating, that stuff. Maybe you can tell me more about Kenya's experience sometime—I mean, if you are willing to, that is."

"Oh, of course. I'd be happy to," I said, fidgeting with the top of my empty coffee cup.

"Great! I look forward to that." He stood up and swung a thumb over his shoulder. "Gotta run. It was nice meeting you," he said to Rowena, "and that's really great news about Kenya. Take care now."

"You too," I said smiling up at him as he turned away from us. I looked over at Rowena who whistled through her teeth.

"Oh, stop," I said.

"Married?" she mouthed.

"I don't know," I said under my breath, "he doesn't wear a ring. But I think if he *was* married, he'd be the type that would wear one."

Rowena nodded as she watched him through the window of the coffee shop walking to his car.

"What do you think?" I said.

"Cute," she said. "*Very* cute. And the best part is he likes you as much as you like him."

"Shut up!"

"No, I know these things. He does. He just hasn't figured out what to do about it yet."

Later that day, my daughter and I were in the woods behind our house scouting for a tree on which to carve the face of the girl she had drawn for me in the studio. I located one tree with a large patch of bark missing from it just about at eye level. I was standing back sizing it up.

"How about this one?" I asked, slapping my hand against the trunk. "We could get rid of all this underbrush and make a little clearing around it. I like that it's kind of off by itself—nice tall, straight trunk—and best of all, it's an ash." I had read how ash trees linked the spirit world and the real world, and this seemed so appropriate to our purpose. I surveyed the ground around me. "That big stone could serve as a little place to sit and meditate." I looked over at Kenya for a reaction.

"I thought you said it was going to be an altar."

"Oh, well, a lot of things can be an altar, honey. Anything you designate as sacred space is an altar."

She sat down on the ground and stared at me. Her brows inched together. "So why are we doing this again?"

"To honor our Scottish ancestors."

"I have ancestors? I thought just old people had ancestors."

"Everyone has ancestors, Kenny. And it's good to honor them because without them we wouldn't be here."

"Does that make Daddy an ancestor?"

"Yes, I guess it does."

"Okay."

"Okay what?"

"Okay, I'll help then, but I think this rock should be the altar because it's long and flat and we can put things on it, like a nice angel statue for Daddy." She leaned down and brushed the dead leaves away from the surface.

"And we can carve the girl on this side of the tree so it faces the same way," Kenya said, pointing up. "Then we can bring in that stone bench from the front of the house that no one ever uses, and we can put that here so you can sit and look at the tree and the altar and kind of visit if you want to." She looked at me and shrugged.

I grinned at her. "That sounds absolutely grand, sweetie. I love all those ideas."

I bent over the bag I had brought with me and pulled out Kenya's drawing. I unrolled it and squinted back at the tree. I was trying to figure out how much more bark we would need to peel off, and tracing it out with my finger, when I heard something stomping through the woods behind us. I turned around to find Ethan and his friend, Aidan, picking their way towards us.

"What are you doing out here?" Ethan called.

"We're making an altar for Daddy," said Kenya.

"A what?" he said.

"We're honoring the ancestors," Kenya explained.

"O-k-a-ay," said Ethan, his brows arched.

Aidan stood behind Ethan and peered curiously over his shoulder.

"Hi, Aidan," I said. "How's your mom doing? I haven't talked to her in a while."

"She's good," he said, "how big of a thing are you building out here anyway?"

"Well," I said, "nothing too elaborate. We're just trying to create a space to honor our dead, similar to what the ancient shamanic cultures would have done."

Aidan's eyes lit up. "You mean, like, what shamans do?"

I nodded.

"For real?" he asked. "How do *you* know about that, Mrs. B.?"

"Well, I've been practicing shamanism for a number of years. I'm being led to do this work here because—."

"Whoa, Mom!" said Ethan, "TMI. Spare us the gory details, will you?"

"But that's so cool," said Aidan. He looked at Ethan. "Dude, it's like *Otherworlds at War*."

"Dude, no, it isn't. It's like my mom and sister acting totally weird and batshit crazy." He looked at me. "I'm taking Aidan home and then I'm going to work. I only came out here to tell you that Grandma called you a little while ago."

"Oh?"

"I told her you'd call her right back."

"Well, I may not get to it right away, Ethan. How late are you working tonight?"

Ethan was working as a camp counselor with inner city kids who were being given an opportunity to experience the Connecticut countryside.

"I'm done at nine, and then I'm going back over to Aidan's for a party."

"Not too late, sweetie. See you, Aidan. Say hi to your mom for me."

"See you, Mrs. B," Aidan said, "I'll tell her."

"I won't be late," said Ethan, walking away and waving his hand over his shoulder at me.

"And be careful. Drive safely now. Watch those speed limits."

He stopped and turned to me. "Shucks, Ma, does this mean I can't run no red lights, neither?"

I frowned. "You're not at all funny, Ethan."

I could hear him laughing as he and Aidan trudged out of the woods to Ethan's car.

"Wow, man," said Aidan, looking back over his shoulder, "when did your mom become a shaman? I mean, can she throw chain lightning and shit?"

Ethan grabbed Aidan by the elbow and pulled him towards the driveway. "Aid, dude, don't encourage the woman, alright?"

I looked after them, smiling. Before I returned to Kenya's drawing, I closed my eyes and took a moment to put light around Ethan and his car. Then I looked back at the tree and put my hand on the bark.

"You know," I said, "I'm going to have to journey to this guy to get permission to carve him."

"Why did you do that?" asked Kenya.

"Do what?"

"Close your eyes like that just now."

"I was putting protection around Ethan so he stays safe and doesn't hurt anyone."

"Do you do that for me, too?" she asked.

I rolled my eyes. "Do I ever," I said, sighing. "Every bless-ed, *bless-ed* day I do that."

Kenya laughed and patted me on the shoulder. "Poor Mom," she said, "poor old Mom."

While I put together a dinner for Kenya and me, I called my mother. Kenny loved breakfast dinners, so I assembled some eggs, pancake mix, bacon and syrup on the counter and was busy getting out a frying pan when my mother picked up.

"Hello?"

She had this way of answering with a note of hesitancy

in her voice, as if she had never used a telephone before and was unsure what would happen next.

"It's me. You called?"

"Well, hours ago, yes," she said.

"Sorry, I was a little tied up," I said, flipping on the burner.

"I tried to impress upon Ethan the urgency of the situation. He didn't convey that to you?"

"Maybe. What's so urgent?"

"I'm going in for a hysterectomy this week, that's all," she said.

I stopped what I was doing. "A hysterectomy, why?"

"Tumors. Could be fibroid; they won't know until they get in there."

I had some strange image of men with mining gear traipsing up my mother's vagina and peering into the cave of her uterus.

I set down the package of bacon I was holding and shut off the range. "Well, wow, " I said. "I-I don't know what to say."

My mother laughed. It was as if she had already predicted how insensitive I was going to be in this situation. I realized to my dismay that I would need to go and be with her through this. How would I manage it on top of the trial and keeping Kenya stable and finishing my art exhibit?

"You want me to come?" I asked. "I can bring Kenny. Ethan can just stay here by himself—he's got to work anyway."

"Don't trouble yourself, Clare. I know you already have enough on your plate."

Her words were as sharp as a surgeon's tools.

"Mom, don't be so stubborn. You're going to need someone to stay with you."

"It's not necessary. Dean and Mary Lynn are here."

My brother and sister-in-law lived two towns away from my mother.

"Well, I realize they're nearby, but you need someone *there*. You won't be up and around for quite a while."

"I'm perfectly aware of the details of my convalescence," my mother said.

I could feel my temper rising to the top of my head. Were other people's mothers like this? It couldn't just be a straightforward and simple: *I'll come and stay with you, Mom. Well, fine, Clare, I would appreciate that.*

"Look," I said, "what's wrong with me coming there to help out? You act like I'm incompetent or something."

"Clare," my mother said wearily, "please don't make this about you. It has nothing to do with you."

I folded my arms and sulked. I felt like I was about ten years old.

She sighed. "It's all a bit much for me to handle right now."

"That's exactly why I'm offering to help. It's not like I can't take care of you," I said. "What's the problem?"

She was quiet for a while. I imagined she was evaluating my worthiness for the position. Then she sighed.

"Honey," she said, "this is difficult enough. I'm afraid your being here will just make it all that much harder."

She was giving me a taste of my own medicine.

"Oh," I said, realizing for perhaps the first time in my life that I was every bit as annoying to my mother as she was to me. Of course I knew she found me difficult. I could hear that nursery rhyme she used to sing me whenever I acted against her wishes: *Mary, Mary, quite contrary.*

But somehow I never thought for one moment there might be times when she didn't want me around. I didn't say anything for a moment or two, absorbing as best I could the brunt of her rejection.

"Well, when's the operation?" I asked, aiming to cover up the awkwardness.

"Monday morning."

Monday—the same day as my hearing with Cynthia.

What the hell was going on with my planets *that* day, I wondered.

"And Dean's taking you?"

"Everything is all set. You don't have to worry about it."

"Well, I am worried about it! And I would like to feel involved in some way."

My mother sighed again. "Clare, like I said before. It has nothing to do with you. I'm just letting you know."

Her words stung again. Was she still punishing me for how I had acted during her visit? God knows the woman could hang onto resentment as if it had been Crazy-glued to her.

"Oh, well, hey," I said, "drop me a line and let me know how things turn out, will you?"

I heard a sound that might have been my mother clearing her throat. I wasn't sure. But I was sure about the click of the disconnected line when she hung up on me.

"Your plate's been pretty full then," said Lila, as I finished my story.

"Well that's just the Reader's Digest version," I said.

She laughed. "I bet."

She looked completely different to me today. Her hair was pulled back in a tight, thick braid from her ruddy, sunburned face. She had on jeans and a men's dark green polo shirt; her feet were bare. I had come upon her earlier in her garden, mounding furrows of compost around her tomato plants. I probably wouldn't have recognized her if it weren't for those eyes.

"But your journeys sound so rich and transformative— I'm not sure why you came to see me."

She pushed back some strands of hair that had strayed across her forehead and tucked them into her braid. I noticed that even though she had soaped and rinsed her hands three times at the kitchen sink after coming inside, they were still stained brown in the cracks of her fingers and thumbs.

"I'm feeling so depleted these days," I said. "Like I can't keep this up or something. And lately my journeys have been really flat. I guess that's understandable—I mean, how can I keep expecting my journeys to rescue me time and time again?"

Lila shrugged. "Could be you just need a little tune-up. I go to my teacher for one every six months or so. Personally, I don't think we're wired to run our spiritual engines this much."

She leaned over and lit the bowl of dried sage that was sitting in front of her. She stood and waved the bowl over her head to allow the sweet pungent smoke to waft freely around the room.

"Stand up," she said, beckoning me up with a flapping motion of her hand.

Lila walked around me with the smoking bowl and clapped the air with a large feather.

"There," she said, "that'll get some of the road dust off you." She opened the door to the wood stove behind me and tossed the remnants of the burning bowl inside.

"Now why don't you lie down here while I drum and journey?" she said. "If you want to journey as well and ask your helping spirits how you can begin to feel more empowered, you can do that. Otherwise, just lie there and rest."

I lay down and Lila draped a blanket over me. Then she settled herself on the floor beside me and began to drum.

At first I thought I would just rest. I had had so many journeys of late that were so senseless and meandering, wispy images and thoughts I couldn't hang onto. I had begun to feel slightly panicked that I didn't know how to journey anymore —that the well had gone dry.

But when the drum started, I found myself unspooling like a ribbon into the earth beneath me. I spiraled down through a cavernous tunnel until I landed rather abruptly on the damp muddy bottom of a cave. I could feel the cool, dank mud squishing through my toes. When I looked out of the opening of the cave, I saw a brown and white spotted horse, tossing its head and flapping its tail impatiently as it waited for me.

I'd never met a horse before on my journeys and riding this one seemed very enticing. As I climbed on its back, it raised its head and took off down the path, its hooves beating in perfect time to Lila's drum.

We galloped along, and I could see Eagle circling above me the way he usually did when I traveled through my journeys on foot. After a short time we came to a glassy lake with a cloud of mist simmering at its center. The horse waded into the lake, swam through the water and the cottony mist until we reached the shore of a lush green island.

I dismounted and walked into a grove of trees. I could see a white columned building beyond me in the distance. Eagle flew down and lighted on a nearby tree, as I sat down in the grove next to a woman in white who waited there. She appeared to be some kind of priestess. There was a blue symbol painted on her forehead and a medallion with the same symbol hung around her neck.

"Who are you?" I asked.

"I am Verena," she said. "I came because today marks the beginning of your initiation."

"For what?" I asked.

She raised her hand and gestured towards the temple-looking structure behind us. "All this," she said. "Your life's work."

She acted like I knew what she was talking about.

I looked over at Eagle. "My life's work?" I asked.

"Maybe you should just listen," he said.

Verena bent down and scooped up some earth and invited me to touch it. It felt sticky and heavy like modeling clay. "This is how you craft your life," she said, "this is how you become."

She took a piece of the claylike earth and shaped it into

a medallion, which she breathed into and hung around my neck. She made a mark on my forehead with some oil she took from her pocket, and put another mark on my right palm. She crossed my right palm over my heart, made a spiral shape on my left palm and placed that over my stomach.

Then she stood and laid a cobalt-colored cloak around my shoulders. She rested her hand briefly on the top of my head and smiled down at me.

I realized I still had clay in my hand. When I squeezed my hand around it, it grew hot.

"You've always been more than a sculptor," she said, watching me, "first and foremost, you are a healer. The sculpting is just the form out of which you bring healing."

"A healer? I don't think I'd be very good at that."

"Not true. You are already."

"But people don't seem to like it when I try and help them—they really don't." I was aware of how whiny I sounded.

Verena shook her head. "If you walk in the *shadow* of the healer, you think healing requires taking on someone else's pain. Healing isn't about thinking you can live someone else's life better than they can."

I felt like she was talking about my mother, maybe even Kenya. I struggled to understand her.

"Healing entails a clarity about what is being asked of you," Verena said, "A deep respect for that. Otherwise it is just a painful struggle. Right now, for instance, what is it your mother is asking you to do?"

"Well, I think my mother would like it if I just kept my mouth shut for a change."

"Then honoring that is *her* healing. What is your daughter asking?"

"Probably just that I love her no matter what."

"Then that is *her* healing."

"That seems awfully simple," I said.

"It *is* very simple."

I smiled. "But, there's still the matter of my legal problems. That doesn't seem so simple."

"It stops being simple when you give your power away
to it," she said nodding. "That's what makes you vulnerable."

"What can I do?"

"Take back your power, put a light of protection
around it, and then cloak yourself so no one can find it."

I felt the cloak around my shoulders glisten and inten-
sify in color. It almost seemed alive.

"Is that what this is for?" I asked, plucking at the luminescent fabric with my fingers.

I heard and felt the drumbeat shift into a callback.
Verena's form got more watery and began to fade.

"It is for many things," I heard her say as I turned and
saw my horse and Eagle waiting to bring me back.

When I opened my eyes and looked up, I found Lila
sitting and staring at me.

"Well?" she said.

"Yeah, that was pretty interesting," I said, gathering the
blanket around me as I sat up. It was 85 degrees outside, but I
still felt so chilly.

"So you got some answers then, good. Okay, let me
first tell you what my journey revealed, and then we'll see how
the two journeys fit together. Alright?"

I nodded.

"What I see first is you, swimming furiously inside a
big wave. The wave tosses you and you tumble around and
around. You struggle and struggle, but what is happening to
you—rather than you drowning or losing strength—is that you
are becoming polished and shaped and ultimately nourished
by the water. After a time I see you coming up, flying high
above the wave and reaching out with your arms for the air.
The wind picks you up in its arms and carries you to a circle
of fire, where it places you down to dry yourself.

"When you stand up; the ordeal is over. And it seems
like now you must begin your work. A tall, willowy woman

gives you a blue cloak. You thank her and she blesses your forehead. Then you bend down and you scoop up these little balls of clay from the earth and shape them. You dip them in water and shape them some more. Then you put them on a tray almost like cookies or animal crackers or something." Lila paused to laugh at this image.

"Next I see you sliding these 'cookies' into the fire— you take them out and blow on each of them and then put them back again and you keep doing this. When you bring them out finally, they are brightly colored; they kind of shimmer and vibrate with energy. It seems they have a power that is healing and transformative for whomever touches them."

Lila leaned back and closed her eyes as if to recapture the details of her journey.

"A crowd of people comes and stands around. Your daughter is there. You give her one of these power objects, and then more people come, and you hand one to each of them. Some people hang them around their necks and some place them in their pockets. Some hold them against their heart or their head. Everyone is helped and healed by them in some way."

She looked at me. "Now I know you said you were a sculptor. Do you ever make jewelry or power objects like this?

"Ah, no," I said. My voice cracked.

"Well, I think it seems like a pretty cool idea, don't you?"

I shrugged. "I don't know," I said.

"Here's what I like about it," she continued, crossing her legs under her and leaning forward. "You are using all four elements here—earth, water, fire and air—to empower these objects and transmute the experience within them. They each seem to be imbued with the energy of some experience, a journey or ordeal that each person has gone through. Somehow each marks the person's triumph over that ordeal, do you see? This is the classic story of the wounded healer, Clare— that's your archetype. You learn; you heal. You heal; you teach others. And in doing so, you heal yourself even more. Very, very cool, don't you think?"

"I gu-ess."

She smirked. "You guess?"

"Look, I'll tell you the same thing I told this priestess who showed up on my journey. I'm not a healer. I suck at that kind of thing. Even my mother knows that—she told me she would heal better after her operation if I wasn't around."

"Listen, Clare, all your discomfort with being who you are comes straight *from* your relationship with your mother. Do you see? Your mother has done you a big, big favor by never recognizing you for who you are. Why else would you have been so motivated to declare yourself, to fight for your identity—over and over again? Remember that image I saw of you in the wave, spinning around and around?"

My eyes welled with tears.

"My guides say you can heal everything that is wrong between you and your mother once you find the gratitude you owe her for having assumed the role of spoiler in your life. Those are not easy shoes to fill—especially when its someone you love as much as your mother loves you."

Lila reached behind herself and handed me a tissue. "Are you alright?" she asked.

I nodded and dabbed at my eyes.

"As far as her illness is concerned, you can do more by listening to your mother than anything else. This illness is not about you, so stop trying to fix it. They said you would under-stand that. Do you?"

The words Lila's guides used were the same words my mother had used when we spoke over the phone. I smiled weakly. "I do."

Lila nodded. "On the matter of your hearing, I get this sweeping motion." She moved her arm across the space be-tween us. "Almost like it is being brushed aside. And they said an interesting thing. These matters are never determined by the courts, they say. That is just an illusion people have. You should enter the process relying not so much on the skill of your attorney or the kindness of the judge but on the power of your helping spirits—they are the ones who protect you. Cloak anything you feel is vulnerable to the process, and put your power animal on guard duty. Can you do that?"

"I can, yes. I was given a cloak on my journey as well."

"That's awesome," said Lila. She wagged her finger at me. "Don't forget to use it."

I nodded.

"Okay, now here's the hard part," she said. "Your spirits tell me you need to send blessings to Cynthia because you are giving away your power by being angry with her."

We looked at one another, and I made a face as I swallowed this bitter little pill of advice.

"Blessing her releases you from all this and that's what you want, right?" asked Lila, smiling sweetly.

I sighed and rolled my eyes. This little nugget had Eagle stamped all over it. "Yeah, yeah," I said wearily. "I'm on it."

It rained for the next two days and when the morning of the hearing arrived, the air outside felt heavy and blanket-thick.

"Yuck," I said, getting into my car and turning the air conditioning on full blast.

As I drove to the courthouse, I secured my energetic cloak around me, and carefully tucked all my power into its sumptuous folds.

I had been working hard on all I'd been given to do to ensure a positive outcome to the hearing. Even giving blessings to Cynthia, which didn't come easily. I had asked Eagle how I should do this, and he showed me a plate piled high with what looked like coins of blue light. I was to present one of these coins to her everyday until the case was settled.

For the last two days, I had felt light and untroubled about the hearing, but from the time I had gotten out of bed, my stomach was in knots, and my lungs felt tight again. All my faith and power seemed to be melting away in the heat.

There was a parking space in front of the playground that was located down the street from the courthouse. I sat in the car with the engine running and the cool air blasting, watching the children run around in the sweltering heat. A bevy of young mothers stood nearby in shorts and tank tops chatting with one another.

I decided, as I looked at them, that their lives were perfect. Maybe it was the firmness of their long, tanned legs or the flatness of their stomachs, the fine houses, secure futures and loving husbands I was certain each one of them had. Maybe it was the leisurely summer day they seemed to be enjoying, while I was scheduled to duke it out in court with my dead husband's girlfriend.

I would have gladly traded places with any one of them, and I would have been willing to use every dime of the financial assets I was currently trying to wrangle back from Cynthia to do it.

"Shit," I said, shaking my head. "Get a grip, Clare."

I closed my eyes and took a deep breath.

"I am grateful for my life," I said, with just the slightest hint of insincerity. "I *love* my life just as it is. It is neither good nor bad, but perfect in every way, even if I can't see it."

I opened my eyes and looked back at the same young mothers who were now huddled together laughing. I couldn't help noticing what perfect bust lines they each had and how lustrous their hair looked.

"My life is neither good nor bad," I repeated, still staring at them, "even if I can't see it."

"And I *most* surely cannot," I said, as I reached across the passenger seat for my papers and handbag. Suddenly, there was a knock on the car window. I turned to see Hal making a spiraling motion with his finger. I rolled my window down.

"Yeah?"

"We need to talk," he said, leaning down to speak into the open window. His curly, cropped hair was dark with sweat.

"Get in," I said.

He stood up and looked up and down the street at the traffic that whizzed by him.

"Let's just sit over here for a minute," he said, pointing towards the playground.

I got out of the car and followed him to a nearby park bench. My heart was hammering away in my chest. "Hal," I said, "what is it? What's going on?"

"Bit of a development," he said, setting his briefcase down on the sidewalk and wiping his brow with the back of his hand.

"Oh, for fuck sake. Now what?"

Hal smiled. "It's good news, Clare. They're dropping the claim. They want to talk settlement."

"Settlement? Isn't it a little early for that?"

"No, not at all. This is a very positive step. Her lawyer says he has some numbers to discuss, and the indication I'm getting is that they're going to be pretty reasonable, so I suggest we ask for a continuance and see what they have to say."

"B-but, what about the hearing?"

Hal put his foot up on the edge of bench seat and leaned against his knee. "I'll tell the judge the parties are talking, he'll be happy with that, we'll set another date in say, three months, and we'll start negotiating." He grinned. "How's that sound?"

I sat down on the bench and started to cry.

"I'm going to assume those aren't tears of disappointment," he said, reaching into his pocket and handing me a handkerchief.

I took the handkerchief and held it in my lap. I rolled the crisp white edges between my fingertips and looked at the courthouse in the distance. I knew now in my gut that I would never have to set foot in there. Something had shifted. I knew

I would never have to endure what I dreaded most—the hu-
miliation of hashing over Daniel's assets in a public courtroom
with his grieving girlfriend. Between the heat of the day and
the enormous sense of relief I was feeling, my head was
swimming. Swimming with prayers of gratitude.

"God," I said aloud, "I'm so glad this is over."

Hal gave me a puzzled look. "It's not over, Clare.
There are a lot of hurdles still to clear here. First, I suggest we
see what they have to offer—."

I stood up and handed him his handkerchief. "Thanks,
Hal. You did a really great job on this."

"But we still have a long way to go here, Clare."

"Thanks again," I said, laughing and walking to my
car.

"Clare?"

I smiled and waved at him, started my car and drove
away.

Chapter Nine
Hazel: **Wisdom**

In the days after my visit to Lila, the hearing postpone-
ment, and my mother's surgery, I sometimes woke in the quiet
of early morning to a voice I believed was speaking to me in
Gaelic. It spoke in a kind of chant, a hard, decisive rhythm I
couldn't get out of my head, an earworm with an incessant
beat that thrummed away non-stop in my head. From the first
time I heard it, I had the strangest feeling I was listening to a
song I had heard before, one I had perhaps known by heart
and sung myself in a place many centuries away.

As I struggled to compose the poem I hoped to use
with the ancestral sculpture Kenya and I were working on, I
felt like the words of this song were chromosomal strains
running up and down my veins, and if I were only to prick my
fingertip and hold it to the blank page, the lyrics would spill
out before my eyes.

I lay on my back on the floor of my studio, an empty pad of paper at my side. God, I thought to myself, if I were a poet and had to do this kind of thing full time, I'd want to kill myself. I wondered if this experience was what made poets go mad--having poems fed to them in a dying language they didn't speak when by rights they should be sleeping peaceably or minding their own business.

There was a tap on the door.

"It's open," I yelled.

"Whoops," said Dill, poking his head into the room. "Did I interrupt a journey?"

"A journey would imply that I was either going or getting somewhere. Neither of which is occurring here." I sat up and pushed the hair back from my face.

"Napping?"

I smiled, "No, just trying to write this stupid poem. Why do you think people choose to become poets anyway? Is it because they're masochistic and they want to devise a really sinister way of tormenting themselves to death?"

"That would imply they have a choice in the matter. I think poets are poets because they have to be."

"Well, it's a hell of a way to make a living. Sculpting is much, *much* easier, and I never thought I'd hear myself saying that." I poked myself on the forehead. "I need to get this thing out of here."

"Okay," said Dill, sitting cross-legged on the floor nearby. "Let's do some surgery on it, shall we?" The turquoise shirt he was wearing made his blue eyes crackle.

I told Dill about the Gaelic chant that was waking me each dawn. I tapped out the rhythm on the floor with the top of my pen. He cocked his head to the side and closed his eyes.

"Are the words sad?"

"Um, well, solemn, I'd say, not particularly sad. There's a kind of wisdom in the words, a knowing."

"Why is it being said?"

I closed my eyes. "Well, it's—it's kind of like a pronouncement, a declaration of some sort. No, wait a minute! Dill, it's a *prayer*! I think it's a prayer that honors the dead."

"Good. Who's saying it?"

"I see a figure in a dark robe. He's raising his arms up as he speaks. A monk or a priest, a Druid maybe."

"And what does the prayer ask for?"

I lay back on the floor and closed my eyes tighter. "Let's see. Well, I think it releases the dead from their ties to the earth. It kind of ushers them on...."

Dill was silent. The swishing sound outside of cars driving by and the hissing sound of the air conditioning broke the stillness of the room with an odd syncopation.

Suddenly the whole point of the chant dropped into my brain with a thunk. I sat up and looked at Dill.

"I need to write out this prayer and then say it in order to release those souls that died in the spilling, you know, the suicide ritual I told you about? This prayer is some kind of ancient practice—the survivors do the work to usher the souls of the departed back to the spirit world. Otherwise, they wander."

"Psychopomp," said Dill.

"What?"

"Psychopomp. It's a kind of ceremony that helps the dead reach the spirit world."

"How do you know that?" I asked.

"I know a lot of things."

"You know what else, Dill? I've been *seeing* things lately, too. These white, hazy things keep appearing just outside my field of vision and when I look in their direction, they disappear. What do you think that means?"

"I think it means you need to have your eyes examined."

"Or, my head maybe, huh?"

"That, too. So you think this is your great-great-great Uncle Angus trying to get your attention?"

I laughed. "I don't know. He always was a pesky sort

of fellow."

"Sounds like you have your work cut out for you."

I made a stroke across my throat from ear to ear. "Oh, no pun intended, right?"

Dill laughed as he got up from the floor. "Your family is intense, man."

"Aye, we're a craggy bunch, lad."

He laughed at my bad Scottish accent.

"Hey, thanks for helping anyway," I called after him.

"Who, me?" asked Dill, as he closed the door behind him, "I didn't do anything. I just make the coffee around here."

By the time I returned home from the studio, I had a beginning. The poem wasn't a Shakespearean sonnet by any means, but I felt like it expressed the appropriate sentiments:

> *May their souls be called pure*
> *And remembered for courage.*
> *May their deeds be found holy*
> *So the dark will not flourish.*
>
> *May their lives be called noble*
> *By those who come after.*
> *May their steps be strong and sure*
> *So their children will not falter.*

I felt excited and ready to do a ceremony around the words, so that the souls of my ancestors would rest and my daughter and my daughter's children would not be troubled by an ancient legacy.

I pulled into the driveway and found Ethan standing beside his car. This was the one we had bought together after I traded in Daniel's car. The hood was raised and the top half of his body was hidden behind it.

"Hey," I said, "what's up with your car?"

"It keeps crapping out on me whenever I stop at a traffic light. I went onto the Car Talk website and got some information. I decided to try a few things."

"Ooh, I'm not sure that's such a good idea, honey. You don't know anything about cars."

"Of course I do. I read all about it."

"Sweetie, take it down to Les and see what he says. I don't want you making matters worse."

Ethan poked his head around the hood and frowned at me. "Mom," he said, "it doesn't take a genius to work on a car. I know what I'm doing."

I crossed my eyes. "No, see, that's just it, Ethan. You *don't* know what you're doing. You need to take it to the mechanic."

"Mom, you're really harshing my mood here. Just let me take care of it, alright?"

His head and shoulders became obscured again behind the raised hood.

I sighed, unable to think of anything to say in response to him. This was the point where as a parent I had to just let go. Let him learn his lessons his way, I thought. And may heaven shower me with medals of valor whenever I reached the pearly gates. Parenting was certainly not for the faint of heart.

I figured while I had him somewhat cornered, however, I'd raise another subject on which I hadn't been able to make any headway.

"So have you gone and registered for your classes?"

"Negative," he said.

"Don't you think it would be a good idea to do that before you get closed out of everything you want to take?"

Ethan reached down into a bag of tools at his feet, selected three different-sized wrenches, laid them out in his palm and scrutinized each one carefully. "That would be assuming there's anything I want to take," he said.

"Look, honey, I know you don't want to go to Middleton State, and I know you don't want to commute, but as I've told you over and over again—this is just a temporary solution until we can get you into a school you like better. And besides that, it's giving me some much needed breathing room with tuition expenses until I can, sort of, get my financial affairs straightened out."

He stood up straight and looked at me. "If it's just a temporary solution, why does it matter if I go or not? I'd much rather spend my time doing something I want."

"What does that mean?"

"Well, I'm thinking about going to a trade school."

"Trade school? Ethan, where the hell are you getting these ideas?"

He narrowed his eyes at me. "I'm getting them from me," he said.

He leaned down and started tapping at something with the wrench. I could tell by the way he was moving the tool and knitting his brows, he had no idea what he was doing, though he was trying very hard to look like he did.

"Honey, you're a very smart kid. Don't think for one minute because you didn't get into the schools you wanted that you should give up on the idea of college."

Ethan slammed the wrench on the driveway.

"Christ! I'm not giving up! Why do you immediately assume this is just some lame-ass idea of mine?"

"Well, what are you saying—this seems so short-sighted and unsuitable."

"Mom! I thought if I learned a trade, I would always have something to fall back on. I don't want to be one of the thousands of college graduates roaming around looking for work. I thought if I learned a skill, I could support myself through school and take my time deciding what I want to do. I'm not even asking for your help. I have some money saved and Grandma said she'd help—."

"Wait, whoa! You told Grandma about this?"

"I called her the other night to see how she was doing.

We got to talking; she asked me what I was doing in the fall and I told her my idea."

"You tell your Grandma about your plans before you even talk to me? Well, thanks so much, Ethan, that's ever so...so *loyal* of you!"

Ethan looked up at the sky and sighed. "I'm telling you now, aren't I? Aren't I?" He held out his hands in exasperation. "What difference does it make who finds out first? What are you, twelve?"

I stared at him. He was so big and so small at the same time. So mature and wise. So wet behind the ears. My eyes welled and I bowed my head and shook it. After a moment, I looked up at him, smiling.

"Okay, sweetie. You're right. Why don't you take a break and come and tell me what you're thinking about?"

He grinned and wiped his hands on his jeans. Ethan, always so quick to forgive and let you back in. I tried not to frown at the swipes of grease he was making on his pants and shirtsleeve. I could tell he was very excited about his idea, and I had to try not to ruin it now. I had to listen.

We walked side by side to the kitchen door of the house.

"There's a program in automotive restoration," he was saying, grinning from ear to ear, "You get cars from junk yards and restore them and sell them at a profit. Or you can work for these collectors who don't know how to restore the cars themselves but love to spend money on them. Mom, you're making that face again."

"What face?"

"The I-think-he's-probably-lost-his-mind face."

"No, son, I'm not. I'm listening. Go on."

One week after Hal asked for a continuance, he called to say he had received an offer to settle from Cynthia. My heart sank when I heard it.

"So, I let her keep the big-ass house, and she gives me $150,000? What kind of a deal is that?"

"Well, looking at her financial affidavit, she and Daniel put $250,000 down on a $300,000 property, and took out a mortgage for $50,000 in both of their names. But the $250,000 isn't all Daniel's money. Cynthia claims that $75,000 of that money came from her. So Daniel's contribution to the down payment less his responsibility on the mortgage is the offer."

"And she can prove all that?"

"The bank statements look pretty straightforward. The funds came from an account that was steadily accumulating capital long before Daniel ever withdrew any money out of your investment portfolio."

I had a sickening feeling in my stomach. I put my hand up to my neck and rubbed it nervously. I could feel my carotid artery thrumming beneath my fingers.

"But I thought Daniel paid for the house," I said, liking my version better.

"No, not entirely, it seems," said Hal.

"Well, where the frig is the rest of it? There's like, $200,000 or more unaccounted for." I said.

"I don't know, Clare. But Cynthia doesn't seem to have it."

"Well, where would it be?"

I could hear Ethan's door open upstairs. I scurried into the mudroom and closed the door behind me.

"I'm not sure you're ever going to be able to piece together the money trail, Clare. A lot of dead-ends here. I've done the standard bank account searches, and found nothing. They have these forensic accountants who do this kind of thing—find hidden assets--but they're not cheap—you want to go that route?"

"I *know* Cynthia has the money."

"Well, as it stands, you're not going to be able to prove that, Clare. Listen, this is a good offer. She's basically return-ing every cent Daniel put into the house—minus his obligations—and *this* for a house that has probably lost value in a declining real estate market. I'm telling you, you wouldn't get a dime more than this in court, and you might well get less."

"But why would she do that? Why would she offer me more than she had to? Does that make sense to you? Something is very fishy here, and I'm not giving in until I know what it is."

I exploded from the mudroom and slammed the door behind me. I hung up the phone, and paced around the kitchen, distractedly making tea with two mugs and three bags, ranting to myself all the while. I didn't feel I could just walk away from more than $200,000 without putting up a fight. And yet I really didn't want to return to the venomous bite of my anger either. I had been following Lila's advice and the counsel of my journeys, and making the effort to send blessings instead of resentment to Cynthia. But all that good intention seemed impossible now under the circumstances.

I poured water into one of the teacups and sat down at the table. The tea and I both steeped. I didn't think it was unreasonable to try and locate the other sizeable portion of the money. I decided I would journey to Eagle later, and see what he had to say. If I *were* being unreasonable and spiteful, Eagle would tell me so. I had no doubt about that.

In the meantime, Kenya and I were working diligently on the altar in the woods. I had grown to love the ash tree we were carving and spoke to him often. He told me his name was Finn.

I had taken a journey and asked permission to use his trunk as part of this memorial, and Finn had told me he *loved* adornment. I said that the carving would not be deep and that humans sometimes had pictures drawn on them in the form of tattoos. He answered that not only did he really want a tattoo of his own, but that he would be honored to be of service in this way because my ancestors were his ancestors. I asked

how that was so and he said that it was the world of his ancestors which had given way to mine and that linked us together.

Nature spirits never ceased to amaze me, and I had
grown quite fond of Finn. I brought him water and tobacco
and cornmeal as gifts, and tied green and gold ribbons (at his
request) around his trunk. I sang to him while I worked, and
always hugged him hello and goodbye.

Kenya would roll her eyes and say: "Mom, if you want
me to do this, you're going to have to stop acting like that.
Seriously, you're weirding me out."

We took turns carving the face in the tree. First, I
roughed it out, and then she worked on the features a bit. She
extended the shape of the hair, which made it much more
dramatic. I worked at refining the face more, and Kenya
smoothed out the mouth.

I couldn't believe how quickly she picked up the skill
of carving, and how much emotional weight her contributions
lent to the piece. Even the slightest stroke of the tool in her
hand created resonance and power. It was just as Lila said it
would be.

Back and forth we went. The rule was to not complain
about what each person changed about the other's work, but to
give the process over completely once you put down your
tools—like when I spent hours and hours detailing the eyes
and Kenny altered them completely.

I came into the clearing where she was still working
and was startled by the change she had made in the girl's
expression. I had directed the eyes off slightly to the right, but
my daughter made them look directly at whoever approached
the tree. It sent chills up my spine when I looked at that carving.

We stood beside one another staring at the sculpture as
it stared back at us.

"You've got those eyes completely right, Kenny," I
said.

"I didn't want her to seem so far away. I wanted her to

seem more like she was right here," she said.

"You did it," I said, smiling at her, "and it's just right."

"I think maybe the one eye is a little bigger than the other one, though."

"Well, maybe, but only just slightly. The thing is, you don't want to change the look in those eyes, because they are so perfect. You run the risk of ruining them if you go in and try to make them more symmetrical. I say, it's done, sweetie. A little more smoothing on this cheek, a little stain to make it pop, and that's about it."

I looked down to find several clusters of ants dragging huge crumbs away from the base of the tree in their tiny mouths.

"What's all this? Were you eating something out here?"

"Oh, I brought Finn some of my Pop Tart," she said.

I burst out laughing, put my arm around her, and kissed her on the forehead. She smiled back at me.

We stood arm in arm, gazing at our work.

"Well, we did it, Ken," I said, finally.

Kenya smiled and tucked her face in my neck.

"Yay," she said.

My mother was recuperating from her hysterectomy, but very slowly. Her doctor's prognosis was that she would be fine. The uterine fibroids had all been benign. The doctor said that once she bounced back from the physical duress of the operation itself, my mother would be right as rain.

But she didn't bounce back. She stayed in bed and slept and slept.

"About 18 hours a day," my sister-in-law, Mary Lynn, said.

"Does she have anything to read?" I asked. "She loves to read."

"I've gotten her stacks of books from the library. She hasn't even touched them."

"DVD's? She likes some of those HBO series. Has she been watching her shows?"

"Clare, she's completely disengaged. I asked the doctor about it and he prescribed some Zoloft for her after they spoke, but it doesn't seem to have changed anything."

"So she's depressed then? Maybe that's kind of normal after hysterectomy."

"I don't know what to tell you, but this doesn't seem normal, Clare. I wouldn't have even called you but Dean's away on a trip and I thought someone should do something."

"Well, I'll call her again and see what I can find out, but she's been very evasive with me—she always says she's resting."

"Well, that's just it—she always is."

"Right."

I called my mother and after two rings her voicemail clicked on. I tried again an hour later and again an hour after that. I tried after dinner and later that night and the following morning.

Then I got a brainstorm. I tapped on Ethan's door.

"Have you spoken to Grandma recently?" I said, opening the door a crack.

He was at his desk, playing a game on his computer. "Yeah, last night," he said over his shoulder."

"How did she sound?"

"About the same,' he said. He took his hands off the keyboard and swiveled around in his chair to look at me. "I guess the doctor's been keeping her on a lot of pain meds. It makes her really groggy."

"Is that what she told you?"

"Yeah."

"Do you have your cell handy?"

Ethan raised one eyebrow. "Why?"

"I need you to call her for me, please."

"Why, what's wrong?"

"Well, it's just a guess, but I think she's screening her

calls, and apparently I'm not on her A-list. I need to talk to her."

Ethan reached into his jeans pocket and pulled out his cell phone. He squinted at the screen, punched a couple of buttons and waited. "Gram? Hey, Gram, it's me, Ethan. I'm good. You? That's good. Hey, my mom wants a word with you, okay?" He handed me the phone and gave me a stern "be nice" look.

I took the phone from him and closed his door.

"Hi!" I said, in a tone of forced cheeriness.

"So, what, you're checking up on me?"

"Yes, I guess I am. How's it going there?"

I padded downstairs in my flip-flops. *Thwip! Thwip! Thwip!*

"I'm getting by," she said.

"Are you?"

"Well, of course. What else would I be doing?"

I pushed open the kitchen door and sat down on the porch step, thinking the warm afternoon breeze might help me focus.

"You sound perturbed."

"Perturbed?"

"Well, okay, exasperated?"

"Clare, I'm doing the best I know how here. I'm recuperating from a bit of an ordeal."

"Mary Lynn tells me you're sleeping an awful lot. Are you getting up and around as well? That's awfully important too, you know."

"I'm re*cov*ering, alright? If that means I have to sleep all day and night, then that's what I'm doing."

I heard a muffled noise like cloth being dragged across the mouthpiece of the receiver. For a moment I thought she might go to sleep on me right then and there.

"Well, why would you need to sleep all day and night, Mother? It's almost three weeks since your operation."

"It's not just the operation! You have no idea of the

magnitude of this experience. You're not the same person at the end as you were at the beginning."

"Well, of course you're the same. It's not like you had a frontal lobotomy."

"Clare!" said my mother. Her voice was shrill. "I'm telling you I'm not the same! There's much, much more to this than you know. It's not at all what they tell you going in."

"Okay, okay, sorry. Just tell me what you mean by that. How are you not the same?"

She thought for a moment. "I don't know. It's like when they took something out they put something in. Something...foreign."

"What?"

"What I mean is, it doesn't feel like me anymore down there. I think they might have left an instrument in there or something."

The men in mining gear came to mind again. I imagined a pickaxe leaning up against the wall of my mother's uterus.

"Oh, mom, I don't know. Did you ask the surgeon about it?"

"I did."

"And?"

"He laughed at me and said, I can assure you, Lois, I left nothing behind! I thought to myself, well, you can say that again, mister!"

I almost laughed, but thought better of it. "Mom, you sound really angry and upset. And I'm not saying you shouldn't be, I just think maybe you should go see a therapist or something."

"Oh, Clare, I don't go to those kind of people."

"Well, what about when Kenny was having problems? You were like the first one on my case about sending her to a therapist!"

"And you told me to mind my own business."

I sighed and watched the birds darting in and out of the

feeder that hung over the porch.

"Okay, that's beside the point. I'm only saying that there are professionals who know about the emotional toll something like a hysterectomy has on women and they can help you sort it out. You can't sleep for the rest of your life."

"I don't want to talk about it," she said, "I have to go."

"Oh, what, you have a hot lunch date or something?"

There was a pin-dropping silence.

"Clare, do me a favor," my mother said finally. "Don't call me. And don't use Ethan's phone to call me either. You're not helpful. You're sarcastic and self-centered and I really don't have the patience to cope with any of your nonsense right now."

Click!

I took the phone from my ear and stared at it. I don't know what I expected it to reveal to me, but if it had been a mirror, I might not have liked what I saw.

I totally deserved that, I thought. My mother was in trouble and I was being such a shit about it. I wanted to help, but I really didn't want it to require anything from me—like patience, for example.

Lila would tell me I needed to allow my mother to be in this process, no matter how strange it seemed to me, that I should listen and listen more, until I heard what it was my mother was trying to say:

It's like when they took something out they put some-thing in. Something...foreign.

I had read in *The Shamanic Handbook* that people who had surgery sometimes experienced soul loss and what were known as intrusions—displaced energy that didn't belong to them. I didn't know how much I understood it, but I thought if I got myself the hell out of the way, I might just be able to help my mother.

"She's in a transitional space," said Eagle of my

mother. "People are always uncomfortable in transition. In-between spaces are places of power and possibility—anything can happen there."

He was sitting on a rock ledge, looking down at me.

"Well, what can I do to help her transition out of it?" I asked.

"Your mother hasn't given you permission to help her."

"I know that, and I don't really understand why, because I would like to help her," I said.

Eagle flitted his wings and ruffled his back. I waited until he settled down again. "You want to help in *your* time, not hers," he said. "You keep putting your foot on the accelerator. Maybe she needs to be where she is."

I thought about that. What he was saying had a ring of truth in it—not like a tinkling dinner bell ring of truth, but more like a twanging iron gong of truth.

"Well, how do I change that then? What do I do?"

Eagle hopped up the face of the rock ledge and looked out into the distance. He poked his head under his wing and started grooming himself.

I grew impatient. "You're ignoring me," I said.

"You haven't taken your foot off the gas."

"Now you're sounding like my mother."

"Aren't you fortunate to have us?" he asked. "Otherwise, how would you know when you were overstepping your bounds?"

I sighed. "Okay, fair enough. I will keep my foot off the gas. I will wait and listen until she asks for my help. But when she does—if she does—will I know what to do?

"You will know."

"Thank you," I said. "Now, I also want to know what to do about the offer from Cynthia. It is much less than what I thought it would be, and I don't understand how that can be. Is there something going on behind the scenes that I'm not seeing? Some kind of deception?"

"The woman is not deceiving you. She is just trying to

find a resolution."

"Should I accept her offer then?"

"Whether you accept or reject it is entirely up to you."

"But there's so much money missing."

Eagle flew to the ground in front of me. I sat down.

"Maybe you should examine how much importance you are placing on this money," he said. "How much you are investing in this tug of war. There is another meaning to the phrase: *it is much less than what I thought.*"

The iron gong clanged again. I *was* kind of invested in winning just to win—in besting Daniel's paramour. And yes, the sum of the settlement was becoming a bit of an obsession for me. What amount *would* I be satisfied with? What magic number would "settle" the matter?

"It's the principle of the thing," I said, having nothing better to say.

"What principle is that?"

"She has something I need, something that belongs to me."

"That is neither a principle, nor is it true," he said. "It is the universe that answers all your needs. It is the universe that finds the point of balance in all matters. Ask only that the settlement be fair and balanced, and it will be. That is more important than the sum."

I sighed. It was hard to decide what irritated me more in that moment, that Eagle was so dead-on right *once again*, or that he was asking me to do more impossible crap.

I wearily nodded my consent. The next thing I knew we were flying over a terrain of lush green hills and valleys. The landscape looked like a big velvet pincushion. We flew lower, skimming the ground, and I reached out to touch the plushness.

We landed in front of a faery cave. A great hazel tree grew out of the knoll behind the cave, its branches arching down over the opening.

Seated at the opening was a leprechaun, counting hazel

nuts at a long wooden table. He was wearing a pair of pince-nez and a velvet suit and cap exactly the color of the grassy knoll behind him.

"Why is he counting nuts?" I asked Eagle.

"Those aren't just any nuts," said Eagle. "They are hazel nuts, which are considered to be the source of wisdom. Wisdom is the most precious of all the virtues to the faeries."

"Ah," I said. "So, who is he?"

"This is your prosperity guide, Liam, " said Eagle.

Prosperity guide, I thought. *Now* we're getting somewhere.

"State your case," said Liam, not bothering to look up from the figures he was toting up in his book.

"My case?"

"Two women, one man," said Eagle, speaking on my behalf. "Man deceased. A sum to be divided between the women."

Liam plopped some nuts in the pan of a brass scale that sat at the end of the table. The arm of the scale tipped down. Then he put some nuts in the other pan and the arm lifted back.

Liam looked at me over his glasses. "Tell the story," he said.

"The story?"

"In your own words."

"Well," I said, "it all began a few days after my husband died. I was going through the desk in his study, trying to get his papers in order, and I discovered that he had been having a relationship with another woman."

While I spoke, the leprechaun moved nuts back and forth between the pans. Occasionally, he added some from the pile on the table. The piles grew and shrank, as if under time-lapsed photography.

"I felt very betrayed," I said.

"By whom? By your husband, the woman, or yourself?"

"Well, I didn't know the woman, so, not by her. But by him, yes, for lying and taking money that belonged to both of us, and by myself, too, for being so blind. I don't think I wanted to see the truth."

A blur of nuts passed between the trays.

"Anyway, I found out that the money he took had been used to buy a house that the other woman now lives in, but at least half of the money seems to have disappeared altogether."

Liam didn't seem interested in this tidbit.

"Are you harboring resentments?" he asked.

I looked at Eagle. "Well, some," I said. "I'm working on it."

Hazel nuts were moved from pan to pan in a cartoon-like flurry.

"Do you have fears about the outcome?"

"Yes, I suppose."

"What are they?"

"Well, I'm afraid I won't be able to send my kids to college, and that I may have to sell my house, that I won't have any savings in the end, that—."

"She is afraid the other woman will benefit at her expense," interrupted Eagle.

Liam took a lump of nuts from one pan and placed it into the other so that the second pan began to sag lower.

"Bloody hell," I said to Eagle. "You know, I've been working on that. Aren't good intentions worth anything here?"

No nuts were moved from Cynthia's sagging pan, which swayed heavily under its own weight.

"We are only trying to demonstrate to you the mechanics of the thing," Eagle said. "If you invest your energy in emotions that give you currency, like joy and compassion...."

"Bling!" said the scale as it came more into balance.

"Gratitude and trust," said Eagle, as Liam placed a fat cluster of nuts onto the high side of the scale.

"And especially love and forgiveness," said Eagle, "you will profit more. It's universal law."

The pans of the scale stood even now.

"Okay," I said, "you've proved your point."

"Then you agree to embrace these principles?" asked Liam.

I nodded.

"That will be verified," he said, returning to his book of numbers.

I thanked Liam for his help and climbed onto Eagle's back again.

"What did he mean by 'verified'?" I asked, as we flew away.

"The faeries are very exacting," he said. "They like *certainty*."

I waited until the day of the full moon to perform the ceremony that would consecrate the ancestral altar. Kenya had agreed to come along.

"Don't make me do anything though, Mom," she said.

"You don't need to, Ken. Being a witness is a very important role in ceremony."

I recited the verses of the poem I had written and circled the ash tree three times, spreading rose petals and lavender as I walked.

The woods around us felt alive with activity, or should I say, curiosity? As I began to recite the chant, we heard a sudden crashing through the trees not far away. I turned.

"Mom?" said Kenya.

"It's alright," I said, "it's just a tree falling over."

Kenya moved next to me, chewing her nails.

I knelt down and began to bury some things I had gathered together for the ceremony. There were a few charms I had pulled off an old bracelet of mine: a musical note that signified joy and song, a peace symbol for eternal rest, and a heart to honor our blood connection to the ancestors. I buried as well a baby shoe of Kenya's to represent the footsteps of the youngest member of the ancestral line, and my best find, a stone I had brought back from a trip that Daniel and I made to Scotland 22 years ago. I was told in a journey that this stone would energetically link the site of the shrine to the land of our ancestors.

I buried each item and stated aloud the intention and hope that came with it—peace, joy, love, honor and belonging.

"May we remember that we are children of the earth and may there always be land to love beneath our feet."

There was a soft bleating nearby, and we looked up to find a family of deer observing us. Their ears were all fanned out, their dark liquid eyes wide and piercing.

"Holy crap, are they going to attack us or something?" asked Kenya.

"No. It's just your power animal paying us a visit, Ken. You should feel honored."

Kenya smiled and made a soft whistling noise. They all turned their heads in unison and stared at her. "That was deer for hello," she explained.

"Thanks, I never would have known."

I went back to work, carefully burrowing a long hole under the base of the ash tree as I'd been shown to do in my journey. This was the exit through which any wandering souls of our ancestors could leave the earth. I smudged the opening of the hole and then stood back and began to rattle.

I closed my eyes and saw a thread of light emerging from the distance. It ran through the stone I'd buried at the base of the tree and then back out through the tunnel I had dug. It spiraled around the trunk of the tree and went straight into the sky. An opening rimmed with angels appeared in the clouds. The beam of light thickened and brightened. Shots of light pulsed upwards and disappeared through the opening, and then the band of light broke up and faded. The air crackled and sparked, and then quieted.

I opened my eyes, and breathed deeply.

"That was weird," said Kenya.

"What was?"

"All those crows. Didn't you see them?"

"I had my eyes shut."

"Well, all these crows came from out of nowhere and landed in Finn's branches and then they just took off and flew way up in the sky."

"That's pretty cool."

"I can't believe you didn't hear them. They were making a huge racket up there."

As I had been instructed in my journey, I placed a round stone the size of a human head against the opening of the tunnel and pushed it down into the earth.

"Our work is done," I said, brushing the dirt from my hands. "And so may it be."

I gave Finn a few tender pats on his trunk and started to gather up my things.

"Here, Kenny, sprinkle some tobacco around for Finn."

"Thanks, Finn," said Kenya, as she tossed pinches of tobacco through the air. "My deer family left, Mom."

"I noticed."

"They said they just stopped by to say hello."

"Did they now?"

"And that they were starving."

"Starving? What, with all the hostas they've been chowing down on?"

"Yes, two said they wanted carrots, one said he'd like some celery and the little one asked for popcorn."

"Popcorn?"

"Yeah. I thought I could just bring that out to them right now and then we could get in the car and go to Skipper Jack's for lunch."

"Seems like that starving thing is pretty prevalent with you deer types."

"Mom, I'm totally in need of some nachos!"

"Totally in need, eh? Well, we can't have that, now can we?"

As we headed toward the house, I could hear the barred owl calling: "*Who, who who-who! Who cooks for you?*"

Chapter Ten
Alder: **Release**

I felt like I had a lot to remember now if I was ever going to accomplish all of the changes that my guides were suggesting. I wanted to be more loving, trusting, grateful and forgiving. I also wanted to learn how to listen better.

So I made myself a touchstone, using the idea Lila had given me from her journey. I took a small disk of clay and worked it with some water I had drawn from the brook in my woods. I blew into the clay my wishes and prayers for prosperity and balance and pressed my thumbprint into the back. I overlaid it with beads and tiny pieces of clay I had cut into symbols. Then I fired it.

I glazed it, blew more prayers into the clay and then fired it again. The final glaze was a metallic midnight blue, which I accented with gold leaf. I strung it onto a black silk cord and wore it daily. Whenever I felt stressed or rattled about something, I held the medallion in my hand and pressed my thumb into the indentation on the back. I don't exactly know why, but it helped steady me.

I felt like once I understood more about the nature of its power, I would make one for Kenya and Ethan.

I was waiting for Ethan to come home from a party and fell asleep on the couch. When the phone woke me, I jumped up and ran to it, feeling startled and disoriented. A late night comedy show was on the TV and the clock read 12:13. My heart was pounding as I grabbed the receiver.

"Ethan?"

"Mom!" he shouted, his voice oddly pitched and broken. "Aidan's been in an accident!"

"Oh, my God," I said, still fuzzy with sleep, "are you two alright?"

"I'm fine," he said. "But Aidan is hurt. I think it might be bad. I should never have let him drive home, Mom. He had too much to drink."

It was then I realized he was crying.

"Where are you, sweetie? I'll come." I slipped my feet into my sandals. I went into the kitchen to find my keys.

"You know that hill by the old gas station?"

"Tremont?"

He didn't know street names. Like his father, he described locations with landmarks.

"I don't know, near where Craig Willis used to live. You know. There's a big pond near the bottom of the hill?"

My mind whirred. Craig. Craig. I could picture the house where I had dropped Ethan off for play dates. What was the name of that road? *Stil*-something.

"Mom, I can't get to him," Ethan was saying. "His car is on its side. I've been to the passenger window rapping and rapping, but he's unconscious or something. He won't answer me!"

"Ethan, listen, sweetie, you have to call 911. Tell them you're near Stilson Farms Road on Tremont. They'll find you."

"I already called them. They're on their way."

"Good, honey. That's good. I'm getting in the car now and you can call me on the cell if you need to, alright? It's going to be fine, Ethan. Everything's going to be fine."

"I don't think so, Mom," he said, crying harder now. "It's all my fault. He was drinking and I shouldn't have let him go."

"No, Ethan. It's no one's fault. Please try and calm down. I'll be there in five minutes."

I was inside the garage getting into my car as I hung up. I tossed the portable phone onto the seat beside me and hit the garage door opener. My hand was shaking so badly, I could barely get the key into the ignition.

Kenya was asleep; she would be fine, I thought, as I backed out of the garage. I probably should have left her a note, and I considered running back upstairs, but my hand went ahead and put the car into drive and my foot pressed down on the accelerator. Right now, I just needed to give my full attention to what was happening with Ethan and Aidan.

I started praying as I made my way up the driveway and out onto the dark, damp streets. As I rolled down the window, I could hear sirens crying faintly in the distance.

"May Aidan be safe," I whispered. I prayed for light and protection to find him. In my mind I could see him, lying silent and still in the cradle of his crumpled car. I could see Ethan at the window, rapping and calling to no avail. I started to cry.

I had known Aidan since the boys were five. He and Ethan were best friends from kindergarten on. And I knew his mother, Sally, since the days when we were both room mothers. I thought about all the snacks and room decorations and dioramas we had created together over the years, including the time we made Roman gladiator costumes for the boys' 4th grade history project. The foil-covered cardboard we used to construct breastplates and helmets had made the children look more like alien insects than soldiers. I remembered Sally, crying with laughter, as we snapped pictures.

"Oh, dear God," I said, wiping the tears from my face. "I can't believe this is happening."

When I turned the corner onto Tremont, I could see a cluster of emergency vehicles ahead of me, flashing their red, white and blue lights. I had to squint my eyes in order to focus. As I approached the scene, a female police officer from the town stepped out of the wild glare of lights and walked toward me.

"My son is the boy who called 911. He's around here somewhere," I said, pointing to the crowd in front of us.

"You're Ethan's mom?" she asked.

I nodded.

"Why don't you pull over here? I'll walk up with you."

"Thank you," I said.

I parked and got out of my car.

"I'm Clare Blakely," I said to the policewoman.

"Officer Pannacelli," she said, shaking my hand.

"Is Sally Whitford here yet?" I asked as we walked up the road. I was trying to pick Ethan out from the crowd standing near the crash site, but the flashing lights were blinding me.

"Unfortunately, we haven't been able to reach the parents yet," the policewoman said.

"I think I might have Sally's cell phone number," I offered.

"We've been calling the cell, but she hasn't picked up yet. Hey, Pete," she called to one of the other police officers. "This is Ethan's mother."

"Officer Denton," he said, as he shook my hand.

The policewoman walked back to her post down the road.

"We have one of the officers talking to Ethan now,"

Denton said, "He's pretty shaken up, so we've been working with him, trying to talk him down a bit."

"But he wasn't involved in the accident?"

"No, no, he was following the Whitford boy. Trying to make sure he got home alright."

We stared at one another, unable to comment on this road that had been paved with Ethan's good intentions.

"They're best friends, Ethan and Aidan," I said. "How *is* Aidan? Ethan said he was unconscious."

"We don't know, yet, ma'am. We're still trying to get him out of there. How about if you wait right here and I'll have someone bring Ethan to you."

"That would be great."

He disappeared into the weird mix of light and dark, noise and confusion. I could hear the shouts of the paramedics and the beeping of an emergency vehicle as it backed up, trying to get a better angle on the wreck. Somewhere in the blackness beyond the commotion he had created, lay Aidan.

Something brushed against my elbow, and I turned, expecting it to be Ethan, but no one was there to meet my gaze. I touched my elbow as if to recreate the sensation and felt a quick, strange buzzing inside my ears. Someone or something had definitely taken hold of my arm just then as if to get my attention, as if asking for my help. I reached my hand out and felt an odd thickness in the air. I pulled my hand back quickly and rested it, almost protectively, against my breastbone, my fingers groping nervously for the cool smoothness of my medallion.

"Mom?"

I turned. "Oh Ethan, sweetie."

He leaned wearily into my arms and put his head on my shoulder. "I should have driven him home myself," he said, his wet face soaking into my tee shirt.

"It's alright, Ethan," I said, patting his back, which was as hot and clammy as the times when he was a baby and awoke from a nightmare or fever. "Aidan is a strong boy. He'll come out of this just fine. You wait and see."

Ethan continued to cry softly into my shoulder. The depth of his emotion amazed me. He had always been a jovial, upbeat kid with a thick exterior. Upset and disappointment rolled away easily. He hadn't even cried like this when his father died. But then maybe his grief for Daniel was coming out through what was happening now. I thought about something I heard once, how one grief compounded another if the first one had not been resolved.

But why was I thinking like that? Why was I suddenly equating Aidan's accident with Daniel's death, as if the two occurrences were the same?

"Aidan's going to be fine, honey," I said, resting my chin on the top of Ethan's head, though I somehow knew in my heart that wasn't true.

We stopped at home briefly and I put some things into a bag—a couple of sweatshirts to combat the hospital air conditioning, my lens case, eyeglasses, water bottles, energy bars and a book. Ethan texted some of Aidan's friends. I wrote a quick note to Kenya and pasted it on her bathroom mirror. Then Ethan and I drove to the hospital so that someone would be there for Aidan, keeping a vigil, until the police located Sally and John Whitford.

Ethan paced the waiting room, while I sat in one of the seats by the entrance, looking up each time someone came in through the automatic doors. I opened my book in my lap, but couldn't read it. I sipped my water, shivered in the icy hospital air and berated myself for not changing out of my shorts into jeans.

Nearly two hours passed, when Aidan's mother, Sally, came through the door alone. Her makeup was smeared under her steely blue eyes, which were shocked wide open as if she's just been hit with a bucket of cold water. She was wearing a bright pink evening dress and silver-strapped high heels, which were making it difficult for her to walk.

I stood up and took hold of her elbow. She wheeled around and looked at me.

"How is he," she said, grabbing both my arms. "What have they told you?"

"They haven't told me anything. I've just been waiting for you. Ethan's here with me."

Sally stepped over to Ethan as if he would be the one with the answers she needed.

"It was you who called 911," she said.

He nodded.

"How is he, Ethan?" she asked, touching his shoulder.

Ethan turned away and started to cry again.

"Ethan," I said, "sweetie, sit down here a minute while I help Mrs. Whitford, okay? Okay, sweetie?"

I eased him into a nearby chair, took Sally by the arm and navigated her towards the admitting desk. "He's in a bit of shock," I said.

Sally stared back over her shoulder at him, as if the true gravity of the situation had just been confirmed.

"This is Aidan Whitford's mother," I said to the admissions clerk. "He was brought in by ambulance about two hours ago."

The woman looked up at the two of us, but said nothing. She stared down at her computer and clicked through a series of screens. "You can go straight back to emergency," she said to Sally. "There's another desk through these double doors. They'll direct you."

"Come with me," said Sally, pulling on my arm.

"I can't leave Ethan," I said.

"Ethan," Sally called across the waiting room. "Come on. We're going to see Aidan."

Ethan leapt from his seat and followed behind us.

A nurse in Emergency directed us to another, smaller waiting room. When Sally asked her how Aidan was, she was told that the doctor would be in to speak with us shortly.

"From my experience, their idea of 'shortly' isn't exactly short," I said under my breath, as the nurse walked out. I was trying to fill up the space of the waiting and the oppressive, sickening apprehension over Aidan's wellbeing with any light, casual banter I could muster. "So where's John?" I asked.

"Good question," said Sally, twisting her lips into a sideways smirk.

I gave her a puzzled look.

She folded her arms, crossed one leg over the other and began swinging it with pretended carelessness. Sally had a kind of girlish energy about her that I always found endearing. She had a slim, athletic body, white-blond hair, and high cheekbones that accentuated her piercing blue eyes.

"Well, is he on his way here, then, or--?"

"No, actually," she said, looking up at the ceiling with sudden interest, as if it had just dripped water on her, "John and I are separated. He went back to England to rekindle an old flame."

"What?"

"An old girlfriend resurfaced," she said, flashing me a tight smile. "Who knew?"

I took her hand. "God, I'm so sorry, Sal," I said, "I-I don't know what to say. I had no idea."

I glanced over at Ethan who was staring at me, alarmed and dismayed, like he couldn't believe how crass I was being. I gave him a helpless shrug.

"It's okay. Ethan probably knows all about it, don't you, honey?" asked Sally.

He nodded and looked at the floor.

"You didn't say anything to *me* about it," I said to him.

"Well, I wasn't supposed to, Mom. Aidan asked me not to!" Ethan rolled his eyes and stuffed his hands into the front pocket of his hoodie. "Christ!"

I felt embarrassed and reached down to the floor for my water bottle. As I bent over, the medallion I wore swung out of the zippered opening of my sweatshirt.

Sally reached over and took the pendant into her hand. "God, that's gorgeous. Where did you get it?"

"I made it," I said.

"Clare, you are so talented. This is beautiful."

"I'll make you one," I said.

Her eyes lit up. "You will? Really? I would *love* that." She let go of the medallion and squeezed me on the arm. Then she turned away and scanned the hallway nervously.

"Listen, Sally, did anyone call John?"

She shook her head.

"Well, it's none of my business but someone should call him, you know? Do you want me to do it?"

"No,' she said, rummaging through the small silver evening bag she had carried into the hospital, "as far as I'm concerned, he gave up his right to know about us." She pulled out a tissue and wiped her nose.

She noticed me eying the evening bag and her dressy attire.

"I was on a *date*," Sally said, snapping the bag shut. She rolled the Kleenex around in her fingers. The tips were painted hot pink to match her dress. "I found an old college boyfriend of mine on Facebook and I called him up." She laughed. "I'm so ridiculous." She closed her eyes and dabbed them. "God, oh God," she whispered into her tissue, "where's my Aidan? Why won't they tell me where my Aidan is?" She started to rock back and forth and sob.

I put my arm around her shoulder.

"The doctor's coming," I said, desperate with hope that I might actually be right. I stared into the empty hallway outside the waiting room door, "he'll be here any second."

"Which one of you is Mrs. Whitford?" asked a doctor in hospital greens.

All three of us stood up at the same time.

"I am," said Sally, shaking the hand he offered.

"Dr. Mathias," he said. He looked at Ethan and me. "And you are?"

"Family," said Sally, "they're my family. This is my sister, Clare and my nephew, Ethan."

Ethan looked at me and knitted his brows. His eyes darted from Sally to the doctor.

"How do you do," said the doctor, shaking our hands. "Let's all sit down then, shall we?"

We sat down in three connecting chairs, holding onto one another. Outside the door, a young woman lingered, waiting for the doctor to finish so that she might enter. She had an odd pointed face that reminded me of a mouse. She carried a clipboard against her small flat chest and peered into the room, blinking. When she caught my eye, she looked down and moved furtively from the door. It was then I knew. Something in her inability to meet my gaze told me what was about to happen.

I squeezed Sally's hand and swallowed hard. I couldn't find my breath. I reached out my other hand and grabbed Ethan's forearm.

Somewhere, nearby, there were words being said, and beyond that a sound that howled in my ears.

A kind of barrage fell from the doctor's mouth like missiles spitting from the belly of a plane. "At first we hoped...but then we couldn't...and then...and then...too much damage...too far gone...nothing more we could do." It felt like the whole room was under siege.

"Stop!" I said suddenly. "Please just stop."

Doctor Mathias stopped and looked at me as if I'd slapped him.

"It's too much!" I said. "She can't take it in right now!" I felt if I could just shut him up, it would be easier. Sally was on one side of me, hanging onto my sweatshirt with both of her fists, shouting and sobbing. Ethan sat on the other side of me, crying into his hands.

The mousy woman with the clipboard leaned tentative-

ly out of the shadow of the hallway and peered into the light
of the doorway with detached curiosity. "*Please*," I said to the
doctor, "just leave us alone for a few minutes, will you? I
gestured at the woman in the hall. "And can you take her with
you?"

During the next several days, I spent a lot of time on
the phone. I arranged for different friends to stay with and take
care of Sally, when I wasn't there to do it myself. As soon as
she was able, I had her go through her address book and the
high school directory with a highlighter and I called every
single person with a streak of yellow through his name.

I never knew I was so good at delegating. Nearly everyone I called, said: "what can I do?" And every one of them
got a task. There were more calls to be made, motel rooms to
be arranged for out of town relatives and people to be picked
up at the airport. A cadre of women came and cleaned Sally's
house, except for Aidan's room, which Sally wanted to be kept
exactly as he had left it. Neighbors shopped and baked and
stocked the refrigerator and cupboards.

It was Ethan who organized Aidan's friends and class-
mates. They appeared on schedule to walk, feed, and play with
the dog. Ethan, Alex and Matt washed Sally's car, mowed the
lawn and weeded the garden. Matt's father showed up later
that evening to mend the broken riser and railing on front
porch steps.

I was surprised at Ethan's steadiness in the days after
Aidan died, but that was how Ethan operated. Give him something to do and he instantly felt better. It took him out of his
grief and gave him a purpose. He had even thought to gather
some friends together to create a tribute for Aidan's funeral.

John Whitford's parents called him with the news that
his son Aidan was dead. I was grateful I wasn't asked to make
that call. I imagined myself doing something awful like blaming him for Aidan's death. The mind went to such places in

times like these: if only Aidan's parents hadn't separated, maybe this terrible thing wouldn't have happened. Maybe the boy wouldn't have been inspired to steal the case of beer out of his mother's garage and take it to the party with him. And maybe he wouldn't have felt like he needed to drink half of it himself in order to numb the confusion and sadness over his father leaving.

I was certain that no one would be required to state the obvious to John Whitford. He would probably be blaming himself for Aidan's death every day for the rest of his life.

The day before the funeral, I went to the dry cleaners to pick up Sally's black dress and pant suit. On my way home, I stopped by the scene of the accident. I brought a can of Dr. Pepper, the soda I always kept in the house for Aidan, and a G.I. Joe action figure, because I remembered how much the boys loved playing with those when they were little.

What struck me as soon as I got out of the car was how quiet it was there. It was as if the usual summer sounds were holding their tongues in that place. No air currents rippled across the pond or through the ribboned bouquets of flowers and notes left by Aidan's friends, though it was a cool and breezy afternoon. No birdsong filtered down from the trees, though I could see many birds sitting solemnly in the branches and on the telephone lines overhead. No neighborhood children played and laughed in the nearby yards that were filled with abandoned toys and play sets.

As I walked under the alder tree that Aidan's car had struck, I felt the density of the surrounding trees hit me in the face. The energy was different here. I sat on the ground and deposited my gifts, and then straightened up all the other mementos that had been heaped haphazardly around the base of the tree. I tossed away some stray sticks and leaves that cluttered the ground and smoothed out the soil.

I leaned down to read a note attached to one of the

bouquets. "Hold a seat for me in heaven, dude," it read. My heart felt so heavy in that moment, I thought it might just plop out of my chest onto the ground. I took in a ragged breath.

"Oh, Aidan," I said. "What a dear, sweet boy you were."

I felt a small pressure on my left hand just then, the same as I had felt on my arm the night of the accident. A chill ran up the length of my arm and down my back. It felt like the touch of someone's hand, only lifeless in its weight, as if a small sack of flour had simply slumped against my hand. *Dead weight*, I thought. When I lifted my hand slowly upwards I could sense a resistance there, something that hung in the air like a heavy dampness. I checked the skin on the back of my hand to see if it were wet. It was bone dry.

"Aidan?" I said.

I felt a hollow nudge against my shoulder.

"Aidan, you don't belong here anymore, sweetie. You need to leave this place."

A sudden weight sunk against my leg, as if he were trying to sit on my lap. I could feel him clinging to my shoulder again. It was then I knew Aidan wasn't asking to stay; he was asking me to help him leave.

My mind went into a mild panic, darting through everything I had read about death and dying, everything I had learned from Eagle, Eamon, Sumeh, and Bear. I took hold of my medallion, closed my eyes and asked what I should do. The only word I heard was *ceremony*. But, I'm not ready, I protested. *Go and prepare*, they answered. *The time is now*.

The sound of a car pulling slowly onto the shoulder of the road startled me out of my meditation. I looked back. Someone I didn't recognize waved at me behind the tinted windshield.

The car door opened and Jack Woods unfolded his tall frame from the seat of his Subaru station wagon.

"Hey," he said.

The hair on my skin was standing on end. "Hey," I

said, feeling the shock of having both Aidan and Jack Woods materialize out of thin air in the same minute.

He walked down the hill to the tree and crouched next to me.

"So sad, this," he said, motioning toward the tree with his hand.

"Way beyond sad," I said. "I haven't figured out yet what to call it. No word is enough."

"Aidan was such a great kid," said Jack.

My eyes filled up with tears. "He was," I said. "I don't know how Sally is going to endure it."

"Only child, isn't he?"

I nodded.

"That's tough," he said, shaking his head.

"I don't know, you could probably have twenty kids and it wouldn't hurt any less. It rips your heart out to lose your baby."

"That's true," he said. "You almost lost one yourself, didn't you?"

"What? Oh, Kennie, you mean? Yeah, I guess I could have lost her. At one point, I certainly thought I had. But we were lucky." I smiled.

Jack Woods rested his hand on my arm. "It wasn't all luck. You handled everything just right in that situation. You kept your head. I've seen those things go very, very wrong. But I really think you *did* save Kenya's life."

I could feel myself blushing under the sincerity of his words and the intensity of his stare. I looked down and folded my arms.

"Well, thank you. I just wish we hadn't lost this one," I said, indicating with a nod of my head the place where Aidan lost his life.

"I brought him a medal," said Jack, opening his broad hand to show me. "When Aidan was in eighth grade I went to bat for him to get the Good Citizen's award, but there were too many politics working against it."

I stretched my mind back to Ethan and Aidan's eighth grade graduation and remembered that the school superintendent's daughter had won that year. I nodded.

"I remember," I said.

Jack laid the keystone-shaped medal in a little niche at the base of the alder tree.

"There you go, Aidan," he said. "A little late, but no less well-deserved."

I was touched by his thoughtfulness. I brushed the tears away from my face.

"Can I help you up, or are you staying for awhile?" he asked, extending a hand.

"Oh, I should probably get back. I have Sally's funeral garb in the car." I grabbed Jack Woods' hand, and almost couldn't believe the strength of it as he pulled me up. I took a second to let go.

He touched my elbow. "Are you alright?"

I smiled weakly. "I'm fine, I guess. I'm--I'm kind of feeling like I saw a ghost here a little while ago. Just before you came. I'm not sure what to make of it."

"Who, Aidan?"

I nodded and wiped my tears again.

Jack reached into his pocket, withdrew a neatly folded handkerchief, and handed it to me.

"He's here," I said. "I felt him. I think he was asking for my help." I dabbed my eyes with Jack's handkerchief and laughed. "You probably think I'm crazy."

"No, I don't think you're crazy at all."

"I need to figure out what to do for him. I have to get him out of here—send him on to where he belongs." I looked up in the sky as if the place where Aidan belonged would suddenly show itself.

"Well, you're the one for the job," Jack said, smiling down at me.

"Why do you say that?"

"You wouldn't be asked to do something you couldn't.

You wouldn't be put on the spot like that." Jack Woods beamed at me, his entire face caught in a puddle of yellow light that splashed down through the trees.

"You think?" I crossed one arm over my chest. The other hand drifted nervously to the base of my neck. I could not get over how handsome this guy was.

"Oh, I'm one hundred percent certain," he said.

When I reached Sally's house, her brother, Ron, met me at the door.

"I was hoping you would get here soon," he said. "Maybe you can speak to her. My mother and I are having a time of it."

"Oh? Why, what's wrong?"

"I don't know. She keeps going on about Aidan—something about how he's not at peace. I can't make any sense of it. My mom's with her now."

"Alright," I said, handing him Sally's clothes, "I'll talk to her."

I found Sally and her mother on the deck with two full glasses of iced tea sitting in front of them.

"Hey, Sal. Hi, Mrs. Petersen."

"Please, just call me Beth," said Sally's mom, as she stood up. "Can I get you something to drink, Clare?"

Sally reached out, grabbed my hand and pulled me into the Adirondack chair beside hers.

"I'm fine. Thanks," I said.

Sally's mother slid open the door from the deck and disappeared into the house. I looked at Sally, whose face was raw from crying.

"I don't see how I can go tonight," she said, "all those people. I don't see how I'll get through it."

I nodded.

"And all these decisions," she said, " the funeral service, the burial, the headstone. How can a person make those

kind of decisions at a time like this? Are they kidding me?"
She started to cry.

I squeezed her hand.

"I keep trying to tell them. He's my child. I have to be
here for him. That's the only thing that matters. Not all this
other stuff. I have to be here for Aidan. Do you understand?"

"I do."

"You *do*?" She took my hand and pressed her cheek to
it. "I'm so glad you said that, because I don't think anyone else
understands." Her beautiful face was streaked with tears, her
blue eyes even more sea-like. "He's not at peace, you know,"
she whispered.

"I know," I said. I took hold of her hand in both of
mine and turned my chair to face hers. "Hey, Sal, remember
when we used to babysit for each other when the boys were
little?"

She smiled sadly and nodded.

"Well, how about if I take care of Aidan for you this
evening? I'll watch over him and make sure everything's okay
and that way you can be free to do what you need to do."

She gave me a deep stare. "He's in trouble, Clare," she
said.

I nodded. "He is a bit, yes."

Her eyes opened wider and she took hold of my arms.
"Do you think maybe you could help him?"

"I don't know. Perhaps."

"My family thinks I'm crazy, but I know what I'm
talking about. I'm his mother. I *know* these things."

Over the years we had known one another, Sally and I
had shared many books from the shelves of the New Age/
Spirituality section of the bookstore. I had always felt that
Sally was very intuitive. It didn't surprise me that, even
through the depth of her grief, she could still sense what was
happening to Aidan.

"Let me sit with him tonight. Okay? You go on and get
dressed and go to the funeral home. Everyone will want to see

you there. You're the only one who can say all the things Aidan would want to tell them."

She gave me a doubtful smile.

"John will be there."

"Of course he will. But I think you two can come together over this. Despite your differences, Aidan is something you will always share."

"I made him promise to come alone," she said.

"Good for you."

Sally sighed.

"So many people," she said, shaking her head. "I'm not sure I'm up to it."

"Then just take one of them at a time. Think of it as one person. One lo-o-ong person."

Sally laughed. "You're so funny," she said, hugging me.

As I started to break away, Sally grabbed me and held me tighter. "Thank you for hearing me, Clare," she said. "Thank you so, so much."

"You are getting better at listening," said Eagle. "You see, when you are open to receive, things come."

"Thanks, I wasn't exactly anticipating anything like this, though," I said. "Help me understand what has happened to Aidan. Why did he leave us?"

Eagle's form shimmered. I felt him move closer and land on my shoulder.

"In death, you leave your body, not your life," he said. "The life of the soul goes on."

"Okay, then why did he leave his body?"

"It was a crossroad, this way or that. There are countless such choices in life. *You* measure them in weight, but they are all the same."

I frowned. "Sorry, but I can't get my mind around that. Aidan's death is a deep, deep loss to many of us. He had everything in front of him. I mean, why so young?"

Eagle moved closer. I felt his strength wrap around my shoulders like a shawl.

"He still has everything in front of him. That doesn't change. The soul is ageless. Sixty-five years, forty years, ten years, all the same. This soul you think of as a boy is older than most. And he is a great teacher. Everyone who knew him will be taught something invaluable."

"What will Ethan be taught?"

"Your son will come to understand that the preciousness of life lies not in the past but in the promise of what it can become."

"And Sally?"

"The mother will realize that her path is much broader than the one she originally chose."

"And me?"

Eagle flew upwards with a great flutter of his wings, as if he were breaking out of a trap.

"For you, this is a doorway to a place that has been calling you for a very long time."

It was dusk when I reached the place where Aidan died. Eagle had given me careful instructions, and there was only a small window of time to carry them out before night fell. I had scribbled everything down onto a sheet of paper, which I could now barely read. One thing I hadn't thought of was to bring a flashlight.

First, I was to call Rowena, who had agreed to come and help me. She had some distance to drive and I worried about her making it in time. As I waited for her to arrive, I laid out a smudge pot filled with dried sage, my lighter, a rattle, and some candles. I cleared a circular space about eighteen inches in diameter and made a ring around it with all the gifts and pictures and letters that had been left by Aidan's friends and visitors.

I was told to sing to Aidan, so I rattled softly and sang a song I used to sing to my kids when they were little.

Soon, Rowena's car approached and slowed to a stop nearby, the tires biting at the gravel along the shoulder of the road.

"Sorry to drag you all the way out here," I said, as she stepped out of her car.

"Oh, that's alright," said Rowena, coming over to survey the ceremonial space I had laid out in front of the alder tree, "I might say it's the strangest thing you ever asked of me, but I know if I wait five minutes, you'll make a liar out of me."

"I need someone to witness the work," I said, lighting the smudge pot.

"I understand," she said, kneeling beside me and putting her hand on my back. "I'm honored you asked."

"Okay, can you light these candles?" I said, handing her the lighter.

"Jeez, I hope the neighbors don't call the fire department on us."

"I already cloaked the area," I said, waving smoke on myself as I made three clockwise circles around the tree. "Here, let me smudge you."

Rowena stood up and held out her arms. "Does that mean they can't see us? Oh my God, that's so cool. I always wanted to be invisible."

"Alright, now. Remember when I got you your power animal?"

"Yes, it was a white bull, I think."

"Exactly. When I start rattling, I want you to close your eyes and call your power animal here. Then, I want you to ask him to stay with you and protect you. Is that clear?"

"Crystal."

"Alright, here we go," I said, picking up my rattle and closing my eyes.

The first thing I did was to call Eagle to me. This time when he appeared over my shoulder, he seemed grayer somehow. Everything, in fact, seemed duller in this space, without the bright luminosity I'd come to expect from my journeys to the lower world. This was the non-ordinary realm of the earth, also known as the middle world.

Eagle flew towards me and then broke the barrier between us, flying straight into my back. I felt his wings spread out inside my shoulders and his head enter my head.

I looked around for Aidan. He was a lanky, good-looking boy with his mother's cheekbones and a thick crop of blond bangs that always dipped into his hazel eyes. I found him standing in the center of the road, holding up his car keys and shrugging.

"I can't find my car," he said.

"They took the car away, Aidan," I said. "It was totaled."

"*I* did that?"

"You did, sweetie."

Aidan slumped his shoulders and kicked at the dirt with his sneaker, "*Man*, that sucks," he said, "How am I going to get home now?"

"Hey, Aidan," I said. "Come stand over here where I can see you."

He came obligingly and stood where I pointed, in the center of the circle I had cleared for him in the dirt.

"Remember when I met you here before?"

"You brought me a soda," he said, smiling.

"I did. And I told you something, didn't I? I told you you couldn't stay here anymore. Do you remember?"

He hung his head. "I messed up," he said.

"No, Aidan, you absolutely did not mess up. You just lost your way. I'm here to help you find it again. Will you let me do that for you?"

He nodded.

"Good, Aidan," I said. "That's good."

I looked up and asked my spirit guide, Sumeh, to create a portal for Aidan to step into the world where he now belonged. What came in response were two golden ribbons of light that descended in spirals from the sky like long yellow curls. Each ribbon was pulled to earth by an angel who brought it to the spot where Aidan stood. The ribbons encircled one another and merged into a high column of light that surrounded Aidan and the angels who now hovered behind each shoulder. When I looked up again, I could see a tall, thin man in a white suit coming down a long winding staircase inside the shaft of light.

Aidan looked up too. "Grandpa!" he said, laughing. "What are you doing here?"

"I came to get *you*, Champ," said the man, smiling and holding out his arms.

Aidan stretched both of his hands up over his head and began to float away towards the man, the column of light rising as they both moved heavenward. I waited until I saw them disappear. Then the sky closed over.

"Goodbye, Aidan, sweet, sweet boy," I said. "Rest in peace."

I sighed and wiped the tears from my face. "Thank you, Sumeh," I said aloud. "Thank you, Eagle and White Bull. Thank you, helping spirits. All is done. And so may it be."

I stopped rattling and opened my eyes. I looked over at Rowena, whose face was sparkling with tears in the candlelight.

"That was awesome," she said.

Three days after Aidan's funeral, I stopped by Sally's with a present. I hollered into the house through the screen door.

"Hey, Sally?"

"I'm in here, Clare."

She was sitting at the kitchen table nursing a cup of tea when I came in.

Every time I saw her now, I felt somewhat amazed. So,

I thought, you do live on after such a tragedy. You actually do.

"You look pretty," she said, as I entered the kitchen.

"Me?" I said. "Give me a break." I sat down in the chair next to her.

"No, you do." She took hold of my wrist and squeezed it.

"How *are* you?" I asked.

Sally shrugged. "Oh, I'm pretty worn out."

"Are you getting any sleep?"

She shook her head. "I really hate going to sleep, because I know when I wake up, the first thing I'll remember is that Aidan is dead, and it's like losing him all over again."

I put my hand on top of hers. "Oh, honey, I'm sorry. I'm so sorry."

We stared at the tears standing in one another's eyes.

"You've been such a help, Clare. You don't know how much. And you were a help to Aidan as well."

I nodded. "I hope so. I think he's better now. It was as if he got stuck in the moment of the accident or something."

"He *was* stuck," said Sally. "I could feel it."

I smiled. "You were so deeply connected to him. Remember how you two always got ear aches and stomach aches together?"

Sally laughed. "I know. I even sprained my ankle after he broke his playing baseball, remember? Would you like a cup of tea, Clare?"

I shook my head.

"Sally," I said, "I wanted to tell you what happened the other night while everyone was at the funeral home. I went back to the crash site, and I helped Aidan pass over. Your dad came down and took him up to heaven. I saw them go."

"Daddy was there?" Sally whispered.

"Yes. Aidan called him Grandpa. And he called Aidan Champ."

Sally put her hand up to her mouth and began to cry. "Yes," she said, nodding, "Daddy always called him Champ.

When my dad was alive and Aidan was little, Aidan followed him around like a puppy. They adored each other." She took my hand. "Oh, Clare, I feel so much better knowing they're together. You can't know what this means to me."

I reached into my pocket. "Here, before I forget, I brought you something," I said, handing her a medallion much like mine, although hers was ovular in shape and had been glazed in aquamarine and silver.

She gasped. "Oh, my gosh, Clare, it's so beautiful! You *made* this for me? It's amazing." She put the cord over her neck and patted the medallion proudly against her. "I love it!" she said, laughing in her girlish way.

"Listen," I said, "you see this little depression here on the back? That's Aidan's thumbprint. I brought this clay with me the morning of the funeral and I pressed it onto Aidan's thumb before they closed the casket. It's a touchstone. This way, you'll always have a connection to him."

Sally rubbed her thumb gently against the indentation on the back. She wrapped her fist around it, closed her eyes and pressed the fist against her heart.

A few moments passed. Then she leaned over and put her arms around me. "I will never, ever be able to thank you enough for all you've done for Aidan and me," she said.

"Don't be silly," I said hugging her back, "I'm glad I could help."

"It's more than just help," she said. "You've given me a peace in my heart I thought I never would have again as long as Aidan was gone."

Later that evening I was sitting on the porch swing, staring up into the sky. The sun had set so beautifully. I thought about Aidan being part of that peach and lavender sky, and how I might want to use those colors as a glaze for the next medallion I made.

The screen door opened and Ethan stepped out onto

the porch. He sat down in the chair beside the swing, and I could tell by the look on his face he wanted to tell me something important.

He leaned over in his seat, elbows on his knees.

"I want to go visit Grandma," he said. "I've thought about this ever since she had her surgery, and I-I really think she needs help."

"You're right," I said. "She does need help."

He watched me and waited. "So can I go?"

I looked at him and smiled, my heart so full of love for him. When had he become so grown-up?

"You know what?" I said. "Let's all go. What do you say? We could drive there."

"Really," he said. "Seriously?"

"Really," I said. "We can leave the day after tomorrow."

Chapter Eleven
Oak: **Strength**

Being back in the house where I grew up had its good points and its bad. One of the good points was that I got to walk every afternoon to a little stream in the nearby woods where I had spent many hours as a child.

It was no longer as shady as I remembered, due to the fall of two large oaks that now lay crisscrossed on the ground in a state of noble decay. The stream where I had hidden and tossed many a secret object or lucky stone burbled more quietly.

But it still had that splendid green coolness to it, the sense of magic rendered by the over arching trees, the mossy rocks, and clumps of nodding ferns. In my childhood, I had spent hours here talking to the faeries, leaving them my trea-sures. In my teenage years, I had sought a different kind of refuge, climbing and perching on the lichen-crusted rocks, my bare toes dangling into the chattering stream, my head swimming with thoughts of boys and the smoke of my sneaked cigarettes.

The bad points of being in the house again were the many facets of my mother's decline. The house reeked with the smell of stagnant air and spoiled food. I cleaned the refrigerator and pantry to no avail the first day after we arrived. I shut off the air conditioning downstairs and opened up all the windows, but the stifling heat of a Midwest summer's end worked against me. I dragged fans out of the basement, cleaned them and distributed them throughout the ground floor. After a few days, the smell was not as bad, but it still kind of socked you in the face every time you came in the door.

My children groaned.

"Mom, it's so hot in here," said Ethan. "Before it just smelled. Not it's hot *and* it stinks."

My sister-in-law, Mary Lynn, shrugged. "I've tried to figure it out. Dean thinks it's a dead mouse."

"Terrific," I said. "Does Mom have any idea what it is?"

Mary Lynn shook her head. "She can't smell it."

"Of course not," I said, "she's been living upstairs for the last month."

The second problem was the general disrepair of the house. The driveway was full of potholes, the basement full of junk, the yard full of weeds, and the roof full of leaks. I sent the kids out to tackle the yard. I figured I could get Dean to order some gravel for the driveway and help me clean out the basement, but the roof had me worried.

Whenever I wasn't worrying about the roof, I worried about my mother. She had no appetite and flaked suspiciously at her food with a fork, as if she expected to find lice in it. She reminded me of a child with food issues—the oatmeal is too lumpy, the eggs are too runny, I don't eat anything green. She had an unending supply of candy I could never locate the source of. I began to suspect there was a hidden portal to Hershey, Pa. under her bed. She refused to come downstairs, and ate (or should I say, dissected) her meals on a bed tray. Once every few days, I was able to coax her into the shower so I could change the sheets on her bed and freshen up her room.

The kids, to their credit, spent most of the day with her, especially Ethan. He was enormously patient and loving to my mother, reading to her, watching movies and playing cards and board games with her. My children filled my mother's room with chatter and activity, so that she slept much less, talked more, and even laughed occasionally.

But I knew she wasn't herself. Her eyes had a hollow, nobody-home look that made me feel hopeless about her recovery. Whenever I stared into those eyes, I half expected to find two telltale gas gauges with their needles on E.

I called my cousin Dave, who was a carpenter, and asked him to come over and look at the roof.

The following night, he clanged into the driveway in his wheezy black pick-up.

"Bonesy!" he said, as he stepped out of his truck.

"Hey, Dink," I called from the porch.

Kenya looked up at me with surprise. "What did you just call each other?"

"Those are our childhood nicknames," I said. "Mine was Bonesy because I was skinny and his was Dinky because he was so little."

We both looked at Dave whose height and weight had expanded considerably since his youth. He now was a burly, ruddy-faced hulk with no neck, Popeye arms and a beer belly of staggering heft.

Kenya sized up Dave's girth. "*He* was little?" she said.

"Kennie!" I said. "Be nice."

"No seriously," she said, "what happened to you?"

Dave stepped up onto the porch and patted her shoulder with his mitt-like hand. "A lot of years and too many beers, young lady," he said.

He reached over and gave me one of his bear hugs. "I see she's inherited your tact, Clare."

I laughed. "It would appear so."

We went in through the screen door and made our way to the back of the house where the worst of the leaks lived.

"Holy crap," said Dave, as we walked into the kitchen, "were you cooking road kill in here?"

I frowned. "Oh," I said, "sorry. Welcome to the smell that will not die."

Dave sniffed again and wrinkled his nose. "God, it's more than a smell, Clare. It's like a demonic being. Did you call an exterminator?"

"Do you really think I need to?"

Dave walked to the center of the kitchen and sniffed again. "Jesus. I got a buddy who does Hazmat Control for the county. You want me to call him?"

"C'mon, Dink," I said, "it's not that bad."

Dave nodded. "Oh, it's bad, Bonesy. If the roof is half as bad as this smell, I say, you demolition the whole place and start over."

Kenya's eyes grew wide. "Mom, is he serious?" she whispered.

"Cousin Dave is never serious, Kennie," I laughed.

"Dink, you mean," she said.

"Right." I said, "Dink."

Dave walked around the ground floor, eyes aloft, looking at leaks. He stopped upstairs to say hello to my mother and Ethan, crawled around the attic for a while, and then dragged a ladder off the side of his truck and climbed up onto the roof.

"I think I can patch it," he said, coming down the ladder to where I stood below, leaning my weight against the bottom rungs.

"Really?"

"Yeah. There's one bad spot over the back porch. That's why she's getting water into the kitchen and den. I won't really know until I strip all the shingles off, but that's the worst of it."

"How soon can you come?"

"I can probably find some time next week to do it. I'll get 'er done. Your mom should have called me sooner, though."

"Well," I said, "she's been kind of out of it lately."

"Boy, you can say that again," said Dave, tugging at the cable on the extension ladder. "It's like she's had the stuffing knocked out of her."

I nodded and smiled weakly. The ladder clattered as it collapsed to half its size.

Dave swiped his brow with one thick forearm and shook his head.

"I mean, I don't know who that woman is in the bed upstairs," he said, "but she ain't my Aunt Lo, I'll tell you that."

"Mom, I thought you liked soft-boiled eggs," I said, as I picked up the bed tray to carry it downstairs. "You didn't even touch these."

"They tell you not to eat a lot of eggs these days," she said, smoothing the covers across her lap.

"Oh, for heaven's sake, a couple of eggs aren't going to hurt you. How about if I leave the fruit and cottage cheese? Can you manage that?"

"I'm really not hungry, Clare," she said, holding her stomach. "I'm still full from last night."

I rolled my eyes. "C'mon, you ate like two bites of dinner. And I even made ham and lentil soup, which you love."

She wrinkled her nose and shook her head. "It didn't agree with me. I think it's better if I don't eat just now."

I sighed and set the tray down on the edge of the bed. "Listen, Mom, you have to meet me halfway here," I said. "I can't do this by myself."

She looked away and stared out the window, rolling the edges of the sheet in her pale hands. At first I thought she was choosing to ignore me, but then she turned and looked at me with those vacant building eyes. "Clare, I don't want to hurt your feelings, because I can see that you mean well, but this is exactly why I didn't want you to come here in the first place."

"What do you mean? I'm just trying to bring back some semblance of order into your life!"

"I never asked you to do that," she said. "I don't really *want* you doing that."

"Oh, okay, Mom, great!" I said. "Well, here's a news flash: your roof is leaking! The tile in the kitchen is buckling, the ceiling in the den is crumbling onto the floor. Your mail is unopened, your bills are overdue, the house is filthy, and there's some incredibly bad smell downstairs that, by the way, do you have any idea what the hell that is down there that's smelling so bad?"

"Clare," my mother said, "if any of this mattered to me, I'd have it fixed inside of a week. Do you really imagine I need *you* to handle it for me?"

I put the bed tray onto the floor and took its place on the edge of the bed. "Of course, you don't need me to handle these things, but the point is, you're not handling them, and this whole place is falling down around your ears. I mean, the porch was completely overrun with spider webs the day we arrived. There were weeds this high in the yard. It looked like the Munsters lived here. And what's with Dean, for Christ's sake, letting it get to this level? I know he's working and all, but it's like he's got his head up his ass or something, sending poor Mary Lynn over here all the time, and—!"

"Good God!" shouted my mother. "Will you just shut up? I'm so sick of listening to you go on and on about the state of this house, like it's some terrible burden that's been placed on your weary shoulders. Nobody asked you to take this on, Clare. I think you of all people should understand how it feels to have someone coming into your house and criticizing the way you're handling things. You didn't like it very much when I came and visited you last spring. In fact, you disliked it so much, you asked me to leave, didn't you?"

I looked down at the floor. "Yes," I mumbled.

"Well, I'm not going to do that, because I don't want to hurt the kids' feelings. They've been wonderful company and a real boost to my spirits. But if you keep upsetting me like this, Clare, I mean it, I *will* ask you to go."

When she finally finished shouting at me, she took a deep, gasping sigh and looked down at the sheets. She folded her arms and put one shaking hand up to her bottom lip, as if she were afraid more unbridled rage might come spewing out.

I had come to my mother's house, thinking I could do something meaningful for her, thinking I could help her get back on her feet again. But in two weeks time, I had only succeeded in making her feel angry and resentful. Once again, I found I could do nothing to please her, and it made me feel hopeless.

After a moment, I sighed and stood up. "Fine," I said. "I'll try not to upset you anymore."

I bent down and picked up the breakfast tray from the floor. "I'm going out later on. Can I get you anything?"

"No," said my mother. "Can you shut the door please?"

I turned back to see her sliding down into the cocoon of her bed. She rolled over with her back to me and pulled the covers up over her head.

It was 9:00 in the morning. My children were still asleep, and my mother had most likely joined them in slumber. I sat mulling over everything my mother had said while I drank my tea. Then I kicked off my flip-flops, put on some sneakers and sun block and walked down the road to the woods.

The simmering heat of the day broke away as I stepped under the deep green canopy of the woods. I reached my favorite stream, and sat down on a rock.

When I made the decision to come here, it seemed like such an inspired idea. Even the car trip from Connecticut had been wonderful. My children and I sang and laughed and joked in a way we hadn't for a very long time. It made us think of other road trips when Daniel was still with us. Granted, they were not all good experiences; oftentimes, we got lost and argued over directions.

But, on the way to Ohio, my kids and I laughed about those times, as if to say to one another: that was then, this is now. We are past it and we have healed.

As soon as we arrived at my mother's, however, the mood shifted. I struggled with Ethan over my approach to his grandmother's care and his own.

"She just wants to relax, Mom. You're creating all this disruption around her with your cleaning and complaining. You haven't spent five minutes talking to her, except when you want to nag her about something."

Ethan didn't seem to require my mother's life to be anything different from what it was. He knew as well as I did that she was struggling, but somehow he didn't judge it. He sat on her bed day after day, telling her jokes and stories, playing his guitar and singing silly songs about Clementine who had number nine shoes and a bullfrog named Jeremiah. He made trips to Blockbuster for movies he thought she would like, and read to her from a collection of Agatha Christie mysteries he had brought along with him on the trip.

I thought in my adult way that the seriousness of my mother's situation was lost on him, but now, after my mother's upbraiding of me this morning, I thought maybe Ethan had it all figured out.

I put my fingers into the water, and was shocked at the

icy coldness of it. Maybe it would soothe my throbbing head, I thought, putting my wet fingers up to my temples. As I did this, I heard the tinkling of wind chimes and looked up, thinking I would find some hanging in the overhead branches. But the branches above me were empty and still.

I thought I could have imagined it, but then the sound came again, as if on cue, crystalline and melodic, part laughter and part song. I felt a soft breeze rush up to me like a child and throw its thin arms around my neck.

When I was young, my friends and I used to believe that the faeries came to this place, that their laughter sounded like little bells and if you caught them unaware, you might even see them. I smiled and closed my eyes, remembering the hours I had spent here, talking to the faeries and leaving little gifts.

"Thank you for the gifts," I heard a voice say, and when I opened my eyes I could just make out the watery form of a tall, translucent woman leaning against the oak on the other side of the stream. She was pale blue-white in color with long auburn hair, the rich color of bark. Bright, gleaming leaves sprouted from the ends of each wavy strand.

"Faery folks live in oaks," I thought to myself.

If I looked harder, she disappeared into the bark of the tree, but when I allowed my eyes to go slightly off focus, she became visible again.

"You're welcome," I said, "I was never quite sure anyone was there to receive them."

She smiled and nodded. "Sing the song," she said.

"Oh dear, let me think of it first," I said, laughing, as I tried to recall the lyrics of a song my mother had sung to me when I was a child and that I had sung here at this brook many times.

White coral bells
Upon a slender stalk.
Lilies of the valley
deck my garden walk.

Oh, how I wish
that you could hear them ring.
That will happen only
when the faeries sing.

My eyes welled with tears as I sang the words.

"Sing that song to your mother," said the faery woman.

I rolled my eyes. "Oh, I don't think so, " I said. "My mother and I are no longer at a place where I could do that."

She frowned. "Why not?"

I shrugged. I didn't know what to say.

The faery woman parted from the tree and sat down on a nearby moss-covered rock. I swore I saw it sink like a cushion under her as she sat, and yet I could not imagine her willowy form bearing any weight whatsoever. Meanwhile, my own butt was feeling pretty sore from the hard, uneven surface I was seated on. I shifted a bit to get more comfortable.

"If you sing that song to your mother," she said, "she will tell you a story."

I frowned. "I'm not five years old anymore," I said. "I don't have that kind of relationship with my mother."

A chickadee flew down and sat in the branches of the faery woman's hair. She didn't seem to mind.

"You are trying to help your mother," she said, her face filled with concern.

I nodded wearily.

"But you are trying to help your mother by creating order in her life," she said, "and that will not work here."

"So I've been told," I said.

"The source of the disorder is within her, not around her."

I could see her point. "Well, what can I do?" I asked.

She cocked her head as if she were listening to a voice from above. The wind whistled through the overhead branches of the oak. The faery nodded. "There is a piece missing from her. It was taken a long time ago."

"Not during the surgery?" I asked.

The faery shook her head. "The surgery disrupted and unearthed a grief she had buried away there. It was the memory of being attacked when she was a young woman."

As she spoke, my hand moved protectively to my own belly, and I knew in that instant—almost as if it had happened to me—that my mother had been raped as a girl. Even though she had never told me this, I knew somehow it was true.

Suddenly, everything that had occurred since her operation made perfect sense. My mother was grieving the loss of something she had never been allowed to grieve before. Perhaps it was the loss of her innocence, her own volition, or sense of security in the world. Perhaps it was this loss that had made her so critical and wary of my own headstrong nature, my childhood willfulness and independent spirit.

I recalled how unreasonably cautious she had always been when I was a teenager, how she constantly warned me about boys and never allowed me to walk home alone at night. She used to have my father drive me everywhere, to and from school dances, football games, and the movies, much to my supreme embarrassment, while my girlfriends casually walked home in the dark.

I looked across the brook at the faery woman. She put one delicate foot into the water that ran between us and poked at a flat black stone with her toe. "Take this stone and put it in on the high shelf of the oak tree. The spirit of the wind will bring your mother's soul piece back here and blow it into the stone. Then you must place the stone under her mattress for three days. Her spirit will reabsorb the energy and she will be well again."

"Seriously?" I asked. My heart was pounding so hard I had to put my hand over it to steady myself.

She nodded.

"My mother is very angry with me right now. She sort of insisted I stop trying to intervene."

"We know what she said. Think of it as an offering. If

your mother does not want it, her spirit will not take it."

I sighed with relief and nodded. "Okay," I said, "I understand."

"Now," she said, "you must do three things." The faery began to count on her long fingers. "One, put clean white sheets on your mother's bed before placing the stone, then remove and wash the sheets after three days, and bring the stone back here. Two, journey to your helping spirits regarding the importance of the white sheets. And three, sing your mother the song."

"What, like out loud, you mean?" I asked.

"Yes, out loud," she said.

I lay awake well past midnight, listening to the unexpected thunderstorm that blew into town. The wind puffed and gusted and rattled the shutters and windows. I struggled to honor my mother's wishes and resisted checking the ceiling in the den, though I was not certain it would hold through another storm.

A loud sudden banging, most likely a slamming door, finally jolted me out of bed, and I padded downstairs to close the windows and check up on things.

Outside, the dark trees were swaying wildly in the streetlight, and I watched them, spellbound. Their motion was something between a prayer and a dance, a movement that felt like the dizzying walk I'd been doing all night through my past, carefully reframing every struggle I'd ever had with my mother.

"Watch out," she was forever saying. "Be careful. Don't buck the system. Don't step out of line." All her old adages to which I'd responded tiredly: "Leave me alone. You don't know what you're talking about. I'm not like you."

Everywhere I looked, there was my mother, moving cautiously through her life. Once upon a time, she had not been so vigilant. It only needed to be once.

My mother had the habit of holding her head a little to the side when she walked, her chin raised just so. I always thought it demonstrated a touch of haughtiness about her. But I was wrong—the tilt of her head was a mark of her uncertainty. It helped her maintain her balance on the precarious tightrope she walked between the denial that she had ever been violated in the first place and the fear it would one day happen again.

The next morning, I stood at the living room window, sipping my tea and surveying the effects of the thunderstorm. Shredded leaves and broken branches littered the front yard and street.

I thought about the flat black stone from the brook that I'd placed in the ample crevice of the biggest oak tree, and I wondered if it would still be there. What if the rain had washed it away?

I finished my tea and rinsed the cup out in the sink. I grabbed a handful of oatmeal out of my mother's pantry and dumped it into my pocket. Then I put on my walking shoes and set off for the woods.

The air in the woods was a thick, steamy cloak that clung to my skin as I entered. The brook had a brisker, gushier sound to it; bits of leaves and branches spun in tiny whirlpools and snagged on the rocks and rotting stumps that cluttered the brook bottom.

A sizeable tree branch had fallen off during the night and lay suspended above me, where it had been caught like a child in the arms of a fellow tree. I hopped over the brook and looked up into the oak where my mother's stone had spent the night, noting with surprise that this was the tree that had been struck by lightning during the storm.

I realized that the lightning, the tree, the wind and rain had all brought powerful medicine to the stone, and I was moved again by the generosity of nature, its constant willingness to help. I scooped up the stone and held it in my fist. The energy within it pulsed against my hand like a heart.

I thanked the lightning for its fire, the wind for its strength and the rain for its purity. I thanked the tree for its courage and the wound it had sustained for the sake of my mother's healing. I thanked the faeries and sprinkled oatmeal around the base of the oak. I sang the song my faery helper liked so much, in hopes she would reappear, but the only response I received was from a squirrel that jabbered testily from a nearby tree, as if to say, *hurry home, hurry home, time is wasting*!

I thought I should seek out my ancestral guide, Eamon, during this journey, but when I started down the tunnel to the lower world, I suddenly found myself moving sideways under the ground. I ended up in a quiet dell that was thickly encrusted with moss and dotted with pools of honey-colored light. In the center of the dell was a round pond filled with jumping fish. An overhanging willow tree wept into it. I sat down on a spongy green rock and waited. Soon, a large fish flopped out of the water onto a neighboring rock and transformed into my faery friend.

"Oh," I said, "I was trying to contact my helping spirits."

"I *am* one of your helping spirits," she said, flouncing her tree branch hair. (I swore I could see acorns growing in there.) "I've been with you all your life."

"Wow, no kidding. I didn't know."

"At one time you knew—you don't remember now." She folded her shiny white hands delicately into her lap.

I copied her pose, crossing my legs at the ankles as she did.

"I'm sorry I forgot," I said.

"It happens," she said. "Now then, your mother is the task at hand. Let's look at that, shall we?"

I nodded my agreement.

"The white sheets, which you put on her bed, represent a kind of confinement that your mother has been in for a very long time. Think of it as an identity that does not serve her. She will wrestle with this identity for the next three days, and then she will tell you the story of it. When she tells the story, you will take it from her. You will see yourself putting her story into a container and letting it float away. Then you will give her a new story."

"A new story? But, what if I don't know one?"

"You will need to go and find it," she said. "The horse will take you."

I looked beside me and found the brown and white spotted horse I had ridden during the journey I made at Lila's. Then I looked back at the faery, and recognized the priestess who had appeared in that same journey.

"Verena?" I asked.

"I take many forms," she said, shrugging. "Now go." She made a shooing motion with her hand.

I leapt onto the back of the horse and we took off through the woods. The dense cover of the trees fell away after a moment and we found ourselves in a more hilly terrain. We trotted beside a noisy river and when I looked down, I could see it was filled with rapids.

Then I noticed Eamon, descending a hill on the other side of the river. A cluster of people I assumed were my ancestors followed him. They carried above them on a funeral pyre, a flaming white shroud I knew to be the body of my mother. Eamon directed the group to place my mother's body onto a waiting raft, and then he shoved the raft into the current with his walking stick.

I sat on the back of the horse and watched what unfolded. This was the story I was given to bring back:

The river grabbed the raft in the hook of its wild current. The raft spun in circles and jumped and banged over the rocks. It moved like a timber through a flume, bumping through the shaft of the river until it reached a high waterfall. There, it paused for one moment on the edge, and then it plummeted into the depths below. My heart flopped over as I watched the raft shatter into splinters, and the shroud fly apart in strips.

From inside the mist and spray of the waterfall leapt a huge rainbow-colored fish. He carried my mother in his mouth, like a bear might catch a salmon in his.

As the fish dove back down into the deep water, my mother struggled to breathe. But the rainbow fish taught her how to breathe underwater like him and soon she was calm and content to lie within the rolling arms of the river. He took her home to his family, where she lived in a vast shimmering school that always moved as one fish, surrounding and protecting her wherever she went. After a time she even came to look like them, with a swishy mermaid tail, fins for arms and long reedy hair.

Then one day, her heart longed to be with her family once again in the world above the river's bottom. She told this to the fish and he said, "Then you must go."

"But, I am still a little afraid to return," she said.

"We will never leave you without comfort," said the rainbow fish. "We helped you before and we will help you again, whenever you need us."

When the story ended, I asked my horse to bring me back. As we parted, I thanked him and said how much I liked having a horse as a power animal.

"I am not your power animal," he said. "I am the spirit of your drum."

Ethan lounged in the wingback chair he had dragged upstairs to my mother's bedroom, one long leg swung over the arm. He was tuning the strings of his guitar, a lime green pick pressed between his fingers.

"Do you know any country western songs, Mom?" he

asked, as I walked in, a tray of snacks and sodas in my hand.

"A few, I guess."

"Grandma likes that swear song."

"What?" I said.

My mother started to laugh. "*I Swear*," she said.

"Oh," I said, "the one about the moon and the stars in the sky...that one?"

She nodded.

"Google the lyrics, Ethan. Yeah, that's a beautiful song," I said, sitting on the edge of the bed.

My mother started to sing it and I followed along. We fumbled through the lyrics as best we could.

"Hey, wait, you guys," said Ethan, clicking the keys on his laptop with frustration. "Okay, way off key there. Not too smooth."

My mother and I smiled and kept singing, searching each other's face for the next line and the next. Some of those lines brought tears to our eyes.

"Yoo-hoo," said Ethan rapping on the face of his guitar. "Musical accompaniment here. You're supposed to wait for me, you know."

We ignored him and forged on, laughing at the lines we fudged, filling in other lyrics for the ones we couldn't remember.

"Whoa," said Ethan, "where are the lyrics police when you need them?"

My mother and I finished the song with a flourish. My mother clapped her hands. I looked at Ethan and laughed.

"God," said Kenya from the doorway. She was frowning and blinking her eyes. At two in the afternoon, she had just rolled out of bed. "Who let the dogs out?"

She dragged across the room and flounced onto the empty side of my mother's bed. Her half-closed eyes caught hold of the snack tray. "Ooh," she said, "breakfast!"

"Kennie," I said, "don't eat that. Go make yourself some cereal or something."

"And what would, like, be the difference between popcorn and corn pops?" she asked, stuffing a handful of snack food into her mouth.

Ethan burst out laughing. "Owned," he said.

I gave him my *"you're-not-helping-matters"* look.

"Which one would you rather have milk on?" I asked Kennie.

She rolled her eyes around and around in her head like a cartoon character. "Here's an idea! How about if I have a bowl of popcorn with soda on it instead?"

"Based on all the years you've known me, Kennie," I said, "what do you think my answer to that might be?"

"Owned," said Ethan.

"Shut up!" said Kenya, getting up out of bed and padding leadenly out of the room. "You can't blame a girl for trying," she said.

We all looked after her and then at one another. Ethan shook his head and went back to picking at the strings of his guitar.

"The apple does not fall far from the tree there," said my mother.

"Oh, here we go," I said. "You are not saying you think she is like me."

"Think? There's no think about it. She is you to a tee."

"Owned," said Ethan.

"Ethan, for God's sake," I said, "nobody asked you." I turned back to my mother. "If anything, I think Ethan's more like me," I said.

"Mom," said Ethan. "Holy crap, you're giving me a serious identity crisis!"

My mother burst out laughing. "I don't know why you're having so much trouble remembering, Clare. I'm pretty sure I never dropped you on your head."

"Oooh, good one, Gram," said Ethan.

I started to laugh. "You two are totally ganging up on me here. I'm going to call Ro and ask her opinion. She'll back me up." I waved my fingers at Ethan. "Give me your phone," I said.

"Don't get any germs on it," he said, handing it to me.

"Germs? Listen, I'll have you know, mister, I made every single cell in that body of yours," I said, dialing Rowena's cell number with my thumb.

"Mom, I've made a few on my own in the last eighteen years, alright?"

"Well, you got your all starter cells from me, and don't you forget it!" I said.

"Alright, I won't," said Rowena through the phone.

"Ro!" I said, "settle an argument for us. Which one of my kids is more like me?"

"Ooh," said Rowena, "this is one of those devil or angel questions, isn't it? I'm pretty sure you're not going to like my answer here, Clare. Hate to disappoint."

"What!" I said.

Ethan and my mother looked triumphantly at each other.

"Owned," said my mother, giving my son a wink.

I came in later to say goodnight to my mother and to see if she needed anything.

"No, I'm alright." she said.

As I turned to go, she said: "That was fun today, wasn't it?"

I stopped and looked at her. "It was," I said. "You really seem a lot better."

"I *feel* much better," she said. "I'm not sure why, because I haven't been sleeping much these past couple of days."

I counted the days in my head. "Remind me to change your sheets tomorrow," I said. I still hadn't found a way to sit and sing her the faery song. It made me feel stupid just thinking about it. I couldn't imagine how I was going to launch into it, apropos of nothing.

"It's been a long time since we sang together," I heard myself saying.

My mother smiled and nodded. "We used to sing every night before you went to sleep," she said.

"H-how about if I sing you a song now? Maybe it will help you sleep." I swallowed hard. My heart was pounding like mad in my chest.

My mother looked at me with surprise. Her eyes filled with tears. "That would be lovely, Clare."

I sat down in the wingback chair. "This is one you used to sing to me about the faeries."

And so I began. My mother and I looked at one another as I sang, the same as we had done earlier that day. And our eyes welled with tears the same as before. I was wrong about how hard it would be to sing aloud to my mother. It was the easiest thing in the world.

When I finished, she nodded, unable to speak, her eyes round and liquid. The emptiness that had been there only days before had vanished. Now her eyes were bright and full of warmth and gratitude.

"I sang that song when I was a little girl," she said, dabbing her eyes with a corner of the white sheet. "I loved the faeries. My mother used to warn me they would carry me off some day if I didn't watch out. Sometimes, she probably hoped they would." She twirled her finger in the fringe of her afghan.

"Why would you say that?" I asked.

"Oh, I was *quite* a handful when I was a kid," she said.

"You were? I can't even picture that."

"I had a real wild streak." She laughed. "Anything the other kids dared me to do, I did it!" She snapped her fingers in the air. "The trouble was, as I got older and into my teens, some of the boys mistook my spunkiness for something else."

"Oh," I said, "you mean they thought you were promiscuous?"

She nodded. "There was a boy in town that kind of

took a shine to me. Least that's what I thought. His name was Brian. His family had money. He had a nice car and all that. I thought I had really lucked out. I had all these ideas that he would marry me someday and we would live happily ever after. Big fancy house, expensive clothes, a *maid*!" She laughed. "What did I know? I was a stupid kid.

"One night he asked me to come to his house for a swim. I was thrilled. I had a brand new pink bathing suit I bought myself with the money I made at the ice cream shop. I told my mother I was going out with my girlfriends, and after work Brian picked me up and took me to his house. His parents weren't home, but that didn't bother me. We got in the pool and splashed around—silly stuff. We drank beer from the fridge. He lit candles. It felt really grown-up. I imagined we were married and this was our house. I thought this was what our life would be like someday.

"At some point, I remember, we were in the shallow end of the pool, and he started to play rough. At first I ignored it. Brian was a very polite kid. I thought he was just getting carried away—maybe didn't know his own strength—but then I said, hey, watch it, or something. But he didn't pull back, like I expected he would. Instead, he got rougher, and he took hold of my wrists. He was twisting them really hard until the skin burned and bending them behind my back. He started dunking me and holding me down so that I couldn't come up for air. I got really mad and knee-ed him in the chest, and as soon as I did that, something snapped in him.

"It's funny the things you remember when something terrible happens. What I remember most about that night was all the burning. Even though I was up to my neck in cold water, my insides felt like they were on fire. My lungs and nose and throat burned from inhaling so much water. Every time I screamed, he dunked me down again and when I gasped for air, I choked in more water. I thought I would drown before it was all over.

"He tore my suit off and I remember how it drifted and

bobbed on the water. I watched it move further and further away, imagining I was floating away inside it. I remember the sound of rushing water in my ears every time I went under, the chlorine in my nose, and the taste of the beer in my throat. Any one of those things still makes me sick to my stomach, to this day.

"At some point he jumped out of the water. I found my suit and put it on. I got out of the water and threw up in the grass. Then I threw up again. Brian handed me a beer and said: 'here, this will help.'"

My mother stopped speaking and closed her eyes.

I got up from the chair and sat down on the edge of her bed. I rested my hand on top of hers. In my mind, I did what the faery told me to do next. I imagined myself wrapping my mother's story up in white paper. I tied it with the string of a pink helium balloon, and watched it float away.

"I only told that story once before," she said. "I told your dad before we were married. I thought he should know, thought it might change how he felt about me. But after he heard the story, he said it didn't change anything, and that we didn't ever have to talk about it again."

"Well, thank you for telling me," I said, squeezing her hand.

"It was an awful thing to go through—the shame and disgust, the secrecy. I knew if I publicly accused Brian of raping me, I would end up paying a very big price. My whole family would. So I decided to pretend it never happened.

"Over the past couple of months, I've been realizing that far from making that rape into something that never happened, I enabled it to live on forever. I let it make me into a totally different person. Do you know what I mean?"

I nodded. "You let one night define every day that followed."

My mother's eyes filled with tears. "Yes," she said.

"Well," I said. "Then, you need a new story."

My mother laughed. "I think it's a little late for that."

"It's never too late for a new story. Or a new life."

She frowned and shook her head doubtfully.

I cleared my throat. "Once upon a time," I said, "there was a girl who loved faeries. She dreamed of faeries and talked and sang to them everyday. The girl's mother warned her that if she weren't careful, the faeries would come and take her away. Well, one day, the girl found herself in a terrible, dark place she couldn't get out of. She was backed into a corner with water all around her. She prayed that someone would save her. And, sure enough, that's just what the faeries did."

I felt my mother squeeze my hand.

I continued the story as I had seen it unfold in my journey. The first faery that met my mother was the river that held her in its arms. The second faery was the waterfall that carried her to safety. The third faery was the rainbow fish that taught her how to breathe underwater.

"And on the day it was time for her to return to her family," I said, in closing, "he promised to protect her and keep her safe forever and ever. The end."

My mother squeezed my hand again. Her eyes glistened with tears.

"Good story," she said, nodding her head.

"Aye," I said in my best brogue, "and wasn't it given to me by the faeries themselves?"

The next morning I was in the kitchen, toothbrush in hand, scrubbing the insides of my mother's coffee maker, which made the worst coffee I had ever tasted.

I heard someone coming down the stairs and turned to find my mother, fully dressed, standing behind me, a bundle of white sheets under her arm. I stopped, mid-scrub and stared.

She opened a nearby cabinet and pulled out a brown paper packet, "Here," she said, "you just need to descale it."

"Thanks," I said, still somewhat stunned to see her

standing there. "How are you feeling? Why don't you let me wash those for you?" I said, taking the sheets from her and tossing them into a laundry basket near the basement steps.

My mother walked to the center of the kitchen floor and sniffed the air. "Rotten potatoes," she said.

"Is *that* what that is?"

She bent down and reached into the cabinet under the range top where she kept her pots and pans and withdrew from the back corner a battered pot with a lid. "They say you should store them in a dark place," she said, holding the pot in front of her at arm's length.

"I'll take them out to the garbage can." I said, trying not to breathe as I carried them away. I pushed the screen door open with my foot and headed out towards the alley behind my mother's house.

"Throw the pot away, too!" she called after me.

"Oh, trust me, I'm not removing this lid!"

When I came back inside, I found my mother in the den, hands on her hips, surveying the ceiling.

"When did Dave say he'd be over to fix the roof?" she asked.

"Sometime next week, I think."

"Hand me the phone," said my mother.

I walked to a nearby side table, picked up the portable phone and brought it to her.

She dialed Dave's number and waited.

"Davey? It's your Aunt Lo. I'm good; how are you? Listen, when are you coming by to fix this roof? Unh-huh. No, I think that's too late, Davey, I really do. We took a real hit during this last storm. Unh-huh. Unh-huh. Hey, Davey? Who was it that always let you crash at her house when you were too drunk to let your dad see you? That's right. I know you are. So, we'll see you tomorrow morning, then? Of course, I know it's Sunday. You're going to work all day on the roof here and then you're staying for Sunday dinner. What? Yeah, she's here."

She handed me the phone. "Wants to talk to you," she said, walking breezily out of the room.

"Hello?" I said.

"What the fuck!" said Dave, laughing in the husky way smokers do.

"I know," I said. "Pretty crazy, huh?"

"She's ba-ack!" he said. "Man! I forgot what a wallop she packs when she gets going!"

I hung up the phone and came back into the kitchen, chuckling to myself.

"What?" said my mother, riffling through her bills.

"He said to tell you he'd be over as soon as he reattaches his face."

"Oh, he's ridiculous," she said, flapping her hand. "I saved that boy's life about a hundred times. If Uncle Bill had ever gotten a whiff of the alcohol on that kid's breath, he wouldn't have had a head to reattach it to."

I couldn't stop laughing. Tears filled my eyes. I felt giddy with relief to see my mother back to normal.

"I need to get out to the grocery store today, Clare. I thought I'd make a roast for the kids tomorrow," she was saying, as she sorted her mail into different stacks on the kitchen table. "And a nice chocolate cream pie. Doesn't that sound good? What? Why are you staring at me like that?"

As we made our way to the supermarket, I noticed a huge flea market sign and a crowd of people browsing through aisles of tables and tents.

"What's that flea market like?" I asked my mother. "Looks pretty popular."

"A little bit of everything," she said. "The Linens, Etc. place went out of business last year, so they opened up the parking lot to local vendors."

"Wow," I said. "You want to go?"

My mother raised her eyebrow. "I thought you hated

those things," she said.

I shrugged. "Ah, what the hell," I said. "It might be fun."

I swung the car into the adjacent lot, and we got out. The sun was blazing hot, but the sky was clear blue and the humidity had broken. A warm breeze blew through the market stalls, rustling the colorful garments on display.

From the minute I stepped out of the car, I picked up the steady thud of a drumbeat, which seemed so out of context that I stopped and looked over at my mother. "Is it me, or is someone drumming?" I asked.

"Oh," she said, reaching into the backseat for her handbag. "It's probably the guy who makes native drums. He comes here sometimes."

"No kidding!" I said. "Can we go?" I sounded as if I were ten years old.

My mother looked at me, amused. "Sure," she said, following behind me as I made a beeline for the drumming.

My mother soon veered off towards a large stall with used clothing. "I'll catch up to you in a bit," she called, waving her hand.

I waved back and made my way through the crowds until I found him. I had expected to find a Native American seller, but the drummer was a young man in his thirties with freckles, green eyes and carrot-colored hair. A copper-skinned woman in a cobalt blue ruffled skirt and red top sat beside him, wrapping beads around the handle of a gourd rattle.

"Hello," she said, looking up and smiling at me, before returning to her handiwork. She had beautiful, dark gleaming eyes, a full mouth and high cheekbones.

The man nodded at me and continued drumming.

The two of them sat near a display of six or eight drums, a crock full of beaters and a circle of rattles arranged like the spokes of a wheel.

"You made these yourself?" I asked.

The redheaded man stopped drumming and got up

from his lawn chair.

"I make the drums and beaters. My wife makes the rattles."

"They're beautiful. May I try out the drums?"

"Of course. The ones along the top are buffalo hide, these are elk, and this one is horse."

I looked down at a large blond-colored drum. I stared at it for a moment and then picked it up. I chose one of the beaters from the jar and began to beat softly on it.

When I closed my eyes, I could see a grey horse standing in a paddock, looking back at me.

"Here," said the man, who was standing at my elbow with another drum in his hand. "My wife says if you want a horse, you should have a wild one."

I looked down. The drum in his hand took my breath away. Its skin was half brown and half white.

I set down the first drum and carefully took the one he offered me. "How did you find this hide?" I asked, rubbing the flat of my hand over it.

"I trained with a native man up in Minnesota. I get most of my hides from him. This was a pinto that died in the wild," he said.

I picked up the beater and played the drum. The sound was round and strong, and it made me grin from ear to ear just hearing it. I knew I had found my drum.

After a moment, I stopped playing and held it to my chest, my arms crisscrossed over the frame. "I'll take it," I said, laughing. "How much is it?"

"That's one-eighty," he said.

"Here," said my mother, who appeared suddenly at my elbow. She gave the man two one hundred dollar bills.

"Mom," I said, "you don't have to do that!"

My mother shook her head. "No, I insist," she said, as the man went to get her change. "I've bought you so many things in your life that weren't right for you, Clare. It feels good to finally give you something you obviously love."

The day before we left Ohio, I made one last trip to the woods.

I found a tree with low, accessible branches and hoisted myself up, climbing as far as I dared through the leafy overhead net. I hung some wind chimes I had bought at the flea market, and secured them to a branch with wire. They looked beautiful, and sounded even better when I dragged them across my fingers.

I also tied a strip of flowery pink cloth onto one of the branches to keep the prayer of my mother's recovery alive.

Then I descended carefully to the ground, sprinkled rose petals from my pocket into the brook and sat by the water for a while, drumming quietly.

I didn't see the faery again, though I squinted my eyes and sang her song and waited patiently. It didn't matter. I knew she would show up again if I needed her, just as all of my helping spirits had done throughout this long and troubled year.

In a few months time, it would be one year since Daniel's death, and it seemed that all year my heart had been healing and growing a whole new layer of skin.

But I suppose that was to be expected. If my heart were cut in half, maybe the inside would look just like the concentric rings of a tree, one for each year of life. And like a tree reacting to its own environment, I imagined the outer ring of my heart would be a little wider and the skin a little thicker, because although there had been much rain and cold this year, there had also been a great deal of light.

Chapter Twelve
Willow: **Grace**

Fall was closing in. In a week my sabbatical would be over and I would be back at the university teaching art classes. My class schedule was full this semester with two sections of ceramics and one of sculpture, plus a lab on glazing techniques. I would only have one weekday free, and limited room to schedule Kenya's own classes and tutoring.

She had asked to take guitar and wood carving in addition to the Algebra, Science, English and Social Studies tutoring she was getting from two unemployed college graduates I had hired to each work one day a week with her. Kenya and I had also decided to take a yoga class together.

Ethan was still unsettled, and had taken a job delivering pizzas for a local shop while he contemplated his next move. He had wanted to stay in Ohio and look after my mother, but she wouldn't hear of it.

"You need to be with kids your own age," she said, "not hanging out with some crazy old lady who can't find her glasses."

I drove down to Middleton in order to get my studio ready for the following week and to check on all the supplies I had ordered. I was sorting through some boxes in the hallway when the department head, Leslie Brill, came up behind me.

"Clare," she said, "you came back!"

She hugged me tightly. Leslie was a short, overweight woman with a round florid face and watery green eyes. Every time I saw her, she seemed to be racing somewhere. She reminded me of the rabbit in *Alice in Wonderland*.

"W-why wouldn't I be back?" I asked.

"Well, you know Tal and Gina both left, right?" She put her hand on her waist. She was breathing heavily as if she had just run across campus.

"I heard. Are you okay? Do you want some water or something?" I handed her my water bottle. She waved away my offer.

"Just like that they went," she said, snapping her fingers. "No warning from either of them. It's got me scrambling to fill their slots, I'll tell you. If you had decided not to come back, I don't know what I would have done."

"Oh, I'm sure you'd have managed," I said lightly. "Lots of people out there looking for jobs right now."

"So, then, you *were* thinking about leaving?"

"Well, no, Leslie, I wasn't. I was just saying—."

"You've been through a lot of changes, Clare, we understand that." She took my elbow in her hand. "You're not the same person you were before. It wouldn't have been unexpected."

"Oh, well. I guess. I hadn't really thought about it that way," I said, looking with casual interest into one of the cartons at my feet. "So listen, with Tal out of the picture, what's been happening with the gallery show we were planning for November? Do you have a replacement?"

Leslie looked up and closed her eyes. "Oh, God," she said, "I completely forgot about the show. Can you go it alone?"

I shook my head. "I didn't come close to finishing the amount of work I'd planned to do last year. But I can maybe find someone else, if you like. Somebody local—non-faculty?"

"That's fine! Great. Have them send me a proposal next week, can you?"

"Ah, sure. No problem."

Leslie hugged me again. "You're wonderful. I can always rely on you, Clare," she said, "It's so good to have you back."

"Thanks, Leslie. I appreciate that."

We smiled and waved to each other, as she trudged off down the hallway, her heels clicking on the linoleum. I peered again into a carton of clay at my feet and sighed.

"Fuck," I said.

Leslie was right, of course. I wasn't the same person. The thought that I would simply pick up again at Middleton where I'd left off a year ago, was unrealistic, and, if I were honest with myself, completely unappealing. I hadn't confront-ed the feelings of resistance that had been churning around in my stomach for the last several weeks. I needed to think about who I was now, and what kind of a life suited me, because the person I was before Daniel died, no longer existed.

I pulled out a shrink-wrapped block of clay and checked the date stamp on the side. Sometimes the supplier sent old stock, and I always wanted to make certain the clay we worked with was fresh.

Maybe that's what I needed to do with my life right now—demand fresh new clay to work with and nothing less.

"May new and wonderful things come into my life," I said, reaching down to slice open a carton of ceramic glazes.

"Wow, what luck!" said someone behind me. "I can't believe I'm running into you like this."

I turned around to find Jack Woods waving a slip of yellow paper in his hand and grinning at me.

I was so startled, I backed up against the box I was unpacking and almost fell into it. He reached out and took my arm to steady me. We both started laughing.

"Are you okay? Jeez, I don't usually have such an alarming effect on women," he said.

"Well, you're really starting to weird me out," I said, straightening my shirt. "You keep materializing in the most unexpected places." I took the paper from his hand. "What's this?"

"I wanted to sign up for your ceramics class, but it's closed out. Do you think you could let me in?" He was rocking back and forth on his heels, like a young suitor, hands clasped behind his back.

"Now, why would you want to take ceramics?" I asked.

"I'm taking a course in art therapy this semester, and I thought it would be good to take an art class alongside it."

I nodded. "Interesting. Wouldn't you be better off taking a drawing or painting class?"

"Maybe, but I've always wanted to take ceramics," he said.

"Really?"

"Yes. Definitely."

"Now why is that?"

He cleared his throat. "Why? Well...." He rubbed the sleeve of his shirt across his forehead. "Wow, you really have some strict interrogation techniques for your prospective students, don't you?"

We both started to laugh again.

"No, seriously," he said, loosening his tie. "I'm like sweating here. Is this normal procedure for latecomers?"

"I'm sorry. I was really just curious."

"Well, as it turns out, I collect pottery. I thought if I tried my hand at it, I might appreciate the things I've collected a bit more. Have a greater sense of their artistry."

"Good answer," I said, taking the pen he offered, "I'll sign your waiver."

"Thanks," he said. "I probably owe you a coffee or something for that."

"You probably do." I handed him his waiver and pen.

He cleared his throat. "Are you free now, by any chance?"

"I'm not, actually. I've got to go through all these supplies and clean out my studio. Get everything in order." I shrugged.

Jack looked down at the boxes. "Can I help you move these?" he asked.

"Wow, that would be great. The janitor just dropped them here because he didn't have his keys with him. This is my studio here," I said, pointing behind us.

He spent a few minutes dragging boxes from the hallway into my studio. I tried to help him, but he insisted on doing it all himself.

I stood watching him with my arms folded. Each time he left the room, I shook my head and laughed to myself. I needed to call Rowena. She was never going to believe this.

"There," said Jack, putting the last one down inside the door. "Anything else I can do for you?"

"No. That was a huge help. You're very kind."

"Oh, I was just trying to suck up to the teacher," he said lightly, brushing some dust off his slacks.

"I don't think so," I said.

He looked up at me with his sparkly brown eyes. We stared at one another for a moment and my heart started to thrum.

"You helped me because you're a kind and thoughtful person. I've noticed that about you. You were kind to Kennie and kind to Aidan, too," I said. "I admire that."

He smiled and looked down. "Oh, well, I was taught to be kind to others. My dad was a very generous guy, and I try to honor that, you know, carry on the good he brought to his life—now that he's gone."

"That's lovely," I said. "I should suggest that idea to my kids—maybe they can each think of something to carry on from their father."

"It's helped me to live that way—tying the past to the future," he said, looking intently at me as if strands of disconnected past and future threads were waving visibly in my eyes.

I stared back at him. "You're a deep guy, Mr. Woods," I said. "Anybody ever tell you that?"

He shrugged. "Deep is where things get really interesting," he said. "Don't you agree?"

I smiled. "I do."

He nodded as if he had learned something just then or gained some reassurance he was looking for. "And that's the other reason I wanted to sign up for your class," he said.

"Oh, I see how it is," I said, laughing.

"Look," he said, "I'd just like to get to know you better is all, and I think, if I'm right about this, I think you would like to know me better, too. Am I right?"

I blushed and looked down at my feet. I wiggled my toes around the strap of my sandals and cleared my throat. "I would say you were right about that, yes."

"I knew it!" he said, triumphantly shaking his fist. He was grinning like a teenage boy as he turned to leave the studio.

"Hey, don't forget about that coffee you owe me," I said.

He stood in the doorway and looked at me for another moment. "Oh, I won't forget," he said.

Then he walked away down the hall, whistling and waving his yellow slip of paper proudly in his hand.

When I got back to my car after unpacking all my supplies and putting my studio into order, I noticed there was a message from Sally on my cell phone. We hadn't spoken in a few weeks and I was anxious to hear how she was doing. In her voicemail, she said she had a favor to ask me. I called her back before leaving the parking lot.

It was a beautiful, balmy day outside but the inside of my car was sweltering. I was sweaty and tired from all the work I had done. I opened the car door for some air, turned sideways in the car seat and stuck my feet out onto the asphalt.

"Oh, Clare," Sally said, "it's great to hear from you!"

"How are you doing?" I asked.

"I'm doing okay," she said. "Not great, but okay. And I think that's enough for right now."

"Sally, I think that's more than enough. I think it's amazing."

"Well, you really helped me a lot. I'm not sure I'd be where I am without you."

My eyes welled. "Well, thanks, Sally," I said, getting out of the hot car and heading towards the grass nearby. "It didn't seem like all that much." I spotted a weeping willow tree waving its tasseled branches over the ground and walked over to sit beneath it.

"It was, and that's kind of what I was calling you about. I belong to this grief support group for parents who have lost their children, and the sessions are pretty tough, but I've gotten close to a few of the other mothers. I told them about all you did for Aidan and me, and we decided we would like to have you come and talk to us."

"Me? What about?" I asked.

"About death and the after-life and where souls go. We want to understand where our children have gone, and how we can stay connected to them, but still go on with our lives."

I reached up and took hold of a willow branch that brushed across my head in the breeze. "Wow. That's a lot, Sally," I said. "I'm not sure I'm the one for the job though."

"Oh, you're the one for the job, Clare," said Sally. "That's the only part I'm sure about."

I looked up into the shelter of the willow and the blue

sky beyond it. I thought about the prayer I had whispered to myself earlier, asking for new things to come into my life. What sense would it make to say no to Sally's request?

"Alright," I said. "Give me a day or so to figure out what to do and how to do it."

"Oh, thank you, Clare! Come and have tea with me on Saturday morning, and we'll plan it out."

I ended the call and lay back on the cool grass.

"Okay, wise old willow," I said. "How do I help Sally's group?"

The willow shuddered its long limbs in the breeze. The sunlight glinted off its green tasseled branches.

"You do what I do—you cry for the ones who can't cry for themselves."

"And that helps?" I asked.

"Compassion always helps. It's puts suffering into a form that can be digested."

"Is that it?"

"Teach them how to journey."

"I love that he's so chivalrous. You can't find guys like that these days. And he clearly has a good sense of humor. He's interested in the same things you are. He's cute as hell. I mean, what's not to like?" asked Rowena. "I think this is good stuff here, Clare. I think this is very good stuff."

Rowena had come over for dinner. We were sitting out on my front porch swing, sipping wine while the pasta sauce bubbled on the stove.

"Well, we don't know what his intentions are. Maybe Jack Woods is just a kind and friendly person," I said, popping a cracker into my mouth.

"Don't be ridiculous. '*I'd like to get to know you better and I think you would like to know me better, too?*' Are you kidding me, Clare? This guy wants to go to bed with you."

"Ro! For pity's sake," I said, looking into the windows

beside the swing. "My kids will hear you."

"Look, haven't I always been good at spotting the ones who had the hots for you?"

"Yes, and they were usually the biggest dweebs in town. Most of the time, I didn't actually *want* to know that these guys had the hots for me. Remember Clark Langtree? He made a whistling sound when he breathed. Right? What was that about?"

Rowena laughed. "Deviated septum or something."

"Or something. And Adam Carmichael? He was a rocker—but not in a good way. He rocked back and forth when he talked to you. And he was always hitching his pants up with his wrists."

Rowena closed her eyes and shook with laughter. "God, you have such a good memory. How do you remember all this stuff?"

"Because you told me these guys were in love with me! I felt responsible for them, Ro. I still worry about them—I mean, how did they get on in life? I picture Adam with a bunch of little sons who also rock and hitch—in perfect unison."

"Not to be outdone by those Whistling Langtrees," said Rowena, dabbing her eyes.

"No, of course not."

Rowena refilled our wine glasses. "So tell me what else has been happening. Any word from Hal?"

"Only to pressure me about making a decision on Cynthia's offer."

Rowena leaned back and crossed her arms. "And what *is* your decision?"

"I don't know yet. I keep feeling like I want more answers. Like something is missing, and I need to know what that is before I can make the right decision."

Rowena sighed and looked out at the cars going by my house. "You want to know what I think?" she said.

"You're going to tell me anyway, aren't you?" I said,

slicing more cheese from the wedge of cheddar we were eating.

"Well, yeah," she said. "Look, I don't think it matters what you don't know. I don't think it matters what Daniel was up to or where the rest of the money went. I think it matters more that you move on now and be done with all this. Start the new life you were given when Daniel died. I say, take her offer and end it."

I nodded. "There's something about that idea that appeals to me. Don't think there isn't. I'm just not there yet. Something keeps holding me to this struggle."

"Like what?"

I sipped my wine. "It feels like knowing more will finally settle things and bring me a sense of relief."

"I don't know. I hope you're right," said Rowena, "But, personally, I think information is highly overrated. Maybe you're not supposed to know all about what was going on behind the scenes. Maybe it wouldn't change anything— maybe it's irrelevant."

"Maybe," I said, getting up to put a pot of water on the stove. I slid my feet into my flip-flops and patted Rowena on the arm. "Listen, I hear you. I'll think about what you said."

"You better," said Rowena, stacking a slice of cheese between two crackers. "People pay good money for that shit."

I thought if I made a model of the carving Kenya and I had done on the birch tree in the woods, I might have enough pieces to fill the show I was having at the university in November. I took my drawing pad and some pencils and tramped out to the woods to make a copy, but I stopped midway on the path when I saw Ethan sitting on the stone bench, head in hands.

I stood still, watching him for a moment, wondering whether it was best to invade his privacy and go and sit with him, or just leave him alone. After a moment I quietly turned to go but didn't feel like I could leave. I thought about the day Aidan had come out to the woods, perhaps the last time I'd seen him, how goofy and boyish he had been. How utterly endearing as always. It was no wonder Ethan missed him. *I* missed him.

"I know you're there, Mom," said Ethan, not turning.

"Oh, I'm sorry, Ethan. I was about to leave but then I started thinking about Aidan."

Ethan looked at me. "Yeah, me too," he said.

I went to the bench and set my things down. "Slide over," I said.

"There's not a shitload of room here, you know."

"There's enough," I said, sitting down and putting my arm around Ethan's shoulder.

The two of us stared at the carved tree with its scattering of offerings underneath. Kenya liked to bring flowers and pretty stones to leave here. I always brought a pocketful of lavender or tobacco.

"You're very lucky, Ethan," I said. "You've had a rich life filled with good people."

"I'm not exactly passing into the great beyond yet, Mom," said Ethan, looking at me with a raised eyebrow.

"No, I know you're not, Ethan. But you've still been lucky."

"I don't know," said Ethan, "I'm not really feeling the lucky thing right now."

"Doesn't mean it isn't true."

Ethan shook his head and bent forward, one elbow on each knee.

"Lost is pretty much what I feel," he said.

I kissed him on the side of his head. "You're not lost, sweetie. You're right here."

"You're not listening to me, Mom."

We stared at one another. I made a puzzled expression. "I thought I was."

"No, you're doing that thing you always do where you

just gloss over what people are saying and put your own spin on it. That doesn't make it so, Mom."

"Oh, I'm sorry. Tell me what you mean by lost then. What are you lost about?"

"Duh! My dad and my best friend both die in the same year. How fucked up is that?"

"You're right. It's pretty fucked up," I said.

"I should have driven him home, Mom. I've been over it a hundred times in my head."

"Oh, Ethan," I said, pulling him closer, "the world in which you drive Aidan home the night he died is a world that doesn't exist. The only world you have is this one right here, the one without him."

"But I don't want this world, Mom. I don't want a world without Aidan and Dad. I just don't." His eyes spilled over with tears.

"It's hard living without the people we love, but that doesn't mean we can't do it. In a way, I think we owe it to Dad and Aidan to live our lives better than we did before, to live for us and them, too. Do you know what I mean?"

Ethan sniffed, wiped his face with the back of his hand and said nothing.

"I was talking to Mr. Woods yesterday. You remember him from Hillington? Well, his dad died when he was a teenager, and what he does is try to live out some of the things his dad taught him about being kind and helping others. He feels that honors his memory and carries on his father's life. Maybe if you thought about what Dad and Aidan each taught you or about emulating the best parts of who they were, you might feel better about living in a world without them. It would be a way of keeping some part of them alive."

Ethan pressed his palms against his eyes. "I don't know. Everything kind of seems like a waste."

"Life can seem that way," I said, "I've felt that way plenty of times."

"Have you?"

"Sure," I said.

"So, what do you do about it?"

I didn't say anything for a while. I thought about his question and the two of us sitting there together. I looked over at Finn and the carving Kenya had helped me with. I could point out every stroke that was hers, and it seemed like a little miracle on that tree.

"Do you remember when I was sick a couple years ago?" I asked.

He nodded.

"Did you know that I almost died?"

He looked up at me. "You?"

"Me," I said. "I could actually feel myself slipping away from my life. It was like standing on the edge of a chasm. One night I was going to sleep and I saw myself staring down into that chasm. It was so mesmerizing; I couldn't take my eyes off of it. I was really tired and I had this thought that if I fell asleep right then, I wouldn't be able to stop myself from falling in. It seemed like it would be so easy just to do that—so freeing. And then all of a sudden I did. I started to fall and fall, but then the air blew up and held me. I kept getting handed from one updraft to the other, and they kept asking me, do you want us to keep holding you or let you fall? I said, no, I didn't want to fall. And then this great wind blew up from below and I landed back up on the ground above."

Ethan was staring into my face. "Then what happened?"

"Then I walked away from the edge and I never went back. I realized death was a choice. And I decided I wanted to live."

"Are you saying Aidan and Dad chose to die?"

"I don't know. Ethan. I'm trying to tell you what seemed so clear to me in that moment. Maybe it's not so clear anymore. I think the line between this world and the next is so thin, you know, and our hold here so tenuous. I don't think it's a failure to let go, because it takes enormous strength and courage to keep living. Life is a choice, but we have to keep choosing it."

"Choose it or lose it?"

I started to laugh. "I guess so."

Ethan shook his head. "Wow, Mom," he said, "way to shoot the crap out of my existential moment."

I had spoken to Dill about showing his work along with mine in the art show at the university. He was reluctant at first, but I talked him into letting me photograph about ten random pieces from his shop that I thought would make a wonderful exhibit.

"You just don't see them as exhibit-worthy. But promise me you'll look at the photos first and then decide."

I photographed twelve of his best pieces against a dark green backdrop that made the copper components in them sing. I presented them to Dill in a beautiful binder with plastic sleeves over each one of the photographs.

"Wow. This is my shit?" he asked. "Looks pretty good. Looks *damn* good." He paged through the binder, nodding and smiling.

"So?" I asked. "Do I need to guilt-trip you into this by telling you if you don't join me, I won't be able to show either?"

"No," he said. "I'll do it. I'm just not sure how to thank you for taking the time to do all this. I never would have done this myself."

"I know," I said, "but you don't need to thank me. We help each other out—right?"

"You went to a lot of trouble," he said. He was now paging through the booklet for the third time.

"I did not! I do this kind of thing all the time. But if you really, really feel indebted, you *can* do me a big favor."

He grinned. "Oh, here it comes."

I tugged on his sleeve. "I want you to help me figure

out what to put in my show. It's all a big mish mash right now.
I have some older pieces I did almost two years ago. I have the
shapeshifting piece I did of the eagle man. Then I've got this
Icarus thing I did and the tree carving I've started working on
in clay and copper, not to mention some new sketches I've
been doing over the last month that I could put into clay. I'm
just in a muddle about how to bring it all together."

"Alright," he said, following me into my studio.

I pulled the covers off some sculptures I had stored up
on the shelf—one of Sumeh, one of Bear and me. Then I
unveiled the head and shoulders of a half eagle, half man
sculpture, to which I had added beading and gold leaf. In the
center of the room on a pedestal was Icarus, my three dimen-
sional poem of Daniel. There was a partially finished tree
trunk in clay and copper wiring, which was cut away at the
back so that it could be mounted on the wall. Coils of roots
hung down from one corner and two branches reached up and
over one side, framing the face carved into the trunk. As I had
worked on it, I realized that the face that wanted to come out
was not the face of the girl Kenya and I had carved together,
but the face of Finn, the spirit inside the tree.

"I'm adding silk leaves to the branches," I said. "And
then there's these sketches I did while I was in Ohio that I'm
thinking of putting into clay." I flipped open my sketchpad.
One was of a horse head carved inside the frame of a drum;
the other was a drawing of my faery friend, Verena. I tore the
horse out of the book and laid the drawings beside one
another. "I'm thinking the horse head will be a wall mount."

Dill looked at everything carefully, but still said nothing. He had his arms folded across his chest, one hand holding
onto his ponytail, a posture I had seen him take before. It
seemed to help him think.

I went over to the Icarus sculpture and brushed some
stray flecks of dried clay from the base. "I feel like this piece
is the star of the show and I'm hoping I can find a central
theme that will pull all these other pieces around it." I looked

over at Dill again and waited. He knitted his brows and scratched his forehead. Then he went back and looked at all the pieces again.

"Okay," he said after awhile. "I don't think you're going to like what I have to say."

"I'm not?"

"I don't know. To me, that piece," he said, pointing to the one I still had my hand on, the one of Daniel, "isn't the star of the show. I don't even think it *belongs* in the show."

"You're kidding?"

"No, I don't even see you in this piece—it's like you're not at home here. But, you're completely present in all these other ones. This one of Icarus feels flat to me—no mojo—you know what I mean? All these others, though, like this one of the bear cradling the woman in his lap—I mean, it's like some weird, powerful take on the Pieta. And the look of wisdom and tenderness here on this dude's face—who is this, by the way?" He pointed to the bust of Sumeh.

"Uh, that's my spirit guide."

"Your spirit guide? Man—*he's* the star of the show, Clare, not this dude." He flicked his thumb at Icarus.

We were quiet for a few moments while I let his words sink in. They sunk quietly without any resistance. I knew what he said was right.

Dill walked over to the Icarus sculpture. He picked it up off the stand and took it over to the shelf. Then he brought the bust of Sumeh to the center of the room and slid it onto the pedestal. He lined up the other pieces around it—Bear, Eagle, and Finn, and the drawing of the horse—and propped up my sketchpad so that Verena and her wild hairdo could join the group. "That's your show, Clare."

Dill pointed to the winged man I was calling "Icarus Ascending." "This you need to let go of. This is the thing that was jamming up your signals. You had to get him out of your head, and you did that, but this isn't who you are. It's who you used to be."

My eyes teared up. "You think? What makes you so sure?"

"Because I pay attention to things," he said, pointing to those laser blue eyes of his. "I'm a jungle fighter, Clare—not much escapes my notice."

I had expected to hear from Hal. The continuance he had secured for us in July would end soon, and I hadn't yet come to any decision on Cynthia's offer.

My cell phone rang as I was leaving my studio. I saw Hal's name on the screen. "Bloody hell," I said, "here we go."

I clicked a button. "Hal," I said.

"Clare. Listen, have you made any decisions about the offer?"

"No, I haven't, no. I've been trying not to think about it actually."

"Well, that seems like a wise plan," said Hal. "I'm going to have to talk to the judge in a week or so, you know?"

"I know, I know."

There was a pause while Hal and I both waited for me to say something more.

"Well, I have a bit of an offer here from Cynthia I'm not sure you're going to like." he said. "I think they're just trying to move things along."

"More money?" I asked.

"No, not more money. Cynthia is suggesting a meeting between the two of you—no lawyers."

I cleared my throat. "A meeting? What for?"

"To discuss the settlement, I would presume. You should take her up on it."

"Well, Hal, it's not like an offer to go shopping for shoes together. We don't even know each other."

"In a manner of speaking you know each other pretty well, Clare. Look, you want my advice? Save yourself a lot of headaches and legal fees, sit down with her and hammer something out. You need to move on, Clare."

"Jeez, if I had a nickel for everybody who keeps telling me that," I said.

"Well enough said then," said Hal. "I have a cell phone number for her. Do you want it or not?"

So here I was.

We were meeting at Dunkin' Donuts. The whole thing could not have been tackier. I arrived a half hour early, purchased a cup of tea at the counter, and then walked up and down the row of booths and tables, carefully examining each one to determine which offered me the best vantage point. The optimal seat for this encounter was clearly the one at the table in the corner but a small woman in a dark suit had already taken it.

I sat down at the table diagonally in front of hers and took out my book, which I already knew I would not be able to read. The book—which was only a prop really—was written by a highly respected author and had won the Man Booker Prize. I had spent some time selecting it as one that would suggest a certain level of sophistication in the person reading it. The cover was elegant, the title mysterious-sounding, and I hoped some of its mystique would rub off on me.

I had also been selective about what I wore, deciding finally on a pair of black trousers, a black cashmere cardigan, a white blouse and flat shoes, to which I had added the diamond stud earrings Daniel had bought me for our first anniversary, a gold bangle bracelet, and a lavender scarf.

I had put some of Kenya's styling gel in my hair and spiked it out a bit, then softened the edges with a hairdryer. I put on extra eyeliner to accentuate my steel gray eyes and a pale shade of lipstick to tone down my too wide mouth.

The book and the tea were in front of me, my fingers pressed against the pages of the paperback to keep it from flopping closed. I lifted my head as someone came in the door and felt the woman behind me lift hers. We both stared at the two teenage boys who came in arguing about how many donuts they could buy with the money they had between them. Then I felt her staring at me.

I turned in my seat to look at her.

"Clare?" she said.

"Cynthia?"

We both laughed. "I was so early," she said, "I didn't even think—." She stood up and walked over to me, her hand extended.

"Me, too," I said, shaking her hand. "I didn't think you would be here so soon."

We stopped and stared at one another. I was startled by the resemblance between us. She was a smaller woman, about six inches shorter and finer-boned. Her hair was long and curly, the way I used to wear mine. Her eyes were lighter, but her mouth and the structure of her face were very similar. The skin tone and hair color were the same.

"Well, may I join you?" she asked. She smiled shyly in an effort to hide her awkwardness, as I did the same.

"Of course," I said, "although I think yours is the better table."

"Well, let's take that one then," she said cheerfully, as if we were about to sit down to a game of cards.

I gathered my things together, walked back to her table and sat down. After the flurry of our meeting and laughing and me moving my things, we settled into our seats, smiled at one another and then had no idea what to say. We both looked down at the table between us.

"So," she said, looking at her hands, which were nervously cradling her tea.

"So," I said, sighing.

I looked up at Cynthia and saw that her eyes were filled with tears. Oh Lord, I thought. I wasn't expecting this. Was she going to launch into some big sob story with me?

She sniffed and dabbed her eyes with the back of her

hand. "Look at me. You probably think I'm about to launch into some big sob story here."

"No. Not at all," I said. "It's difficult. Why don't we both take a deep breath and just try and get through it?"

She nodded and I waited. She took a sip of tea and cleared her throat.

"I'm so sorry about all this," she said. "I wasn't working with a full story."

"Join the club," I said, and then regretted interrupting her with my bitter remark.

She inhaled and shut her eyes. "I'd like to begin at the beginning, if that's alright?"

"Go on," I said.

"I met Daniel through work. I work for a company that installs integrated office systems, and we were doing a job for Strickner, Hall, and Goldblatt."

"How long ago was this?" I asked.

"Two years ago. Anyway, I used to keep to myself and eat my lunch in the employee's kitchen, and after a few weeks, Daniel started coming in and eating his lunch there too."

The idea of Daniel eating in the employee lunchroom at his brokerage firm rather than joining his cronies for a three martini lunch at one of Hartford's executive hangouts was so out of character, it made his premeditated conquest of this woman almost laughable.

"I knew he was married, but he told me that his wife was very ill. He said he just wanted someone to talk to and couldn't share any of what he was going through with his colleagues. So that's how we began. He actually talked a lot about you. He told me about your art and how talented you were, what a great cook you were and a good mother. He seemed very proud of you and heartbroken to be losing you."

It was nice to know that my husband spoke well of me to his mistress. It was creepy to learn he used my illness to invoke sympathy and ingratiate himself with her. It was a little like being handed a gift-wrapped box of dog poop.

"We went from lunches to dinners," she continued, "and spent a lot of time talking. I knew I was developing feelings for him and thought it was probably best if I broke things off between us. Initially, he agreed. But, then he kept asking me out to dinner. He left me gifts that I returned to him. And then, sometime around August, he came and told me they were putting you into hospice."

I sat back as if the force of this revelation had literally shoved me into the seat. Healthwise, things didn't start to turn around for me until the fall of that year, but I guess the suspense was really getting to Daniel. He jumped to what he assumed was my foregone conclusion.

"God, that's wrong on so many levels," I said, shaking my head in disbelief. "So, did I actually die?"

"In November." she said.

I began to laugh. "I'm sorry," I said. "I'm just thinking how bummed out he must have been when I started to get better, and here he was already committed to this other—you know, story."

She stared at me, without cracking a smile.

I cleared my throat. "When did you realize I was still alive?"

"When I read his death notice. I know—stupid, right? I hadn't heard from Daniel that weekend. He was supposed to be home for dinner on Saturday. I called and called his cell, and then I finally called the office Monday to track him down. His secretary told me. I went to the newspaper to see where the service was being held. I think I read the part that said 'survived by his loving wife, Clare' about forty-seven times. And then of course your papers came, saying you were filing suit."

"When you say 'home' for dinner, do you mean your place?"

Her face flushed with embarrassment. "Oh, yes, we were living together. I mean, at least I thought we were. He traveled a lot, but I guess that was when he was home with you."

"Yes, there was travel on my end as well," I said. "So where did my children fit into this story? You knew about them, surely?"

"Yes," she said. "What he said was that your mother had taken custody of them, and that she had been caring for them during the months you were sick. He said she never liked him and had talked you into requesting that the kids be turned over to her after your death. And that he had complied because he thought it was best for them."

"Jeez, I'm disappointed in him," I said. "He lifted that part right out of *Terms of Endearment*."

Again, Cynthia didn't laugh. "I consoled him," she said. "I consoled him through all of this. And he *made it up*." Her eyes welled with tears.

I frowned. Yes, I felt kind of sorry for her, but after all, hadn't he killed my character off in order to give her the starring role? And what about my kids? I leaned across the table.

"What did he imagine he was doing? Was he going to just walk away from his kids?" I asked, barely disguising my indignation.

"No, he would never have done that. He kept saying he hoped he would regain visitation rights and that someday they would be able to come and stay with us, but all that was very delicate and he had to be careful. He said he was trying his best to get back into your mother's good graces, but if she found out about me, it would destroy his chances of ever seeing his kids again. Obviously, I respected the seriousness of the situation. He was only able to be with me part of the time because the kids needed him. The plan was that I would live in the house in Arizona and he would fly back and forth. I was all set to move out there when it happened."

"Dear God," I said. "What a fucking mess he created here. It's like something a child would do. How did he think he was ever going to get away with this?"

She shook her head. "I-I don't know," she said.

"And how was he planning to finance the whole thing —living in two states? What about his job?"

"He was waiting for some investment to pan out."

"I beg your pardon?"

"He had given a good bit of seed money to some start-up. An electronics company, I think. A couple of weeks before Daniel died, he got some news that things weren't going so well with the investment."

"Wait, does the name Jerry Bender figure into this story by any chance?"

"Yes, his investment partner was a guy named Jerry. Both of them put money into this venture, apparently. But it didn't work out, and Daniel was really, really upset."

I sat back and shook my head. Jerry Bender—now why hadn't I seen that coming? Jerry was an old college buddy, a get-rich-quick-schemer and a total loser, and he and Daniel made a very lethal combination. Daniel had lost money years before on a new type of home insulation that Jerry's brother-in-law was developing. It was going to revolutionize the industry and make millions, they said, until Jerry's brother-in-law realized that someone else had already patented his "secret ingredient". I called Jerry the Nowhere Man because that's where all his schemes eventually ended up—nowhere.

"Well, that explains a lot," I sighed. "I'll have Hal look into it."

I sat shaking my head, trying to absorb everything Cynthia had just told me.

Cynthia watched me. "I've shocked you," she said.

"Oh, I don't know about that. I've ceased being surprised at the level of folly Daniel was capable of. I actually feel kind of sorry for him."

Cynthia looked surprised. "What he did was terrible, Clare. I had no idea he was someone who would do something like that to his family."

"Well, he lied to you, too, didn't he?" I said.

"It's not the same," said Cynthia. "What he did to you

was un*con*scionable."

I stared at her. She was being completely sincere with me. She had more compassion for me than I had for her. Did I really deserve it?

"Thanks for saying that," I said.

"Listen, I think you should be aware of something else," said Cynthia. "I'm pretty sure Kenya knows about me."

"Knows about you? Why? How?"

"She apparently took Daniel's cell phone after he died. She said she found it in his coat."

I blinked and stared down at the table. "Shit. I figured there had to be another cell phone, but I never found it."

Cynthia nodded. "Well, Kenya had it. She called it Daddy's secret phone. She kept it because I think she thought she might actually be able to talk to him on it. I guess that sounds crazy."

"No," I said, "it sounds totally like Kenya. So you spoke to her then?"

"Yes. I spoke to her a number of times actually. Please don't be upset with me. I think she kept calling me because she missed Daniel, and she knew that I knew him. She never really asked me how—maybe she picked up all the frantic messages I'd left during the two days after Daniel died. I don't know. I haven't spoken to her for some months. I closed the account."

"What would she say to you when she called?"

"She would ask me if I knew the same things about Daniel that she knew. Did I know that he made really good pancakes? Did I know he liked to play Trivia? Did I know what his favorite color was? Those kinds of things. I'm sorry. I should never have answered the phone in the first place, but I thought it was probably you calling, and I figured, let's just get all this out in the open right now. But it was Kenya, missing her dad, and I just couldn't hang up on her, or ignore her."

Cynthia and I looked at one another. "I-I understand," I said. "I'm sure you did the right thing."

"I never wanted to cause more harm than—well, you know—than was already done," said Cynthia, pushing a stray curl out of her eyes. "When the papers first came, I was on my way to Arizona. I shoved them into my bag and didn't look at them for weeks. Then I got this lawyer out there to look at them, and he said I should play hardball, you know? I was afraid, and so, at first, I listened to him, but then somewhere along the line, I just realized how stupid it all was. I had no quarrel with you—you were going through enough already. It made no sense to me to fight with you—over anything."

"You're right," I said, feeling sheepish for all the months I had unjustly vilified this woman.

"I've done a lot of thinking this year and a lot of healing," said Cynthia. "I want to move forward with my life now, but I don't want to do that without settling things with you first. I want there to be peace between us, and for the settlement to be fair and equitable. If nothing else, I think we should be able to manage that. I've brought all the paperwork." She leaned down and reached into a canvas tote bag that sat on the floor under her chair, her brown curly hair and pearls necklace flopping forward as she bent. "I wanted to bring them here myself so you could see that the offer I made is really and truly all the money there is."

Cynthia put a stack of papers on the table between us. "Would you like to go through these figures with me?"

"No," I said, "I think we can settle all this without going through the details. I don't think either of us would really relish that little exercise."

"Then, you'll take the settlement?" Cynthia asked.

"I will, but I have some things I need to say to you. What I'd planned to say when I came here isn't really relevant now because I've learned a lot by talking to you, and I want to thank you for having the courage to suggest what I couldn't— that the two of us meet like this. And I agree with you, I think that we can manage to create a certain peace between us. Would you like another cup of tea?"

Cynthia shook her head. "No, I'm good," she said.

I sat for a while putting my thoughts together and Cynthia sat quietly across from me, waiting and watching.

"I've been very unfair to you. I've blamed you for something that wasn't really your fault to begin with. I hope you can forgive me for that—for being uncivil to you."

Cynthia smiled and nodded.

"Daniel was in a very desperate place when he met you, and all of us suffered from the fallout of that desperation. What Daniel told you wasn't entirely fabricated. I did almost die two years ago—I came very, very close actually. What I realize now is that not all of me survived that experience. Some part of me did die—the part that was Daniel's wife. And he knew it. I'm ashamed to say what I'm going to say next—I never truly mourned Daniel—not because I couldn't grieve, but because I didn't have anything *to* grieve. I felt no true loss when Daniel died—we were already over—he was already gone. All I felt was rage at what he had done, how he had lied and jeopardized the security of our family, and the only loss I really felt was the money he'd taken. Maybe that's why I focused so much energy on it. I don't know, but I've never really missed Daniel—I still don't. Do you? Do you ever miss him?"

Cynthia picked up her cup and swirled around the dark liquid that remained in the bottom, as if she were trying to read the leaves. "I do. There are times when I miss him so terribly. Despite everything that happened, I do. When Daniel first died, I was completely lost. I had no job, no home. I was living in this strange place where I knew no one. I kept feeling if Daniel hadn't died, everything would be all right. And yet, I knew it wouldn't have been—it would never have been all right. The end was always waiting to happen. And that just made me so sad."

Her eyes welled with tears.

"I'm sorry," I said. "I feel like you ended up with all the grief I should have had."

She stared at her hands, turning a rumpled tissue around and around in her fingers. "The grief was deep. It took a long time to get to the bottom."

"So, what will you do now?" I asked.

"Go back to Arizona. It's a good place to make a new start—not the new start I'd originally planned, but I think I'm up for it." She smirked and shook her fists with feigned determination and then laughed at herself.

I had to admit I liked her. She was a kind and sweet person, and in the best of circumstances she would have made a good companion for Daniel, or a good friend for me. Our connection to one another was a weird and sad one, but we had been able to make something of it. We had taken the painful experience that bound us together and come through it with grace.

That night I made Creole shrimp and rice for dinner. I set the table for four and lit candles and laid out colorful cotton napkins.

"What's all this?" asked Ethan as he took his seat at the table. "Company coming?"

"No, I set a place for Dad. He used to like my shrimp and rice."

Ethan paused and stared for a moment at the chair across from him where Daniel used to sit. Then he took his seat and shook out the folds of his napkin. "You're losing it, Mom," he said.

Kenya came in and looked at Daniel's place setting. "Is Aunt Ro coming to dinner?" she asked.

"No, apparently *Dad* is joining us," said Ethan, in a tone typically used around the mentally unstable. "Isn't that right, Mom?"

"I thought it would be nice to include him, that's all," I said. "He's still part of our family, isn't he?"

Kenya nodded. "Don't pay any attention to Ethan,

Mom. He's just being a dick."

"Kenya, really," I said, "you don't need to say things like that."

My daughter lifted the bowl of rice and began to pile some onto her plate. "Just stating the obvious," she said.

"You're such a little bitch," said Ethan, throwing a roll at Kenya, which hit her squarely on the side of her head.

Kenya picked up the roll and was about to launch it back, when I reached across the table and grabbed her arm. "Will you two *please* stop it?" I said. "What is the matter with you?"

"Kenya's just showing off because Dad's here," said Ethan, shoveling a fork full of rice into his mouth.

I rolled my eyes and sighed and quietly rested my hands on either side on my placemat. "Who would like to say grace?" I asked.

Ethan stopped eating, his fork poised between his plate and his mouth, and looked at me. "We're saying grace now? Holy crap, Mom, what's gotten into you?"

"I'm just trying to have a nice dinner to kind of mark some of the changes that have occurred in this family, and I'm trying to do that in a respectful and ceremonial way, which obviously is way beyond your level of maturity, Ethan."

Kenya burst out laughing. "Ha, ha," she said.

"Sorry, Mom," Ethan said. "I didn't realize."

"That's alright," I said.

"But, we really should have Dad say grace. After all, he's our guest."

I closed my eyes. "Ethan, please."

"I'm kidding, Mom. I'm kidding, okay? Want *me* to say grace?"

"Yes, that would be lovely."

Ethan folded his hands solemnly in front of his plate and closed his eyes. An angelic expression came over his face. "Dearly beloved," he began.

I struggled not to smile.

"We are gathered here so that this shrimp and this rice may be eaten in peace without disruption or unwanted gastric distress. May there be no food fights or curse words spoken, this at the behest of our cook, Clare. And let us honor our cook while we're at it, folks, shall we, for creating this lovely meal for us? Heck of a job there, Mom! We would also like to honor Dan Blakely for having traveled the farthest to get here. Way to go, Dad! And so, without further ado—by the powers vested in me—I ask you all to raise your forks on high—."

"Alright, alright. Honestly, Ethan," I said, unfolding my hands and placing my napkin in my lap.

"I said *rai-aise* those forks on high, children!" Ethan shouted, his arm aloft.

"Ethan, enough."

"What, I thought it was cool what he said," said Kenya. "Can I do it next time?"

"Don't worry, I'll never ask either of you again." I picked up the platter of shrimp and started spooning some onto my plate.

Kenya and Ethan fist-bumped over the table.

"I was trying to create a certain atmosphere, but you two can't be serious about anything," I said, handing the platter to Kenya. "Kennie, you can't just eat rice and bread for dinner."

Kenya took the platter with a frown and began to inspect the contents, finally choosing one shrimp and sliding it cautiously onto her plate as if it might leap up and bite her on the nose.

"What's the big serious deal?" asked Ethan.

"I have made some decisions. For starters, I have decided that we will no longer have any secrets in this family— that secrets can cause problems and hurt feelings between people. I was hoping that we could all agree to a policy of full disclosure around here—."

"*Now* what did you do?" asked Ethan, turning to Kenya.

"Me?" shouted Kenya.

"Ethan, Kennie didn't do anything. No one has done anything wrong. I just feel we need to get some things out on the table."

Ethan took a gulp of water and set down his glass. "This ought to be good," he said, rolling his eyes.

"Kenya," I said gently, "Sweetie, I know you have a cell phone that used to belong to Dad."

"See," said Ethan, "I *knew* this was about her."

"It's not about Kenya!" I said. I turned my attention back to Kenya. "Honey, I don't care that you have the phone or that you didn't tell me about it. I just want to be sure you understand why Dad had that phone and who it was you were speaking to."

Kenya sat back in her seat and gaped at me. "How do you know about my phone?" she asked.

"Okay, it's not your phone, first of all, and I found out that you have it from the person you used to talk to on it."

"You talked to Dad's girlfriend?" asked Kenya.

"Oh, crap," said Ethan, "here we go."

"What do you mean here we go?" said Kenya. "What the hell do you know about Daddy's girlfriend?"

"I know the whole story. I heard Mom telling Gram about it one night."

Kenya leaned over the table towards Ethan. "Shut up," she said, "what did you hear?"

"Hello? Yoo hoo," I said, "Could I be a part of this conversation?"

They both stared at me and sat back quietly in their seats.

"Now," I said, "yes, there was a woman that Dad became involved with, and her name is Cynthia, and I have met her, and I think she is a very nice person—."

"Did we get the money back?" asked Ethan.

"What money?" asked Kenya.

"She stole money from us," Ethan said.

"Ethan!" I said. "She did not steal any money from us! Dad took some money that belonged to the family and used it to buy a house with Cynthia. I had to go through some legal channels to get the money returned, but it's all been settled amicably, and no one stole anything, is that clear?"

They nodded.

"What I want you both to understand is that what happened between Dad and me was just that—between Dad and me. Daddy loved both of you and loved being your father and that would never have changed."

"We know that," they both said in unison.

"Well, alright then. Good. Now, is there anything you would like to ask me about this?"

"What does she look like?" asked Kenya, leaning over the table and resting her chin on her palm.

"Well," I said, frowning at the question, "actually, she kind of looks like me, only like, shorter."

"What? So, she's like Mini Me?" said Ethan. He looked at the empty place setting at the end of the table. "Dad, you totally lack imagination, dude."

"Ethan!"

"Mom, Jesus, chill already. I'm just trying to lend a little humor to a tense situation here. Is anybody going to eat the rest of the shrimp?"

I waved it towards him with my hand. "So, is there *anything* else either of you would like to say?"

"Yeah," said Ethan, "I'm going to Cambodia in three weeks."

"Ethan, please stop joking around." I slid a forkful of rice and shrimp into my mouth.

"I'm not joking," he said.

"So I have to let him go," I said to Eagle, "he took what I said to heart and now he's trying to honor Aidan's generosity and Daniel's sense of adventure by doing humanitarian work on the other side of the world. I mean, I'm honored he listened to me, and he's absolutely doing the right thing for them and for him."

"But not the right thing for you?" asked Eagle.

"Of course not. I'm worried sick."

"If something is good for the soul of one it is good for the soul of all. Everything is united at that level of experience," Eagle said.

"Yeah, I'm not really feeling it," I said, and I pictured Ethan in my mind for the hundredth time, up to his knees in leech-infested mud, digging the foundation of a clean water facility in rural Cambodia. If the statistics on the number of children who died each year from unsafe drinking water weren't enough to convince me of the integrity of this endeavor, what chance did Eagle have? Part of me was deeply proud of Ethan's courage and commitment. The other part of me was saying, okay, yeah, but why my kid?

"I seem to just get adjusted to one thing and something new comes along," I said wearily.

"Life is not an endurance contest, dear one," said Eagle. I felt him lifting off and pulling me with him as he flew. We were clearly moving towards the upper world. I lay back and floated upwards, safe in the folds of Eagle's wings.

I thought I would probably be meeting my father, but it was Daniel who stood beside Sumeh when I arrived at the gate to the upper world. He looked very clean and polished, like he had just stepped out of the shower. His hair was combed off his forehead the way it always was before he blew it dry, and it had lost its threads of gray.

"Sit, sit," said Sumeh, gesturing with his hands like a Jewish grandmother.

The three of us sat down on a cluster of flattened stones the size of tree stumps.

"You have done good work," Sumeh said to me, nodding and smiling.

I shrugged. "Alright," I said.

"It isn't a small thing," he said, "this man's soul has been freed by it."

I looked at Daniel—he was sitting with his hands quietly resting in his lap. I wasn't sure I had ever seen him so calm.

"Accepting what is difficult and painful," said Sumeh, "and making it the foundation for something loving and whole is the greatest skill one can master."

"Well, I had lots of help," I said. "Lots."

"Clare," said Daniel, "I wanted to tell you that you don't need to worry about Ethan. I'll be with him on his trip, protecting him the whole way. You have other things you need to do now."

"I do?"

Sumeh nodded. "You do."

"Oh no, not some new crisis du jour?" I asked.

"No crisis," said Sumeh. "Realize that by freeing Daniel, you have also freed yourself. You have made space for a new part of yourself to come forward—to become. Are you ready?"

"I guess so, but what exactly am I becoming?"

"We keep telling you," said Sumeh, "everyone keeps telling you. Your life is showing you. Why can't you see it?"

I shrugged. "Sometimes I need a brick to fall on my head."

Sumeh stood up abruptly. "Then you must go and find out."

Daniel stood as well and hugged me, "Thank you, Clare. Please entrust me to take care of Ethan."

"I do," I said.

He smiled and walked away with Sumeh.

"Be happy, Daniel," I said.

He turned and waved.

Eagle was pacing along the top of the gate, fluffing his wings with a series of quick shudders. I climbed onto his back and we dropped from the sky onto the ground of the lower world. We landed in a field and I could see Verena and Eamon standing nearby in front of a large hill. As I approached, I could see that the hill was a massive mound of fist-sized rocks.

Before I even greeted them, Verena turned and disappeared into the crevices between the rocks, Eamon following close behind her. Eagle and I squeezed through after them. Inside the cairn I was surprised to find a large, echoey space the size of a domed sports arena. Thousands of round passageways covered the inside walls, giving the space a honeycombed effect, and I felt as if I were standing inside an enormous beehive.

I became aware of a vibrant humming. The whole cairn seemed to be pulsing with life. Verena held up her hands and ascended smoothly to the top of the dome as if she were riding on a cherry picker. Then she disappeared into one of the passageways, and soon reappeared, accompanied by a young woman in a green dress. The two of them floated down to the floor of the cairn.

The young woman walked up to me and held out her hands. One palm was branded with the figure of the sun, the other with the figure of the earth. Her eyes were like pools of water, her hair like seaweed. There was a tattoo of a shimmering moon emblazoned on her forehead. Her green dress was sewn from a heavy homespun material, and around her neck she wore a gold amulet covered in symbols I did not understand. She was silent and mysterious, belonging to a time and place I could not name, but when I looked into her face, I felt like I was looking into a mirror.

"She *is* you," said Verena. "She has been with us since the time you were a girl. We raised her and cared for her."

"Why did we separate?"

"You wanted to taste the world; she did not. She preferred the realm within, where you spent a lot of time as a child. But as you came into your adolescence, you rejected the world within; you wanted to explore the world around you and all it had to offer, and why should you not have? Now you have come full circle; now you have learned that life in the material world cannot always be easily endured without the wisdom and comfort of this one—the world of the spirits. If you walk the path of the shaman, you must be prepared to straddle both worlds—to live neither fully in one nor the other, but to occupy the space between as if it were the only place you knew you could belong."

I nodded. "This has become a world I cannot live without now." I looked at everything around me—my guides, my missing self, and the enormous protective hive in which we stood. "I see that clearly, and have learned it through the living of my life, but I feel like this world is spilling out into everything else now, everything I do and every person I meet. I can't contain it and leave it here any longer. I have to find a way to take something of this world back with me every time I leave a journey."

"That is the challenge and the life purpose of the shaman," said Eamon. "You are walking in the footsteps of many who have already traveled this path. But you must walk it in your own way. Focus on your own growth and wholeness. Everything else will follow from that."

And with these words, Verena plucked two golden strands of light from her hair and handed one to Eagle. They began to sew together the woman in the green dress and me, Eagle flying in and out of Verena's arms, the two of them entwining their singing threads into beautiful stitches that looked like Celtic knots running down the sides of my torso and legs. At some point I felt myself and the woman in green melt into one person. I looked down and smoothed my palms over the green fabric of my dress. I picked up my hands and looked at them; they were branded with symbols that were sunken deep into my flesh. I picked up the amulet that swung heavily against my chest. It was inscribed with words written in the ancient alphabet of the trees.

But I could read the message perfectly now. It said:

"Walk into the world and you will lose your heart. Walk into your heart and you will find the whole world."

Up a Tree

A Shamanic Handbook

Lesson One
Take a Shamanic Journey

This is a very basic journey to help you get started. Journeying is the foundation of shamanic practice. It provides a safe and rich container for exploration of the spirit world and the inner realms.

- You will need the following things: a quiet room, an uninterrupted space of 20-30 minutes, a comfortable place to lie down, a light blanket, a bandana or eye covering, a shamanic drumming CD, MP3, or audio tape, and a journal in which you can record your journey. You will undertake this journey with the purpose of locating a power animal.

- Lie on the floor in a comfortable position. You may want to put a pillow under your knees or head. Cover yourself with the blanket and your eyes with the bandana. Turn on the drum recording.

- Remember a place where a special tree grows. Think, for instance, of places around your house, places from your childhood or a vacation spot you loved. Imagine yourself standing in front of this tree. Familiarize yourself with its size, form, trunk, and branches. You may wish to climb it or wrap your arms around it. Explore the tree for several minutes.

- Now kneel down and look for a hole at the base of the tree. This hole will begin to expand and your body collapse as you send your spirit down below the tree. Make your way through this tunnel under the tree. You may wish to follow a root down to the bottom. As you lower yourself, the ground will begin to open and expand into an underground space. This is the lower world. Follow the form of the earth as it opens and changes into rock forms, a waterfall, perhaps, a pool or cave. Keep moving until you come out into the open. (Do not be surprised to see sunlight or sky.)

- See, hear or sense everything that is happening around you. You may wish to feel your way with your hands. Try and learn as much about your environment as you can. You may for instance sense you are standing in water because your feet feel cold and wet. You may hear or feel the wing of a bird nearby. You may see a hill covered with bluebells in front of you. You may smell or sense a large animal nearby.

- Follow your senses. If you encounter an animal, watch (or sense) it for a while, and then ask if it is your power animal. (A rule of thumb is that the animal will keep reappearing while others may come and go. If you see it three times, it is likely to be the one.) When you find the right animal, it will let you know.

- Sit down and get comfortable. Ask the animal why it has offered to be your power animal. Hear or sense the answer. You might want to ask how this animal will protect and help you. You might want to ask the animal for advice on a problem or situation in your life. You may ask it for a gift that will symbolize something you need to remember about yourself. Put the gift into your pocket for safekeeping.

- You may stay with your power animal until you hear the callback of the drum. Your power animal may wish to show you around the lower world or take you on a quest. When the drumbeat shifts into a series of slow thumps, it is time to return to the room. Thank your power animal and tell it you will meet again soon.

- Make your way back by reversing the way you came. You will move much more quickly as the drumbeat becomes more hurried. When you reach the base of your special tree, begin to bring movement back to your toes and fingers and then open your eyes.

•   Record your journey.

Tip: if your initial journey is a "bust" and you feel that you are one of those special people who "can't" journey, think again. This practice is encoded in your DNA, and it is simply a matter of training yourself back to a skill on which our planetary life was forged. We all daydream and are used to directing our fantasies as we wish for them to happen. In the beginning you can rely on this same skill. If you are meeting with nothing but blank empty space in your journey experiences, create the kind of journey you would like to have. Make it unfold just like a daydream. Continue to create what is happening in the journey space with your imagination, until one day you will realize that something unplanned has taken place and you are not making this up!

Suggestion: Now that you have a power animal, don't forget to use it! Power animals don't like to be forgotten, once they are invoked. Call upon their special skills to help you out in tricky situations. All animals have special ways of disguising themselves when they don't want to be seen, defending themselves when they are threatened, or calling attention to themselves when they need to get noticed. Ask your power animal to lend you these skills when you require them, and, just as your mom always told you, don't forget to say thank you!

Creative Exercise: Find a nice flat or smooth stone that is no larger than the size of your palm. Using paint pens, draw an image or symbol of your power animal on the surface. (Chinese characters make a beautiful and unique way of doing this.) Carry the stone in your pocket or put it in a special place where you will see it often.

Lesson Two
Take a Walking Journey

To everyone else, it will seem like you are just out getting some air. Little do they know that not only are you working those thigh muscles, you are also on a spirit quest!

• You'll need a comfortable pair of walking shoes. A place to walk and forage: a park, natural preserve, beach or wooded area is best, but if you can only manage your backyard or the streets of your town, that's okay, too. A question or issue from your life that needs some clarity. About 30-40 minutes of your time. A journal in which to record your journey.

• Avoid framing your question as a yes and no answer. Two reasons: one, there's a general reluctance within the spirit world to muck with the free will of humans. (Otherwise, it isn't free will anymore.) Secondly, the spirit world is always game for a good gritty slog through the sort of crises we humans like to avoid if we can. They don't judge things as good or bad, and so will answer as positively as they know how with a resounding yes to every choice put to them. (Not always *good*, despite what they say.) A better way to word your question is: What am I not seeing? What am I learning through this experience? Or, what do I need to remember?

• Venture out with little expectation. You want to have as clear a mind as possible. Shamans call this being a "hollow bone." Remain open to sights and sounds around you. Take note of everything that happens, particularly if it seems unusual. Think of each "happening" as part of a story or metaphor. If you encounter any animal (particularly non-domesticated), take note of how it is behaving.

- Now ask to locate a stone that will hold a picture or image that responds in some way to your question. Let your vision kind of float over the ground beneath you. If it seems to snag on any particular stone, approach the stone and ask if it holds the answer to your question. You will need to sense its answer with your gut or intuition. If the answer is positive, ask if you may take the stone, and will you need to return it once you have found your answer? (I always feel if nature is respecting my free will, I should respect its.) If the answer is negative, move on until you get a positive response.

- Before you remove the stone, notice how and where it is situated—the context. Then, take your stone in your hands and turn it over. Notice the overall shape, texture, and color. Does this information tell you anything? Now look at the surface for any patterns, faces or images. (You might notice wavy lines or concentric circles, a spiral, the shape of a fist, an owl's face, etc.) What do the images remind you of? What do they tell you about the issue at hand?

- Record your entire journey and make a list of all the things you saw and heard and learned on your walk. You may wish to draw illustrations.

Tip: If you're having trouble converting the patterns and images you see on your stone into a sensible message, try free association. (Remember that exercise psychiatrists do with ink blots?) The idea behind free association is that it takes you out of your left brain (thinking mind) and into your right brain (creative imagination). What is the first word that pops into your head? What does that word make you think of, and so on? Imagine that the message on your stone is located at the center of a labyrinth inside your head. Pretend you are walking toward the center of that labyrinth on a concentric path of linked words. Keep walking on words until you locate your message.

Suggestion: Make the messages you receive from the spirit world into mantras. When a situation into which you previously sought insight occurs, and emotions arise, recite the mantra again and again, breathing deeply and releasing.

Creative Exercise: Think of a metaphor that brings to mind a message from spirit. Say that the message "You are free" makes you think of a butterfly. "Let go of the past" may make you think of an open hand. Now get some pliable plastic-coated wire, a few sheets of newspaper and a package of plaster of Paris strips (you can buy these in an art store.) Create a 3D image of the metaphor in wire. Stuff the wire with shredded newspaper if necessary. Soak the plaster of Paris strips in water. Layer over the strips and mold to your wire sculpture. Let dry. Cover with words, colored paper, pictures, paint, buttons, charms, etc. to create a collage that speaks your message.

Lesson Three
Take Flight

The upper world is another realm worth exploring. This is the home of spirit guides and angelic beings, saints and mystics, gods and goddesses, as well as family members who have passed on.

- You will need: 20-30 minutes of journey time, a quiet place where you won't be disturbed, a light blanket and eye covering, a drumming CD or MP3, a part of your life that needs a healing, a journal to record your experience.

- Healing doesn't always mean finding relief from a physical ailment, although illness can certainly be an outcome of imbalance. Shamans, like many practitioners of energy medicine, believe that all imbalances (discord, depression, confusion, misfortune, etc.) begin on a spiritual (energetic) level. Think of an area of your life that is not flowing naturally or moving in a desirable direction. In what way do you feel depleted or stuck?

- Lie down and cover yourself with your blanket. Put some covering like a bandana over your eyes. Start your drum recording.

- Return to the special tree you used when you journeyed to the lower world. Call your power animal to you and ask for its guidance to the upper world. Even four-legged power animals and sea creatures have inventive ways of getting to the upper realm! The two of you might be provided with a staircase, a tall tree, a low cloud or a beanstalk to climb. Make your way into the sky until you discover an opening of some sort: a doorway, portal or gate. Step into that opening and proceed until you encounter a spirit being.

- Ask if this is your spirit guide. If the answer is no, ask to be taken to your spirit guide. Remember how to intuit responses. You may hear, see or sense the answer. (You may have to create or assume it just to keep things rolling!) Follow this being until you have located the spirit who will guide you in the upper world. Ask what name he or she wishes to be called.
- Sit down and speak to your guide about which area of your life feels out of balance. Ask what you can do to feed your soul and heal the spiritual imbalance that lies at the heart of this issue.
- Ask for an activity—something you can do—that will shift the imbalance. Ask for a gift that will remind you to choose a different approach. Ask for any other clarity you need in order to heal this imbalance.
- When you hear the callback, thank your guide. Make your way back from how you came to the upper world. Float comfortably and easily back to earth. Begin to move your toes and fingers. Open your eyes.
- Record your journey.

Tip: You have been given a virtual gift by your guide. Find or make a replica of that gift to wear or carry in your pocket. Also: a nice reciprocal gesture is to think of a virtual gift you can take back to your guide the next time you meet. (Good manners work everywhere in the world.)

Suggestion: Devote some area of your home to your ancestors. This may take the form of a wall of pictures, an altar laid with family faces and memorabilia, or a large collage. Most native medicine wheels place the ancestors in the north direction, so you may wish to choose a north-facing wall or room in your house. Collect stories and details about your ancestors. Go back as many generations as you can. Consider this place in your home to be sacred space, where you can observe family traditions and conduct ceremony. Without your ancestors, their triumphs and struggles, you would not be here. Thank them for giving you your life.

Creative Exercise: This is a little transmutation ceremony you can do to shift the energy of any problem situation. You will need a smooth flat stone about two or three inches across, a paint pen, a bowl of rainwater, a sprig of sage and a container to burn it in. Lie back in a quiet room with your eyes closed. You may or may not wish to play your drumming CD. Settle back quietly and take several deep breaths. Hold the nature of the imbalance in your mind. Observe the feelings it brings up within you without judgment. Place the stone on the area of your body that holds the root of the imbalance. Hold it there until you feel the energy draw out of you and seep into the stone. When you are finished, sit up, turn off the drum recording, and place the bowl of water in front of you. Cleanse the stone asking the water to wash away the energy of these emotions. Dry it gently with a towel. Light the sprig of sage in a fireproof and heavy bottom container. When it catches, blow out the flame. It will send up a fragrant smoke that you will dowse your stone in, asking the smoke to transmute or neutralize the imbalance. Now lie back once more and place the stone again on the affected area you held it to previously. Ask the spirit of the stone (or your power animal) to provide you with a word, a symbol or pictograph that indicates for you a healing or new beginning in the situation. Sit up and using your paint pen, inscribe the symbol onto your stone.

Lesson Four
Strike a Better Accord

We all have regrets about our relationships. There are wounds and misunderstandings, resentments and irritations—things we carry that no longer matter and yet, weigh heavily on our hearts. The dynamic within relationships is just energy, and it takes the intention of only one member of any relationship to shift or transmute that energy from discordant to harmonic.

- You will need: your drum recording or your own drum (you will beat it at a pace of 120 beats per minute), a space of 20-30 minutes, a quiet room where you won't be disturbed, a comfortable place to lie or sit, a light blanket to cover you, and a bandana for your eyes. Have a journal nearby for recording the details of this journey.
- Enter the journey with the intention of healing the discord between you and another person in your life. (Remember, it is not important that this person share your intention. Once you change how you feel, the energy will shift and the dynamic between you will heal.) Go to the tree you use to meet up with your power animal. Enter the lower world the same way. When you arrive in the lower world, call your power animal to you. Explain the purpose of your journey.
- Hear or sense what your power animal has to say about what is out of balance in the relationship you wish to heal. Ask for a metaphor or symbol that will describe the dynamic as it is now. Ask what will correct this imbalance. Ask for a healing of the relationship.
- Follow your power animal to an open neutral space within the lower world. Allow your power animal to direct the proceedings. See the spirit of the other per-

son come into the space. He or she will arrive escorted by an animal spirit. Let the meeting evolve as your spirit animal sees fit. Perhaps there will be some exchange of gifts or the return of power that one party appropriated from the other.

- Say your goodbyes and return with your power animal to the place where you met. Ask what it is you are supposed to remember about this person or your relationship with him (or her)—a truth you may have previously missed.
- Thank your power animal and go back the way you originally came until you come out by the base of your chosen tree.
- Begin to move your fingers and toes. Slowly come back to the room. Record your journey.

Tip: Suppose you return from your journey without as much insight or clearance as you had hoped for. That's okay. We don't always need to "know" what is operating as long as we still carry the intention of releasing it. When "bad" or hurt feelings arise from the relationship in question, just adopt the following mantra: "whatever is operating within these feelings belongs in the past and no longer matters. I fully forgive and freely release the past."

Suggestion: There is a familiar custom of going to church to light candles for a family member who was sick or in trouble. This is a beautiful practice that symbolizes the vigil, or watch, we pledge to keep until a particular cause finds resolution. If there is a chapel or church with votive candles you can light, that is fine, but you can also light one in your home. You can buy votive candles in tall glass holders that actually burn for about 3 days. Light it with your wish for a healed relationship and allow it to burn to the end. (For safety reasons, put the candle inside a fireplace or in a bathtub whenever you leave the house.)

Creative Exercise: It isn't healthy or kind to carry bad feelings, no matter how entitled to them you feel you are. Here's an exercise to release those feelings. Sit down and write a letter that expresses every emotion you have about your painful experiences with another person. You are free to say anything you like here, but keep it more about how you feel rather than what you think about the other person. When you feel you have said everything you need to say, tear up the letter and burn the pieces outside in a small fireproof container. Take the ashes and put them into a small square of cloth (about 5" X 5"). You may wish to add some things that are tokens of the relationship or an experience you had with this person. Sprinkle with tobacco or cornmeal—typically given as thanks to the elements of nature that have volunteered to take this bundle from you. Tie up the bundle securely. At the time of the full moon (when the moon is in a state of release), either drop the bundle into a river or lake or bury the bundle (on public or open land). A good burying spot is an "in-between space"—where water meets land, where tree or stone meets earth, or some type of crossroad. Thank the earth or water for taking your bundle (burden) from you. Sprinkle more tobacco, cornmeal, or lavender over the spot. Acknowledge and speak the words: It is done.

Lesson Five
Seek Greater Clarity

Sometimes spring cleaning entails more than dusting behind the furniture or washing the windows. Our homes get cluttered energetically as well—from an excess of dense emotions like grief or anger, from unchecked flows of natural or manmade elements such as water or electricity, from death or a long illness, and from too much physical debris. Take a journey through your house with a helping spirit to discover where the imbalances lie and learn how to correct them.

- You'll need 20-30 minutes of time, a quiet, comfortable place to lie down, a bandana and a light blanket. Keep your journal handy for recording the results.
- When you hear the drumbeat, lie down and close your eyes. If you have a fireplace in your home, imagine yourself in front of it now. Notice there is a fire burning brightly inside it. The ancient Celts believed that the hearth was a portal to the spirit world. Make use of that portal by staring into the fire and calling forth your power animal. (If you don't have a fireplace, think about where you would like to have one and imagine it there.)
- When your power animal arrives, tell it that you would like to clear your house of any stuck or congested energy. Ask your power animal to identify and call forth a protector for your house. This protector may take the form of another power animal or a spirit being such as an angel.
- Travel from room to room, intuiting and observing all that is said and done in diagnosing and curing any imbalances. Sometimes your helping spirits will do the work themselves. Sometimes they will advise you to

do something.

- Ask to be shown the heart of your home and what you can do to honor it and keep it energetically sound.
- When the house has been cleared and protected, go outside and walk around the land on which your house or apartment building is situated to determine if there is any energy surrounding your home that also needs to be corrected or removed.
- The callback drumbeat will let you know when it is time to finish. Thank your helping spirits and watch them exit through the fireplace portal. Record your journey.

Tip: Keep spaces clear of displaced energies by burning sage or using open bowls of salted or scented water. Orange, rose or lavender water all have clearing properties. (Soak fruit peels or flowers in water 2 or 3 days. Strain before using.)

Suggestion: Dreams can also be used as portals to the spirit world. If you have had a dream you don't understand, reenter the dreamspace and ask your power animal to join you there in order to help decipher the meaning.

Creative Exercise: Create an altar in the heart of your home. Cover it with a cloth of some powerful color or design. Honor the protecting spirit of your home with a small figurine or picture. Place objects on the altar, such as a stone from an energetically powerful spot or something that symbolizes an important event or person. Don't forget to leave gifts there for your protecting spirit as a gesture of thanks. And keep a candle burning!

Lesson Six
Leave the Past in the Past

In this journey, you will have the opportunity to heal your ancestral line from past to present. Just as individual souls carry experience from one lifetime into another, families do as well, and when we, the newest members of our family enter life, we agree to bear and hopefully resolve at least some of those persistent issues. Notice how many problems are said to *run* in families: obesity, addiction, depression, cancer, arthritis, heart disease, and so on.

Do you find that you exhibit the same fears and inhibitions as your parents or grandparents? These can be examples of ancestral imbalance, and here we will address them with a classic shamanic journey known as the dismemberment journey, a potent healing mechanism used by shamans across every continent for many centuries.

- You will need 30-40 minutes (or more) of journey time, the usual *accoutrements* of a drum recording, quiet place, light blanket, bandana, and a family issue that you would like to heal. Keep your journal handy. Light a candle to mark the sacredness of the process.
- Journey to the lower world in the usual manner and meet up with your power animal. Ask this helping spirit to take you to meet your ancestral guide. The role of the ancestral guide is to direct and oversee the healing of your family line. Once you meet this spirit, you may want to take some time and ask who this guide is and why he or she has come forward as the chosen representative of your lineage.
- Present your guide with the family issue you wish to address through this process. Ask the guide to take you

to meet with family members who have had direct experience with this matter. Determine, *if you can,* the identity of these family members and their relationship to you.

- Interview each family member who appears in order to garner his or her particular viewpoint or involvement in the issue. Aim to uncover in particular any aspect of the issue that the family may have kept secret. Secrets have tremendous energy and lend endurance to the problem. Ask family members about their regrets and what legacies they would have preferred to leave behind.

- Return to your guide and ask that you be allowed to stand in as the representative of your family in the healing of the pattern. Your guide will direct you through a healing process that may be assisted, if necessary, by your power animal. This process may involve immersion in water, burning, burial or the disassembling and reassembling of your body parts—some death/rebirth cycle.

- When the healing and restoration of your body has ended in the journey, thank your guides and family members for their help. Ask if there is anything else you need to understand before you go.

- Answer the callback of the drumbeat by returning to the room. Record the findings and experience of your journey.

Tip: Tell your family secrets. This might seem counterintuitive, but secrets perpetuate unhealthy and destructive patterns within families. Tell friends and family about your journey and what you learned. If you are handy with a pen, you may want to write this family saga out in story form for the benefit of your children, grandchildren, cousins, or siblings.

Suggestion: Educate yourself about the history of your particular lineage. Cultural tragedies such as war, atrocities, diaspo-ras, ethnic cleansing, famine, natural disasters and other dev-astations have resounding impact on individual family lines, creating unique and painful memories, wounds, stigmas and debilitation. Ask your ancestral guide to explain how these events specifically impacted your family.

Creative Exercise: It is always good to seal the work you do in non-ordinary reality with a real world ritual or ceremony. Make a bundle of things that represent people in your family who were affected by the pattern you are releasing (particular-ly those who appeared in the journey). Photocopies of old photographs, funeral cards, a letter, newspaper article or a trinket of some kind are typical examples. Add to the bundle things that represent what needs to be released. Copies of medical records or death certificates, a replica of a war medal or symbol of your ancestors' life work, a label from a favored alcoholic beverage, a cigarette packet, etc. might signify the specific family issue. Sprinkle in items that represent what your ancestors wished they had left behind (e.g., sweetness, love, hope). You might use for instance, sugar, dried rose petals or some religious talisman. When you have completed your bundle, tie it securely and find a place in nature that will willingly accept and transmute it. Likely places are a body of water, a crevice in the rocks, a hollowed out tree, a hole in the ground. Offer the bundle at the time of the full moon. Leave an offering of tobacco, lavender, corn, or another token of thanks to the elements and nature spirits that were willing to accept your bundle.

Lesson Seven
What is Lost Can Be Found

In shamanic terms, we call it *soul*, but in common language, we might call it strength, energy, power, heart, or even love. In a situation where one person feels guilty about leaving another, a parent feels her child will not thrive in the world, a child feels he cannot garner enough attention from his distracted parent, or one person feels they have more advantage in a relationship, a piece of soul is sometimes extended or dropped in order to resolve the imbalance.

Conversely, in an instance where an insecure parent has a child that seems more sturdy and resilient, a jealous lover fears abandonment, or an addict feels constantly at a loss to cope, soul energy can sometimes be taken in order for the weaker party to feel more in control.

The truth is that everyone loses in this type of exchange. One individual cannot benefit from the vitality or essence of another. When soul is given away or lost, it burdens rather than helps, and threatens the balance and health of the relationship.

- In this journey, you will need the following: 30 minutes of drumming in a quiet place where you won't be disturbed, a bandana and a light blanket, a pillow for your head. You will want to keep a record of the relationships that are mentioned here, so have your journal on hand.
- Go to the lower world and contact your power animal. Explain that you would like to rectify all of the soul swapping that's played a part in your relationships to date. Your power animal will take you to a place where you will be able to see or learn the names of people to

whom you have given a part of your soul. For instance, you might find yourself at the opening of a cave where people in your past and present will emerge one by one. As they appear, you will ask your power animal to explain the reasons why you gave away soul to this person.

- Next you will want to ascertain whose soul parts you are carrying. Ask your power animal to help you identify the people to whom these soul parts belong. Ask whether these parts were given or taken, and why.

- As each relationship should be taken separately in order to give the restoration process the focus it deserves, you may be required to take subsequent journeys in order to complete this work. For now, choose the one relationship you most want to heal. Allow your power animal to guide you through a ceremony or ritual that will accomplish the rescue and return of any displaced soul parts. The ritual process may involve the exchange of forgiveness or gifts, perhaps the promise to behave differently toward that person. It may involve returning to the time and place where a soul part was lost. It may involve a trip to the upper world if the person you are meeting has passed out of this life.

- Returned soul parts are usually given to some helping spirit for safekeeping. Beyond giving up custody of the soul part you are carrying, you have no role in its restoration.

- When the process is complete, you may choose to work on other relationships in which soul parts have been misappropriated, or you may choose to return and do the work at another time. Hold the intention to rectify any discrepancies you may have uncovered.

- Thank your helping spirits and return to the room with the callback.

Tip: Sometimes it's hard to shift the dynamic that exists between you and another person. Sometimes it's hard to forgive. Whenever you get stuck or attached to a particular perception, it can benefit you to look at things from another perspective. Shapeshifting is a great tool for changing the way you see things. Shamans do it to garner wisdom from nature and break down the tyranny of the ego. Take a journey and ask your power animal to suggest an aspect of nature into which you can shapeshift. It might be a plant, an animal, a stone or an element. Experience life through the eyes and wisdom of this part of nature. What do you learn?

Suggestion: If you give a virtual gift to someone in your journey space, you can seal and reinforce the healing by giving them a gift in ordinary reality. It does not have to be the same gift and you do not have to tell them what it represents for the gesture to be effective.

Creative Exercise: Make a collage of your soul. Draw a shape on a piece of watercolor paper that represents your soul. Tear pieces of colored paper or pictures from a magazine or newspaper that represent your unique strengths and talents, and label them as such. One might say: my artistic nature. Another might say: my spiritual strength or my deep connection to nature, and so on. Fill up as much of the shape as you feel you can. What parts are missing? Where did they go? Ask your power animal how you can restore them.

(Sometimes you cannot restore or even remember your lost strengths and powers, but a shamanic practitioner can help you access and integrate these parts through the process of soul retrieval. Doing an Internet search of your area will help you to locate a practitioner. Sandra Ingerman provides a comprehensive list on her website: www.shamanicteachers.com)

Lesson Eight
What to Wear to a Cloak and Dagger Affair

The world can sometimes feel like a precarious place to live. You may occasionally feel the need for protection from all sorts of risks, people and things that seem to threaten the stability of your power, health and wellbeing. Remember, you can always secure protection for yourself, your possessions and your loved ones simply by asking. Here is a journey to help you do that:

- You will need about 10 minutes for this journey, a quiet time and space, a bandana, a drum recording, and perhaps a light blanket to cover yourself. Keep a journal handy to record your journey.
- Go to the lower world and contact your power animal. Ask how you can protect what is precious to you in times of threat.
- Your power animal may actually give you a cloak or energetic garment to wear. It may provide you with a special staff, wand, or sword to carry with you for protection.
- Ask how and when you are to use this special protective equipment and how to care for it. And then ask your power animal to bless it.
- Thank your power animal. Return to the room and record your findings.

Tip: Cloaking or protecting yourself and your loved ones should be a quick and easy visual exercise. Even if you do not feel or are aware of an imminent threat, protecting whatever you value—most particularly your own personal power—is a good daily exercise. Keep it a simple and visual exercise that takes no more than 5 or 10 seconds.

Suggestion: Wishing someone well or sending him a blessing is another way of protecting your power. Instead of sending anger, jealousy, or fear someone's way, choose to send a blessing instead. If you are connected to being angry or in a state of dissonance with people, it is the same thing as giving away your power to them!

Creative Exercise: Pack up your sorrows and give them all to the earth. When we bury our dead, we let them go and relinquish them to the earth from which they came. You can perform a similar ritual with any emotional detritus you've been hauling around with you. Take a square of colorful paper (gift wrap works nicely). Into the paper create a beautiful and colorful pattern of leaves, petals and flowers. As you release each onto the paper, blow prayers and blessings into them. You are breathing life into forgiveness instead of sorrow and regret. Add sage for purification. Wrap up this package with a string or cord and burn it. Bury the ashes in the earth and sprinkle tobacco or cornmeal over the burial site for thanks to the elements for taking and transmuting your sorrow. Sing it away as you release it fully. It is done!

Lesson Nine
Getting the Horse in Front of the Cart

Prosperity is not just about money. Prosperity means the unobstructed flow of all that you desire in life—health, wealth, love, harmony, and joy. The basic universal law of attraction is this: that which is like unto itself is drawn. Being morose and unhappy will not bring joy and laughter into your life. Fear of lack will only engender more lack. Don't play the "if only" game. If only I had a sweetheart, if only I had more money, if only I were thinner, *then* I'd be happy. That's putting the cart before the horse. Be happy and appreciative of everything you do have and everything you are *now*. Expressing love and joy will attract more of what you want into your life. In this journey you will meet a prosperity guide who will help you devote yourself to thoughts and emotions that are more harmonic and resonant with your desires.

- You will need about 20-30 minutes of journey time, the usual accoutrements of a drum recording or your own drum, a quiet place, light blanket, bandana, and the intention to heal an aspect of your life that is not how you want it to be. Keep your journal handy.
- Travel to the lower world and meet your power animal. Ask your power animal to take you to meet your prosperity guide. (It may be another power animal, a faery or spirit guide.) When you meet your guide, greet it, and ask its name.
- Present your issue—the area of your life in which you would like to feel more fulfilled. State both how the matter stands now and how you would like it to be. Ask your guide what particular thoughts and emotions obstruct or prevent your true desires from flowing to you.

- Stay for a moment with each obstructing thought and emotion. Ask your guide: do these thoughts reflect the truth? Do these emotions reflect my true nature? What is the truth? What is my true nature?
- Now ask that the obstructing or counterproductive thoughts and emotions you have been harboring be transmuted. Ask your guide to take you to a magic pond. Imagine each thought and emotion is a stone that you drop one by one into the pond. Watch them each sink like lead to the bottom. As the magic waters of the pond transmute them into buoyant thoughts and emotions, each will bounce to the surface and float towards you. They will look like beautiful blown-glass balls. Scoop them up and put them into your pocket.
- Thank your guide for his help and make your way back to the room. Record your findings.

Tip: They say you attract more bees with honey. Positive emotions have ten times the power as negative emotions, and you have the free will to choose which emotion you lend to every situation. Remember, love is more powerful than fear; appreciation trumps discontent, and kindness dissolves anger.

Suggestion: Take whichever truths and insights revealed to you by your guide and convert them into a mantra that will help you to keep your renewed perspective. (Example: I am loving and loveable. The past is past. I move forward freely into the arms of love.)

Creative Exercise: One of the reasons why it is sometimes so hard to change negative feelings is because they are invisible and formless. This exercise will give shape to your fears, resentments and frustrations through the creation of an effigy. Take a sheet of newspaper. Scribble onto the newspaper with a dark pen all the negative feelings you harbor about a situation. Write until you have no more to say. Then, take the sheet and tear it longwise into 1-inch strips. Stack the strips so that the ends are fairly even. Now, fold the bundle of strips over in half. At the fold, grab about two inches of length between your fingers and tie it with a string. Take the strips that hang below the string and divide them into three sections, as if you were about to braid. The middle section should be thicker than the outer two sections. Tie the thicker section with a string about 5 inches below the first string. Tie each of the two remaining sections about an inch from the ends. You may now see that you are making a paper doll similar to the yarn dolls you might have made in elementary school. All that remains for you to do now is tie off each of the legs with string at the ankles of the doll. (Your newspaper doll will have string secured at the neck, waist and wrists as well.) Now cast the doll into a fire asking that the fire transmute your negative feelings into more positive ones. May the beauty of the fire lift your spirit higher!

Lesson Ten
Never Say Never

Most of us assume that it is too late to heal old wounds, or say what was never said, once someone dies. Thankfully, this isn't true. You needn't let the death of a loved one stand in the way of achieving peace.

This journey involves a trip to the upper world. It is an opportunity for you to heal the differences and misunderstandings between you and a loved one who has passed into the afterlife. It also offers you a chance to express your love and forgiveness and receive love and forgiveness in return.

Think about someone close to you who is deceased. If you were given 20 minutes to sit and speak with them again, what would you say?

- You will need about 20-30 minutes of journey time, a drum recording (or your own drum), a quiet room, a light blanket, and an eye cover. Have a journal on hand.
- When the drumming begins and you are lying down comfortably, return to the special tree you use whenever you journey to the lower world. Call your power animal to you. Climb the branches into the sky. Keep climbing until you come to a gate. Knock on the gate and ask that your upper world guide come to meet with you.
- When your upper world guide appears, greet him and ask to be taken to a place where you can speak with your deceased loved one. Follow your guide to the meeting place where your loved one awaits you. Regardless of the problems that existed in the past, you

should greet this person with love.

- Ask or tell your loved one anything you want to convey. Hear what he or she has to say in response. Spend time with this. Say what is in your heart. You may need to rely on the advice of your guide to steer the dialogue towards a positive result—remember, that is the intention here. You might ask, for instance, to view the relationship from the standpoint of your loved one.
- Give your loved one a gift. Ask for a gift in return. Part with an expression of love and forgiveness.
- Return to the room and slowly open your eyes. Take notes.

Tip: Send peace to obtain peace. Each day, you may send this Gaelic blessing to your loved one:

> *Deep peace of the running waves to you.*
> *Deep peace of the quiet earth to you.*
> *Deep peace of the flowing air to you.*
> *Deep peace of the smiling stars to you.*
> *Deep peace of the Shining Ones to you.*

Suggestion: Seal this journey by creating a little altar to honor your loved one. Decorate it with colors and objects or replicas of things that were important to them, things that tell the story of a life now passed. Honor that life. Allow your loved one the right to his or her mistakes and shortcomings—we all have them. Allow your loved one the right to have left his or her body. Burn a candle for three days. As you blow this candle out at the end of each day, release any residual emotional pain still associated with this relationship. Thank this person for being a part of your life.

Creative Exercise: You can create a talisman that brings you strength in difficult situations. Start with some modeling

compound that air-dries in a day or two and will harden easily
without kiln firing or baking. Make a disk that fits nicely in
the center of your palm (1-2 inches in diameter.) Decorate it
with other clay pieces or inscribe it with any designs you
might find appropriate. Smudge it with burning sage to clear it
of any negative energy. Bless it with water from a favorite
pond or stream, lake, ocean or river. Allow it to dry outside in
a special place. Ask the wind to lend its strength and power to
your talisman. When it is dry, paint it with tempura or acrylic
paint. When it is finished, you may carry it in a pocket or
purse. You may wish to keep it by your bedside for when you
have trouble sleeping. In a moment of stress, hold it in your
hand and rub it with your thumb, asking that the strength
rendered to it by the "flowing air" be yours.

Lesson Eleven
Faery Tales Can Happen to You

Faeries are the angels and custodians of the natural world, and they make wonderful allies. While they are known to be mysterious and elusive, they will generally respond quite favorably to sincere overtures of friendship from humans.

We forget sometimes that we too are part of the natural world and not something apart from it. We are as much of the earth as a tree, a flower, a bee, or a mountain. The more we can feel we are an integral part of our natural surroundings, the more we can connect to the faery kingdom.

- Make this journey on your own land, a park or natural setting nearby. You may want to take a drum or rattle along with you. Bring something pretty to leave behind like a shiny stone or a charm, a piece of sea glass or a flower. Also carry with you some item of thanks—faeries like milk, nuts, raisins, and berries.

- When you walk through nature, be sensitive to the way different areas feel. Find an area that you are drawn to more than others. It may be a moist and mossy place, a waterfall, a cove of rocks by the ocean, a majestic oak tree, a beautiful garden landscape, or a mountaintop. It only matters that there is something special or unique in the way it feels to you.

- Sit down in the space you have selected and get comfortable. Drum or sing if you wish. Lovingly observe, smell and hear everything that is going on around you. Butterflies, birds, and other animals sometimes act as the cloak (disguise) of a faery spirit. Feel yourself blend in and become a part of this setting.

- When you feel ready, close your eyes all or part of the way. Ask the faeries who live in this place to show you how they see their surroundings. You may notice a heightening of the light, the appearance of rainbows, other spheres of existence, or the sensation of sitting inside a dome. You may hear music. Stay with this consciousness for a while. Observe and enjoy the tranquility.

- Now choose to shapeshift into some part of your surroundings. Become, for instance, the water, the tree, the sand, a rock, or the breeze. As you remain in this other consciousness, you may experience a greater level of connectedness to the nature around you. You may also be able to observe the faeries that tend and care for this land and everything in it.

- Thank the faeries for the work they do to create harmony and balance in our world. Add to the beauty of your surroundings by leaving the pretty object you brought. Leave a gift for the faeries and nature spirits.

Tip: If you find yourself in a beautiful place and you want to leave a gift, but have none at the ready, a song, a poem, or a nature painting is always a great gesture of reciprocation. To create a nature painting, pick at random from what is close at hand: stones, twigs, moss, flowers, leaves, etc. Make a circular or square border on the ground and assemble the found objects inside it like a collage.

Suggestion: Faeries are wonderful advocates and generous, powerful beings. If you have a problem you want help with, ask the faeries for assistance by hanging a colorful prayer tie, or cloughtie, onto a tree branch. And remember, once you give a problem to the faeries, you shouldn't continue to feed it negativity. Faeries create harmony with joy and gratitude. You are wise to do the same.

Creative Exercise: Build a special garden or enhance an existing one to honor the faery folk. Include something shiny and reflective that will catch the sun and moonlight, like glass or water; something soft, like moss or a ground creeping plant like thyme or phlox; an element of sound such as a fountain, chimes, or a fluttering wind sock; flowers that will attract hummingbirds and butterflies; something fragrant like lilies of the valley, roses, or lilacs; and something with nooks and crannies like stacked rocks or a birdhouse. Add texture, color, and depth, but don't overdo it. Faeries like simple, thoughtful beauty that reflects an appreciation for nature.

Lesson Twelve
We Could All Use a Little Saving

Faeries, as Earth's angels, are the great conservators of the life force of our planet. They value and protect energy and power in ways we have yet to comprehend. Humans can sometimes be rather inept managers of their own power and soul, and have been known to make poor trade-offs. ("For what will it profit a man if he gains the whole world, but forfeits his soul?") It is thought that one of the services faeries can provide for lost soul parts is something called soul raising or soul saving. This beautiful work was originally envisioned and taught by the Celtic shaman and scholar, Tom Cowan.

To see if the faeries are holding and keeping a part of your soul (a piece of yourself you once let go of, like an unexplored talent or desire), make a journey and meet your faery guide, or what is sometimes known as a co-walker.

- You will need 20-30 minutes to complete this journey. Find a quiet place where you won't be disturbed. Have a light blanket, an eye cover and journal at the ready. Put on your drum recording.
- Ask your power animal to take you to a cairn or faery mound in ordinary reality, where you can meet your co-walker. (You may or may not have actually known this place as a faery dwelling, but it will be one that is familiar to you.) Your power animal will show you the entrance into the cairn or mound. Follow it to the hollow place inside.
- You will either be met by your faery guide or by an emissary who will take you to your co-walker. Ask your co-walker to name an experience in your life in which he or she played an important and protective

role.

- Ask your co-walker if the faeries are holding any soul parts that belong to you. Ask when and how they were lost and whether it is time for them to come back. (The faeries will be reluctant to return any parts they feel you may not be prepared to receive.)
- If you are told it is not time for the part(s) to be returned, ask what growth or changes might pave the way for a future reunion. Express your interest in having the part(s) returned to you and vow to return periodically to see if the time has arrived.
- If you are told it is time, ask to meet the soul part and be given an understanding of why and when it was lost. Ask what changes and responsibilities the reunion will incur.
- Allow your faery guide and power animal to restore your soul part to you and ask if there is anything you need to do or remember going forward.
- Thank the faeries for caring for your soul part and your guides for restoring it to you.
- Return to the room and record your journey.

Tip: On another journey, ask what is the quickest way of connecting to your faery guide for protection and insight. Circumstances don't always provide a quiet room for meditation and journey, so it is good to have a gesture or signal you can use to call up the guidance available from your co-walker anytime you require it.

Suggestion: The faeries love celebration and music. Mark the homecoming of your soul part with a special ceremony. Go to a favorite place in nature. Bring along a picnic and offerings. Sing a song, play music, dance, drum or recite a poem for the faeries.

Creative Exercise: Paint and decorate a birdhouse or a beautiful shell for the faeries to live inside. Hang it outside your door or dangle it from a tree in your garden. When you acknowledge and honor the presence of the faeries, you open your life to magic and wonder!

Acknowledgments

I could not have written this book without the guidance of the gifted and wise teachers with whom I have been blessed to study shamanism, in particular, Sandra Ingerman and Tom Cowan, who teach not only by what they say and do, but by who they are.

I cannot fail to credit the spirit allies and guides who have been by my side since my very first journey. To my power animals, spirit guides, faery guides and helping spirits all—thank you for allowing me to see with your eyes, hear with your ears, speak with your voice, perceive with your hearts and walk with your strength!

I have been graced with two wonderful sons, Ryan and Seth, who, though they do not walk the same path, are, nonetheless, deeply proud of the work and my commitment to it. Your admiration—though I am not easy to explain to your friends—means everything to me.

To my writing group, who were the first readers and critics of this book—Sari Bodi, Lisa Clair, Linda Howard, Russ Miller, and Ray Rauth. Thank you for every suggestion, criticism and praise you gave to the crafting of this manuscript. You helped me beyond measure to feel my way through the telling of this tale.

Thanks also to my smart and careful readers, Bracken Burns, Elise Broach and Nancy Murphy, the moral support of my oldest and dearest friend, Janice Lawry, the overwhelming generosity of Denise and Jon Guerringue, Jon, in particular, for his technical help and his boatload of patience. I'm also grateful for the legal insights of Bill O'Neill.

Thank you, Journeywomen: Gail Gorelick, Denise Guerringue and Lucy Walker for your sassiness, your fierceness, your friendship and your wisdom.

To Judith Bird, for her exquisite cover art, Deb Moran for her skilled graphic design, and Joan Bennett, for her heartfelt photography. Together, you women created a beautiful gift-wrap for this book!

To every one of my students and clients, who, each day, generously entrust me with the most blessed and miraculous work a human being could ever dream of.

Deep Peace and Gratitude to All of You!

About the Author

Jane Burns is a shamanic practitioner and teacher who lives and works in Southbury, CT. Her Reiki and shamanic practice are inspired and shaped by Celtic myth and lore. Her website is: www.journeystothesoul.com.

CPSIA information can be obtained at www.ICGtesting.com
Printed in the USA
LVOW10s1813180416

484152LV00019B/1296/P